The Breaker

MINETTE WALTERS

The Breaker

BCA

LONDON NEW YORK SYDNEY TORONTO

This edition published 1998
by BCA
by arrangement with Macmillan
An imprint of Macmillan Publishers Ltd

CN 3846

Typeset by SetSystems Ltd, Saffron Walden, Essex
Printed and bound in Great Britain by
Clays Ltd, St Ives plc

For Marigold and Anthony

Acknowledgements

With particular thanks to
Sally and John Priestley of *XII Bar Blues*
and Encombe House Estate.

Chapman's Pool   Emmetts Hill   Quarry Valley   St Alban's Head

Eastern Perspective

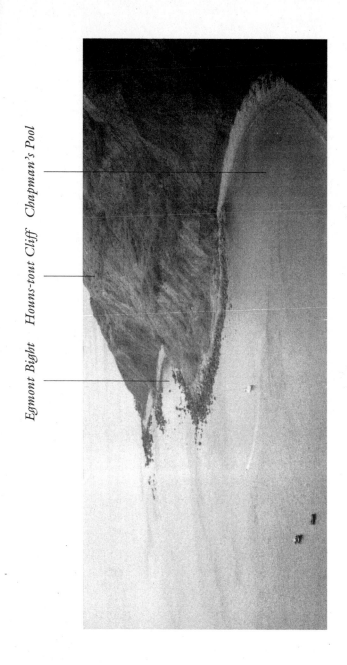

Egmont Bight Houns-tout Cliff Chapman's Pool

Western Perspective

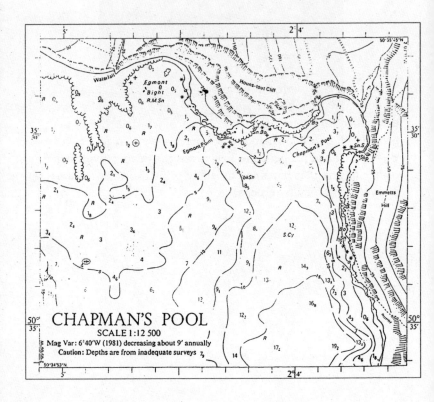

CHAPMAN'S POOL
SCALE 1:12 500
Mag Var: 6°40'W (1981) decreasing about 9' annually
Caution: Depths are from inadequate surveys

Sunday, 10 August 1997 – 1.45 a.m.

SHE DRIFTED with the waves, falling off their rolling backs and waking to renewed agony every time salt water seared down her throat and into her stomach. During intermittent periods of lucidity when she revisited, always with astonishment, what had happened to her, it was the deliberate breaking of her fingers that remained indelibly printed on her memory, and not the brutality of her rape.

Sunday, 10 August 1997 – 5.00 a.m.

THE CHILD sat cross-legged on the floor like a miniature statue of Buddha, the grey dawn light leeching her flesh of colour. He had no feelings for her, not even common humanity, but he couldn't bring himself to touch her. She watched him as solemnly as he watched her, and he was enthralled by her immobility. He could break her neck as easily as a chicken's, but he fancied he saw an ancient wisdom in her concentrated gaze, and the idea frightened him. Did she know what he'd done?

Prologue

Extract from: *The Mind of a Rapist* by Helen Barry

THE most widely held view is that rape is an exercise in male domination, a pathological assertion of power, usually performed out of anger against the entire sex or frustration with a specific individual. By forcing a woman to accept penetration, the man is demonstrating not only his superior strength but his right to sow his seed wherever and whenever he chooses. This has elevated the rapist to a creature of legendary proportions – demoniacal, dangerous, predatory – and the fact that few rapists merit such labels is secondary to the fear the legend inspires.

In a high percentage of cases (including domestic, date and gang rape) the rapist is an inadequate individual who seeks to bolster poor self-image by attacking someone he perceives to be weaker than himself. He is a man of low intelligence, few social skills, and with a profound sense of his own inferiority in his dealings with the rest of society. A deep-seated fear of women is more common to the rapist than a feeling of superiority, and this may well lie in early failure to make successful relationships.

Pornography becomes a means to an end for such a person because masturbation is as necessary to him as the regular fix is to a heroin addict. Without orgasm the sex-fixator experiences nothing. However, his obsessive nature, coupled with his lack of achievement, will make him an unattractive mate to the sort of woman his inferiority complex demands, namely a woman who attracts successful men. If he has a relationship at all, his partner will be someone who has been used and abused by other men which only exacerbates his feelings of inadequacy and inferiority.

It could be argued that the rapist, a man of limited intelligence, limited sensation and limited ability to function, is more to be pitied than feared, because his danger lies in the easy ascendancy society has given him over the so-called weaker sex. Every time judges and newspapers demonize and mythologize the rapist as a dangerous predator, they merely reinforce the idea that the penis is a symbol of power . . .

Chapter One

THE WOMAN LAY on her back on the pebble foreshore at the foot of Houns-tout Cliff, staring at the cloudless sky above, her pale blonde hair drying into a frizz of tight curls in the hot sun. A smear of sand across her abdomen gave the impression of wispy clothing, but the brown circles of her nipples and the hair sprouting at her crotch told anyone who cared to look that she was naked. One arm curved languidly around her head while the other rested palm-up on the shingle, the fingers curling in the tiny wavelets that bubbled over them as the tide rose; her legs, opened shamelessly in relaxation, seemed to invite the sun's warmth to penetrate directly into her body.

Above her loomed the grim shale escarpment of Houns-tout Cliff, irregularly striped with the hardy vegetation that clung to its ledges. So often shrouded in mist and rain during the autumn and winter, it looked benign in the brilliant summer sunlight. A mile away to the west on the Dorset Coast Path that hugged the clifftops to Weymouth, a party of hikers approached at a leisurely pace, pausing every now and then to watch cormorants and shags plummet into the sea like tiny guided missiles. To the east, on the path to Swanage, a single male walker passed the Norman chapel on St Alban's Head on his way to the rock-girt crucible of Chapman's Pool whose clear blue waters made an attractive anchorage when the wind was light and offshore. Because of the steep hills that surround it, pedestrian visitors to its beaches were rare, but at lunchtime on a fine weekend upwards of ten boats rode at anchor there, bobbing in staggered formation as the gentle swells passed under each in turn.

A single boat, a thirty-two foot Princess, had already nosed in through the entrance channel, and the rattle of its anchor chain over its idling engines carried clearly on the air. Not far behind, the bow of a Fairline Squadron carved through the race off St Alban's Head, giving the yachts that wallowed lazily in the light winds a wide berth in its progress towards the bay. It was a quarter past ten on one of the hottest Sundays of the year, but out of sight around Egmont Point the naked sunbather appeared oblivious to both the shimmering heat and the increasing likelihood of company.

The Spender brothers, Paul and Daniel, had spotted the nudist as they rounded the Point with their fishing rods, and they were now perched precariously on an unstable ledge some hundred feet above her and to her right. They took it in turns to look at her through their father's expensive binoculars which they had smuggled out of the rented holiday cottage in a bundle of T-shirts, rods and tackle. It was the middle weekend of their two weeks' holiday, and as far as the elder brother was concerned, fishing had only ever been a pretext. This remote part of the Isle of Purbeck held little attraction for an awakening adolescent, having few inhabitants, fewer distractions and no sandy beaches. His intention had always been to spy on bikini-clad women draped over the expensive motor cruisers in Chapman's Pool.

'Mum said we weren't to climb the cliffs because they're dangerous,' whispered Danny, the virtuous ten-year-old, less interested than his brother in the sight of bare flesh.

'Shut up.'

'She'd kill us if she knew we were looking at a nudie.'

'You're just scared because you've never seen one before.'

'Neither've you,' muttered the younger boy indignantly. 'Anyway, she's a dirty person. I bet loads of people can see her.'

Paul, the elder by two years, treated this remark with the scorn it deserved – they hadn't passed a soul on their way round Chapman's Pool. Instead, he concentrated on the wonderfully accessible body below. He couldn't see much of the woman's face because she was lying with her feet pointing towards them, but the magnification of the lenses was so powerful that he could see every other detail of her. He was too ignorant of the naked female form to question the bruises that blotched her skin, but he knew afterwards that he wouldn't have questioned them anyway, even if he'd known what they meant. He had fantasized about something like this happening – discovering a quiescent, unmoving woman who allowed him to explore her at his leisure, if only through binoculars. He found the soft flow of her breasts unbearably erotic and dwelt at length on her nipples, wondering what it would be like to touch them and what would happen if he did. Lovingly he traversed the length of her midriff, pausing on the dimple of her belly button, before returning to what interested him most, her opened legs and what lay between them. He crawled forward on his elbows, writhing his body beneath him.

'What are you doing?' demanded Danny suspiciously, crawling up beside him. 'Are you being dirty?'

''Course not.' He gave the boy a savage thump on the arm. 'That's all you ever think about, isn't it? Being dirty. You'd better watch it, penis-brain, or I'll tell Dad on you.'

In the inevitable fight that followed – a grunting, red-faced brawl of hooked arms and kicking feet – the Zeiss binoculars slipped from the elder brother's grasp and clattered down the slope, dislodging an avalanche of shale in the process. The boys, united in terror of what their father was going to say, abandoned the fight to wriggle back from the brink and stare in dismay after the binoculars.

'It's your fault if they're broken,' hissed the ten-year-old. 'You're the one who dropped them.'

But for once his brother didn't rise to the bait. He was more interested in the body's continued immobility. With an awful sense of foreboding it dawned on him that he'd been masturbating over a dead woman.

Chapter Two

THE CLEAR WATERS of Chapman's Pool heaved in an undulating roll to break in rippling foam around the pebble shore of the bay. By now three boats were anchored there, two flying the red ensign – *Lady Rose*, the Princess, and *Gregory's Girl*, the Fairline Squadron; the third, *Mirage*, a French Beneteau, flew the tricolour. Only *Gregory's Girl* showed any sign of real activity with a man and a woman struggling to release a dinghy whose winching wires had become jammed in the ratchet mechanism of the davits. On *Lady Rose*, a scantily clad couple lounged on the flying bridge, bodies glistening with oil, eyes closed against the sun, while on *Mirage*, a teenage girl held a video camera to her eye and panned idly up the steep grassy slope of West Hill, searching for anything worth filming.

No one noticed the Spender brothers' mad dash around the bay, although the French girl did zoom in on the lone male walker as he descended the hillside towards them. Seeing only with the tunnel vision of the camera, she was oblivious to anything but the handsome young man in her sight, and her smitten heart gave a tiny leap of excitement at the thought of another chance encounter with the beautiful Englishman. She had met him two days before at the Berthon Marina in Lymington when, with a gleaming smile, he'd told her the computer code for the lavatories, and she couldn't believe her good luck that he was here ... today ... in this shit-hole of boring isolation which her parents described as one of England's gems.

To her starved imagination he looked like a longer-haired

version of Jean-Claude Van Damme in his sleeveless T-shirt and bottom-hugging shorts – tanned, muscled, sleek dark hair swept back from his face, smiling brown eyes, grittily stubbled jaw – and in the narrative tale of her own life, romanticized, embellished, unbelievably innocent, she pictured herself swooning in his strong arms and capturing his heart. Through the intimacy of magnification she watched his muscles ripple as he lowered his rucksack to the ground, only for the lens to fill abruptly with the frantic movements of the Spender brothers. With an audible groan, she switched off the camera and stared in disbelief at the prancing children who, from a distance, appeared to be showing enthusiastic delight.

Surely he was too young to be anybody's father?

But . . . A Gallic shrug . . .

Who knew with the English?

Behind the questing mongrel which zigzagged energetically in pursuit of a scent, the horse picked its way carefully down the track that led from Hill Bottom to the Pool. Tarmac showed in places where the track had once been a road, and one or two sketchy foundations among the overgrown vegetation beside it spoke of buildings long abandoned and demolished. Maggie Jenner had lived in this area most of her life but had never known why the handful of inhabitants in this corner of the Isle of Purbeck had gone away and left their dwellings to the ravages of time. Someone had told her once that 'chapman' was an archaic word for merchant or pedlar but what anyone could have traded in this remote place she couldn't imagine. Perhaps, more simply, a pedlar had drowned in the bay and bequeathed his death to posterity. Every time she took this path she reminded herself to find out, but every time she made her way home again she forgot.

The cultivated gardens that had once bloomed here had left a lingering legacy of roses, hollyhocks and hydrangeas amid the weeds and grasses, and she thought how pleasant it would be to have a house in this colourful wilderness, facing south-west towards the channel with only her dog and her horses for company. Because of the threat of the ever-sliding cliffs, access to Chapman's Pool was denied to motorized traffic by pad-locked gates at Hill Bottom and Kingston, and the attraction of so much stillness was a powerful one. But then isolation and its attendant solitude was becoming something of an obsession with her, and occasionally it worried her.

Even as the thought was in her head, she heard the sound of an approaching vehicle, grinding in first gear over the bumps and hollows behind her, and gave a surprised whistle to bring Bertie to heel behind Sir Jasper. She turned in the saddle, assuming it was a tractor, and frowned at the approaching police Range Rover. It slowed as it drew level with her and she recognized Nick Ingram at the wheel before, with a brief smile of acknowledgement, he drove on and left her to follow in his dusty wake.

The emergency services had rushed into action following a nine-nine-nine call to the police from a mobile telephone. It was timed at 10.43 a.m. The caller gave his name as Steven Harding and explained that he had come across two boys who claimed a body was lying on the beach at Egmont Bight. The details were confused because the boys omitted to mention that the woman was naked, and their obvious distress and garbled speech led Harding to give the impression that 'the lady on the beach' was their mother and had fallen from the cliff while using a pair of binoculars. As a result the police and coastguards acted on the presumption that she was still alive.

Because of the difficulty of retrieving a badly injured person from the foreshore, the coastguards dispatched a Search and Rescue helicopter from Portland to winch her off. Meanwhile, PC Nick Ingram, diverted from a burglary investigation, approached via the track that skirted the inappropriately named West Hill on the eastern side of Chapman's Pool. He had had to use bolt cutters to slice through the chain on the gate at Hill Bottom and, as he abandoned his Range Rover on the hard standing beside the fishermen's boatsheds, he was hoping fervently that rubber-neckers wouldn't grab the opportunity to follow him. He was in no mood to marshal petulant sightseers.

The only access from the boatsheds to the beach where the woman lay was by the same route the boys had taken – on foot around the bay, followed by a scramble over the rocks at Egmont Point. To a man in uniform, it was a hot and sweaty business, and Nick Ingram, who stood over six feet four inches and weighed upwards of sixteen stone, was drenched by the time he reached the body. He bent forward, hands on knees, to recover his breath, listening to the deafening sound of the approaching SAR helicopter and feeling its wind on his damp shirt. He thought it a hideous intrusion into what was obviously a place of death. Despite the heat of the sun, the woman's skin was cold to the touch and her widely staring eyes had begun to film. He was struck by how tiny she seemed, lying alone at the bottom of the cliff, and how sad her miniature hand looked waving in the spume.

Her nudity surprised him, the more so when it required only the briefest of glances about the beach to reveal a complete absence of towels, clothes, footwear or possessions. He noticed bruising on her arms, neck and chest, but it was more consistent with being tumbled over rocks on an incoming tide, he thought, than with a dive off a clifftop. He stooped again over the body, looking for anything that would indicate how it had got there, then retreated rapidly as the descending stretcher spiralled dangerously close to his head.

The noise of the helicopter and the amplified voice of the winch-operator calling instructions to the man below had attracted sightseers. The party of hikers gathered on the clifftop to watch the excitement while the yachtsmen in Chapman's

Pool motored out of the bay in their dinghies to do the same. A spirit of revelry was abroad because everyone assumed the rescue wouldn't have happened unless the woman was still alive, and a small cheer went up as the stretcher rose in the air. Most thought she'd fallen from the cliff; a few thought she might have floated out of Chapman's Pool on a lilo and got into difficulties. No one guessed she'd been murdered.

Except, perhaps, Nick Ingram who transferred the tiny, stiffening body to the stretcher and felt a dreadful anger burn inside him because Death had stolen a pretty woman's dignity. As always, the victory belonged to the thief and not to the victim.

As requested by the nine-nine-nine operator, Steven Harding shepherded the boys down the hill to the police car which was parked beside the boatsheds where they waited with varying degrees of patience until its occupant returned. The brothers, who had sunk into an exhausted silence after their mad dash round Chapman's Pool, wanted to be gone, but they were intimidated by their companion, a twenty-four-year-old actor, who took his responsibilities *in loco parentis* seriously.

He kept a watchful eye on his uncommunicative charges (too shocked to speak, he thought) while trying to cheer them up with a running commentary of what he could see of the rescue. He peppered his conversation with expressions like: '*You're a couple of heroes . . .*' '*Your mum's going to be really proud of you . . .*' '*She's a lucky lady to have two such sensible sons . . .*' But it wasn't until the helicopter flew towards Poole and he turned to them with a smile of encouragement, saying: 'There you are, you can stop worrying now. Mum's in safe hands,' that they realized his mistake. It hadn't occurred to either of them that what appeared to be general remarks about their own mother applied specifically to the 'lady on the beach'.

'She's not our mum,' said Paul, dully.

'Our mum's going to be *really* angry,' supplied Danny in his piping treble, emboldened by his brother's willingness to abandon the prolonged silence. 'She said if we were late for lunch she'd make us eat bread and water for a week.' (He was an inventive child.) 'She's going to be even angrier when I tell her it's because Paul wanted to look at a nudie.'

'Shut up,' said his brother.

'*And* he made me climb the cliff so he could get a better look. Dad's going to kill him for ruining the binoculars.'

'Shut *up*.'

'Yeah, well, it's all your fault. You shouldn't have dropped them. *Penis*-brain!' Danny added snidely, in the safe knowledge that their companion would protect him.

Harding watched tears of humiliation gather in the older boy's eyes. It didn't take much reading of the references to 'nudie', 'better look', 'binoculars' and 'penis-brain' to come up with a close approximation of the facts. 'I hope she was worth it,' he said matter-of-factly. 'The first naked woman I ever saw was so old and ugly, it was three years before I wanted to look at another one. She lived in the house next to us and she was as fat and wrinkled as an elephant.'

'What was the next one like?' asked Danny with the sequential logic of a ten-year-old.

Harding exchanged a glance with the elder brother. 'She had nice tits,' he told Paul with a wink.

'So did this one,' said Danny obligingly.

'Except she was dead,' said his brother.

'She probably wasn't, you know. It's not always easy to tell when someone's dead.'

'She was,' said Paul despondently. 'Me and Danny went down to get the binoculars back.' He unravelled his bundled T-shirt to reveal the badly scratched casing of a pair of Zeiss binoculars. 'I – well, I checked to make sure. I think she drowned and got left there by the tide.' He fell into an unhappy silence again.

'He was going to give her the kiss of life,' said Danny, 'but her eyes were nasty, so he didn't.'

Harding cast another glance in the older brother's direction, this time sympathetic. 'The police will need to identify her,' he said matter-of-factly, 'so they'll probably ask you to describe her.' He ruffled Danny's hair. 'It might be better not to mention nasty eyes or nice tits when you do it.'

Danny pulled away. 'I won't.'

The man nodded. 'Good boy.' He took the binoculars from Paul and examined the lenses carefully before pointing them at the Beneteau in Chapman's Pool. 'Did you recognize her?' he asked.

'No,' said Paul uncomfortably.

'Was she an old lady?'

'No.'

'Pretty?'

Paul wriggled his shoulders. 'I guess so.'

'Not fat then?'

'No. She was very little, and she had blonde hair.'

Harding brought the yacht into sharp focus. 'They're built like tanks, these things,' he murmured, traversing the sights across the bay. 'Okay, the bodywork's a bit scratched but there's nothing wrong with the lenses. Your dad won't be that angry.'

Maggie Jenner would never have become involved if Bertie had responded to her whistle, but like all dogs he was deaf when he wanted to be. She had dismounted when the noise of the helicopter alarmed the horse and natural curiosity had led her to walk him on down the hill while the rescue was under way. The three of them rounded the boatsheds together and Bertie, overexcited by all the confusion, made a beeline for Paul Spender's crotch, shoving his nose against the boy's shorts and breathing in with hearty enthusiasm.

Maggie whistled, and was ignored. 'Bertie!' she called. 'Come here, boy!'

The dog was a huge, fearsome-looking brute, the result of a night on the tiles by an Irish wolfhound bitch, and saliva drooled in great white gobbets from his jaws. With a flick of his hairy head, he splattered spittle across Paul's shorts and the terrified child froze in alarm.

'BERTIE!'

'It's all right,' said Harding, grabbing the dog by the collar and pulling him off, 'he's only being friendly.' He rubbed the dog's head. 'Aren't you, boy?'

Unconvinced, the brothers retreated rapidly to the other side of the police car.

'They've had a tough morning,' explained Harding, clicking his tongue encouragingly and walking Bertie back to his mistress. 'Will he stay put if I let him go?'

'Not in this mood,' she said, pulling a lead from her back trouser pocket and clipping one end into the collar before attaching the other end to the nearest stirrup. 'My brother's two boys adore him and he doesn't understand that the rest of the world doesn't view him in quite the same way.' She smiled. 'You must have dogs yourself, either that or you're very brave. Most people run a mile.'

'I grew up on a farm,' he said, stroking Sir Jasper's nose and studying her with frank admiration.

She was a good ten years older than he was, tall and slim with shoulder-length dark hair and deep brown eyes that narrowed suspiciously under his assessing gaze. She knew exactly what type she was dealing with when he looked pointedly at her left hand for the wedding ring that wasn't there. 'Well, thanks for your help,' she said rather brusquely. 'I can manage on my own now.'

He stood back immediately. 'Good luck then,' he said. 'It was nice meeting you.'

She was all too aware that her distrust of men had now

reached pathological proportions, and wondered guiltily if she'd jumped to the wrong conclusion. 'I hope your boys weren't too frightened,' she said rather more warmly.

He gave an easy laugh. 'They're not mine,' he told her. 'I'm just looking after them till the police get back. They found a dead woman on the beach so they're pretty shook up, poor kids. You'd be doing them a favour if you persuaded them Bertie's just an overgrown hearthrug. I'm not convinced that adding canophobia to necrophobia all in one morning is good psychology.'

She looked undecidedly towards the police car. The boys did look frightened, she thought, and she didn't particularly want the responsibility of inspiring a lifelong fear of dogs in them.

'Why don't we invite them over,' he suggested, sensing her hesitation, 'and let them pat him while he's under control? It'll only take a minute or two.'

'All right,' she agreed half-heartedly, 'if you think it would help.' But it was against her better judgement. She had the feeling that once again she was being drawn into something she wouldn't be able to control.

It was after midday by the time PC Ingram returned to his car to find Maggie Jenner, Steven Harding and the Spender brothers waiting beside it. Sir Jasper and Bertie stood at a distance, secure in the shade of a tree, and the aesthete in Nick Ingram could only admire the way the woman displayed herself. Sometimes he thought she had no idea how attractive she was; other times, like now, when she placed herself side by side with natural, equine and human beauty, demanding comparison, he suspected the pose was deliberate. He mopped his forehead with a large white handkerchief, wondering irritably who the Chippendale was and how both he and Maggie managed to look so cool in the intolerable heat of that Sunday morning.

They were looking at him and laughing, and he assumed, in the eternal way of human nature, they were laughing at him.

'Good morning, Miss Jenner,' he said with exaggerated politeness.

She gave a small nod in return. 'Nick.'

He turned enquiringly to Harding. 'Can I help you, sir?'

'I don't think so,' said the young man with an engaging smile. 'I think we're supposed to be helping you.'

Ingram was Dorsetshire born and bred and had no time for wankers in dinky shorts, sporting artificial tans. 'In what way?' There was a hint of sarcasm in his voice that made Maggie Jenner frown at him.

'I was asked to bring these boys to the police car when I made the emergency call. They're the ones who found the dead woman.' He clapped his hands across their shoulders. 'They're a couple of heroes. Maggie and I have just been telling them they deserve medals.'

The 'Maggie' wasn't lost on Ingram although he questioned her enthusiasm for being on Christian-name terms with such an obvious poser. She had better taste, he thought. Ponderously, he shifted his attention to Paul and Danny Spender. The message he had received couldn't have been clearer. Two boys had reported seeing their mother fall from a cliff while using a pair of binoculars. He knew as soon as he saw the body – not enough bruises – that it couldn't have fallen, and looking at the boys now – too relaxed – he doubted the rest of the information. 'Did you know the woman?' he asked them.

They shook their heads.

He unlocked his car door and retrieved a notebook and pencil from the passenger seat. 'What makes you think she was dead, sir?' he asked Harding.

'The boys told me.'

'Is that right?' He examined the young man curiously then deliberately licked the point of his pencil because he knew it would annoy Maggie. 'May I have your name and address, please, plus the name of your employer if you have one?'

'Steven Harding. I'm an actor.' He gave an address in London. 'I live there during the week, but if you have trouble getting hold of me you can always go through my agent, Graham Barlow of the Barlow Agency.' He gave another London address. 'Graham keeps my diary,' he said.

Bully for Graham, thought Ingram sourly, struggling to suppress rampant prejudices against pretty boys . . . Chippendales . . . Londoners . . . actors . . . Harding's address was Highbury, and Ingram would put money on the little poser claiming to be an Arsenal fan, not because he'd ever been to a match but because he'd read *Fever Pitch*, or seen the movie. 'And what brings an actor to our neck of the woods, Mr Harding?'

Harding explained that he was in Poole for a weekend break and had planned to walk to Lulworth Cove and back that day. He patted the mobile telephone that was attached via a clip to his waistband, and said it was a good thing he *had* otherwise the boys would have had to hoof it to Worth Matravers for help.

'You travel light,' said Ingram, glancing at the phone. 'Aren't you worried about dehydrating? It's a long walk to Lulworth.'

The young man shrugged. 'I've changed my mind. I'm going back after this. I hadn't realized how far it was.'

Ingram asked the boys for their names and addresses together with a brief description of what had happened. They told him they'd seen the woman on the beach when they rounded Egmont Point at ten o'clock. 'And then what?' he asked. 'You checked to see if she was dead and went for help?'

They nodded.

'You didn't hurry yourselves, did you?'

'They ran like the clappers,' said Harding, leaping to their defence. 'I saw them.'

'As I recall, sir, your emergency call was timed at 10.43, and it doesn't take nearly three-quarters of an hour for two healthy lads to run round Chapman's Pool.' He stared Harding down. 'And while we're on the subject of misleading information, perhaps you'd care to explain why I received a message saying two boys had seen their mother fall from a clifftop after using a pair of binoculars?'

Maggie made a move as if she was about to say something in support of the boys, but Ingram's intimidating glance in her direction changed her mind.

'Okay, well, it was a misunderstanding,' said Harding, flicking his thick dark hair out of his eyes with a toss of his head. 'These two guys' – he put a friendly arm across Paul's shoulders – 'came charging up the hill shouting and yelling about a woman on the beach beyond the Point and some binoculars falling, and I rather stupidly put two and two together and made five. The truth is, we were all a bit het-up. *They* were worried about the binoculars and *I* thought they were talking about their mother.' He took the Zeisses from Paul's hands and gave them to Ingram. 'These belong to their father. The boys dropped them by accident when they saw the woman. They're very concerned about how their dad's going to react when he sees the damage, but Maggie and I have persuaded them he won't be angry, not when he hears what a good job they've done.'

'Do you know the boys' father, sir?' asked Ingram, examining the binoculars.

'No, of course not. I've only just met them.'

'Then you've only their word that these belong to him?'

'Well, yes, I suppose so.' Harding looked uncertainly at Paul and saw the return of panic in the boy's eyes. 'Oh, come on,' he said abruptly. 'Where else could they have got them?'

'Off the beach. You said you saw the woman when you rounded Egmont Point,' he reminded Paul and Danny.

They nodded in petrified unison.

'Then why do these binoculars look as if they've fallen

down a cliff? Did you find them beside the woman and decide to take them?'

The boys, growing red in the face with anxiety about their peeping Tom act, looked guilty. Neither answered.

'Look, lighten up,' said Harding unwarily. 'It was a bit of fun, that's all. The woman was nude so they climbed up for a better look. They didn't realize she was dead until they dropped the binoculars and went down to get them.'

'You saw all this, did you, sir?'

'No,' he admitted. 'I've already told you I was coming from St Alban's Head.'

Ingram turned to his right to look at the distant promontory topped by its tiny Norman chapel, dedicated to St Alban. 'You get a very good view of Egmont Bight from up there,' he said idly, 'particularly on a fine day like this.'

'Only through binoculars,' said Harding.

Ingram smiled as he looked the young man up and down. 'True,' he agreed. 'So where did you and the boys run into each other?'

Harding gestured towards the coastal path. 'They started shouting at me when they were halfway up Emmetts Hill, so I went down to meet them.'

'You seem to know the area well.'

'I do.'

'How come, when you live in London?'

'I spend a lot of time here. London can be pretty hellish in the summer.'

Ingram glanced up the steep hillside. 'This is called West Hill,' he remarked. 'Emmetts Hill is the next one along.'

Harding gave an amiable shrug. 'Okay, so I don't know it *that* well, but normally I come in by boat,' he said, 'and there's no mention of West Hill on the Admiralty charts. This whole escarpment is referred to as Emmetts Hill. The boys and I ran into each other approximately there.' He pointed towards a spot on the green hillside above them.

Out of the corner of his eye, Ingram noticed Paul Spender's frown of disagreement but he didn't remark on it.

'Where's your boat now, Mr Harding?'

'Poole. I sailed her in late last night but as the wind's almost non-existent and I fancied some exercise' – he favoured Nick Ingram with a boyish smile – 'I took to my legs.'

'What's the name of your boat, Mr Harding?'

'*Crazy Daze*. It's a play on words. Daze is spelt D-A-Z-E, not D-A-Y-S.'

The tall policeman's smile was anything but boyish. 'Where's she normally berthed?'

'Lymington.'

'Did you come from Lymington yesterday?'

'Yes.'

'Alone?'

There was a tiny hesitation. 'Yes.'

Ingram held his gaze for a moment. 'Are you sailing back tonight?'

'That's the plan, although I'll probably have to motor if the wind doesn't improve.'

The constable nodded in apparent satisfaction. 'Well, thank you very much, Mr Harding. I don't think I need detain you any longer. I'll get these boys home and check on the binoculars.'

Harding felt Paul and Danny sidle in behind him for protection. 'You will point out what a good job they've done, won't you?' he urged. 'I mean, but for these two, that poor little woman could have floated out on the next tide and you'd never have known she was there. They deserve a medal, not aggro from their father.'

'You're very well informed, sir.'

'Trust me. I know this coast. There's a continuous south-south-easterly stream running towards St Alban's Head, and if she'd been sucked into that the chances of her resurfacing would have been nil. It's got one hell of a back eddy on it. My guess is she'd have been pounded to pieces on the bottom.'

Ingram smiled. 'I meant you were well informed about the woman, Mr Harding. Anyone would think you'd seen her yourself.'

Chapter Three

'WHY WERE YOU so hard on him?' asked Maggie critically as the policeman shut the boys into the back of his Range Rover and stood with eyes narrowed against the sun watching Harding walk away up the hill. Ingram was so tall and so solidly built that he cast her literally and figuratively into the shade, and he would get under her skin less, she often thought, if just once in a while he recognized that fact. She only felt comfortable in his presence when she was looking down on him from the back of a horse, but those occasions were too rare for her self-esteem to benefit from them. When he didn't answer her, she glanced impatiently towards the brothers on the back seat. 'You were pretty rough on the children, too. I bet they'll think twice before helping the police again.'

Harding disappeared from sight around a bend, and Ingram turned to her with a lazy smile. 'How was I hard on him, Miss Jenner?'

'Oh, come on! You all but accused him of lying.'

'He *was* lying.'

'What about?'

'I'm not sure yet. I'll know when I've made a few enquiries.'

'Is this a male thing?' she asked in a voice made silky by long-pent-up grudges. He had been her community policeman for five years, and she had much to feel resentful for. At times of deep depression, she blamed him for everything. Other times, she was honest enough to admit that he had only been doing his job.

'Probably.' He could smell the stables on her clothes, a musty scent of hay dust and horse manure that he half-liked and half-loathed.

'Then wouldn't it have been simpler just to whip out your willy and challenge him to a knob-measuring contest?' she asked sarcastically.

'I'd have lost.'

'That's for sure,' she agreed.

His smile widened. 'You noticed then?'

'I could hardly avoid it. He wasn't wearing those shorts to disguise anything. Perhaps it was his wallet. There was precious little room for it anywhere else.'

'No,' he agreed. 'Didn't you find that interesting?'

She looked at him suspiciously, wondering if he was making fun of her. 'In what way?'

'Only an idiot sets out from Poole for Lulworth with no money and no fluid.'

'Maybe he was planning to beg water off passers-by or telephone a friend to come and rescue him. Why is it important? All he did was play the good Samaritan to those kids.'

'I think he was lying about what he was doing here. Did he give a different explanation before I got back?'

She thought about it. 'We talked about dogs and horses. He was telling the boys about the farm he grew up on in Cornwall.'

He reached for the handle on the driver's door. 'Then perhaps I'm just suspicious of people who carry mobile telephones,' he said.

'Everyone has them these days, including me.'

He ran an amused eye over her slender figure in its tight cotton shirt and stretch jeans. 'But you don't bring yours on country rambles whereas that young man does. Apparently he leaves everything behind except his phone.'

'You should be grateful,' she said tartly. 'But for him, you'd never have got to the woman so quickly.'

'I agree,' he said without rancour. 'Mr Harding was in the right place at the right time with the right equipment to report a body on a beach and it would be churlish to ask why.' He opened the door and squeezed his huge frame in behind the wheel. 'Good day, Miss Jenner,' he said politely. 'My regards to your mother.' He pulled the door to and fired the engine.

The Spender brothers were in two minds who to thank for their untroubled return home. The actor because his pleas for tolerance worked? Or the policeman because he was a decent bloke after all? He had said very little on the drive back to their rented cottage other than to warn them that the cliffs were dangerous and that it was foolish to climb them, however tempting the reason. To their parents he gave a brief, expurgated account of what had happened, ending with the suggestion that, as the boys' fishing had been interrupted by the events of the morning, he would be happy to take them out on his boat one evening. 'It's not a motor cruiser,' he warned them, 'just a small fishing boat, but the sea bass run at this time of year and if we're lucky we might catch one or two.' He didn't put his arms round their shoulders or call them heroes, but he did give them something to look forward to.

Next on Ingram's agenda was an isolated farmhouse where the elderly occupants had reported the theft of three valuable paintings during the night. He had been on his way there when he was diverted to Chapman's Pool and, while he guessed he was wasting his time, community policing was what he was paid for.

'Oh God, Nick, I'm so sorry,' said the couple's harassed daughter-in-law who, herself, was on the wrong side of seventy. 'Believe me, they did *know* the paintings were being auctioned. Peter's been talking them through it for the last twelve months but they're so forgetful, he has to start again from scratch every time. He has power of attorney, so it's all quite legal, but, honestly, I nearly *died* when Winnie said she'd called you. And on a *Sunday*, too. I come over every morning to make sure they're all right but *sometimes . . .*' She rolled her eyes to heaven, expressing without the need for words exactly what she thought of her ninety-five-year-old parents-in-law.

'It's what I'm here for, Jane,' he said, giving her shoulder an encouraging pat.

'No it's not. You should be out catching criminals,' she said, echoing the words of people across the nation who saw the police only as thief-takers. She heaved a huge sigh. 'The trouble is their outgoings are way in excess of their income and they're incapable of grasping the fact. The home help *alone* costs over ten thousand pounds a year. Peter's having to sell off the family silver to make ends meet. The silly old things seem to think they're living in the 1920s when a housemaid cost five bob a week. It drives me mad, it really does. They ought to be in a home, but Peter's too soft-hearted to put them there. *Not* that they could afford it. I mean *we* can't afford it, so how could they? It would be different if Celia Jenner hadn't per-suaded us to gamble everything on that beastly husband of Maggie's but . . .' She broke off on a shrug of despair. 'I get so angry sometimes I could scream, and the only thing that stops me is that I'm afraid the scream would go on for ever.'

'Nothing lasts for ever,' he said.

'I know,' she said mutinously, 'but once in a while I think about giving eternity a hand. It's such a pity you can't buy arsenic any more. It was so easy in the old days.'

'Tell me about it.'

She laughed. 'You know what I mean.'

'Should I order a post-mortem when Peter's parents finally pop their clogs?'

'Chance'd be a fine thing. At this rate I'll be dead long before they are.'

The tall policeman smiled and made his farewells. He didn't want to hear about death. *He could still feel the touch of the woman's flesh on his hands* . . . He needed a shower, he thought, as he made his way back to his car.

The blonde toddler marched steadfastly along a pavement in the Lilliput area of Poole, planting one chubby leg in front of the other. It was 10.30 on Sunday morning so people were scarce, and no one took the trouble to find out why she was alone. When a handful of witnesses came forward later to admit to the police that they'd seen her, the excuses varied. '*She seemed to know where she was going.*' '*There was a woman about twenty yards behind her and I thought she was the child's mother.*' '*I assumed someone else would stop.*' '*I was in a hurry.*' '*I'm a bloke. I'd have been strung up for giving a lift to a little girl.*'

In the end it was an elderly couple, Mr and Mrs Green, who had the sense, the time and the courage to interfere. They were on their way back from church and, as they did every week, they made a nostalgic detour through Lilliput to look at the art deco buildings that had somehow survived the post-war craze for mass demolition of anything out of the ordinary in favour of constructing reinforced concrete blocks and red-brick boxes. Lilliput sprawled along the eastern curve of Poole Bay and, amid the architectural dross that could be found anywhere, were elegant villas in manicured gardens and art deco houses with windows like portholes. The Greens adored it. It reminded them of their youth.

They were passing the turning to Salterns Marina when Mrs Green noticed the little girl. 'Look at that,' she said disapprovingly. 'What sort of mother would let a child of that age get so far ahead of her? It only takes a stumble and she'd be under a car.'

Mr Green slowed. 'Where's the mother?' he asked.

His wife twisted in her seat. 'Do you know, I'm not sure. I thought it was that woman behind her, but she's looking in a shop window.'

Mr Green was a retired sergeant major. 'We should do something,' he said firmly, drawing to a halt and putting the car into reverse. He shook his fist at a motorist who hooted ferociously after missing his back bumper by the skin of his teeth. 'Bloody Sunday drivers,' he said, 'they shouldn't be allowed on the road.'

'Quite right, dear,' said Mrs Green, opening her door.

She scooped the poor little mite into her arms and sat her comfortably on her knee while her eighty-year-old husband drove to Poole police station. It was a tortuous journey because his preferred speed was twenty miles an hour and this caused mayhem in the one-way system round the Civic Centre roundabout.

The child seemed completely at ease in the car, smiling happily out of the window, but once inside the police station, it proved impossible to prize her away from her rescuer. She locked her arms about the elderly woman's neck, hiding her face against her shoulder and clung to kindness as tenaciously as a barnacle clings to a rock. Upon learning that no one had reported a toddler missing, Mr and Mrs Green sat themselves down with commendable patience and prepared for a long wait.

'I can't understand why her mother hasn't noticed she's gone,' said Mrs Green. 'I never allowed my own children out of sight for a minute.'

'Maybe she's at work,' said the woman police constable who had been detailed to make the enquiries.

'Well, she shouldn't be,' said Mr Green reprovingly. 'A child of this age needs her mother with her.' He pulled a knowing expression in WPC Griffiths's direction which resolved itself into a series of peculiar facial jerks. 'You should get a doctor to examine her. Know what I'm saying? Odd people about these days. Men who should know better. Get my meaning?' He spelled it out. 'P-A-E-do-*fills*. S-E-X criminals. Know what I'm saying?'

'Yes, sir, I know exactly what you're saying, and don't worry' – the WPC tapped her pen on the paper in front of her – 'the doctor's at the top of my list. But if you don't mind we'll take it gently. We've had a lot of dealings with this kind of thing and we've found the best method is not to rush at it.' She turned to the woman with an encouraging smile. 'Has she told you her name?'

Mrs Green shook her head. 'She hasn't said a word, dear. To be honest, I'm not sure she can.'

'How old do you think she is?'

'Eighteen months, two at the most.' She lifted the edge of the child's cotton dress to reveal a pair of disposable trainer pants. 'She's still in nappies, poor little thing.'

The WPC thought two years old was an underestimation, and added a year for the purposes of the paperwork. Women like Mrs Green had reared their children on terry towelling and, because of the washing involved, had had them potty-trained early. The idea that a three-year-old might still be in nappies was incomprehensible to them.

Not that it made any difference as far as this little girl was concerned. Whether she was eighteen months old, two years old or three, she clearly wasn't talking.

With nothing else to occupy her that Sunday afternoon, the French girl from the Beneteau, who had been an interested observer of Harding's conversations with the Spender brothers, Maggie Jenner and PC Ingram through the video camera's zoom lens, rowed herself into shore and walked up the steep slope of West Hill to try to work out for herself what the mystery had been about. It wasn't hard to guess that the two boys had found the person who had been winched off the beach by helicopter, nor that the handsome Englishman had reported it to the police for them, but she was curious about why he had re-emerged on the hillside half an hour after the police car's departure to retrieve the rucksack he'd abandoned there. She had watched him take out some binoculars and scan the bay and the cliffs before making his way down to the foreshore beyond the boatsheds. She had filmed him for several minutes, staring out to sea, but she was no wiser, having reached his vantage point above Chapman's Pool, than she'd been before and, thoroughly bored, she abandoned the puzzle.

It would be another five days before her father came across the tape and humiliated her in front of the English police . . .

At six o'clock that evening the Fairline Squadron weighed anchor and motored gently out of Chapman's Pool in the direction of St Alban's Head. Two languid girls sat on either side of their father on the flying bridge, while his latest companion sat, alone and excluded, on the seat behind them. Once clear of the shallow waters at the mouth of the bay, the boat roared to full power and made off at twenty-five knots on the return journey to Poole, carving a V-shaped wake out of the flat sea behind it.

Heat and alcohol had made them all soporific, particularly the father who had overexerted himself in his efforts to please his daughters, and after setting the autopilot he appointed the elder one lookout before closing his eyes. He could feel the daggers of his girlfriend's fury carving away at his back and, with a stifled sigh, wished he'd had the sense to leave her behind. She was the latest in a string of what his daughters called his 'bimbos' and, as usual, they had set out to trample on the fragile shoots of his new relationship. Life, he thought resentfully, was bloody . . .

'Watch out, Dad!' his daughter screamed in sudden alarm. 'We're heading straight for a rock.'

The man's heart thudded against his chest as he wrenched the wheel violently, slewing the boat to starboard, and what his daughter had thought was a rock slid past on the port side to dance in the boisterous wake. 'I'm too old for all of this,' he said shakily, steering his three hundred thousand-pound boat back on to course and mentally checking the current state of his insurance. 'What the hell was it? It can't have been a rock. There are no rocks out here.'

The two youngsters, eyes watering, squinted into the burning sun to make out the black, bobbing shape behind them. 'It looks like one of those big oil drums,' said the elder.

'Jesus wept,' growled her father. 'Whoever let that wash overboard deserves to be shot. It could have ripped us open if we'd hit it.'

His girlfriend, still twisted round, thought it looked more like an upturned dinghy but was reluctant to voice an opinion for fear of attracting any more of his beastly daughters' derision. She'd had a bucketful already that day, and heartily wished she had never agreed to come out with them.

'I bumped into Nick Ingram this morning,' said Maggie as she made a pot of tea in her mother's kitchen at Broxton House.

It had been a beautiful room once, lined with old oak dressers, each one piled with copper pans and ornate crockery, and with an eight-foot-long, seventeenth-century refectory table down its middle. Now it was merely drab. Everything worth selling had been sold. Cheap white wall and floor units had replaced the wooden dressers and a moulded plastic excrescence from the garden stood where the monks' table had reigned resplendent. It wouldn't be so bad, Maggie often thought, if the room was cleaned occasionally, but her mother's arthritis and her own terminal exhaustion from trying to make money out of horses meant that cleanliness had long since gone the way of godliness. If God was in his heaven, and all was right with the world, then he had a peculiar blind spot when it came to Broxton House. Maggie would have cut her losses and moved away long ago if only her mother had agreed to do the same. Guilt enslaved her. Now she lived in a flat over the stables on the other side of the garden, and made only intermittent visits to the house. Its awful emptiness was too obvious a reminder that her mother's poverty was her fault.

'I took Jasper down to Chapman's Pool. A woman drowned in Egmont Bight and Nick had to guide the helicopter in to pick up the body.'

'A tourist, I suppose?'

'Presumably,' said Maggie, handing her a cup. 'Nick would have said if it was someone local.'

'Typical!' snorted Celia crossly. 'So Dorset will foot the bill for the helicopter because some inept creature from another county never learnt to swim properly. I've a good mind to withhold my taxes.'

'You usually do,' said Maggie, thinking of the final reminders that littered the desk in the drawing room.

Her mother ignored the remark. 'How was Nick?'

'Hot,' said her daughter, remembering how red-faced he had been when he returned to the car, 'and not in the best of moods.' She stared into her tea, screwing up the courage to address the thorny issue of money, or more accurately lack of money, coming into the riding and livery business she ran from the Broxton House stableyard. 'We need to talk about the stables,' she said abruptly.

Celia refused to be drawn. 'You wouldn't have been in a good mood either if you'd just seen a drowned body.' Her tone became conversational as a prelude to a series of anecdotes. 'I remember seeing one floating down the Ganges when I was staying with my parents in India. It was the summer holidays. I think I was about fifteen at the time. It was a horrible thing, gave me nightmares for weeks. My mother said . . .'

Maggie stopped listening and fixed instead on a long black

hair growing out of her mother's chin which needed plucking. It bristled aggressively as she spoke, like one of Bertie's whiskers, but they'd never had the kind of relationship that meant Maggie could tell her about it. Celia, at sixty-three, was still a good-looking woman with the same dark brown hair as her daughter, touched up from time to time with Harmony colour rinses, but the worry of their straitened circumstances had taken a heavy toll in the deep lines around her mouth and eyes.

When she finally drew breath, Maggie reverted immediately to the subject of the stables. 'I've been totting up last month's receipts,' she said, 'and we're about two hundred quid short. Did you let Mary Spencer-Graham off paying again?'

Celia's mouth thinned. 'If I did it's my affair.'

'No it's not, Ma,' said Maggie with a sigh. 'We can't afford to be charitable. If Mary doesn't pay then we can't look after her horse. It's as simple as that. I wouldn't mind so much if we weren't already charging her the absolute minimum but the fees barely cover Moondust's fodder. You really must be a bit tougher with her.'

'How can I? She's almost as badly off as we are, and it's our fault.'

Maggie shook her head. 'That's not true. She lost ten thousand pounds, peanuts compared with what we lost, but she knows she only has to turn on the waterworks for half a second and you fall for it every time.' She gestured impatiently towards the hall and the drawing room beyond. 'We can't pay the bills if we don't collect the money, which means we either decide to hand everything over now to Matthew and go and live in a council flat or you go to him, cap in hand, and beg for some kind of allowance.' She gave a helpless shrug at the thought of her brother. 'If I believed there was any point in my trying, I would, but we both know he'd slam the door in my face.'

Celia gave a mirthless laugh. 'What makes you think it would be any different if I tried? That wife of his can't stand me. She'd never agree to keeping her mother-in-law and sister-in-law in what she chooses to call the lap of luxury when her real pleasure in life would be to see us destitute.'

'I know,' said Maggie guiltily, 'and it serves us right. We should never have been rude about her wedding dress.'

'It was difficult not to be,' said Celia tartly. 'The vicar nearly had a heart attack when he saw her.'

Her daughter's eyes filled with humour. 'It was the greenfly that did it. If there hadn't been a plague of the blasted things the year they got married, and if her wretched veil hadn't collected every single one in a twenty-mile radius while she walked from the church to the reception . . . What was it you called her? Something to do with camouflage.'

'I didn't call her anything,' said Celia with dignity. 'I congratulated her for blending so well into her surroundings.'

Maggie laughed. 'That's right, I remember now. God, you were rude.'

'You found it funny at the time,' her mother pointed out, easing her bad hip on the chair. 'I'll talk to Mary,' she promised. 'I can probably bear the humiliation of dunning my friends rather better than I can bear the humiliation of begging off Matthew and Ava.'

Chapter Four

Physical/psychological assessment of unidentified toddler: 'Baby Smith'

Physical: The child's general health is excellent. She is well nourished and well cared for, and is not suffering from any disease or ailment. Blood test indicates minute traces of benzodiazepine (possibly Mogadon) and stronger traces of paracetamol in her system. There is no evidence of past or recent abuse, sexual or physical, although there is some evidence (see below) that she has suffered past, continuing or recent psychological trauma. The physical evidence suggests that she was separated from her parent/guardian within 3–4 hours of being found – most notably in terms of her overall cleanliness and the fact that she hadn't soiled herself. In addition she showed no signs of dehydration, hypothermia, hunger or exhaustion which would have been expected in a child who had been abandoned for any length of time.

Psychological: The child's behaviour and social skills are typical of a two-year-old, however her size and weight suggest she is older. She presents evidence of mild autism although knowledge of her history is needed to confirm a diagnosis. She is uninterested in other people/children and reacts aggressively when approached by them. She is overly passive, preferring to sit and observe rather than explore her environment. She is unnaturally withdrawn and makes no attempt to communicate verbally, although will use sign language to achieve what she wants. Her hearing is unimpaired and she listens to everything that's said to her; however, she is selective about which instructions she chooses to obey. As a simple example, she is happy to point to a blue cube when asked, but refuses to pick it up.

While she is unable or unwilling to use words to communicate, she resorts very quickly to screams and tantrums when her wishes are thwarted or when she feels herself stressed. This is particularly evident when strangers enter the room, or when voices rise above a monotone. She invariably refuses any sort of physical contact on a first meeting but holds out her arms to be picked up on a second. This would indicate good recognition skills, yet she evinces a strong fear of men and screams in terror whenever they intrude into her space. In the absence of any indication of physical or sexual abuse, this fear may stem from: unfamiliarity with men as a result of being raised in a sheltered, all-female environment; witnessing male aggression against another – e.g. mother or sibling.

Conclusions: In view of the child's backward development and apparent stress-related disorders, she should not be returned to her family/guardians without exhaustive enquiries being made about the nature of the household. It is also imperative that she be placed on the 'at risk' register to allow continuous monitoring of her future welfare. I am seriously concerned about the traces of benzodiazepine and paracetamol in her bloodstream. Benzodiazepine (strong hypnotic) is not recommended for children, and certainly not in conjunction with paracetamol. I suspect the child was sedated, but can think of no legitimate reason why this should have been necessary.

N.B. Without knowing more of the child's history, it is difficult to say whether her behaviour is due to: (1) autism; (2) psychiatric trauma; (3) taught dependence which, while leaving her ignorant of her own capabilities, has encouraged her to be consciously manipulative.

Dr Janet Murray

Chapter Five

IT HAD BEEN a long twenty-four hours and WPC Sandra Griffiths was yawning as her telephone started to ring again at noon on Monday. She had done several local radio and television interviews to publicize Lily's abandonment (named after Lilliput where she was found), but although the response to the programmes had been good, not one caller had been able to tell her who the child was. She blamed the weather. Too many people were out in the sunshine; too few watching their sets. She stifled the yawn as she picked up the receiver.

The man at the other end sounded worried. 'I'm sorry to bother you,' he told her, 'but I've just had my mother on the phone. She's incredibly het-up about some toddler wandering the streets who looks like my daughter. I've told her it can't possibly be Hannah, but' – he paused – 'well, the thing is we've both tried phoning my wife and neither of us can get an answer.'

Griffiths tucked the receiver under her chin and reached for a pen. This was the twenty-fifth father to phone since the toddler's photograph had been broadcast, and all were estranged from their wives and children. She had no higher hopes of this one than she'd had of the previous twenty-four but she went through the motions willingly enough. 'If you'll answer one or two questions for me, sir, we can establish very quickly whether the little girl is Hannah. May I have your name and address?'

'William Sumner, Langton Cottage, Rope Walk, Lymington, Hampshire.'

'And do your wife and daughter still live with you, Mr Sumner?'

'Yes.'

Her interest sharpened immediately. 'When did you last see them?'

'Four days ago. I'm at a pharmaceutical conference in Liverpool. I spoke to Kate – that's my wife – on Friday night and everything was fine, but my mother's positive this toddler's Hannah. It doesn't make sense though. Mum says she was found in Poole yesterday, but how could Hannah be wandering around Poole on her own when we live in Lymington?'

Griffiths listened to the rising alarm in his voice. 'Are you phoning from Liverpool now?' she asked calmly.

'Yes. I'm staying in the Regal, room number two-two-three-five. What should I do? My mother's beside herself with worry. I need to reassure her that everything's all right.'

And yourself, too, she thought. 'Could you give me a description of Hannah?'

'She looks like her mother,' he said rather helplessly. 'Blonde, blue eyes. She doesn't talk very much. We've been worrying about it but the doctor says it's just shyness.'

'How old is she?'

'She'll be three next month.'

The policewoman winced in sympathy as she put the next question, guessing what his answer was going to be. 'Does Hannah have a pink cotton dress with smocking on it and a pair of red sandals, Mr Sumner?'

It took him a second or two to answer. 'I don't know about the sandals,' he said with difficulty, 'but my mother bought her a smocked dress about three months ago. I think it was pink – no, it *was* pink. Oh God' – his voice broke – 'where's Kate?'

She waited a moment. 'Did you drive to Liverpool, Mr Sumner?'

'Yes.'

'Do you know roughly how long it will take you to get home?'

'Five hours maybe.'

'And where does your mother live?'

'Chichester.'

'Then I think you'd better give me her name and address, sir. If the little girl *is* Hannah, then she can identify her for us. Meantime I'll ask Lymington police to check your house while I make enquiries about your wife here in Poole.'

'Mrs Angela Sumner, Flat Two, The Old Convent, Osborne Crescent, Chichester.' His breathing became laboured – *with tears?* – and Griffiths wished herself a million miles away. How she hated the fact that, nine times out of ten, she was the harbinger of bad news. 'But there's no way she can get to Poole. She's been in a wheelchair for the last three years and can't drive. If she could, she'd have gone to Lymington to check on Kate and Hannah herself. Can't I make the identification?'

'By all means, if that's what you prefer. The little girl's in the care of a foster family at the moment, and it won't harm her to stay there a few more hours.'

'My mother's convinced Hannah's been abused by some man. Is that what's happened? I'd rather know now than later.'

'Assuming the little girl is Hannah, then, no, there's no evidence of any sort of physical abuse. She's been thoroughly checked and the police doctor's satisfied that she hasn't been harmed in any way.' She glossed over Dr Murray's damning psychological assessment. If Lily were indeed Hannah Sumner, then that particular issue would have to be taken up later.

'What kind of enquiries can you make about my wife in Poole?' he asked in bewilderment, reverting to what she'd said previously. 'I told you, we live in Lymington.'

The hospital kind . . . 'Routine ones, Mr Sumner. It would

42

help if you could give me her full name and a description of her. Also the type, colour and registration number of her car and the names of any friends she has in the area.'

'Kate Elizabeth Sumner. She's thirty-one, about five feet tall and blonde. The car's a blue Metro, registration F52 VXY, but I don't think she knows anyone in Poole. Could she have been taken to hospital? Could something have gone wrong with the pregnancy?'

'It's one of the things I'll be checking, Mr Sumner.' She was flicking through the RTA reports on the computer while she was talking to him, but there was no mention of a blue Metro with that registration being involved in a road accident. 'Are your wife's parents living. Would they know where she is?'

'No. Her mother died five years ago and she never knew her father.'

'Brothers? Sisters?'

'She hasn't got anyone except me and Hannah.' His voice broke again. 'What am I going to do? I won't be able to cope if something's happened to her.'

'There's no reason to think anything's happened,' said Griffiths firmly, while believing the exact opposite. 'Do you have a mobile telephone in your car? If so I can keep you up to date as you drive down.'

'No.'

'Then I suggest you break your journey at the halfway mark to ring from a callbox. I should have news from Lymington police by then, and with luck I'll be able to set your mind at rest about Kate. And try not to worry, Mr Sumner,' she finished kindly. 'It's a long drive from Liverpool, and the important thing is to get yourself back in one piece.'

She put through a call to Lymington police, explaining the details of the case and asking for a check to be made of Sumner's address, then as a matter of routine dialled the Regal Hotel in Liverpool to enquire whether a Mr William Sumner had been registered in room two-two-three-five since Thursday. 'Yes, ma'am,' said the receptionist, 'but I can't put you through, I'm afraid. He left five minutes ago.'

Reluctantly, she started on the list of hospitals.

For various reasons, Nick Ingram had no ambitions to move away from his rural police station where life revolved around community policing and the hours were predictable. Major cases were handled thirty miles away at County HQ Winfrith, and this left him free to deal with the less glamorous side of policing which for 95 per cent of the population was the only side that mattered. People slept sounder in their beds knowing that PC Ingram had zero tolerance for lager louts, vandals and petty thieves.

Real trouble usually came from outside, and the unidentified woman on the beach looked like being a case in point, he thought, when a call came through from Winfrith at 12.45 p.m. on Monday, 11 August. The Coroner's Office at Poole had ordered a murder inquiry following the post-mortem, and he was told to expect a DI and a DS from headquarters within the hour. A scene of crime team had already been dispatched to search the beach at Egmont Bight but Ingram was requested to stay where he was.

'I don't think they'll find anything,' he said helpfully. 'I had a bit of a scout round yesterday but it was fairly obvious the sea had washed her up.'

'I suggest you leave that to us,' said the unemotional voice at the other end.

Ingram gave a shrug at his end. 'What did she die of?'

'Drowning,' came the blunt response. 'She was thrown into the open sea after an attempt at manual strangulation which failed. The pathologist guestimates she swam half a mile to try and save herself before she gave up from exhaustion. She was fourteen weeks pregnant, and her killer held her down and raped her before pitching her over the side.'

Ingram was shocked. 'What sort of man would do that?'

'An unpleasant one. We'll see you in an hour.'

Griffiths drew a series of blanks with the name Kate Sumner – there was no record of her at any hospital in Dorset or Hampshire. It was only when she made a routine check through Winfrith to see if there was any information on the whereabouts of a small blonde woman, aged thirty-one, who appeared to have gone missing from Lymington within the last forty-eight hours that the scattered pieces of the jigsaw began to come together.

The two detectives arrived punctually for their meeting with PC Ingram. The sergeant, an arrogant, pushy type with ambitions to join the Met, who clearly believed that every conversation was an opportunity to impress, went down like a lead balloon with his rural colleague and Ingram was never able afterwards to remember his name. He talked in bullet points 'reference a major investigation' in which 'speed was the essence' before the murderer had a chance to get rid of evidence and/or strike again. Local marinas, yacht clubs and harbours were being 'targeted' for information on the victim and/or her killer. Victim identification was the 'first priority'. They had a possible lead on a missing IC/1 female, but no one was counting chickens until her husband identified a photograph and/or the body. The second priority was to locate the boat she'd come off and give forensics a chance to strip it top-to-bottom in search of non-intimate samples that would connect it to the body. Give us a suspect, he suggested, and DNA testing would do the rest.

Ingram raised an eyebrow when the monologue came to an end but didn't say anything.

'Did you follow all that?' asked the sergeant impatiently.

'I think so, si-rr,' he said in a broad Dorsetshire burr, resisting the temptation to tug his forelock. 'If you find some of her hairs on a man's boat that'll mean he's the rapist.'

'Near enough.'

'That's amazing, sir-rr,' murmured Ingram.

'You don't sound convinced,' said DI Galbraith, watching his performance with amusement.

He shrugged and reverted to his normal accent. 'The only thing that non-intimate samples will prove is that she visited his boat at least once, and that's not proof of rape. The only useful DNA tests will have to be done on her.'

'Well, don't hold your breath,' the DI warned. 'Water doesn't leave trace evidence. The pathologist's taken swabs but he's not optimistic about getting a result. Either she was in the sea too long and anything useful was flushed away or her attacker was wearing a condom.' He was a pleasant-looking man with cropped, ginger hair and a smiling, freckled face that made him look younger than his forty-two years. It also belied a sharp intelligence that caught people unawares if they were foolish enough to stereotype him by his appearance.

'How long was long?' asked Ingram with genuine curiosity. 'Put it this way, how does the pathologist know she swam half a mile? It's a very precise estimate for an unpredictable stretch of water.'

'He based it on the condition of the body, prevailing winds and currents, and the fact that she must have been alive when she reached the shelter of Egmont Point,' said John Galbraith, opening his briefcase and extracting a sheet of paper. 'Victim died of drowning at or around high water which was at 1.52 a.m. British Summer Time on Sunday, 10 August,' he said, skip-reading the document. 'Several indicators, such as evidence of hypothermia, the fact that a keeled boat couldn't have sailed too close to the cliffs and the currents around St Alban's Head suggest she entered the sea' – he tapped the page with his finger – 'a *minimum* of half a mile west-south-west of where the body was found.'

'Okay, well assuming the minimum, that doesn't mean she swam half a mile. There are some strong currents along this part of the coast, so the sea would have caused her eastward drift. In real terms she would only have swum a couple of hundred yards.'

'I presume that was taken into account.'

Ingram frowned. 'So why was she showing evidence of hypothermia? The winds have been light for the last week and the sea's been calm. In those conditions, an average swimmer could cover two hundred yards in fifteen to twenty minutes. Also, the sea temperature would have been several degrees higher than the night air, so she'd be more likely to develop hypothermia on the beach than she would in the water, especially if she was naked.'

'In which case she wouldn't have died from drowning.'

'No.'

'So what's the point you're making?' asked Galbraith.

Nick shook his head. 'I don't know except that I'm having trouble reconciling the body I saw with what the pathologist is saying. When the lifeboat crew at Swanage fished a corpse out of the sea last year, it was black with bruises and had swelled to twice its normal size.'

The DI consulted the paper again. 'Okay, well there's a time constraint. He says the time of death must have coincided with high water to leave it stranded on the beach as the tide receded. He also makes the argument that if she hadn't reached the shelter of Egmont Point before she drowned, the body would have been pulled under by back eddies and towed out round St Alban's Head. Put those two together and you have your answer, don't you? In simple terms she must have died within yards of the shore and her body was stranded shortly afterwards.'

'That's very sad,' said Ingram, thinking of the tiny hand waving in the spume.

'Yes,' agreed Galbraith who had seen the body in the mortuary and was as moved by the unnecessary death as Ingram was. He found the constable easy to like. But then he always preferred policemen who showed emotion. It was a sign of honesty.

'What evidence is there that she was raped if everything useful was flushed away?'

'Bruising to the inside of her thighs and back. Rope marks on her wrists. Bloodstream full of benzodiazepine . . . probably Rohypnol. Do you know what that is?'

'Mmm. The date-rape drug . . . I've read about it . . . haven't come across it, though.'

Galbraith handed him the report. 'It'll be better if you read it yourself. They're preliminary notes only, but Warner never commits anything to paper unless he's pretty damn sure he's right.'

It wasn't a long document and Ingram read it quickly. 'So you're looking for a boat with bloodstains?' he said, laying the pages on the desk in front of him when he'd finished.

'Also skin tissue if she was raped on a wooden deck.'

The tall policeman gave a doubtful shake of his head. 'I wouldn't be too optimistic,' he said. 'He'll hose down the deck and the topsides the minute he gets into a marina and what the sea hasn't already taken, fresh water will finish off.'

'We know,' said Galbraith, 'which is why we need to get a move on. Our only lead is this tentative identification which, if it's true, suggests the boat she was on might have come from Lymington.' He took out his notebook. 'A three-year-old kid was found abandoned near one of the marinas in Poole yester-day and the description of the missing mother matches our victim. Her name's Kate Sumner and she lives in Lymington. Her husband's been in Liverpool for the last four days but he's on his way back now to make the identification.'

Ingram picked up the incident report he'd typed that morning and squared it between his large hands. 'It's probably just coincidence,' he said thoughtfully, 'but the guy who made the emergency call keeps a boat in Lymington. He sailed it into Poole late on Saturday night.'

'What's his name?'

'Steven Harding. Claimed to be an actor from London.'

'You think he was lying?'

Ingram shrugged. 'Not about his name or his occupation, but I certainly think he was lying about what he was doing there. His story was that he'd left his boat in Poole because he fancied some exercise, but I've done a few calculations and by my reckoning there's no way he could have made it on foot in time to make the call at 10.43. If he was berthed in one of the marinas then he'd have to have taken the ferry to Studland but as the first crossing isn't until seven that means he had to cover sixteen-odd miles of coastal path in just over three hours. If you take into account that a good percentage is sandy beach and the rest is a roller-coaster ride of hills, I'd say it was an impossibility. We're talking an average of over five miles an hour and the only person I can think of who could sustain that sort of speed on that kind of terrain is a professional marathon runner.' He pushed the report across. 'It's all in there. Name, address, description, name of boat. Something else that's interesting is that he sails into Chapman's Pool regularly and knows everything there is to know about the back eddies. He's very well informed about the seas round here.'

'Is he the one who found the body?'

'No, that was two young lads. They're on holiday with their parents. I doubt there's any more they can tell you but I've included their names and the address of their rented cottage. A Miss Maggie Jenner of Broxton House talked to Harding for an hour or so after he made the call, but he doesn't appear to have told her much about himself except that he grew up on a farm in Cornwall.' He laid a hand the size of a dinner plate on the report. 'He was sporting an erection, if that's of any interest. Both Miss Jenner and I noticed it.'

'Jesus!'

Ingram smiled. 'Don't get too excited. Miss Jenner's a bit of a looker, so it may have been her that brought it on. She has that effect on men.' He lifted his hand. 'I've also included the names of the boats that were anchored in the bay when the body was found. One was registered in Poole, one in Southampton and the third was French, although it shouldn't be too hard to find. I watched it leave yesterday evening and it was heading for Weymouth so I guess they're on holiday and working their way along the coast.'

'Good work,' said Galbraith warmly. 'I'll be in touch.' He tapped the pathologist's report as he turned to go. 'I'll leave this with you. Maybe something will strike you that hasn't struck any of us.'

Steven Harding woke to the sound of a dying outboard motor, followed by someone banging his fist on the stern of *Crazy Daze*. It was at its permanent mooring, a buoy in Lymington river, and was well out of reach of casual visitors unless they had a dinghy of their own. The swell was sometimes unpleasant, particularly when the Lymington to Yarmouth ferry went past on its way to the Isle of Wight, but it was affordable, private and suitably remote from prying eyes.

'Hey, Steve! Get up, you bastard!'

He groaned as he recognized the voice, then rolled over in his bunk, pulling the pillow over his head. His brain was splitting from a piledriver of a hangover and the last person he wanted to see at crack of dawn on Monday morning was Tony

Bridges. 'You're banned from coming aboard, arsehole,' he roared angrily, 'so bugger off and leave me alone!'

But *Crazy Daze* was sealed up as tight as a can of beans and he knew his friend couldn't have heard him. The boat tilted as Tony climbed aboard after securing his dinghy next to Harding's on the aft cleat.

'Open up!' he said, hammering on the companionway hatch. 'I know you're in there. Have you any idea what time it is, you stupid sod? I've been trying to get you on your mobile for the last three hours.'

Harding squinted at his watch. Three ten, he read. He sat bolt upright and banged his already aching head on the planked ceiling. 'Fucking Ada!' he muttered, crawling off his bunk and stumbling into the saloon to pull the bolt on the hatch. 'I was supposed to be in London by midday,' he told Tony.

'So your agent keeps telling me. He's been calling me non-stop since 11.30.' Tony pulled back the main hatch and dropped down into the saloon, sniffing the ripe atmosphere with an expression of distaste. 'Ever heard of fresh air?' he asked, pushing past his friend to open the forward hatch in the cabin and create a through draft. He looked at the rumpled sheets and wondered what the hell Steve had been doing. 'You're a bloody fool,' he said unsympathetically.

'Go away. I'm sick.' Harding groaned again as he slumped on to the port settee in the saloon and dropped his forehead into his hands.

'I'm not surprised. It's like an oven in here.' Tony handed him a bottle of mineral water from the galley. 'Get some of this into you before you die of dehydration.' He stood over him until he'd downed half the bottle then lowered himself on to the facing settee. 'What's going on? I talked to Bob and he said you were supposed to be crashing at his place last night and catching the early train to town this morning.'

'I changed my mind.'

'So I gather.' Tony looked at the empty bottle of whisky on the table between them and the photographs scattered across its surface. 'What the hell's up with you?'

'Nothing.' He pushed the hair out of his eyes with a frown of irritation. 'How did you know I was here?'

Tony jerked his head towards the stern. 'I spotted your dinghy. Also I've tried everywhere else. Graham's after your blood in case you're interested. He's pissed off that you missed the audition. It was in the bag, according to him.'

'He's lying.'

'Your big chance, he said.'

'Fuck that!' said Harding dismissively. 'It was a bit part in a kids' TV series. Three days' filming with spoilt brats to make something I wouldn't be seen dead in. Only idiots work with children.'

Malice stirred briefly in Tony's eyes before he cloaked his anger behind a harmless smile. 'Is that a dig at me?' he asked mildly.

Harding shrugged. 'No one forced you to be a teacher, mate. It was your choice.' He rocked his flattened palm. 'Your funeral when the little bastards finally do your head in.'

Tony held his gaze for a moment then picked up one of the photographs. 'So how come you don't have a problem with this kind of crap?' he said, jabbing his finger at the image. 'Doesn't this count as working with kids?'

No answer.

'You're being exploited by experts – *mate* – but you can't see it. You might as well sell your arse in Piccadilly Circus as let perverts drool over tacky porno pics of you in private.'

'Shut it,' growled Harding angrily, touching his fingertips to his eyelids to suppress the pain behind them. 'I've had enough of your bloody lectures.'

Tony ignored the note of warning. 'What do you expect if you keep behaving like an idiot?'

An unfriendly smile thinned the other man's lips. 'At least

I'm up front about what I do' – his smile broadened – 'in every respect.' He stared Bridges down. 'Unlike you, eh? How's Bibi these days? Still falling asleep on the job?'

'Don't tempt me, Steve?'

'To do what?'

'Shop you.' He stared at the photograph in a confusion of disgust and jealousy. 'You're a fucking deviant. This kid's barely fifteen.'

'Nearly sixteen . . . as you damn well know.' Harding watched him tear the photograph to shreds. 'Why are you getting so het up about it?' he murmured dispassionately. 'It's only acting. You do it in a movie and they call it art. You do it for a mag and they call it pornography.'

'It's cheap filth.'

'Wrong. It's *exciting* cheap filth. Be honest. You'd swap places with me any day. Hell, the pay's three times what you get as a teacher.' He raised the bottle of mineral water to his mouth and tilted his head back, smiling cynically. 'I'll talk to Graham,' he said, wiping his wet lips with the back of his hand. 'You never know. A little guy like you might go down a wow on the Internet. Paedophiles like 'em small.'

'You're sick.'

'No,' said Harding, dropping his head into his hands, energy spent. 'Just broke. It's inadequate bastards who jerk off over my pictures who're sick.'

Chapter Six

Forensic Pathology Report
UF/DP/5136/Interim: Ref: GFS/Dr J. C. Warner

- General description: Natural blonde – 30 yrs (approx) – height 5′
  – weight: 6 st 12 lbs – blue eyes – blood group O – excellent
  health – excellent teeth (2 fillings; RL wisdom removed) – no
  surgical scars – mother of at least one child – 14 weeks pregnant
  (foetus male) – non-smoker – small traces of alcohol in blood –
  consumed last meal approx 3 hrs before drowning – contents of
  stomach (other than sea water): cheese, apple – pronounced
  indentation 3rd finger L-hand indicates recent presence of ring
  (wedding or otherwise).

- Cause of death: Drowning. The evidence **prevailing conditions** –
  wind, tide, rocky shoreline; **good condition of body** – had she
  entered the sea on or near the shoreline she was obviously
  determined enough to save herself, and while there is some post-
  mortem bruising, there is not enough to suggest that the corpse
  remained long in the water after death – points to her coming off a
  boat in the open sea, alive, and swimming for some considerable
  time before exhaustion led to drowning within shelter of land.

- Contributory factors in victim's death: 0.5 litres of sea water in
  stomach – fingertip bruising either side of voicebox, indicative of

attempted manual strangulation – residual benzodiazepine in bloodstream and tissues (Rohypnol?) – bruising and abrasions to back (pronounced on shoulder blades and buttocks) and inside of thighs, indicative of forced intercourse on a hard surface, such as a deck or an uncarpeted floor – some blood loss from abrasions in vagina (vaginal swabs negative, either due to prolonged immersion in sea water or assailant using a condom) – severe fingertip bruising on upper arms, indicative of manual restraint and/or manual lift (possibly inflicted during ejection from boat) – incipient hypothermia.

- Condition of body: Death had occurred within 14 hrs of being examined – most likely time of death: at or around high water at 1.52 a.m. BST on Sunday, 10 August (see below) – general condition good, although hypothermal evidence, condition of skin and vasoconstriction of the arterial vessels (indicative of prolonged stress) suggests victim spent considerable time in the sea before drowning – extensive abrasions to both wrists, suggesting she was bound with rope and made efforts to release herself (impossible to say whether she succeeded, or whether her killer released her prior to drowning her) – two fingers on L-hand broken; all fingers on R-hand broken (difficult at this stage to say what caused this – it may have been done deliberately or may have happened accidentally if the woman tried to save herself by catching her fingers on a railing?) – fingernails broken on both hands – post-mortem bruising and grazing of back, breasts, buttocks and knees indicate the body was dragged to and fro across rocks/pebbles prior to being stranded.

- Ambient conditions where found: Egmont Bight is a shallow bay, inaccessible to boats other than keel-less vessels such as ribs/ dinghies (lowest recorded depth = 0.5 m; variation between low and high water = 1.00–2.00 m). Kimmeridge Ledges to the west of Egmont Bight make sailing close to the cliffs hazardous and sailors steer well clear of the shoreline (particularly at night when that part of the coast is unlit). Due to a back eddy, a continuous SSE stream runs from Chapman's Pool towards St Alban's Head, which suggests victim was inside the shelter of Egmont Point before she died and was stranded on the shoreline as the tide receded. Had she drowned farther out, her body would have been swept round the Head. SW winds and currents mean she must have entered the water WSW of Egmont Bight and was towed along the coast in an easterly direction as she swam towards the shore. In view of the above factors,* we estimate the victim entered the sea a minimum of 0.5 miles WSW of where the body was found.

- Conclusions: The woman was raped and subjected to a manual strangulation attempt before being left to drown in the open sea. She may also have had her fingers broken prior to immersion with the possible aim of hampering her efforts to swim towards the shore. She was certainly alive when she entered the water, so the failure to report her fall overboard suggests her killer expected her to die. The removal of distinguishing features (wedding ring, clothing) suggests a premeditated intent to hinder an investigation should the body surface or be washed ashore.

***NB:** In view of the fact that she came so close to saving herself, it is possible that she made the decision to jump while the boat was still in sight of land. However, both the failure to report her 'missing overboard' and the evidence of premeditation leaves little room for doubt that her death was intended.

***Rohypnol** (manufactured by Roche) Much concern is being expressed about this drug. A soluble, intermediate-acting hypnotic

* These estimates are calculated on what an average swimmer could achieve in the conditions.

These conclusions are predicated on the rape taking place on board a boat, most probably on deck.

Difficult at this stage to say to what extent the benzodiazepine would have affected her ability to operate. Further tests required.

compound – known on the street as the 'date-rape drug', or more colloquially as a 'roofie'. It has already been cited in several rape cases, two being 'gang-rape' cases. Very effective in the treatment of severe and disabling insomnia, it can induce sleep at unusual times. Used inappropriately – easily dissolved in alcohol – it can render a woman unconscious without her knowledge, thus making her vulnerable to sexual attack. Women report intermittent bouts of lucidity, coupled with an absolute inability to defend themselves. Its effects on rape victims have been well-documented in the US where the drug is now banned: temporary or permanent memory loss; inability to understand that a rape has taken place; feelings of 'spaced-out' disconnection from the event; subsequent and deep psychological trauma because of the ease with which the victim was violated against her will (often by more than one rapist). There are enormous difficulties in bringing prosecutions because it is impossible to detect Rohypnol in the bloodstream after seventy-two hours, and few victims regain their memories quickly enough to present themselves at police stations in time to produce positive semen swabs or benzodiazepine traces in the blood.

***NB:** The UK police lag well behind their US counterparts in both understanding and prosecution of these types of cases.

J. C. Warner

Chapter Seven

SALTERNS MARINA LAY at the end of a small cul-de-sac off the Bournemouth to Poole coastal road, some two hundred yards from where the Greens had rescued the blonde toddler. Its approach from the sea in a pleasure craft was through the Swash Channel and then via the North Channel which allowed a passage between the shore and the numerous moored boats that flew like streamers from the buoys in the centre of the bay. It was a popular stopping-off place for foreign visitors or sailors setting out to cruise the south coast of England, and was often crowded in the summer months.

An enquiry at the marina office about traffic in and out over the previous two days, 9/10 August, produced the information that *Crazy Daze* had moored there for approximately eighteen hours on the Sunday. The boat had come in during the night and taken a vacant berth on 'A' pontoon, and the nightwatch-man had recorded the arrival at 2.15 a.m. Subsequently, when the office opened at 8.00 a.m., a man calling himself Steven Harding had paid for a twenty-four-hour stay, saying he was going for a hike but planned to be back by late afternoon. The harbour master remembered him. 'Good-looking chap. Dark hair.'

'That's the one. How did he seem? Calm? Excited?'

'He was fine. I warned him we'd need the berth again by the evening and he said, no problem, because he'd be heading back to Lymington by late afternoon. As far as I recall he said he had an appointment in London on Monday – this morning in other words – and was planning to catch the last train up.'

'Did he have a child with him?'

'No.'

'How did he pay?'

'Credit card.'

'Did he have a wallet?'

'No. He had the card tucked into a pocket inside his shorts. Said it was all you needed these days to go travelling.'

'Was he carrying anything?'

'Not when he came into the office.'

No one had made a note of *Crazy Daze*'s departure, but the berth was empty again by 7.00 p.m. on Sunday evening when a yacht out of Portsmouth had been logged in. On this initial enquiry, there were no reports of an unaccompanied toddler leaving the marina, or a man taking a toddler away with him. However, several people pointed out that marinas were busy places – even at eight o'clock in the morning – and anyone could take anything off a boat if it was wrapped in something unexceptional like a sleeping bag and placed in a marina trolley to transport it away from the pontoons.

Within two hours of Lymington police being asked to check William Sumner's cottage in Rope Walk, another request came through from Winfrith to locate a boat by the name of *Crazy Daze* which was moored somewhere in the tiny Hampshire port's complex of marinas, river moorings and commercial fishing quarter. It took a single telephone call to the Lymington harbour master to establish its exact whereabouts.

'Sure I know Steve. He moors up to a buoy in the dog-leg, about five hundred yards beyond the yacht club. Thirty-foot sloop with a wooden deck and claret-coloured sails. Nice boat. Nice lad.'

'Is he on board?'

'Can't say. I don't even know if his boat's in. Is it important?'

'Could be.'

'Try phoning the yacht club. They can pick him out with binoculars if he's there. Failing that, come back to me and I'll send one of my lads up to check.'

William Sumner was reunited with his daughter in Poole police station at half-past six that evening after a tiring two hundred and fifty-mile drive from Liverpool, but if anyone expected the little girl to run to him with joyful smiles of recognition, they were to be disappointed. She chose to sit at a distance, playing with some toys on the floor, while making a cautious appraisal of the exhausted man who had slumped on a chair and buried his head in his hands. He apologized to WPC Griffiths. 'I'm afraid she's always like this,' he said. 'Kate's the only one she responds to.' He rubbed his red eyes. 'Have you found her yet?'

Griffiths moved protectively in front of the little girl, worried about how much she understood. She exchanged a glance with John Galbraith who had been waiting in the room with her. 'My colleague from Dorset Constabulary Headquarters, DI Galbraith, knows more about that than I do, Mr Sumner, so I think the best thing is that you talk it through with him while I take Hannah to the canteen.' She reached out an inviting hand to the toddler. 'Would you like an ice cream, sweetheart?' She was surprised by the child's reaction. With a trusting smile, Hannah scrambled to her feet and held up her arms. 'Well, that's a change from yesterday,' she said with a laugh, swinging her on to her hip. 'Yesterday, you wouldn't even look at me.' She cuddled the warm little body against her side and deliberately ignored the danger signals that shot like Cupid's arrows through her bloodstream, courtesy of her frustrated thirty-five-year-old hormones.

After they'd gone, Galbraith pulled forward a chair and sat facing Sumner. The man was older than he'd been expecting, with thinning dark hair and an angular, loose-limbed body that he seemed unable to keep still. When he wasn't plucking nervously at his lips, he was jiggling one heel in a constant rat-a-tat-tat against the floor, and it was with reluctance that Galbraith took some photographs from his breast pocket and held them loosely between his hands. When he spoke it was with deep and genuine sympathy. 'There's no easy way to tell you this, sir,' he said gently, 'but a young woman, matching your wife's description, was found dead yesterday morning. We can't be sure it's Kate until you've identified her but I think you need to prepare yourself for the fact that it might be.'

A look of terror distorted the man's face. 'It will be,' he said with absolute certainty. 'All the way back I've been thinking that something awful must have happened. Kate would never have left Hannah. She adored her.'

Reluctantly, Galbraith turned the first close-up and held it for the other man to see.

Sumner gave an immediate nod of recognition. 'Yes,' he said with a catch in his voice, 'that's Kate.'

'I'm so sorry, sir.'

Sumner took the photograph with trembling fingers and examined it closely. He spoke without emotion. 'What happened?'

Galbraith explained as briefly as possible where and how Kate Sumner had been found, deeming it unnecessary at this early stage to mention rape or murder.

'Did she drown?'

'Yes.'

Sumner shook his head in bewilderment. 'What she doing there?'

'We don't know but we think she must have fallen from a boat.'

'Then why was Hannah in Poole?'

'We don't know,' said Galbraith again.

The man turned the photograph over and thrust it at Galbraith, as if by putting it out of sight he could deny its contents. 'It doesn't make sense,' he said harshly. 'Kate wouldn't have gone anywhere without Hannah, and she hated sailing. I used to have a Contessa 32 when we lived in Chichester but I could never persuade her to come out on it because she was terrified of turning turtle in the open sea and drowning.' He lowered his head into his hands again as the meaning of what he'd said came home to him.

Galbraith gave him a moment to compose himself. 'What did you do with it?'

'Sold it a couple of years ago and put the money towards buying Langton Cottage.' He lapsed into another silence which the policeman didn't interrupt. 'I don't understand any of this,' he burst out then in despair. 'I spoke to her on Friday night and she was fine. How could she possibly be dead forty-eight hours later?'

'It's always worse when death happens suddenly,' said the DI sympathetically. 'We don't have time to prepare for it.'

'Except I don't believe it. I mean, why didn't someone try to save her? You don't just abandon people when they fall overboard.' He looked shocked suddenly. 'Oh, God, did other people drown as well? You're not going to tell me she was on a boat that capsized, are you? That was her worst nightmare.'

'No, there's no evidence that anything like that happened.' Galbraith leaned forward to bridge the gap between them. They were on hardbacked chairs in an empty office on the first floor and he could have wished for friendlier surroundings for a conversation like this one. 'We think Kate was murdered, sir. The Home Office pathologist who performed the post-mortem believes she was raped before being deliberately thrown into the sea to die. I realize this must be a terrible shock to you, but you have my assurance that we're working round the clock to find her killer and if there's anything we can do to make the situation easier for you, we will of course do it.'

It was too much for Sumner to take in. He stared at the detective with a surprised smile carving ridges in his thin face. 'No,' he said, 'there's been a mistake. It can't have been Kate. She wouldn't have gone anywhere with a stranger.' He reached out a tentative hand for the photograph again, then burst into tears when Galbraith turned it over for him.

The wretched man was so tired that it was several minutes before he could stem his weeping but Galbraith kept quiet because he knew from past experience that sympathy more often exacerbated pain than ameliorated it. He sat quietly looking out of the window which faced towards the park and Poole Bay beyond, and only stirred when Sumner spoke again.

'I'm sorry,' he said, striking the tears from his cheeks. 'I keep thinking how frightened she must have been. She wasn't a very good swimmer which is why she didn't want to go sailing.'

Galbraith made a mental note of the fact. 'If it's any comfort, she did everything in her power to save herself. It was exhaustion that beat her, not the sea.'

'Did you know she was pregnant?' Tears gathered in his eyes again.

'Yes,' said Galbraith gently, 'and I'm sorry.'

'Was it a boy?'

'Yes.'

'We wanted a son.' He took a handkerchief from his pocket and held it to his eyes for several moments before getting up abruptly and walking to the window to stand with his back to Galbraith. 'How can I help you?' he said then in a voice stripped of feeling.

'You can tell me about her. We need as much background information as you can give us – the names of her friends, what she did during the day, where she shopped. The more we know the better.' He waited for a response which never came. 'Perhaps you'd rather leave it until tomorrow? I realize you must be very tired.'

'Actually, I think I'm going to be sick.' Sumner turned an ashen face towards him, then, with a small sigh, slid to the floor in a dead faint.

The Spender boys were easy company. They demanded little from their host other than the odd can of Coke, occasional conversation and help with threading their hooks with bait. Ingram's immaculate fifteen-foot dayboat, *Miss Creant*, sat prettily on the surface of a calm turquoise sea off Swanage, her white topsides turning pale pink in the slowly setting sun and a fine array of rods bristling along her rails like porcupine quills. The boys loved her.

'I'd rather have *Miss Creant* any day than a stupid cruiser,' said Paul after helping the mighty policeman launch her down the Swanage slip. He had allowed the boy to operate the winch at the back of his ancient Jeep while he himself had waded into the sea to float her off the trailer and make her fast to a ring on the slip wall. Paul's eyes had gleamed with excitement because boating was suddenly more accessible than he'd realized. 'Do you reckon Dad might buy one? Holidays would be great if we had a boat like this.'

'You can always ask,' had been Ingram's response.

Danny found the whole idea of sliding a long wriggling ragworm on to a barbed point until the steel was clothed in something resembling a wrinkled silk stocking deeply repugnant and insisted that Ingram did the business for him. 'It's alive,' he pointed out. 'Doesn't the hook hurt it?'

'Not as much as it would hurt you.'

'It's an invertebrate,' said his brother, who was leaning over the side of the boat and watching his various floats bob on the water, 'so it doesn't have a nervous system like us. Anyway, it's near the bottom of the food chain so it only exists to be eaten.'

'Dead things are the bottom of the food chain,' said Danny. 'Like the lady on the beach. She'd've been food if we hadn't found her.'

Ingram handed Danny his rod with the worm in place. 'No fancy casting,' he said, 'just dangle it over the side and see what happens.' He leaned back and tilted his baseball cap over his eyes, content to let the boys do the fishing. 'Tell me about the bloke who made the phone call,' he invited. 'Did you like him?'

'He was all right,' said Paul.

'He said he saw a lady with no clothes on and she looked like an elephant,' said Danny, joining his brother to lean over the side.

'It was a joke,' said Paul. 'He was trying to make us feel better.'

'What else did he talk about?'

'He was chatting up the lady with the horse,' said Danny, 'but she didn't like him as much as he liked her.'

Ingram smiled to himself. 'What makes you think that?'

'She frowned a lot.'

So what's new?

'Why do you want to know if we liked him?' asked Paul, his agile mind darting back to Ingram's original question. 'Didn't *you* like him?'

'He was all right,' said Ingram, echoing Paul's own answer. 'A bit of a berk for setting out on a hike on a hot day without any suntan lotion or water, but otherwise okay.'

'I expect they were in his rucksack,' said Paul loyally, who hadn't forgotten Harding's kindness even if his brother had. 'He put it down to make the telephone call then left it there because he said it was too heavy to lug down to the police car. He was going to pick it up again on his way back. It was probably water that was making it heavy.' He looked earnestly towards their host. 'Don't you think?'

Ingram closed his eyes under the brim of his cap. 'Yes,' he agreed, while wondering what had been in the rucksack that meant Harding hadn't wanted a policeman to see it. Binoculars? Had he seen the woman, after all? 'Did you describe the lady on the beach to him?' he asked Paul.

'Yes,' said the boy. 'He wanted to know if she was pretty.'

There were two hidden agendas behind the decision to send WPC Griffiths home with William and Hannah Sumner. The first derived entirely from the child's unfavourable psychiatric report and was intended to safeguard her welfare; the second was based on years of statistical evidence that showed a wife was always more likely to be murdered by her husband than by a stranger. However, because of the distances involved and the problems of jurisdiction – Poole being Dorsetshire Constabulary and Lymington being Hampshire Constabulary – Griffiths was advised that the hours would be long ones.

'Yes, but is he *really* a suspect?' Griffiths asked Galbraith.

'Husbands are always suspects.'

'Come on, guv, he was definitely in Liverpool because I phoned the hotel to check, and it's a hell of a long way from there to Dorset. If he's driven to and fro twice in five days, then he's done over a thousand miles. That's a hell of a lot of driving.'

'Which may explain why he fainted,' was Galbraith's dry response.

'Oh, great!' she said sarcastically. 'I've always wanted to spend quality time with a rapist.'

'There's no compulsion, Sandy. You don't have to do it if you don't want to, but the only other option is to leave Hannah in the care of foster parents until we're satisfied it's safe to return her to her father. How about you go back tonight and see how it goes? I've got a team searching the house at the moment, so I'll instruct one of the chaps to stay on and shadow you. Can you live with that?'

'What the hell!' she said cheerfully. 'With any luck, it'll give me a chance to work babies out of my system.'

As far as Sumner himself was concerned, Griffiths was the official 'friend' who was supplied by any police force to a family in distress. 'I can't possibly cope on my own,' he kept telling Galbraith as if it was the fault of the police that he found himself a widower.

'We don't expect you to.'

The man's colour had improved after being given something to eat when he admitted he'd had nothing since a cup of tea at breakfast that morning. Renewed energy had set him chasing explanations again. 'Were they kidnapped?' he asked suddenly.

'We don't think so. Lymington police checked the house inside and out and there's no indication of any sort of disturbance. The neighbour let them in with a spare key so the search was a thorough one. That doesn't mean we're ignoring the possibility of abduction, just that we're keeping an open mind. We're conducting a second search ourselves at the moment, but on the evidence so far it looks as if Kate and Hannah left of their own accord some time after the post was delivered on Saturday morning. The letters had been opened and stacked on the kitchen table.'

'What about her car? Could she have been taken from her car?'

Galbraith shook his head. 'It's parked in your garage.'

'Then I don't understand.' Sumner appeared genuinely confused. 'What happened?'

'Well, one explanation is that Kate met someone when she was out, a friend of the family perhaps, who persuaded her and Hannah to go for a sail in his boat.' He was careful to avoid any idea of a pre-arranged meeting. 'But whether she expected to be taken as far as Poole and the Isle of Purbeck we simply don't know.'

Sumner shook his head. 'She'd never have gone,' he said with absolute certainty. 'I keep telling you, she didn't like sailing. And, anyway, the only people we know with boats are couples.' He stared at the floor. 'You're not suggesting a couple could have done something like this, are you?' He sounded shocked.

'I'm not suggesting anything at the moment,' said Galbraith patiently. 'We need more information before we can do that.' He paused. 'Her wedding ring seems to be missing. We assume it was removed because it could identify her. Was it special in some way?'

Sumner held out a trembling hand and pointed to his own ring. 'It was identical to this one. We had them engraved inside with our initials. "K" entwined with "W".'

Interesting, thought Galbraith. 'When you're ready, I'd like a list of your friends, particularly the ones who sail. But there's no immediate hurry.' He watched Sumner crack his finger joints noisily, one after the other, and wondered what had attracted the pretty little woman in the mortuary to this gauche, hyperactive man.

Sumner clearly hadn't been listening. 'When was Hannah abandoned?' he demanded.

'We don't know.'

'My mother said she was found in Poole at lunchtime yesterday, but you said Kate died in the early hours of the morning. Doesn't that mean Hannah must have been on board when Kate was raped and was put ashore in Poole *after* Kate was dead? I mean, she couldn't possibly have been wandering around on her own for twenty-four hours before somebody saw her, could she?'

He was certainly no fool, thought Galbraith. 'We don't think so.'

'Then her mother was killed in front of her?' The man's

voice rose. 'Oh my God, I'm not sure I can bear this! She's only a baby, for Christ's sake.'

Galbraith reached out a calming hand. 'It's far more likely she was asleep.'

'You can't know that.'

No, thought Galbraith, I can't. Like everything else in policework, I can only guess. 'The doctor who examined her after she was found thinks she was sedated,' he explained. 'But, yes, you're right. At the moment we can't be certain about anything.' He rested his palm briefly on the man's taut shoulder, then withdrew tactfully into his own space. 'But it really is better to stop tormenting yourself with what might have been. Nothing's ever as bleak as our imagination paints it.'

'Isn't it?' Sumner straightened abruptly and let his head flop on to the chair back so that he was looking at the ceiling. A long sigh whispered from his chest. 'My imagination tells me you're working on the theory that Kate was having an affair, and that the man she went with was her lover.'

Galbraith saw no point in pretending. The idea of an affair that had turned sour was the first they'd considered, particularly as Hannah had apparently accompanied her mother on what-ever journey she had made. 'We can't ignore the possibility,' he said honestly. 'It would certainly explain why she agreed to go on board somebody's boat and take Hannah with her.' He studied the man's profile. 'Does the name Steven Harding mean anything to you?'

Sumner frowned. 'What's he got to do with it?'

'Probably nothing, but he was one of the people on the spot when Kate's body was found and we're questioning every-one connected with her death, however remotely.' He waited a moment. 'Do you know him?'

'The actor?'

'Yes.'

'I've met him a couple of times.' He steepled his hands in

front of his mouth. 'He carried Hannah's buggy over the cobbles at the bottom of the High Street one day when Kate was struggling with some heavy shopping, and she asked me to thank him when we bumped into him about a week later. After that he started popping up all over the place. You know what it's like. You meet someone, and then you see them wherever you go. He's got a sloop on Lymington river and we used to talk sailing from time to time. I invited him back to the house once and he chewed my ear off for hours about some blasted play he was auditioning for. He didn't get the part, of course, but I wasn't surprised. He couldn't act his way out of a paper bag if his life depended on it.' His eyes narrowed. 'Do you think he did it?'

Galbraith gave a small shake of his head. 'At the moment, we're just trying to eliminate him from the inquiry. Were he and Kate friends?'

Sumner's lips twisted. 'Do you mean, were they having an affair?'

'If you like.'

'No,' he said adamantly. 'He's a galloping poof. He poses for pornographic gay magazines. In any case she can't . . . couldn't stand him. She was furious when I took him back to the house that time . . . said I should have asked her first.'

Galbraith watched him for a moment. The denial was overdone, he thought. 'How do you know about the gay magazines? Did Harding tell you?'

Sumner nodded. 'He even showed me one of them. He was proud of it. But then he loves all that. Loves being in the limelight.'

'Okay. Tell me about Kate. How long have you and she been married?'

He had to think about it. 'Getting on for four years. We met at work and married six months later.'

'Where's work?'

'Pharmatec UK in Portsmouth. I'm a research chemist there and Kate was one of the secretaries.'

Galbraith lowered his eyes to cloak his sudden interest. 'The drug company?'

'Yes.'

'What sort of drugs do you research?'

'Me personally?' He gave an indifferent shrug. 'Anything to do with the stomach.'

Galbraith made a note. 'Did Kate go on working after you married?'

'For a few months until she fell pregnant with Hannah.'

'Was she happy about the pregnancy?'

'Oh, yes. Her one ambition was to have a family of her own.'

'And she didn't mind giving up work?'

Sumner shook his head. 'She wouldn't have it any other way. She didn't want her children to be brought up the way she was. She didn't have a father, and her mother was out all day, so she was left to fend on her own.'

'Do you still work at Pharmatec?'

He nodded. 'I'm their top scientist.' He spoke the words matter-of-factly.

'So you live in Lymington and work in Portsmouth?'

'Yes.'

'Do you drive to work?'

'Yes.'

'That's a difficult journey,' said Galbraith sympathetically, doing a rough calculation in his head. 'It must take you – what? – an hour and a half of travelling each way. Have you ever thought of moving?'

'We didn't just think about it,' said Sumner with a hint of irony. 'We *did* it a year ago when we moved to Lymington. And, yes, you're right, it's an awful journey, particularly in the summer when the New Forest's packed with tourists.' He sounded unhappy about it.

'Where did you move from?'

'Chichester.'

Galbraith remembered the notes Griffiths had shown him after Sumner's telephone call. 'That's where your mother lives, isn't it?'

'Yes. She's been there all her life.'

'You too? A born and bred Chichester man?'

Sumner nodded.

'Moving must have been a bit of a wrench, particularly if it meant adding an hour to your journey each way?'

He ignored the question to stare despondently out of the window. 'You know what I keep thinking?' he said then. 'If I'd stuck to my guns and refused to budge, Kate wouldn't be dead. We never had any trouble when we lived in Chichester.' He seemed to realize immediately that his remarks could be interpreted in a number of ways and added what was presumably intended as an explanation: 'I mean, Lymington's full of strangers. Half the people you meet don't even live there.'

Galbraith had a quick word with Griffiths before she left to accompany William and Hannah Sumner home. She had been given time, while the SOCOs finished their search of Langton Cottage, to go home in order to change and pack a bag, and was dressed now in a baggy yellow jumper and black leggings. She looked very different from the severe young woman in the police uniform and Galbraith wondered wryly if the father and daughter would feel more or less comfortable with the Sloppy Joe. Less, he fancied. Police uniforms inspired confidence.

'I'll be with you early tomorrow morning,' he told her, 'and I need you to prod him a bit before I get there. I want lists of their friends in Lymington, a second list of friends in Chichester, and a third list of work friends in Portsmouth.' He ran a tired hand around his jaw, while he tried to organize his memory. 'It would be helpful if he splits those with boats, or with access to boats, from those without, and even more helpful if he separates Kate's personal friends from their joint friends.'

'Okey-doke,' she said.

He smiled. 'And try to get him to talk about Kate,' he went on. 'We need to know what her routine was, how she managed her day, which shops she used, that kind of thing.'

'No problem.'

'*And* his mother,' he said. 'I get the impression Kate forced him to move away from her, which may have caused some friction within the family.'

Griffiths looked amused. 'I don't blame her,' she said. 'He's ten years older than she was and he'd been living at home with Mummy for thirty-seven years before they got married.'

'How do you know?'

'I had a chat with him when I asked him for his previous address. His mother gave him the family home as a wedding present in return for him taking a small mortgage to help her buy a flat in some sheltered accommodation across the road.'

'A bit too close for comfort, eh?'

She chuckled. 'Bloody stifling, I should think.'

'What about his father?'

'Died ten years ago. Up until then it was a *ménage à trois*. Afterwards, a *ménage à deux*. William was the only child.'

Galbraith shook his head. 'How come you're so well informed? It can only have been a very little chat.'

She tapped the side of her nose. 'Sensible questions and a woman's intuition,' she said. 'He's been waited on all his life which is why he's so convinced he won't be able to cope.'

'Good luck then,' he said, meaning it. 'I can't say I envy you.'

'Someone has to look after Hannah.' She sighed. 'Poor little kid. Do you ever wonder what would have happened to you if you'd been abandoned the way most of the kids we arrest are abandoned?'

'Sometimes,' Galbraith admitted. 'Other times I thank God

my parents pushed me out of the nest and told me to get on with it. You can be loved too much as well as too little, you know, and I'd be hard pushed to say which was the more dangerous.'

Chapter Eight

THE DECISION TO question Steven Harding was made at eight o'clock that Monday night when Dorset police received confirmation that he was on board his boat in the Lymington river; although the interview itself did not take place until after nine because the officer in charge, Detective Superintendent Carpenter, had to drive from Winfrith in order to lead it. DI John Galbraith, who was still in Poole, was instructed to make his own way to Lymington and meet his governor outside the harbour master's office.

Attempts had been made to raise Harding on his radio and his mobile telephone but, as both were switched off, the investigating officers had no way of finding out whether he would still be there on Tuesday morning. A call to his agent, Graham Barlow, had elicited only a furious tirade against arrogant young actors 'who are too big for their boots to attend auditions' and who could 'dream on about future representation'.

'Of course I don't know where he'll be tomorrow,' he had finished angrily. 'I haven't heard a cheep out of him since Friday morning so I've sacked the bugger. I wouldn't mind if he was making any money for me but he hasn't worked in months. From the way he talks, you'd think he was Tom Cruise. Ha! Pinocchio's nearer the mark . . . he's certainly wooden enough . . .'

Galbraith and Carpenter met up at nine o'clock. The Superintendent was a tall rangy man with a shock of dark hair and a ferocious frown that made him look permanently angry. His colleagues had ceased to notice it, but suspects were often intimidated by it. Galbraith had already rung through a brief report of his conversation with Sumner, but he went through it again for the Superintendent's benefit, particularly the reference to Harding being 'a galloping poof'.

'It doesn't square with what we've been told by his agent,' said Carpenter bluntly. 'He describes him as sex mad, says he's got girls falling over themselves to get into bed with him. He's a cannabis smoker, a heavy metal fanatic, collects adult movies and, when he's got nothing better to do, sits for hours in strip joints watching the girls shed their kit. He's got a thing about nudity so when he's on his own, either on the boat or in his flat, he prances around bollock-naked. Chances are we'll find him with his dick hanging out when we go aboard.'

'That's something to look forward to then,' said Galbraith gloomily.

Carpenter chuckled. 'He fancies himself – doesn't think he's doing the business unless he's got two birds on the go at one time. Currently there's a twenty-five-year-old in London called Marie, and another called Bibi or Didi, or something similar, down here. Barlow's given us the name of a friend of Harding's in Lymington, one Tony Bridges, who acts as his answering service when he's out at sea, so I've sent Campbell round to have a word with him. If he gets a line on anything he'll call through.' He tugged at his earlobe. 'On the plus side, the sailing lobby speak well of him. He's lived in Lymington all his life, grew up over a chip shop in the High Street, and he's been mucking around in boats since he was ten. He made it to the top of the waiting list for a river mooring just over three years ago – they're like gold dust apparently – whereupon he sank every last cent into buying *Crazy Daze*. He spends his free weekends on her, and the number of man-hours he's put into getting her shipshape would leave lesser men weeping. That's a quote from some fellow in the yacht club. The general consensus seems to be that he's a bit of a lad, but his heart's in the right place.'

'He sounds like a ruddy chameleon,' said Galbraith cynically. 'I mean that's three different versions of the same guy. Arse-bandit, rampant stud, and all-round good bloke. You pays your money and takes your choice, eh?'

'He's an actor, don't forget, so I doubt if any of them are accurate. He probably plays to the gallery whenever he's given a chance.'

'A liar, more like. According to Ingram, he said he grew up on a farm in Cornwall.' Galbraith raised his collar as a breeze blew down the river, reminding him that he had put on light clothes that morning when the air temperature had touched the low thirties. 'Do you fancy him for it?'

Carpenter shook his head. 'Not really. He's a bit too visible. I think our man's more likely to be textbook material. A loner . . . poor work record . . . history of failed relationships . . . probably lives at home with his mother . . . resents her interference in his life.' He raised his nose to sniff the air. 'At the moment, I'd say the husband sounds a more likely candidate.'

Tony Bridges lived in a small terraced house behind the High Street and gave a nod of agreement when the grey-haired detective sergeant at his door asked if he could talk to him for a few minutes about Steven Harding. He had no shirt or shoes on, just a pair of jeans, and he weaved unsteadily down the corridor as he led the way to an untidy sitting room. He was thin and sharp-featured, with a peroxide crew-cut that didn't suit his sallow complexion, but he smiled amiably enough as he gestured DS Campbell through the door. Campbell, who thought he smelt cannabis in the air, had the distinct impression that visits from the police were not unusual and suspected the neighbours had much to put up with.

The house gave the impression of multiple occupancy with

a couple of bicycles leaning against the wall at the end of the corridor, and assorted clothes lying in heaps about the furniture and floor. Dozens of empty lager cans had been tossed into an old beer crate in a corner – left over, Campbell presumed, from a long-dead party – and overflowing ashtrays reeked into the atmosphere. Campbell wondered what the kitchen was like. If it was as rank as the sitting room, it probably had rats, he thought.

'If his car alarm's gone off again,' said Bridges, 'then it's the garage you want to talk to. *They* fitted the sodding thing and I'm sick to death of people phoning you lot about it when he's not here. I don't even know why he bothered to have it put in. The car's a pile of crap so I can't see anyone wanting to steal it.' He picked up an opened Enigma can from the floor and used it to point to a chair. 'Take a pew. Do you want a lager?'

'No thanks.' Campbell sat down. 'It's not about his alarm, sir. We're asking routine questions of everyone who knows him in order to eliminate him from an inquiry, and we were given your name by his agent.'

'What inquiry?'

'A woman drowned on Saturday night and Mr Harding reported finding the body.'

'Is that right? Shit! Who was it?'

'A local woman by the name of Kate Sumner. She lived in Rope Walk with her husband and daughter.'

'Fucking Nora! Are you serious?'

'Did you know her?'

Tony took a swill from the can. 'I knew *of* her but I never met her. She had this thing about Steve. He helped her out once with her kid and she wouldn't leave him alone. It used to drive him mad.'

'Who told you this?'

'Steve of course. Who else?' He shook his head. 'No wonder

he drank himself stupid last night if he's the one who found her.'

'He wasn't. Some boys found her. He made the phone call on their behalf.'

Bridges pondered for several moments in silence, and it was clearly hard work. Whatever anaesthetic he'd taken – cannabis, alcohol or both – he was having trouble getting his mind into gear. 'This doesn't make sense,' he said with sudden belligerence, his eyes focusing on Campbell like two little spy cameras. 'I know for a fact Steve wasn't in Lymington on Saturday night. I saw him Friday night and he told me he was going to Poole for the weekend. His boat was out all Saturday and Sunday which means there's no way he could have reported a drowning in Lymington.'

'She didn't drown here, sir. She drowned off the coast about twenty miles from Poole.'

'Ah, shit!' He emptied the lager can with one swallow then crumpled it between his fist and threw it at the beer crate. 'Look, it's pointless asking me any more questions. I don't know anything about anyone drowning. Okay? I'm a mate of Steve's not his blasted keeper.'

Campbell nodded. 'Fair enough. So, as a mate, do you know if he has a girlfriend down here called Bibi or Didi, Mr Bridges?'

Tony levelled an accusing finger. 'What the hell *is* this?' he demanded. 'Over my dead body are these routine questions. What's going on?'

The DS looked thoughtful. 'Steve isn't answering his telephone so his agent's the only person we've been able to talk to. He told us Steve had a girlfriend in Lymington called Bibi or Didi and he suggested we contact you for her address. Is that a problem for you?'

'TO-ONY!' called a drunken female voice from upstairs. 'I'M WA-AITING!'

'Too right it's a problem,' said Bridges angrily. 'That's Bibi and she's *my* sodding girlfriend, not Steve's. I'll kill the bastard if he's been two-timing me.'

There was the sound of a body slumping on the floor upstairs. 'I'M GOING TO SLE-EP AGAIN, TONY!'

Carpenter and Galbraith travelled out to *Crazy Daze* in the harbour master's rib – a souped-up dinghy with a fibreglass keel and a steering column – captained by one of his young assistants. The night air had become noticeably cold after the heat of the day and both men wished they had had the sense to wear jumpers or fleeces under their jackets. A stiff breeze was funnelling down the Solent, making rigging lines rattle noisily against the forest of masts in the Berthon and Yacht Haven marinas. Ahead of them the Isle of Wight crouched like a slumbering beast against the shadowy sky and the lights from the approaching Yarmouth to Lymington ferry danced in reflection across the waves.

The harbour master had been amused by police suspicion over their fruitless attempts to raise Harding via radio or mobile telephone. 'Do the man a favour! Why should he waste his batteries on the odd chance that you lot want to talk to him? There's no shore power to boats on the buoys. He lights the saloon with a butane gas lamp – claims it's romantic – which is why he prefers a buoy in the river to a pontoon in a marina. That, and the fact that once on board the girls are dependent on him and his dinghy to get them off again.'

'Does he take many girls out there?' asked Galbraith.

'I wouldn't know. I've got better things to do than keep a tally of Steve's conquests. He prefers blondes, I know that. I've seen him with a right little stunner recently.'

'Small, curly blonde hair, blue eyes?'

'Far as I recall, she had straight hair, but don't quote me on it. I'm no good with faces.'

'Any idea what time Steve's boat left on Saturday morning?' asked Carpenter.

The harbour master shook his head. 'I can't even see it from here. Ask at the yacht club.'

'We already have. No luck.'

'Wait till the weekenders come down on Saturday then. They'll be your best bet.'

The rib slowed as it approached Harding's sloop. Yellow light glimmered in the midship portholes and a rubber dinghy bobbed astern in the wash from the ferry. From inside came the faint sound of music.

'Hey, Steve,' shouted the harbour master's lad, rapping smartly on the port planking. 'It's Gary. You've got visitors, mate.'

Harding's voice came faintly. 'Bog off, Gary! I'm sick.'

'No can do. It's the police. They want to talk to you. Come on, open up, and give us a hand.'

The music ceased abruptly and Harding hoisted himself through the open companionway into the cockpit. 'What's up?' he asked, surveying the two detectives with an ingenuous smile. 'I guess this has something to do with that woman yesterday? Were the boys lying about the binoculars?'

'We've a few follow-up questions,' said Detective Superintendent Carpenter with an equally ingenuous smile. 'Can we come on board?'

'Sure.' He hopped on to the deck and reached down to assist Carpenter before turning to help his companion.

'My shift ends at ten,' the lad called to the police officers. 'I'll be back in forty minutes to take you off. If you want to leave earlier call on your mobile. Steve knows the number. Otherwise get him to bring you back.'

They watched him turn away in a wide circle, carving a gleaming wake out of the water as he headed upriver towards the town.

'You'd better come below,' said Harding. 'It's cold out

here.' He was dressed – much to Galbraith's relief – in the same sleeveless T-shirt and shorts he'd been wearing the day before, and he shivered as a wind blew across the salt flats at the entrance to the river. Barefoot himself, he looked critically at the policemen's shoes. 'You'll have to take those off,' he told them. 'It's taken me two years to get the planking looking like this and I don't want it marked.'

Obligingly, the two men unlaced their boots before padding across to the companionway in search of welcome warmth. The atmosphere inside the saloon was still redolent of the previous night's heavy drinking session and, even without the evidence of the empty whisky bottle which stood on the table, neither officer had any difficulty guessing why Harding had described himself as 'sick'. The muted light of the single gas-operated lamp served only to accentuate the hollows in his cheeks and the dark stubble around his unshaven jaw, and the brief glimpse they had of the tumbled sheets in the forward cabin before he closed the door left neither of them in any doubt that he'd spent most of the day sleeping off a ferocious hangover.

'What kind of follow-up questions?' he asked, sliding on to a bench seat at the side of the table and gesturing them to take the other.

'Routine ones, Mr Harding,' said the Superintendent.

'About what?'

'Yesterday's events.'

He pressed the heels of his palms against his lids and rotated them fiercely as if to drive out demons. 'I don't know any more than I told the other guy,' he said, eyes watering as he lowered his hands. 'And most of that was what the boys told me. They reckoned she drowned and got left on the beach. Were they right?'

'It certainly looks that way.'

He hunched forward over the table. 'I'm thinking about making a complaint against that copper. He was bloody rude, made out me and the kids had something to do with the body being there. I didn't mind for myself so much, but I was pretty pissed off for the boys. They were scared of him. I mean, let's face it, it can't be much fun finding a corpse – and then to have some idiot in hobnailed boots making the whole situation worse . . .' He broke off with a shake of his head. 'Matter of fact I think he was jealous. I was chatting up this bird when he came back, and he looked bloody furious about it. I reckon he fancies her himself, but he's such a dozy pillock he hasn't done anything about it.'

As neither Galbraith nor Carpenter rose in Ingram's defence, a silence fell during which the two policemen cast interested glances about the saloon. In other circumstances the light may well have been romantic, but to a couple of law officers intent on spotting anything that might connect its owner to a brutal rape and murder it was worse than useless. Too much of the interior was obscured by shadow and if there was evidence that Kate and Hannah Sumner had been on board the previous Saturday then it wasn't obvious.

'What do you want to know?' asked Harding then. He was watching John Galbraith as he spoke, and there was something in his eye – *triumph? amusement?* – that made Galbraith think the silence had been deliberate. He had given them an opportunity to look, and they had only themselves to blame if they were disappointed.

'We understand you berthed in Salterns Marina on Saturday night and stayed there most of Sunday?' said Carpenter.

'Yes.'

'What time did you tie up, Mr Harding?'

'I've no idea.' He frowned. 'Pretty late. What's that got to do with anything?'

'Do you keep a log?'

He glanced towards his chart table. 'When I remember.'

'May I look at it?'

'Why not?' He leaned over and retrieved a battered exercise book from the clutter of paper on the lid of the chart table. 'It's hardly great literature.' He handed it across.

Carpenter read the last six entries.

09.08.97.	10.09.	*Slipped mooring.*
" "	11.32.	*Rounded Hurst Castle.*
10.08.97.	02.17.	*Berthed, Salterns Marina.*
" "	18.50.	*Slipped mooring.*
" "	19.28.	*Exited Poole Harbour.*
11.08.97.	00.12.	*Berthed, Lymington.*

'You certainly don't waste your words much, do you?' he murmured, flicking back through the pages to look at other entries. 'Doesn't wind speed or course ever feature in your log?'

'Not often.'

'Is there a reason for that?'

The young man shrugged. 'I know the course to everywhere on the south coast so I don't need to keep reminding myself, and wind speed is wind speed. That's part of the beauty of it. Any journey takes as long as it takes. If you're the sort of impatient type who's only interested in arrivals then sailing will drive you nuts. On a bad day it can take hours to go a few miles.'

'It says here you tied up in Salterns Marina at 2.17 on Sunday morning,' said Carpenter.

'Then I did.'

'It also says you left Lymington at 10.09 on Saturday morning.' He did a quick calculation. 'Which means it took you fourteen hours to sail approximately thirty miles. That's got to be a record, hasn't it? It works out at about two knots an hour. Is that as fast as this thing can go?'

'It depends on the wind and the tide. On a good day I can do six knots but the average is probably four. In fact I probably sailed sixty miles on Saturday because I was tacking most of the way.' He yawned. 'Like I said, it can take hours on a bad day, and Saturday was a bad day.'

'Why didn't you use your motor?'

'I didn't want to. I wasn't in a hurry.' His expression grew wary with suspicion. 'What's this got to do with the woman on the beach?'

'Probably nothing,' said Carpenter easily. 'We're just tying up some loose ends for the report.' He paused, assessing the young man thoughtfully. 'I've done a little sailing myself in the past,' he said then, 'and I'll be honest with you, I don't believe it took you fourteen hours to sail to Poole. If nothing else, the offshore winds as the land cooled in the late afternoon would have boosted your speed well over two knots. I think you sailed on past the Isle of Purbeck, perhaps with the intention of going to Weymouth, and only turned back to Poole when you realized how late it was getting. Am I right?'

'No. I hove to off Christchurch for a few hours to do some fishing and have a nap. That's why it took so long.'

Carpenter didn't believe him. 'Two minutes ago you gave tacking as the explanation. Now you're claiming a fishing break. Which was it?'

'Both. Tacking and fishing.'

'Why isn't it in your log?'

'It wasn't important.'

Carpenter nodded. 'Your approach to time seems a little' – he sought a suitable word – 'individualistic, Mr Harding. For example, you told the police officer yesterday that you were planning to walk to Lulworth Cove, but Lulworth's a good twenty-five miles from Salterns Marina, fifty in total if you intended to walk back again. That's an ambitious distance for a twelve-hour hike, isn't it, bearing in mind you told the harbour master at Salterns Marina you'd be back by late afternoon?'

Harding's eyes gleamed with sudden amusement. 'It doesn't look nearly as far by sea,' he said.

'Did you make it to Lulworth?'

'Like hell I did!' he said with a laugh. 'I was completely whacked by the time I reached Chapman's Pool.'

'Could that be because you travel light?'

'I don't understand.'

'You were carrying a mobile telephone, Mr Harding, but nothing else. In other words you set out on a fifty-mile hike on one of the hottest days of the year with no fluids, no money, no sunscreen protection, no additional clothes if you started to burn, no hat. Are you usually so careless about your health?'

He pulled a wry face. 'Look, all right it was stupid. I admit it. That's the reason I turned back after your bloke drove the kids away. If you're interested, the return journey took twice as long as the journey out because I was so damn knackered.'

'About four hours then,' suggested DI Galbraith.

'More like six. I started after they left, which was 12.30 near enough, and got to the marina around 6.15. I drank about a gallon of water, had something to eat then set off for Lymington maybe half an hour later.'

'So the hike out to Chapman's Pool took three hours?' said Galbraith.

'Something like that.'

'Which means you must have left the marina shortly after 7.30 to be able to make the emergency call at 10.43.'

'If you say so.'

'I don't say so at all, Steve. Our information is that you were paying for your berth at eight o'clock which means you couldn't have left the marina until several minutes later.'

Harding linked his hands behind his head and stared across the table at the Inspector. 'Okay, I left at eight,' he said. 'What's the big deal?'

'The big deal is there's no way you could have hiked sixteen miles along a rough coastal path in two and a half hours' – he paused, holding Harding's gaze – 'and that includes the time you must have lost waiting for the ferry.'

There was no hesitation in his reply. 'I didn't go along the coastal path, or not to start off with anyway,' he said. 'I hitched a lift with a couple on the ferry who were heading for the country park near Durlston Head. They dropped me off by the gates leading up to the lighthouse and I got on to the path there.'

'What time was that?'

He shifted his gaze to the ceiling. 'Ten forty-three minus however long it takes to jog from Durlston Head to Chapman's Pool, I suppose. Look, the first time I remember checking my watch yesterday was just before I made the nine-nine-nine call. Up until then I couldn't have given a toss what time it was.' He looked at Galbraith again, and there was irritation in his dark eyes. 'I hate being ruled by the bloody clock. It's social terrorism to force people to conform to arbitrary evaluations of how long something should take. That's why I like sailing. Time's irrelevant and there's bugger all you can do about it.'

'What sort of car did the couple drive?' asked Carpenter, unmoved by the young man's flights of philosophical fancy.

'I don't know. A saloon of some sort. I don't notice cars.'

'What colour?'

'Blue, I think.'

'What were the couple like?'

'We didn't talk much. They had a Manic Street Preachers album on tape. We listened to that.'

'Can you describe them, Mr Harding?'

'Not really. They were ordinary. I spent most of the time looking at the backs of their heads. She had blonde hair and he had dark hair.' He reached for the whisky bottle and rolled it between his palms, beginning to lose his patience. 'Why the hell are you asking me these questions anyway? What the fuck does it matter how long it took me to get from A to B, or who I met along the way? Does everyone who dials nine-nine-nine get the third degree?'

'Just tying loose ends, sir.'

'So you said.'

'Wouldn't it be truer to say that Chapman's Pool was your destination, and not Lulworth Cove?'

'No.'

A silence developed. Carpenter stared fixedly at Harding while he continued to play with the whisky bottle. 'Were there any passengers on board your boat on Saturday?' he asked then.

'No.'

'Are you sure about that, sir?'

'Of course I'm bloody sure. Don't you think I'd have noticed them? It's hardly the *QE2*, is it?'

Carpenter leafed idly through the logbook. 'Do you *ever* carry passengers?'

'That's none of your business.'

'Maybe not, but we've been led to believe you're a bit of a lad.' He lifted an amused eyebrow. 'Legend has it that you regularly entertain ladies on board. I'm wondering if you ever take them sailing with you' – he jerked his head towards the cabin – 'or does all the action take place in there when you're moored up to your buoy?'

Harding took time to consider his answer. 'I take some of them out,' he admitted at last.

'How often?'

Another long pause. 'Once a month, maybe.'

Carpenter slapped the exercise book on to the table and drummed his fingers on it. 'Then why is there no mention of them in here? Surely you have a responsibility to record the names of everyone on board in case of an accident? Or perhaps you don't care that someone might drown because the coast-guards assume you're the only person they're looking for?'

'That's ridiculous,' said Harding dismissively. 'The boat would have to turn turtle for a scenario like that and the log'd be lost anyway.'

'Have any of your passengers ever gone overboard?'

Harding shook his head but didn't say anything. His eyes flickered with open suspicion from one man to the other, tasting their mood in the way a snake flicks his tongue to taste scent on the air. There was something very studied about every movement he made, and Galbraith regarded him objectively, mindful that he was an actor. He had the impression that Harding was enjoying himself, but he couldn't think why this should be unless Harding had no idea the investigation involved rape and murder and was merely using the experience of an interrogation to practise 'method-acting' techniques.

'Do you know a woman by the name of Kate Sumner?' asked Carpenter next.

Harding pushed the bottle aside and leaned forward aggressively. 'What if I do?'

'That's not an answer to my question. Let me repeat it. Do you know a woman by the name of Kate Sumner?'

'Yes.'

'Do you know her well?'

'Well enough.'

'How well is well enough?'

'None of your bloody business.'

'Wrong answer, Steve. It's very much our business. It was her body you saw being winched into the helicopter.'

His reaction surprised them.

'I had a feeling it might be,' he said.

Chapter Nine

AHEAD ACROSS THE WATER, the lights of Swanage gleamed like brilliant jewels in the night. Behind, the dying sun dipped beneath the horizon. Danny Spender was yawning profusely, worn out by his long day and three hours' exposure to fresh sea air. He leaned against Ingram's comforting bulk while his older brother stood proudly at the wheel, steering *Miss Creant* home. 'He was a dirty person,' he confided suddenly.

'Who was?'

'That man yesterday.'

Ingram glanced down at him. 'What did he do?' he asked, careful to keep the curiosity out of his voice.

'He was rubbing his willy with his telephone,' said Danny, 'all the time the lady was being rescued.'

Ingram looked at Paul to see if he was listening but the other boy was too enthralled by the wheel to pay them any attention. 'Did Miss Jenner see him do it?'

Danny's eyelids drooped. 'No. He stopped when she came round the corner. Paul reckons he was polishing it – you know, like bowlers do with cricket balls to make them turn in the air – but he wasn't, he was being dirty.'

'Why does Paul like him so much?'

The child gave another huge yawn. 'Because he wasn't cross with him for spying on a nudie. Dad would be. He was *furious* when Paul got hold of some porno mags. I said they were boring but Paul said they were natural.'

*

Detective Superintendent Carpenter's telephone rang. 'Excuse me,' he said, retrieving it from his jacket pocket and flipping open the mouthpiece. 'Yes, Campbell,' he said. 'Right . . . go on . . .' He stared at a point above Steven Harding's head as he spoke, his inevitable frown lengthened and deepened by the shadows thrown by the gaslight as he listened to his DS's report on his interview with Tony Bridges. He clamped the receiver tight against his ear as the name 'Bibi' was mentioned, and lowered his eyes curiously to the young man opposite.

Galbraith watched Steven Harding while the one-sided conversation proceeded. The man was listening acutely, straining to pick up what was being said at the other end, all too aware that the topic under discussion was probably himself. Most of the time he stared at the table but once or twice he raised his eyes to look at Galbraith, and Galbraith felt a curious empathy with him as if he and Harding, by dint of their mutual ignorance of the conversation, were ranged against Carpenter. He had no sense that Harding was guilty, no intuition that he was sitting with a rapist; yet his training told him that that meant nothing. Sociopaths could be as charming and as unthreatening as the rest of humanity, and it was always a potential victim who thought otherwise.

Galbraith resumed his inspection of the interior, picking out shapes in the shadows beyond the gaslight. His eyes had become accustomed to the gloom and he was able to make out a great deal more now than he had ten minutes ago. With the exception of the clutter on the chart table, everything else was neatly stowed away in lockers or on shelves, and there was nothing to indicate the presence of a woman. It was a masculine environment of wooden planking, black leather seats and brass fittings, and no colour intruded anywhere to adorn its austere simplicity. Monastic, he thought, with approval. His own house, a noisy toy-filled establishment created by a wife who was a power in the National Childbirth Trust, was too cluttered and . . . God forbid, *child-centred!* . . . for an endlessly weary policeman.

The galley which was to starboard of the companionway particularly interested him. It was built into an alcove beside the laddered steps and contained a small sink and Calor-gas hob set into a teak worktop with lockers below and shelves above. His attention had been caught by some articles pushed back into the shadows in the corner and, with the passage of time, he had been able to identify them as a half-eaten lump of cheese in a plastic wrapper with a Tesco's sticker and a bag of apples. He felt the shift of Harding's gaze as it followed his, and he wondered if the man had any idea that a forensic pathologist could detail what a victim had eaten before she died.

Carpenter disconnected and placed the telephone on the logbook. 'You said you had a feeling the body was Kate Sumner's,' he reminded Harding.

'That's right.'

'Could you elaborate? Explain when and why you got this feeling?'

'I didn't mean I had a feeling it was going to be *her*, only that it was bound to be somebody I knew otherwise you wouldn't have come out to my boat.' He shrugged. 'Put it this way, if you do this kind of follow up every time somebody makes an emergency call then it's not bloody surprising the country's awash with unconvicted criminals.'

Carpenter chuckled, although the frown didn't leave his face and remained fixed on the young man opposite. 'Never believe what you read in newspapers, Steve. Trust me, we always catch the criminals who matter.' He examined the actor closely for several seconds. 'Tell me about Kate Sumner,' he invited. 'How well did you know her?'

'Hardly at all,' said Harding with airy unconcern. 'I've met her maybe half a dozen times since she and her husband moved to Lymington. The first time was when she was having trouble pushing her little girl's buggy over the cobbles near the old

Customs House. I gave her a hand with it, and we had a brief chat before she went on up the High Street to do her shopping. After that she always stopped to ask me how I was whenever she saw me.'

'Did you like her?'

Harding's gaze strayed towards the telephone while he considered his answer. 'She was all right. Nothing special.'

'What about William Sumner?' asked Galbraith. 'Do you like him?'

'I don't know him well enough to say. He seems okay.'

'According to him, he sees you quite often. He's even invited you back to his house.'

The young man shrugged. 'So? Loads of people invite me to their houses. It doesn't mean I'm close mates with them. Lymington's a sociable place.'

'He told me you showed him some photographs of yourself in a gay magazine. I'd have thought you'd need to be pretty friendly with a man to do that.'

Harding grinned. 'I don't see why. They're good photos. Admittedly he didn't think much of them, but that's his problem. He's pretty straight is old Will Sumner. Wouldn't show his tackle for anything, not even if he was starving, and certainly not in a gay mag.'

'I thought you said you didn't know him well.'

'I don't need to. You only have to look at him. He probably looked middle-aged when he was eighteen.'

Galbraith agreed with him, which made Kate's choice of a husband even odder, he thought. 'Still, it's an unusual thing to do, Steve, go round showing nude photos of yourself to other guys. Do you make a habit of it? Have you shown them round the yacht club, for example?'

'No.'

'Why not?'

Harding didn't answer.

'Maybe you just show them to husbands, eh?' Galbraith

lifted an enquiring eyebrow. 'It's a great way to convince a man you've no designs on his wife. I mean if he thinks you're gay he'll think you're safe, won't he? Is that why you did it?'

'I can't remember now. I expect I was pissed and he was getting on my nerves.'

'Were you sleeping with his wife, Steve?'

'Don't be stupid,' said Harding crossly. 'I've already told you I hardly knew her.'

'Then the information we've been given that she wouldn't leave you alone and it was driving you mad is completely wrong?' said Carpenter.

Harding's eyes widened slightly, but he didn't answer.

'Did she ever come on board this boat?'

'No.'

'Are you sure?'

For the first time there was genuine nervousness in the man's manner. He hunched his shoulders over the table again and ran his tongue across dry lips. 'Look, I don't really get what all this is about. Okay, somebody drowned and I knew her – not very well, but I *did* know her. Okay – too – I can accept it looks like a bizarre coincidence that I was there when she was found – but, listen, I'm always meeting up with people I know. That's what sailing's about – bumping into guys that you had a drink with maybe two years before.'

'But that's the root of the problem,' said Galbraith reasonably. 'According to our information, Kate Sumner didn't sail. You've said yourself she was never on board *Crazy Daze*.'

'That doesn't mean she didn't accept a spur-of-the moment invitation. There was a French Beneteau called *Mirage* anchored in Chapman's Pool yesterday. I saw her through the boys' binoculars. She was moored up in Berthon at the end of last week – I know that because they have this cute kid on board who wanted to know the code for the lavatories. Well – *Jesus!* – those French guys are just as likely to have met Kate as

I was. Berthon's in Lymington, isn't it? Kate lives in Lymington. Maybe they took her for a spin?'

'It's a possibility,' agreed Carpenter. He watched Galbraith make a note. 'Did you catch the "cute kid's" name, by any chance?'

Harding shook his head.

'Do you know of any other friends who might have taken Kate out on Saturday?'

'No. Like I said, I hardly knew her. But she must have had some. Everyone round here knows people who sail.'

Galbraith jerked his head towards the galley. 'Did you go shopping on Saturday morning before you left for Poole?' he asked.

'What's that got to do with anything?' the Truculence was back in his voice again.

'It's a simple question. Did you buy the cheese and apples that are in your galley on Saturday morning?'

'Yes.'

'Did you meet Kate Sumner while you were in town?'

Harding hesitated before he replied. 'Yes,' he admitted then. 'She was outside Tesco's with her little girl.'

'What time was that?'

'Nine-thirty, maybe.' He seized the whisky bottle again and laid it on its side, placing his forefinger against the neck and turning it slowly. 'I didn't hang around because I wanted to get off, and she was looking for some sandals for her child. We said hi and went our separate ways, and that was it.'

'Did you invite her to go sailing with you?' asked Carpenter.

'No.' He lost interest in the bottle and abandoned it with its open neck pointing directly at the Superintendent's chest like the barrel of a rifle. 'Look, I don't know what you think I've done,' he said, ratcheting up his irritation, 'but I'm damn sure you're not allowed to ask me questions like this. Shouldn't there be a tape recorder?'

'Not when people are merely helping us with our inquiries, sir,' said Carpenter mildly. 'As a general rule, the taping of interviews follows the cautioning of a suspect for an indictable offence. Such interviews can only be conducted in a police station where the proper equipment allows an officer to insert a new blank tape into the recorder in front of the suspect.' He smiled without hostility. 'However, if you prefer, you can accompany us to Winfrith where we will question you as a voluntary witness under taped conditions.'

'No way. I'm not leaving the boat.' He stretched his arms along the back of the settee and gripped the teak edging as if to emphasize the point. The movement caused his right hand to brush against a piece of fabric that was tucked on to the narrow shelf behind the edging strip and he glanced at it idly for a moment before crushing it in his hand.

There was a short silence.

'Do you have a girlfriend in Lymington?' asked Carpenter.

'Maybe.'

'May I ask what her name is?'

'No.'

'Your agent suggested a name. He said she was called Bibi or Didi.'

'That's his problem.'

Galbraith was more interested in what was crushed inside Harding's fist because he had seen what it was. 'Do you have any children?' he asked him.

'No.'

'Does your girlfriend have children?'

No answer.

'You're holding a bib in your fist,' the DI pointed out, 'so presumably someone who's been on this boat has children.'

Harding uncurled his fingers and let the object drop on to the settee. 'It's been there for ages. I'm not much of a cleaner.'

Carpenter slammed his palm on to the table, making the phone and the whisky bottle jump. 'You're annoying me, Mr

Harding,' he said severely. 'This isn't a piece of theatre put on for your benefit, it's a serious investigation into a young woman's drowning. Now you've admitted knowing Kate Sumner and you've admitted seeing her on the morning before she drowned, but if you've no knowledge of how she came to be lying on a shore in Dorset at a time when she and her daughter were assumed to be in Lymington then I advise you to answer our questions as straightforwardly and honestly as you can. Let me rephrase the question.' His eyes narrowed. 'Have you recently entertained a girlfriend on board this boat who has a child or children?'

'Maybe,' said Harding again.

'There's no maybe about it. Either you have or you haven't.'

He abandoned his 'crucifixion' pose to slump forward again. 'I've several girlfriends with children,' he said sulkily, 'and I've entertained them all off and on. I'm trying to remember who was the most recent.'

'I'd like the names of every one of them,' said Carpenter grimly.

'Well you're not going to get them,' said Harding with sudden decision, 'and I'm not answering any more questions. Not without a solicitor and not without the conversation being recorded. I don't know what the hell I'm supposed to have done but I'm buggered if you're going to stitch me up for it.'

'We're trying to establish how Kate Sumner came to drown in Egmont Bight.'

'No comment.'

Carpenter righted the whisky bottle and placed a finger on top of it. 'Why did you get drunk last night, Mr Harding?'

The man stared at the Superintendent but didn't say anything.

'You're a compulsive liar, lad. You said yesterday that you grew up on a farm in Cornwall when the truth is you grew up over a chip shop in Lymington. You told your agent your girlfriend's name was Bibi when in fact Bibi's been your mate's steady girlfriend for the last four months. You told William Sumner you were a poof while everyone else round here seems to think you're Casanova. What's your problem, eh? Is your life so boring that you have to play-act some interest into it?'

A faint flush reddened Harding's neck. 'Jesus, you're a piece of shit!' he hissed furiously.

Carpenter steepled his hands over the telephone and stared him down. 'Have you any objections to us taking a look round your boat, Mr Harding?'

'Not if you've got a search warrant.'

'We haven't.'

Harding's eyes gleamed triumphantly. 'Don't even think about it then.'

The Superintendent studied him for a moment. 'Kate Sumner was brutally raped before being thrown into the sea to drown,' he said slowly, 'and all the evidence suggests that the rape took place on board a boat. Now let me explain the rules about searching premises, Mr Harding. In the absence of the owner's consent, the police have various courses open to them, one of which – assuming they have reasonable cause to suspect that the owner has been guilty of an arrestable offence – is to arrest him and then search any premises he controls in order to prevent the disposal of evidence. Do you understand the implications of what I've just said, bearing in mind that rape and murder are serious arrestable offences?'

Harding's face had gone very white.

'Answer me, please,' snapped Carpenter. 'Do you understand the implications of what I've just said?'

'You'll arrest me if I refuse.'

Carpenter nodded.

Shock was giving way to anger. 'I can't believe you're allowed to behave like this. You can't go round accusing people of rape just so you can search their boats without a warrant. That's abuse of police powers.'

'You're forgetting reasonable cause.' He enumerated points on his fingers. '*One*, you've admitted meeting Kate Sumner at 9.30 on Saturday morning shortly before you sailed; *two*, you've failed to give an adequate explanation of why it took you fourteen hours to sail between Lymington and Poole; *three*, you've offered conflicting stories about how you came to be on the coastal path above where Kate Sumner's body was found yesterday; *four*, your boat was berthed at a time and in the vicinity of where her daughter was discovered wandering alone and traumatized; *five*, you seem unwilling or unable to give satisfactory answers to straightforward questions . . .' He broke off. 'Do you want me to go on?'

Whatever composure Harding had was gone. He looked what he was, badly frightened. 'It's all just coincidence,' he protested.

'Including little Hannah being found near Salterns Marina yesterday? Was that a coincidence?'

'I guess so . . .' He stopped abruptly, his expression alarmed. 'I don't know what you're talking about,' he said, the pitch of his voice rising. 'Oh, shit! I need to think.'

'Well, think on this,' said Carpenter evenly, 'if, when we search the interior of this boat, we discover a single fingerprint belonging to Kate Sumner—'

'Look, okay,' he interrupted, breathing deeply through his nose and making damping gestures with his hands as if it was the detectives who needed calming and not himself. 'She and her kid have been on board, but it wasn't on Saturday.'

'When was it?'

'I can't remember.'

'That's not good enough, Steve. Recently? A long time ago? Under what circumstances? Did you bring them out in your dinghy? Was Kate one of your conquests? Did you make love to her?'

'No, dammit!' he said angrily. 'I hated the stupid bitch. She was always throwing herself at me, wanting me to fuck her and wanting me to be nice to that weird kid of hers. They used to hang around down by the fuelling pontoon in case I came in for diesel. It used to bug me, it really did.'

'So, let me get this straight,' murmured Carpenter sarcastically. 'To stop her pestering you, you invited her on board?'

'I thought if I was polite . . . Ah, what the hell! Go ahead, search the damn boat. You won't find anything.'

Carpenter nodded to Galbraith. 'I suggest you start in the cabin. Do you have another lamp, Steve?'

Harding shook his head.

Galbraith unhooked a torch from the aft bulkhead and flicked the switch to see if it was working. 'This'll do.' He propped open the cabin door and swung the beam around the interior, settling almost immediately on a small pile of clothes on the port shelf. He used the end of his biro to push a flimsy blouse, a bra and pair of panties to one side to reveal some tiny child's shoes nestling together on the shelf. He turned the beam of the torch full on them and stood back so they were visible to Carpenter and Harding.

'Who do the shoes belong to, Mr Harding?'

No answer.

'Who do the women's clothes belong to?'

No answer.

'If you have an explanation for why these articles are on board your boat, Steve, then I advise you to give it to us now.'

'They're my girlfriend's,' he said in a strangled voice. 'She has a son. The shoes belong to him.'

'Who is she, Steve?'

'I can't tell you. She's married, and she's got nothing to do with this.'

Galbraith emerged from the cabin with one of the shoes hooked on the end of his biro. 'There's a name written on the strap, guv, H. SUMNER. And there's staining on the floor in here.' He pointed the torch beam towards some dark marks beside the bunk bed. 'It looks fairly recent.'

'I need to know what caused the stains, Steve.'

In one lithe movement, the young man erupted out of his seat and grabbed the whisky bottle in both hands, swinging it violently to his left and forcing Galbraith to retreat into the cabin. 'Enough, okay!' he growled, moving towards the chart table. 'You're way off beam on this one. Now back off before I do something I'll regret. You've got to give me some space, for Christ's sake. I need to think.'

He was unprepared for the ease with which Galbraith plucked the bottle from his grasp and spun him round to face the teak clad wall while securing his wrists behind his back with handcuffs.

'You'll have plenty of time for thinking when we get you into a police cell,' said the DI unemotionally as he pushed the young man face-down on to the settee. 'I am arresting you on suspicion of murder. You do not have to say anything but it may harm your defence if you do not mention, when questioned, something you later rely on in court. Anything you do say may be given in evidence.'

Had William Sumner not had a key to his front door, Sandy Griffiths would have questioned whether he had ever lived in Langton Cottage because his knowledge of the house was minimal. Indeed, the police constable who had stayed behind to act as her shadow was better informed than he was, having watched the scene-of-crime officers meticulously examine every room. Sumner looked at her blankly each time she asked him a question. Which cupboard was the tea in? He didn't know. Where did Kate keep Hannah's nappies? He didn't know. Which towel or flannel was hers? He didn't know. Could he at least show her to Hannah's room so that she could put the child to bed? He looked towards the stairs. 'It's up there,' he said, 'you can't miss it.'

He seemed fascinated by the invasion of his home by the search team. 'What were they looking for?' he asked.

'Anything that will connect with Kate's disappearance,' said Griffiths.

'Does that mean they think I did it?'

Griffiths eased Hannah on her hip and turned the child's head into her shoulder in a somewhat futile attempt to block her ears. 'It's standard procedure, William, but I don't think it's something we should talk about in front of your daughter. I suggest you take it up with DI Galbraith tomorrow.'

But he was either too insensitive or too careless of his daughter's welfare to take the hint. He stared at a photograph of his wife on the mantelpiece. 'I couldn't have done it,' he said. 'I was in Liverpool.'

At the request of Dorsetshire Constabulary, Liverpool police had already begun preliminary inquiries at the Regal Hotel. It was early days, of course, but the account he'd settled that morning made interesting reading. Despite being a heavy user of the telephone, coffee lounge, restaurant and bar in the first two days, there was a period of twenty-four hours between lunchtime on Saturday and a noon drink in the bar on Sunday when he had failed to make use of a single hotel service.

Chapter Ten

DURING THE TWENTY minutes that he waited in the sitting room at Langton Cottage the following morning to speak to William Sumner, John Galbraith learnt two things about the man's dead wife. The first was that Kate Sumner was vain. Every photograph on display was either of herself, or of herself and Hannah, and he searched without success for a likeness of William, or even of an elderly woman who might have been William's mother. In frustration he ended up counting the pictures that were there – thirteen – each of which showed the same prettily smiling face within its framework of golden curls. Was this the cult of the personality taken to its extreme, he wondered, or an indication of a deep-seated inferiority which needed constant reminders that to be photogenic was a talent like any other?

The second thing he learnt was that he could never have lived with Kate. She delighted, it seemed, in applying frills to everything: lace curtains with frills, pelmets with frills, armchairs with frills – even the lampshades had tassels attached to them. Nothing, not even the walls, had escaped her taste for over-embellishment. Langton Cottage was of nineteenth-century origin with beamed ceilings and brick fireplaces, and instead of the plain white plaster that would have shown these features off to their best advantage, she had covered the walls of the sitting room – probably at considerable expense – with mock Regency wallpaper, adorned with gilt stripes, white bows and baskets of unnaturally coloured fruit. Galbraith shuddered at the desecration of what could have been a charming room and unconsciously contrasted it with the timbered simplicity of Steven Harding's sloop which was currently being put under a microscope by scene-of-crime officers while Harding, exercising his right to remain silent, cooled his heels in a police cell.

Rope Walk was a quiet tree-lined avenue to the west of the Royal Lymington and Town yacht clubs, and Langton Cottage had clearly not been cheap. As he knocked on the door at eight o'clock on Tuesday morning after two hours' sleep, Galbraith wondered how big a mortgage William had had to raise to buy it and how much he earned as a pharmaceutical chemist. He could see no logic behind the move from Chichester, particularly as neither Kate nor William appeared to have any links with Lymington.

He was let in by WPC Griffiths who pulled a face when he told her he needed to talk to Sumner. 'You'll be lucky,' she whispered. 'Hannah's been bawling her head off most of the night, so I doubt you'll get any sense out of him. He's had almost as little sleep as I've had.'

'Join the club.'

'You, too, eh?'

Galbraith smiled. 'How's he holding up?'

She shrugged. 'Not too well. Keeps bursting into tears and saying it's not supposed to be like this.' She lowered her voice even further. 'I'm really concerned about Hannah. She's obviously scared of him. She works herself into a tantrum the minute he enters the room then calms down rapidly as soon as he leaves. I ordered him to bed in the end to try and get her to sleep.'

Galbraith looked interested. 'How does he react?'

'That's the odd thing. He doesn't react at all. He just ignores it as if it's something he's grown used to.'

'Has he said why she does it?'

'Only that, being out at work so much, he's never had a chance to bond with her. It could be true, you know. I get the impression Kate swaddled her in cotton wool. There are so many safety features in this house that I can't see how Hannah was ever expected to learn anything. Every door has a child lock on it – even the wardrobe in her own bedroom – which means she can't explore, can't choose her own clothes or even make a mess if she wants to. She's almost three but she's still sleeping in a cot. That's pretty weird, you know. More like prison bars than a nursery. It's a damned odd way to bring up a child and, frankly, I'm not surprised she's a withdrawn little thing.'

'I suppose it's occurred to you that she might be scared of him because she watched him kill her mother,' murmured Galbraith.

Sandy Griffiths spread her hand and made a rocking motion. 'Except I don't see how he can have done it. He's made a list of some colleagues who can alibi him for Saturday night in Liverpool, and if that holds good then there's no way he could have been shoving his wife in the water at 1.00 a.m. in Dorset.'

'No,' agreed Galbraith. 'Still . . .' He pursed his lips in thought. 'Do you realize the SOCOs found no drugs in this house at all, not even paracetamol? Which is odd considering William's a pharmaceutical chemist.'

'Maybe that's why there aren't any. He knows what goes into them.'

'Mmm. Or they were deliberately cleared out before we got here.' He glanced towards the stairs. 'Do you like him?' he asked her.

'Not much,' she admitted, 'but you don't want to go by what I say. I've always been a lousy judge of character where men are. concerned. He could have done with a good smacking thirty years ago, in my opinion, just to teach him some manners but as things are, he seems to view women as serving wenches.'

He laughed. 'Are you going to be able to stick it out?'

She rubbed her tired eyes. 'God knows! Your chap left

about half an hour ago, and there's supposed to be some relief coming when William's taken away to identify the body and talk to the doctor who examined Hannah. The trouble is, I can't see Hannah letting me go that easily. She clings to me like a limpet. I'm using the spare room to grab kip when I can, and I thought I'd try to organize some temporary cover while she's asleep so I can stay on the premises. But I'll need to get hold of my governor to organize someone locally.' She sighed. 'I suppose you want me to wake William for you.'

He patted her shoulder. 'No. Just point me towards his room. I'm happy to do the business.'

She was sorely tempted, but shook her head. 'You'll disturb Hannah,' she said, baring her teeth in a threatening grimace, 'and I swear to God I'll kill you if she starts howling again before I've had a fag and some black coffee. I'm bushed. I can't take any more of her screaming without mega-fixes of caffeine and nicotine.'

'Is it putting you off babies?'

'It's putting me off husbands,' she said. 'I'd have coped better if he hadn't kept hovering like a dark cloud over my shoulder.' She eased open the sitting-room door. 'You can wait in here till he comes. You'll love it. It has all the makings of a shrine.'

Galbraith heard footsteps on the stairs and turned to face the door as it opened. Sumner was in his early forties, but he looked a great deal older than that today and Galbraith suspected Harding would have been a lot harsher in his description if he could have seen Kate's husband like this. He was unshaven and dishevelled, and his face was inexpressibly weary, but whether from grief or lack of sleep, it was impossible to say. Nevertheless, his eyes shone brightly enough and Galbraith took note of the fact. Lack of sleep did not lead automatically to blunted intelligence.

'Good morning, sir,' he said. 'I'm sorry to bother you again so early but I've more questions to ask, and I'm afraid they won't wait.'

'That's all right. Sit down. I feel I was less than helpful last night but I was so whacked I couldn't think properly.' He took an armchair and left Galbraith to the sofa. 'I've made those lists you wanted. They're on the table in the kitchen.'

'Thanks.' He gave the man a searching look. 'Did you get any sleep?'

'Not really. I couldn't stop thinking about it. It's all so illogical. I could understand if they'd both drowned, but it doesn't make sense that Kate's dead and Hannah's alive.'

Galbraith agreed. He and Carpenter had been puzzling over that very fact most of the night. Why had Kate had to swim for her life while the toddler was allowed to live? The neat explanation – that the boat was *Crazy Daze*, that Hannah *had* been on board but had managed to release herself while Harding was walking to Chapman's Pool – failed to address the questions of why the child hadn't been pushed into the sea along with her mother, why Harding was so unconcerned about her wails being heard by other boat users in the marina that he'd left her on her own, and who had fed, watered and changed her nappy in the hours before she was found.

'Have you had time to go through your wife's wardrobe, Mr Sumner? Do you know if any of her clothes are missing?'

'Not that I can tell ... but it doesn't mean much,' he added as an afterthought. 'I don't really notice what people wear, you see.'

'Suitcases?'

'I don't think so.'

'All right.' He opened his briefcase on the sofa beside him. 'I've some articles of clothing to show you, Mr Sumner. Please tell me if you recognize any of them.' He removed a polythene bag containing the flimsy blouse found on board *Crazy Daze* which he held out for the other man to look at.

Sumner shook his head, without taking it. 'It's not Kate's,' he said.

'Why so positive,' Galbraith asked curiously, 'if you didn't notice what she wore?'

'It's yellow. She hated yellow. She said it didn't suit people with fair hair.' He gestured vaguely towards the door. 'There's no yellow anywhere in the house.'

'Fair enough.' He took out the bags containing the bra and panties. 'Do you recognize either of these as belonging to your wife?'

Sumner reached out a reluctant hand and took both bags, examining the contents closely through the clear plastic. 'I'd be surprised if they were hers,' he said, handing them back. 'She liked lace and frills, and these are very plain. You can compare them with the other things in her drawers, if you like. You'll see what I mean.'

Galbraith nodded. 'I'll do that. Thank you.' He took out the bag with the child's shoes and laid them on his right palm. 'What about these?'

Sumner shook his head again. 'I'm sorry. All children's shoes look alike to me.'

'They have H. SUMNER printed inside the strap.'

He shrugged. 'Then they must be Hannah's.'

'Not necessarily,' said Galbraith. 'They're very small, more suited to a one-year-old than a three-year-old, and anyone can write a name into some shoes.'

'Why would they want to do that?'

'Pretence, perhaps.'

The other man frowned. 'Where did you find them?'

But Galbraith shook his head. 'I'm afraid I can't reveal that at this stage.' He held the shoes up again. 'Would Hannah recognize them, do you think? They may be a pair of cast-offs.'

'She might if the policewoman showed them to her,' said Sumner. 'There's no point in my trying. She screams her head off every time she sees me.' He swept imaginary dirt from the arm of the chair. 'The trouble is I spend so much time at work that she's never had the chance to get to know me properly.'

Galbraith gave him a sympathetic smile while wondering if there was any truth in the statement. Who could contradict him, after all? Kate was dead; Hannah was tongue-tied; and the various neighbours who'd already been interviewed claimed to know little about William. Or indeed, Kate herself.

'To be honest I've only met him a couple of times and he didn't exactly impress me. He works very hard, of course, but they were never ones for entertaining. She was quite sweet, but we were hardly what I'd call friends. You know how it is. You don't choose your neighbours; they get thrust upon you . . .'

'He's not what you'd call sociable. Kate told me once that he spends his evenings and weekends working out formulas on his computer while she watched soaps on the telly. I feel awful about her dying like that. I wish I'd had more time to talk to her. I think she must have been quite lonely, you know. The rest of us all work, of course, so she was a bit of a rarity, staying at home and doing the housework . . .'

'He's a bully. He took my wife to task about one of the fencing panels between our gardens, said it needed replacing, and when she told him it was his ivy that was pulling it down, he threatened her with court proceedings. No, that's the only contact we've had with him. It was enough. I don't like the man . . .'

'I saw more of Kate than I saw of him. It was an odd marriage. They never did anything together. I sometimes wondered if they even liked each other very much. Kate was very sweet but she hardly ever talked about William. To be honest, I don't think they had much in common . . .'

'I understand Hannah cried most of the night. Does she usually do that?'

'No,' Sumner answered without hesitation, 'but then Kate always cuddled her when she was upset. She's crying for her mother, poor little thing.'

'So you haven't noticed any difference in her behaviour?'

'Not really.'

'The doctor who examined her after she was taken to Poole police station was very concerned about her, described her as unnaturally withdrawn, backward in her development and possibly suffering from some sort of psychological trauma.' Galbraith smiled slightly. 'Yet you're saying that's quite normal for Hannah?'

Sumner coloured slightly as if he'd been caught out in a lie. 'She's always been a little bit' – he hesitated – 'well, odd. I thought she was either autistic or deaf so we had her tested, but the GP said there was nothing wrong and just advised us to be patient. He said children were manipulative, and if Kate did less for her she'd be forced to ask for what she wanted and the problem would go away.'

'When was this?'

'About six months ago.'

'What's your GP's name?'

'Dr Attwater.'

'Did Kate take his advice?'

He shook his head. 'Her heart wasn't in it. Hannah could always make her understand what she wanted, and she couldn't see the point of forcing her to talk before she was ready.'

Galbraith made a note of the GP's name. 'You're a clever man, Mr Sumner,' he said next, 'so I'm sure you know why I'm asking you these questions.'

A ghost of a smile flickered across the man's tired face. 'I prefer William,' he said, 'and yes, of course I do. My daughter screams every time she sees me; my wife had ample opportunity to cheat on me because I'm hardly ever at home; I'm angry because I didn't want to move to Lymington; the mortgage on this place is way too high and I'd like to get shot of it; she was lonely because she hadn't made many friends; and wives are more usually murdered by their partners out of fury than by strangers out of lust.' He gave a hollow laugh. 'About the only thing in my favour is a cast-iron alibi and, believe me, I've spent most of the night thanking God for it.'

Under the rules governing police detention, there is a limit to how long a person may be held without charge, and the pressure to find evidence against Steven Harding mounted as the hours ticked by. It was notable more for its absence. The stains on the floor of the cabin, which had looked so promising the night before, turned out to be whisky-induced vomit – blood group A, matching Harding's – and a microscopic examination of his boat failed to produce any evidence that an act of violence had occurred on board.

If the pathologist's findings were right – '*bruising and abrasions to back (pronounced on shoulder blades and buttocks) and inside of thighs, indicative of forced intercourse on a hard surface such as a deck or an uncarpeted floor – some blood loss from abrasions in vagina*' – the wooden planking of the deck and/or saloon and/or cabin should have had traces of blood, skin tissue and even semen trapped between the grooved joints or under rogue splinters of wood. But no such traces were found. Dried salt was scraped in profusion from the deck planking, but while this might suggest he had scrubbed the topsides down with sea water to remove evidence, it was axiomatic that dried salt would be found on a sailing boat.

On the more likely probability that a blanket or rug had been spread on the hard surface before Kate Sumner had been forced on to it, every item of cloth on board was examined with similarly negative results, although it was all too obvious that any such item would have been thrown overboard along with Kate's clothes and anything else connecting her to the boat. Kate's body was re-examined inch by inch, in the hope that splinters of wood, linking her to *Crazy Daze*, had become embedded under her skin, but either the flaying action of the sea on open wounds had washed the evidence away or it had never been there in the first place. It was a similar story with her broken fingernails. If anything had ever been underneath them, it had long since vanished.

Only the sheets in the cabin showed evidence of semen staining but as the bedclothes hadn't been washed for a very long time it was impossible to say whether the stains were the product of recent intercourse. Indeed, as only two alien hairs were discovered on the pillows and bedclothes – neither of which was Kate's although both were blonde – the conclusion was that, far from being the promiscuous stallion portrayed by the harbour master, Steven Harding was in fact a lonely masturbator.

A small quantity of cannabis and a collection of unopened condoms were discovered in the bedside locker, together with three torn Mates wrappers minus their contents. No used condoms were found. Every container was examined for benzodiazepine, Rohypnol and/or *any* hypnotic. No indications were found. Despite a comprehensive search for pornographic photographs and magazines, none were found. Subsequent searches of Harding's car and flat in London were equally disappointing, although the flat contained thirty-five adult movies. All were on general release, however. A warrant was issued to search Tony Bridges' house in Lymington, but there was nothing to incriminate Steven Harding or to connect him or anyone else there with Kate Sumner. Despite extensive inquiries, police could come up with no other premises used or owned by Harding, and bar a single sighting of him talking to Kate outside Tesco's on Saturday morning, no one reported seeing them together.

There was fingerprint and palm evidence that Kate and Hannah Sumner had been on board *Crazy Daze* but too many of the prints were overlaid with other prints, few of which were Steven Harding's, for the SOCOs to be confident that the visit had been a recent one. Considerable interest was raised by the fact that twenty-five different sets of fingerprints, excluding Carpenter's, Galbraith's, Kate's, Hannah's and Steven's – at least five of the sets being small enough to be children's – were lifted from the saloon, some of which matched prints lifted from Bridges' house, but few of which were replicated in the cabin. Demonstrably, therefore, Harding had entertained people on board, although the nature of the entertainment remained a mystery. He explained it by saying he always invited fellow sailors into the saloon whenever he took a berth in a marina and, in the absence of proof to the contrary, the police accepted his explanation. Nevertheless, they remained curious about it.

In view of the cheese and apples in the galley, Kate Sumner's last meal looked like something the police could run with until the pathologist pointed out that it was impossible to link semi-digested food with a particular purchase. A *Tesco's* Golden Delicious, minced with gastric acids, showed the same chemical printout as a *Sainsbury's* Golden Delicious. Even the child's bib proved inconclusive when the fingerprint evidence on the plastic surface demonstrated that, while Steven Harding and two unidentified others had certainly touched it, Kate Sumner had not.

Briefed by Nick Ingram, attention was paid to the only rucksack found on the boat, a triangular black one with a handful of sweet wrappers in the bottom. Neither Paul nor Danny Spender had been able to give an accurate description of it – Danny: 'it was a big black one . . .'; Paul: 'it was quite big . . . I think it might have been green . . .' – but it told them nothing about what it might have contained on Sunday morning or indeed identified it as the one the boys had seen. Steven Harding, who seemed baffled by police interest in his rucksack, claimed it was certainly the one he had been using that day and explained he had left it on the hillside because it had a litre bottle of water in it, and he couldn't be bothered to lug it down to the boatsheds simply to lug it all the way up again. He further said that PC Ingram had never asked him about a rucksack which is why he hadn't mentioned it at the time.

The nail in the coffin of police suspicion was supplied by a cashier at Tesco's in Lymington High Street who had been on duty the previous Saturday.

"'Course I know Steve,' she said, identifying his photograph. 'He comes in every Saturday for provisions. Did I see him talking to a blonde woman and child last week? Sure I did. He spotted them as he was about to leave and he said, "Damn!" so I said, "What's the problem?" and he said, "I know that woman and she's going to talk to me because she always does," so I said, *jealous*-like, "She's very pretty," and he said, "Forget it, Dawn, she's married, and anyway I'm in a hurry." And he was right. She did talk to him, but he didn't hang around, just tapped his watch and scarpered. You want my opinion? He had something good lined up and he didn't want delaying. She looked mighty miffed when he left, but I didn't blame her for it. Steve's a bit of a hunk. I'd go for him myself if I wasn't a grandmother three times over.'

William Sumner claimed to know little about the management of Langton Cottage or his wife's regular movements. 'I'm away from the house for twelve hours a day, from seven in the morning till seven at night,' he told Galbraith as if it were something to be proud of. 'I was much more *au fait* with her routine in Chichester, probably because I knew the people and the shops she was talking about. Things register better when you recognize names. It's all so different here.'

'Did Steven Harding feature in her conversation?' asked Galbraith.

'Is he the bastard who had Hannah's shoes?' demanded Sumner angrily.

Galbraith shook his head. 'We'll get on a lot faster if you

don't keep second-guessing me, William. Let me remind you that we still don't know if the shoes belonged to Hannah.' He held the other man's gaze. 'And, while I'm about it, let me *warn* you that if you start speculating on anything to do with this case, you could prejudice any prosecution we try to bring. And that could mean Kate's killer going free.'

'I'm sorry.' He raised his hands in apology. 'Go on.'

'Did Steven Harding feature in her conversation?' Galbraith asked again.

'No.'

Galbraith referred to the lists of names he had produced. 'Are any of the men on here ex-boyfriends? The ones in Portsmouth, for example. Did she go out with any of them before she went out with you?'

Another shake of the head. 'They're all married.'

Galbraith wondered about the naivety of that statement, but didn't pursue the issue. Instead, he went on to try and build a picture of Kate's early life. It was about as easy as building houses out of straw. The potted history that William gave him was notable more for its gaps than its inclusions. Her maiden name had been Hill, but whether that was her mother's or her father's surname, he didn't know.

'I don't think they were married,' he said.

'And Kate never knew him?'

'No. He left when she was a baby.'

She and her mother had lived in a council flat in Birmingham, although he had no idea where it was, which school Kate had gone to, where she had trained as a secretary or, even, where she had worked before joining Pharmatec UK. Galbraith asked him if she had any friends from that time with whom she had kept in contact, but William shook his head and said he didn't think so. He produced an address book from a drawer in a small bureau in the corner of the room and said Galbraith could check for himself. 'But you won't find anyone from Birmingham in there.'

'When did she move?'

'When her mother died. She told me once that she wanted to put as much distance between herself and where she grew up as she could, so she moved to Portsmouth and rented a flat over a shop in one of the back streets.'

'Did she say why distance was important?'

'I think she felt she'd have less of a chance to get on if she stayed put. She was quite ambitious.'

'For a career?' asked Galbraith in surprise, recalling Sumner's assertion the day before that Kate's one ambition had been to have a family of her own. 'I thought you said she was happy to give up working when she got pregnant.'

There was a short silence. 'I suppose you're planning to talk to my mother?'

Galbraith nodded.

He sighed. 'She didn't approve of Kate so she'll tell you she was a gold-digger. Not in so many words, perhaps, but the implication will be clear. She can be pretty vitriolic when she chooses.' He stared at the floor.

'Is it true?' prompted Galbraith after a moment.

'Not in my opinion. The only thing Kate wanted was something better for her children than she had herself. I admired her for it.'

'And your mother didn't?'

'It's not important,' said Sumner. 'She never approved of anyone I brought home, which probably explains why it took me so long to get married.'

Galbraith glanced at one of the vacuously smiling photographs on the mantelpiece. 'Was Kate a strong character?'

'Oh, yes. She was single-minded about what she wanted.' He gave a lopsided smile as he made a gesture that encompassed the room. 'This was it. The dream. A house of her own. Social acceptance. Respectability. It's why I know she'd never have had an affair. She wouldn't have risked this for anything.'

Yet another display of naivety? Galbraith wondered. 'Maybe

she didn't realize there was a risk involved,' he said dispassion-ately. 'By your own admission, you're hardly ever here so she could easily have been conducting an affair that you knew nothing about.'

Sumner shook his head. 'You don't understand,' he said. 'It wasn't fear of *me* finding out that would have stopped her. She had me wound round her little finger from the first time I met her.' A wry smile thinned his lips. 'My wife was an old-fashioned puritan. It was fear of other people finding out that ruled her life. Respectability *mattered*.'

It was on the tip of the DI's tongue to ask this man if he had ever loved his wife, but he decided against it. Whatever answer Sumner gave, he wouldn't believe him. He felt the same instinctive dislike of William that Sandy Griffiths felt, but he couldn't decide if it was a chemical antipathy or a natural revulsion that was inspired by his own unshakeable hunch that William had killed his wife.

Galbraith's next port of call was The Old Convent, Osborne Crescent in Chichester where Mrs Sumner senior lived in sheltered accommodation at number two. It had obviously been a school once but was now converted into a dozen small flats with a resident warden. Before he went in, he stared across the road at the solidly rectangular 1930s semi-detached houses on the other side, wondering idly which had been the Sumners' before it was sold to buy Langton Cottage. They were all so similar that it was impossible to say, and he had a sneaking sympathy for Kate's desire to move. Being respectable, he thought, wasn't necessarily synonymous with being boring.

Angela Sumner surprised him because she wasn't what he was expecting. He had pictured an autocratic old snob with reactionary views, and found instead a tough, gutsy woman, wheelchair-bound by rheumatoid arthritis, but with eyes that brimmed with good humour. She told him to put his warrant card through her letter-flap before she'd allow him entrance, then made him follow her electrically operated chair down the corridor into the sitting room. 'I suppose you've given William the third degree,' she said, 'and now you're expecting me to confirm or deny what he's told you.'

'Have you spoken to him?' asked Galbraith with a smile.

She nodded, pointing to a chair. 'He phoned me yesterday evening to tell me that Kate was dead.'

He took the chair she indicated. 'Did he tell you how she died?'

She nodded. 'It shocked me, although to be honest I guessed something dreadful must have happened the minute I sat Hannah's picture on the television. Kate would never have abandoned the child. She doted on her.'

'Why didn't you phone the police yourself when you recognized Hannah's photograph?' he asked curiously. 'Why did you ask William to do it?'

She sighed. 'Because I kept telling myself it couldn't possibly be Hannah – I mean, she's such an unlikely child to be wandering around a strange town on her own – and I didn't want to appear to be causing trouble if it wasn't. I phoned Langton Cottage over and over again and it was only when it became clear yesterday morning that no one was going to answer that I phoned William's secretary and she told me where he was.'

'What kind of trouble would you have been causing?'

She didn't answer immediately. 'Let's just say Kate wouldn't have believed my motives were pure if I made a genuine error. You see, I haven't seen Hannah since they moved twelve months ago, so I wasn't 100 per cent sure I was right anyway. Children change so quickly at that age.'

It wasn't much of an answer, but Galbraith let it go for the moment. 'So you didn't know William had gone to Liverpool?'

'There's no reason why I should. I don't expect him to tell me where he is all the time. He rings once a week and drops in occasionally on his way back to Lymington, but we don't live in each other's pockets.'

'That's quite a change, though, isn't it?' suggested Galbraith. 'Didn't you and he share a house before he was married?'

She gave a little laugh. 'And you think that means I knew what he was doing? You obviously don't have grown-up children, Inspector. It makes no difference whether they live with you or not, you still can't keep tabs on them.'

'I have a seven- and five-year-old who already have a more exciting social life than I've ever had. It gets worse, does it?'

'It depends on whether you approve of them spreading their wings. I think the more space you give them, the more likely they are to appreciate you as they get older. In any case, my husband converted the house into two self-contained flats about fifteen years ago. He and I lived downstairs, and William lived upstairs, and days could go by without our paths crossing. We lived quite separate lives, which didn't change much even after my husband died. I became more disabled, of course, but I hope I was never a burden to William.'

Galbraith smiled. 'I'm sure you weren't, but it must have been a bit of a worry, knowing he'd get married one day and all the arrangements would have to change.'

She shook her head. 'Quite the reverse. I was longing for him to settle down but he never showed any inclination to do it. He adored sailing, of course, and spent most of his free time out on his Contessa. He had girlfriends, but none that he took seriously.'

'Were you pleased when he married Kate?'

There was a short silence. 'Why wouldn't I be?'

Galbraith shrugged. 'No reason. I'm just interested.'

Her eyes twinkled suddenly. 'I suppose he's told you I thought his wife was a gold-digger?'

'Yes.'

'Good,' she said. 'I hate having to tell lies.' She raised the back of a gnarled hand to her cheek to wipe away a stray hair. 'In any case there's no point pretending I was happy about it when anyone round here will tell you I wasn't. She *was* a gold-digger, but that wasn't why I thought he was mad to marry her. It was because they had so little in common. She was ten years younger than he was, virtually uneducated and completely besotted by all the material things in life. She told me once that what she really enjoyed in life was *shopping*.' She shook her head in bewilderment that anything so mundane could produce a height of sensation. 'Frankly, I couldn't see what was going to keep them together. She wasn't remotely interested in sailing and refused point-blank to have anything to do with that side of William's life.'

'Did he go on sailing after they married?'

'Oh, yes. She didn't have a problem with him doing it, she just wouldn't go herself.'

'Did she get to know any of his sailing friends?'

'Not in the way you mean,' she said bluntly.

'What way's that, Mrs Sumner?'

'William said you think she was having an affair.'

'We can't ignore the possibility.'

'Oh, I think you can, you know.' She gave him an old-fashioned look. 'Kate knew the price of everything and the value of nothing, and she'd certainly have calculated the cost of adultery in terms of what she'd lose if William found out about it. In any case, she wouldn't have been having an affair with any of William's sailing friends in Chichester. They were all far more shocked by his choice of wife than I was. She made no effort to fit in, you see, plus there was a generation gap between her and most of them. Frankly, they were all completely bemused by her rather inane conversation. She had no opinions on anything except soap operas, pop music and film stars.'

'So what was her attraction for William? He's an intelligent man and certainly doesn't give the impression of someone who likes inane conversation.'

A resigned smile. 'Sex, of course. He'd had his fill of intelligent women. I remember him saying that the girlfriend before Kate' – she sighed – 'her name was Wendy Plater and she was such a nice girl . . . so suitable . . . that her idea of foreplay was to discuss the effects of sexual activity on the metabolism. I said, how interesting, and William laughed and said, given the choice, he preferred physical stimulation.'

Galbraith kept a straight face. 'I don't think he's alone, Mrs Sumner.'

'I'm not going to argue the point, Inspector. In any case, Kate was obviously far more experienced than he was even though she was ten years younger. She knew William wanted a family and she gave him a baby before you could say Jack Robinson.' He heard the reservation in her voice, and wondered about it. 'Her approach to marriage was to spoil her husband rotten, and William revelled in it. He didn't have to do a damn thing except take himself to work every day. It was the most old-fashioned arrangement you can imagine, with the wife as chief admirer and bottle-washer and the husband swanking around as bread-winner. I think it's what's known as a passive–aggressive relationship where the woman controls the man by making him dependent on her while giving the impression she's dependent on him.'

'And you didn't approve?'

'Only because it wasn't my idea of a marriage. Marriage should be a meeting of minds as well as bodies otherwise it becomes a waste ground where nothing grows. All she could talk about with any enthusiasm were her shopping expeditions and who she'd bumped into during the day, and it was quite clear William never listened to a word she said.'

He wondered if she realized William had yet to be eliminated as a suspect. 'So what are you saying? That he was bored with her?'

She gave his question long consideration. 'No, I don't think he was bored,' she said then, 'I think he just realized he could take her for granted. That's why his working day got progressively longer and why he didn't object to the move to Lymington. She approved of whatever he did, you see, so he didn't have to bother spending time with her. There was no challenge in the relationship.' She paused. 'I hoped children would be something they could share, but Kate appropriated Hannah at birth as something that was the preserve of women, and if I'm honest the poor little thing created even more distance between them. She used to roar her head off every time William tried to pick her up, and he soon got bored with her. I took Kate to task about it, as a matter of fact, told her she wasn't doing the child any good by swamping her in mother love, but it only made her angry with me.' She sighed. 'I shouldn't have interfered. It's what drove them away of course.'

'From Chichester?'

'Yes. It was a mistake. They made too many changes in their lives too quickly. William had to pay off the mortgage on my flat when he sold the house across the road, then take out a much larger one to buy Langton Cottage. He sold his boat, gave up sailing. Not to mention flogging himself to death driving to and from work every day. And all for what? A house he didn't even like very much.'

Galbraith was careful to keep the interest out of his voice. 'Then why did they move?'

'Kate wanted it.'

'But if they weren't getting on, why did William agree to it?'

'Regular sex,' she said crossly. 'In any case, I didn't say they weren't getting on.'

'You said he was taking her for granted. Isn't it the same thing?'

'Not at all. From William's point of view she was the perfect wife. She kept house for him, provided him with children and never pestered him once to put himself out.' Her mouth twisted into a bitter smile. 'They got on like a house on fire as long as he paid the mortgage and kept her in the manner to which she was rapidly becoming accustomed. I know you're not supposed to say these things any more but she was awfully common. The few friends she made were quite dreadful ... loud ... over made-up ...' She shuddered. 'Dreadful!'

Galbraith pressed his fingertips together beneath his chin and studied her with open curiosity. 'You really didn't like her, did you?'

Again Mrs Sumner considered the question carefully. 'No, I didn't,' she said then. 'Not because she was overtly unpleasant or unkind, but because she was the most self-centred woman I've ever met. If everything – and I do *mean* everything – in life wasn't revolving around her she manoeuvred and manipulated until it did. Look at Hannah if you don't believe me. Why encourage the child to be so dependent on her unless she couldn't bear to compete for her affections?'

Galbraith thought of the photographs in Langton Cottage, and his own conclusion that Kate Sumner was vain. 'If it wasn't an affair that went wrong, then what do you think happened? What persuaded her to take Hannah on board someone's boat when she hated sailing so much?'

'What a strange question,' the woman said in surprise. '*Nothing* would have persuaded her. She was obviously forced on board. Why should you doubt that? Anyone who was prepared to rape and kill her then leave her child to wander the streets alone would obviously have no qualms about using threats to coerce her.'

'Except marinas and harbours are busy places and there have been no reports of anyone seeing a woman and child being put on board a boat against their will.' Indeed, as far as the police had been able to establish so far, there had been no sightings of Kate and Hannah Sumner at all at any of the access points to boats along the Lymington River. They hoped for better luck on Saturday when the weekenders returned but, meanwhile, they were working in the dark.

'I don't suppose there would have been,' said Angela Sumner stoutly, 'not if the man was carrying Hannah and threatening to hurt her if Kate didn't do what he said. She loved that child to distraction. She'd have done anything to prevent her being harmed.'

Galbraith was about to point out that such a scenario would have depended on Hannah's willingness to be carried by a man, which seemed unlikely in view of the psychiatric report and Angela Sumner's own admission that she screamed her head off every time her own father tried to pick her up, but he had second thoughts. The logic was sound even if the method had varied . . . Hannah had obviously been sedated . . .

Chapter Eleven

Memo

To: Detective Superintendent Carpenter
From: Detective Inspector Galbraith
Date: 12.8.97 – 9.15 p.m.
Re: **Kate & William Sumner**

Thought you'd be interested in the enclosed report/statements. Of the various issues raised, the most telling seem to be:

1. Kate made few friends and those she had came from her own milieu.
2. She appears to have had little interest in her husband's friends/pursuits.
3. There are some unflattering descriptions of her – i.e.: manipulative, sly, deceitful, malicious.
4. William is under stress over money worries.
5. The 'dream house' was clearly Kate's idea but the consensus view is that William made a mistake buying it.
6. Finally, what on earth was the attraction? Did he marry her because she was pregnant?

Some interesting vibes, don't you think?

Witness statement: James Purdy, Managing Director, Pharmatec UK

I've known William Sumner since he joined the company fifteen years ago at the age of twenty-five. I recruited him myself from Southampton University where he worked as an assistant to Professor Hugh Buglass after gaining his MSc. William led the research into two of our pharmaceutical drugs – Antiac and Counterac – which between them represent 12 per cent of the antacid market. He is a valued and valuable member of the team and is well respected in his profession. Until his marriage to Kate Hill in 1994 I would have described William as the eternal bachelor. He had an active social life but his real interests were work and sailing. I remember him telling me once that a wife would never allow him the sort of freedom his mother did. Various young women set their caps at him over the years but he was adroit at avoiding entanglement. I was surprised therefore when I heard that he and Kate Hill were planning to get married. She worked at Pharmatec for some twelve months in '93/'94. I was extremely sorry to hear about her death and have authorized extended leave for William while he comes to terms with his loss and sorts out the care of his daughter. As far as I am aware William was in Liverpool during the weekend of 9/10 August, although I had no contact with him after he left on the morning of Thursday, 7 August. I barely knew Kate Hill-Sumner while she was here and have not seen or heard from her since she left.

James Purdy

Witness statement: Michael Sprate, Services Manager, Pharmatec UK

Kate Hill-Sumner worked as part of my team from May '93 to March '94 when she left the company. She had no shorthand but her typing skills were above average. I had one or two problems with her, principally in relation to her behaviour. This could be very disruptive at times. She had a sharp tongue and was not averse to using it against the other secretaries. I would describe her as a bully who had no qualms about spreading malicious gossip in order to undermine someone she had taken a dislike to. She became particularly difficult after her marriage to William Sumner which she clearly felt gave her an elevated status and, had she not decided to leave voluntarily, I would certainly have sought to have her transferred from my department. I know William only slightly, so cannot comment on their relationship as I have not seen or heard from Kate since she left Pharmatec UK. I know nothing about her death.

Michael Sprate

Witness statement: Simon Trew, Manager, R & D, Pharmatec UK

William Sumner is one of our leading scientists. His most successful research resulted in Antiac and Counterac. We are optimistic that something may come of the project he is working on at the moment, although he has hinted for some time now that he might be leaving us to work for one of our competitors. I believe the pressure to move has been coming from his wife. William took on an expensive mortgage some twelve months ago which he is having trouble honouring and the increase in salary we can offer him does not match the offer from elsewhere. All our employee contracts contain indemnity clauses relating to the unauthorized use of research ideas funded by Pharmatec UK, so if he decides to leave his research will remain with the company. I understand that he is reluctant to abandon the project at what he believes to be a crucial point, however his financial commitments may force his hand sooner than he would like. I have never met Kate Sumner. I joined the company two years after she left, and my relationship with William has always been strictly professional. I admire his experience and expertise but I find him difficult to get on with. He carries a permanent chip on his shoulder because he sees himself as undervalued, and this causes friction within the department. I can confirm that William left for Liverpool on the morning of Thursday, 7 August and that I spoke to him by telephone shortly before he delivered his paper on the afternoon of Friday, 8 August. He appeared to be in good spirits and confirmed a meeting with me for 10.00 a.m. on Tuesday, 12 August. In the event the meeting did not take place. I know nothing about Mrs Sumner's death.

Simon Trew

Witness statement: Wendy Plater, Research Scientist, Pharmatec UK

I've known William Sumner for five years. We were very close when I first joined the company, and I visited him and his mother in Chichester and also went sailing once or twice on his boat. He was a quiet man with a dry sense of humour, and we spent some pleasant times together. He always told me he wasn't the marrying kind, so I was very surprised when I heard that Kate Hill had hooked him. If I'm honest, I thought he had better taste, although I don't think he stood a chance once she set her sights on him. There is nothing nice I can say about her. She was uneducated, vulgar, manipulative and deceitful, and she was out for anything and everything she could get. I knew her quite well before she married and I disliked her intensely. She was a stirrer and a malicious gossiper, and she was never happier than when she was pulling people down to her own level or below. Lying was second nature to her and she told some appalling lies about me for which I have never forgiven her. The sad part is William changed for the worse after his marriage. He's been a right bitch since he moved to Lymington, constantly complaining about the people he works with, disrupting team spirit and whingeing on about how he's been cheated by the company. He made a mistake selling his boat and taking on a huge mortgage, and he's been venting his spleen on his work colleagues. I believe Kate to have been a terrible influence on him; however, I cannot conceive of a single circumstance that would have caused William to have anything to do with her death. The impression I have always had is that he was genuinely fond of her. I was at a disco on Saturday night, 9 August, with my partner, Michael Sprate. I haven't seen or heard from Kate Sumner since she left Pharmatec UK and I know nothing about her murder.

Wendy Plater

Witness statement: Polly Garrard, Secretary, Services, Pharmatec UK

I knew Kate Hill very well. She and I shared an office for ten months while she worked in Services. I felt sorry for her. She had a hell of a life before she moved to Portsmouth. She lived on a run-down council estate in Birmingham, and she and her mother used to barricade themselves behind their front door because they were so terrified of the other tenants. I think her mother worked in a shop and I think Kate learnt her typing while she was still at school, but I can't swear to either. I remember she told me once that she had been working in a bank before her mother died and that they'd sacked her because she took time off to care for her ma. On another occasion she said she resigned voluntarily in order to nurse her mother. I don't know which story is true. She didn't talk much about her life in Birmingham except to say it was pretty rough. She was okay. I liked her. Everyone else thought she was a bit sly – you know, out for what she could get – but I just saw her as an incredibly vulnerable person who was looking for security. It's true she took against people and picked up bits of gossip about them and spread them around, but I'm not convinced she did it from malice. I think it made her feel better about herself to know that other people weren't perfect. I visited her a couple of times after she and William got married, and on both occasions her mother-in-law was there. Mrs Sumner Snr. was very rude. Kate married the son, not the mother, so what business was it of hers if Kate talked with a Brummie accent and held her knife like a pencil? She was always lecturing Kate on how to bring up little Hannah and how to be a good wife, but as far as I could see she was making a success of both without any interference from anyone. The best thing she did was move to Lymington, and I'm really upset she's dead. I haven't seen her for over a year and I know nothing about her murder.

Polly Garrard

**Addendum to report on Hannah Sumner ('Baby Smith')
following conversation with William Sumner (father) and
telephone conversation with Dr Attwater, GP**

Physical: As before.

Psychological: Both father and doctor agree that Hannah's mother
was overprotective and would not allow her to develop naturally by
playing with other children or by being allowed to explore her own
environment and make mistakes. She had some contact with a
mothers' and toddlers' group but, as Hannah's play tends to be
aggressive, her mother chose less exposure to other children rather
than more as a means of dealing with it. Hannah's 'withdrawal' is
manipulative rather than frightened, and her 'fear' of men has
everything to do with the sympathetic reaction it inspires in women
and nothing to do with any real terror. Both father and doctor
describe Hannah as being of below-average intellect, and blame
both this and her mother's overprotectiveness for her poor verbal
skills. Dr Attwater has not seen Hannah since her mother's death;
however, he is confident that my assessment of her does not differ
materially from the assessment he made six months ago.

Conclusions: While I am prepared to accept that Hannah's
backward development (which I believe to be serious) may not be
due to any recent event, I can only reiterate that this child's welfare
must be continuously monitored. Without supervision, I consider it
probable that Hannah will suffer psychological, emotional and
physical neglect as William Sumner (father) is immature, lacks
parental skills and appears to have little affection for his daughter.

Dr Janet Murray

Chapter Twelve

STEVEN HARDING WAS released without charge shortly before 9.00 a.m. on Wednesday, 13 August 1997, when the review officer declined to authorize his continued detention due to lack of evidence. However, he was informed that both his car and his boat would be retained for 'as long as is necessary'. No further explanation was offered for their retention. With the co-operation of the Hampshire Constabulary, he was remanded on police bail to twenty-three Old Street, Lymington, the house of Anthony Bridges, and was ordered to present himself at Lymington police station daily so that a regular check could be kept on his movements.

On the advice of a solicitor, he had made a detailed statement about his relationship with Kate Sumner and his movements over the weekend of 9/10 August, although it added little to what he had already told the police. He explained the fingerprint evidence and the presence of Hannah's shoes on *Crazy Daze* in the following manner:

> They came on board in March when I had the boat lifted out of the water to clean and repaint the hull. *Crazy Daze* was in Berthon's yard, sitting on a wooden cradle, and when Kate realized I couldn't get away from her because I had to finish the painting, she kept coming to the yard and hanging around, making a nuisance of herself and irritating me. In the end, just to get rid of her, I agreed to let her and Hannah climb the ladder and look at the inside while I stayed below. I told them to take

their shoes off and leave them in the cockpit. When the time came for them to climb down again, Kate decided Hannah couldn't manage the ladder so lowered her down to me instead. I strapped Hannah into her buggy but I didn't notice whether or not she was wearing shoes. To be honest I never look at her much. She gives me the creeps. She never says anything, just stares at me as if I'm not there. Some time later I found some shoes in the cockpit with H. SUMNER written on the strap. Even if they were too small to be the ones Hannah was wearing that day, I have no other explanation for their presence there.

Although I knew where the Sumners lived, I did not return Hannah's shoes because I was sure that Kate had left them there deliberately. I did not like Kate Sumner and I did not want to be alone with her in her house because I knew she had a serious crush on me which I did not reciprocate. She was very peculiar and her constant pestering worried me. I can only describe her behaviour as harassment. She used to hang around by the yacht club waiting for me to come ashore in my dinghy. Most of the time she just stood and watched me, but sometimes she'd deliberately bump into me and rub her breasts against my arm. The mistake I made was to visit Langton Cottage with her husband shortly after she introduced me to him in the street at the end of last year. I believe that was the beginning of her infatuation. At no time was I inclined to respond to her advances.

Some time later, at the end of April, I think, I was moored up to the Berthon fuelling pontoon, waiting for the dockie to come and operate the pump, when Kate and Hannah walked down 'C' pontoon towards me. Kate said she hadn't seen me for a while but had spotted *Crazy Daze* and felt like a chat. She and Hannah came on board without invitation which annoyed me. I suggested Kate go into the aft cabin to retrieve Hannah's shoes from the port shelf. I knew there were some clothes belonging to other women in the cabin and I thought it would be a good thing if Kate saw them. I hoped it would make her realize that I wasn't interested in her. She left soon afterwards and when I went into the cabin, I found she'd taken off Hannah's nappy, which was dirty, and had ground the mess into the bedclothes. She had also left the shoes behind again. I believe both acts were done deliberately to show me that she was angry about the women's underclothes in the cabin.

I became seriously concerned about Kate Sumner's harassment of me when she found out where I parked my car and took to setting off the alarm to get Tony Bridges and his neighbours riled with me. I have no proof it was Kate who was doing it, although I am sure it must have been because I kept finding faeces smeared on the driver's handle. I did not tell the police about my suspicions because I was afraid of becoming even more involved with the Sumner family. Instead I sought out William Sumner some time in June and showed him photographs of myself in a gay magazine because I wanted him to tell his wife I was gay. I realize this must seem odd after I had shown Kate evidence that I entertain girlfriends on board *Crazy Daze* but I was becoming desperate. Some of the photographs were quite explicit and William was shocked by them. I don't know what he told his wife but, to my relief, she stopped harassing me almost immediately.

I have seen her in the street maybe five times since June but did not speak to her until the morning of Saturday, 9 August, when I realized I couldn't avoid her. She was outside Tesco's, and we said good morning to each other. She told me she was looking for some sandals for Hannah, and I said I was in a hurry to get off because I was sailing to Poole for the weekend. That was the extent of our conversation. I did not see her again. I admit that I was very aggrieved by her persecution of me, and developed a strong dislike for her, but I have no idea how she came to drown in the sea off the Dorset coast.

A long interview with Tony Bridges produced a corroborative statement. As DS Campbell had predicted, Bridges was known to the Lymington police as a cannabis user but they took a tolerant view of it. 'Once in a while his neighbours complain when he has a party in there, but it's alcohol that makes them raucous, not cannabis, and even the blue-rinse brigade are finally beginning to realize that.' Rather more surprisingly, he was also a respected chemistry teacher at one of the local schools. 'What Tony does in the privacy of his home is his own affair,' said his headmaster. 'As far as I'm concerned, the policing of my colleagues' morals outside school hours isn't part of my job description. If it were, I would probably lose some of my better staff. Tony's an inspirational teacher who enthuses children in a difficult subject. I have a lot of time for him.'

I've known Steven Harding for eighteen years. We attended the same primary and secondary schools and have been friends ever since. He sleeps in my house when his boat's out of commission or during the winter when it's too cold for him to stay on board. I used to know his parents quite well before they moved to Cornwall in 1991 but I have not seen them since. Steve sailed down to Falmouth two summers ago but I don't believe he's made any other visits to Cornwall. He divides his life between his flat in London and his boat in Lymington.

He told me on more than one occasion this year that he was having problems with a woman called Kate Sumner who was stalking him. He described her and her child as weird, and said they scared him. His car alarm kept going off and he told me he thought it was Kate Sumner who was activating it and asked me if he should report it to the police. It was a pretty odd story so I wasn't sure whether to believe him or not. Then he pointed out the faeces on the car door handle and told me how Kate Sumner had wiped her child's nappy on his sheets. I told him that if he brought the police into it it would get worse rather than better and suggested he find somewhere else to park his car. As far as I know, that sorted the problem.

I have never spoken to Kate or Hannah Sumner. Steve pointed them out to me once in the middle of Lymington then dragged me round a corner so we wouldn't have to speak to them. His reluctance was genuine. I believe he found her seriously intimidating. I met William Sumner once in a pub at the beginning of this year. He was drinking alone and invited Steve and me to join him. He knew Steve already because they'd been introduced to each other by Kate after Steve had helped her with her shopping. I left after about half an hour, but Steve told me later that he went back to William's house to continue a discussion they were having about sailing. He said William used to race a Contessa and was interesting to talk to.

Steve's a good-looking bloke and has an active sex life. He has at least two girls on the go at the same time because he's not interested in settling down. He's obsessed with sailing and told me once that he could never get serious about anyone who didn't sail. He's not the kiss-and-tell type and, as I never listen to names, I've no idea who he's got on the go at the moment. When he's not acting, he can always get regular work as a photographic model. Mostly he models clothes, but he's done a few sessions for pornographic magazines. He needs money to fund the flat in London and keep *Crazy Daze* afloat, and that kind of work pays well. He's not ashamed of the photographs but I've never known him show them around. I've no idea where he stores them.

I saw Steve on the evening of Friday, 8 August. He dropped in to tell me he was off to Poole the next day and wouldn't see me again until the following weekend. He mentioned that he had an audition in London on Monday, 11 August, and said he was planning to catch the last train back on Sunday night. Later, a mutual friend, Bob Winterslow, who lives near the station, told me that Steve had rung from his boat to ask if he could borrow a sofa Sunday night in order to catch the first train on Monday morning. In the event he stayed on board and missed his audition. This is standard for Steve. He tends to come and go as he pleases. I became aware that Steve had cocked up when his agent, Graham Barlow, phoned me on Monday morning to say there was no sign of Steve in London and he wasn't answering his mobile phone. I phoned friends to see if anyone knew where he was, then borrowed a dinghy to go out to *Crazy Daze*. I discovered that Steve was badly hungover, and that this was the reason for his non-appearance.

I spent the weekend, 9/10 August, with my girlfriend Beatrice 'Bibi' Gould whom I've known for four months. On Saturday night we went to a 'rave' at the Jamaica Club in Southampton, returning home at approximately 4.00 a.m. We slept through till some time Sunday p.m. I know nothing about Kate Sumner's death, although I am completely sure that Steven Harding had nothing to do with it. He is not an aggressive person.

(Police note: this rave certainly took place, but there is no way of checking whether A. Bridges & B. Gould were present. Rough estimate of numbers at the Jamaica Club on Saturday night: 1,000+.)

Beatrice Gould's statement supported Bridges' and Harding's in all relevant details.

I'm nineteen years old and I work as a hairdresser in Get Ahead in Lymington High Street. I met Tony Bridges at a pub disco about four months ago and he introduced me to Steve Harding a week later. They've been friends for a long time and Steve uses Tony's house as a base in Lymington when he can't stay on his boat for any reason. I've come to know Steve quite well over the time Tony and I have been together. Several of my friends would like to go out with him but he's not interested in settling down and tends to avoid heavy relationships. He's a good-looking bloke and, because he's an actor as well, girls throw themselves at him. He told me once that he thinks they see him as a stud, and that he really hates it. I know he's had a lot of problems in that way with Kate Sumner. He was nice to her once, and afterwards she wouldn't leave him alone. He said he thought she was lonely but that didn't give her the right to make his life a misery. It got to the point that he'd hide behind corners while Tony or I checked to see if she was on the other side. I think she must have been mentally disturbed. The worst thing she did was smear her daughter's dirty nappies on his car. I thought that was completely disgusting and told Steve that he should report her to the police.

I didn't see Steve the weekend of 9/10 August. I went to Tony's house at 4.30 p.m. on Saturday, 9 August, and at about 7.30 p.m. we left for the Jamaica Club in Southampton. We go there a lot because Daniel Agee is a brilliant DJ and we really like his style. I stayed at Tony's until 10.00 p.m. on Sunday night then went home. My permanent address is sixty-seven Shorn Street, Lymington, where I live with my parents but I spend most weekends and some weekday nights with Tony Bridges. I like Steve Harding a lot and I don't believe he had anything to do with Kate Sumner's death. He and I get on really well together.

Detective Superintendent Carpenter sat in silence while John Galbraith read through all three statements. 'What do you think?' he asked when the other had finished. 'Does Harding's story ring true? Is that a Kate Sumner you recognize?'

Galbraith shook his head. 'I don't know. I haven't got a feel for her yet. She was like Harding, a bit of a chameleon, play-acted different roles to suit different people.' He reflected for a moment. 'I suppose one thing in Harding's defence is that when she rubbed someone up the wrong way she did it in spades – really got under their skin in other words. Did you read those statements I sent you? Her mother-in-law didn't like her at all, and neither did Wendy Plater, William's ex-girlfriend, who was cut out of the running by Kate. You could argue it was straightforward jealousy on both counts, but I got the impression there was more to it than that. They used the same word to describe her. Manipulative. Angela Sumner referred to her as the most self-centred and calculating woman she had ever met, and the girlfriend said lying was second nature to her. William said she was single-minded about what she wanted and had him wound round her finger from the first time she met him.' He shrugged. 'Whether any of that means she was stalking a man she became infatuated with, I don't know. I wouldn't have expected her to be so blatant but' – he spread his hands in perplexity – 'she was pretty blatant in her pursuit of a comfortable lifestyle.'

'I hate these cases, John,' said Carpenter with genuine regret. 'The poor little woman's dead but her character's going to be blackened whichever way you look at it.' He pulled Harding's statement across the desk towards him and drummed his fingers on it in irritation. 'Shall I tell you what this smells of to me? The classic defence against rape. *She was panting for it, guv. Couldn't keep her hands off me. I just gave her what she wanted and it's not my fault if she cried foul afterwards. She was an aggressive woman and she liked aggressive sex.*' His frown deepened to a chasm. 'All Harding's doing is laying some neat groundwork in case we manage to bring charges against him. Then he'll tell us her death was an accident . . . she fell off the back of the boat and he couldn't save her.'

'What did you make of Anthony Bridges?'

'I didn't like him. He's a cocky little bastard, and a damn sight too knowledgeable about police interviews. But his and his blousy girlfriend's stories tally so closely with Harding's that, unless they're operating some sort of sick conspiracy, I think we have to accept they're telling the truth.' A sudden smile banished his frown. 'For the moment anyway. It'll be interesting to see if anything changes after he and Harding have had a chance to talk together. You know we've bailed him to Bridges' address.'

'Harding's right about one thing,' said Galbraith thoughtfully. 'Hannah gives *me* the creeps, too.' He leaned forward, elbows on knees, a troubled expression on his face. 'It's codswallop about her screaming every time she sees a man. I was waiting for her father to bring me some lists he'd made, and she came into the room, sat down on the carpet in front of me and started to play with herself. She had no knickers on, just pulled up her dress and got going like there was no tomorrow. She was watching me the whole time she was doing it, and I swear to God she knew exactly what she was about.' He sighed. 'It was bloody unnerving, and I'll eat my hat if she hasn't been introduced to some sort of sexual activity, whatever that doctor said.'

'Meaning you've got your money on Sumner?'

Galbraith considered for a moment. 'Put it this way, I'd says he's a dead cert if, one: his alibi doesn't check out and, two: I can work out how he managed to have a boat waiting for him off the Isle of Purbeck.' His pleasant face broke into a smile. 'He gets under my skin something rotten, probably because he thinks he's so damned clever. It's hardly scientific but, yes, I'd put my money on him any day before Steven Harding.'

For seventy-two hours, local and national newspapers had been carrying reports of a murder inquiry following the finding of a body on a beach on the Isle of Purbeck. On the theory that the dead woman and her daughter had been travelling by boat, sailors between Southampton and Weymouth were being asked to come forward with any sightings of a small, blonde woman and/or a three-year-old child on the weekend of 9/10 August. During her lunch break that Wednesday, a shop assistant in one of the big department stores in Bournemouth went into her local police station and suggested diffidently that, while she didn't want to waste anyone's time, she thought that something she'd seen on Sunday evening might be connected to the woman's murder.

She gave her name as Jennifer Hale and said she'd been on a Fairline Squadron called *Gregory's Girl* belonging to a Poole businessman called Gregory Freemantle.

'He's my boyfriend,' she explained.

The desk sergeant found the description amusing. She'd never see thirty again, and he wondered how old the boyfriend was. Approaching fifty, he guessed, if he could afford to own a Fairline Squadron.

'I wanted Gregory to come and tell you about it himself,' she confided, 'because he could have given you a better idea of where it was, but he said it wasn't worth the bother because I didn't have enough experience to know what I was looking at. He believes his daughters, you see. They said it was an oil drum and woe betide anyone who disagrees with them. He won't argue with them in case they complain to their mother when what he ought to be doing . . .' She heaved the kind of sigh that every potential stepmother has sighed down the ages. 'They're a couple of little madams, frankly. I thought we should have stopped at the time to investigate but' – she shook her head – 'it wasn't worth going into battle over. Frankly, I'd had enough for one day.'

The desk sergeant who had stepchildren of his own gave her a sympathetic smile. 'How old are they?'

'Fifteen and thirteen.'

'Difficult ages.'

'Yes, particularly when their parents . . .' She stopped abruptly, reconsidering how much she wanted to say.

'It'll get better in about five years when they've grown up a bit.'

A gleam of humour flashed in her eyes. 'Assuming I'm around to find out, which at the moment doesn't look likely. The younger one's not too bad, but I'd need a skin like a rhinoceros to put up with another five years of Marie. She thinks she's Elle McPherson and Claudia Schiffer rolled into one, and throws a tantrum if she isn't being constantly petted and spoilt. Still . . .' She returned to her reason for being there. 'I'm sure it wasn't an oil drum. I was sitting at the back of the flying bridge and had a better view than the others. Whatever it was, it wasn't metal . . . although it *was* black . . . it looked to me like an upturned dinghy . . . a rubber one. I think it may have been partially deflated because it was pretty low in the water.'

The desk sergeant was taking notes. 'Why do you think it was connected with the murder?' he asked her.

She gave an embarrassed smile, afraid of making a fool of herself. 'Because it was a boat,' she said, 'and it wasn't far from where the body was found. We were in Chapman's Pool when the woman was lifted off by helicopter, and we passed the dinghy only about ten minutes after we rounded St Alban's Head on our way home. I've worked out that the time must have been about 6.15 and I know we were travelling at twenty-five knots because my boyfriend commented on the fact as we rounded the Head. He says you'll be looking for a yacht or a cruiser but I thought – well – you can drown off a dinghy just as easily as off a yacht, can't you? And this one had obviously capsized.'

Carpenter received the report from Bournemouth at three o'clock, mulled it over in conjunction with a map, then sent it through to Galbraith with a note attached.

Is this worth following up? If it hasn't beached between St Alban's Head and Anvil Point, then it'll have gone down in deep water somewhere off Swanage and is irretrievable. However, the timings seem very precise so, assuming it washed up before Anvil Point, your friend Ingram can probably work out where it is. You said he was wasted as a beat copper. Failing

*him, get on to the coastguards. In fact it might be worth going
to them first. You know how they hate having their thunder
stolen by landlubbers. It's a long shot – can't see where Hannah
fits in or how anyone can rape a woman in a dinghy without
turning turtle – but you never know. It could be that boat off
the Isle of Purbeck you wanted.*

In the event the coastguards happily passed the buck to Ingram,
claiming they had better things to do at the height of the
summer season than look for 'imaginary' dinghies in unlikely
places. Equally sceptical himself, Ingram parked at Durlston
Head and set off along the coastal path, following the route
Harding claimed to have taken the previous Sunday. He walked
slowly, searching the shoreline at the foot of the cliffs every fifty
yards through binoculars. He was as conscious as the coastguards of the difficulties of isolating a black dinghy against the
glistening rocks that lined the base of the headland, and
constantly re-examined stretches he had already decided were
clear. He also had little faith in his own estimate that a floating
object seen at approximately 6.15 p.m. on Sunday evening,
some three hundred yards out from Seacombe Cliff – his guess
at where a Fairline Squadron might have been after ten minutes
travelling at twenty-five knots from St Alban's Head – could
have beached approximately six hours later halfway between
Blackers Hole and Anvil Point. He knew how unpredictable
the sea was, and how very unlikely it was that a partially deflated
dinghy would even have come ashore. The more probable
scenario was that it was halfway to France by now – always
assuming it had ever existed – or twenty fathoms under.

He found it slightly to the east of where he had predicted,
nearer to Anvil Point, and he smiled with justifiable satisfaction
as the powerful lenses picked it out. It was upside down, held
in shape by its wooden floor and seats, and neatly stranded
on an inaccessible piece of shore. He dialled through to

DI Galbraith on his mobile. 'How good a sailor are you?' he asked him. 'Because the only way you'll get close to this little mother is by boat. If you meet me in Swanage I can take you out this evening. You'll need waterproofs and waders,' he warned. 'It'll be a wet trip.'

Ingram invited along a couple of friends from the Swanage lifeboat crew to keep *Miss Creant* on station while he took Galbraith into the shore in his own inflatable. He killed the outboard motor and swung it up out of the water thirty yards from land, using his oars to manoeuvre them carefully through the crops of jagged granite that lay in wait for unwary sailors. He steadied the little craft against a good-sized rock, nodded to Galbraith to get out and start wading, then followed him into the water and used the painter to guide the lightened dinghy on to what passed for a beach in that desolate spot.

'There she is,' he said, jerking his head to the left while he lifted his inflatable clear of the waterline, 'but God only knows what she's doing out here. People don't abandon perfectly good dinghies for no reason.'

Galbraith shook his head in amazement. 'How the hell did you spot it?' he asked, gazing up at the sheer cliffs above them and thinking it must have been like looking for a needle in a haystack.

'It wasn't easy,' Ingram admitted, leading the way towards it. 'More to the point, how the hell did it survive the rocks?' He stooped over the upturned hull. 'It must have come in like this or its bottom would have been ripped out, and that means there won't be anything left inside. Still' – he raised an enquiring eyebrow – 'shall we turn it over?'

With a nod, Galbraith grasped the stern board while Ingram took a tuck in the rubber at the bow. They set it right way up with difficulty because the lack of air meant there was no rigidity in the structure and it collapsed in on itself like a deflated balloon. A tiny crab scuttled out from underneath and slipped into a nearby rock pool. As Ingram had predicted, there was nothing inside except the wooden floorboards and the remains of a wooden seat which had snapped in the middle, probably on its journey to and fro across the rocks. Nevertheless, it was a substantial dinghy, about ten feet long and four feet wide with its stern board intact.

Ingram pointed to the indentations where the screw clamps of an outboard motor had bitten into the wood, then squatted on his haunches to examine two metal rings screwed into the transom planking aft, and a single ring screwed into the floorboarding at the bow. 'It's been hung from davits off the back of a boat at some point. These rings are for attaching the wires before it's winched up tight against the davit arms. That way it doesn't swing about while the host boat's in motion.' He searched the outside of the hull for any sign of a name, but there was none. He looked up at Galbraith, squinting against the setting sun. 'There's no way this dropped off the back of a cruiser without anyone noticing. Both winching wires would have to snap at the same moment and the chances of that happening would be minimal, I should think. If only one wire snapped – the stern wire for example – you'd have a heavy object swinging like a pendulum behind you and your steering would go haywire. At which point you'd slow right down and find out what the problem was.' He paused. 'In any case, if the wires had sheered they'd still be attached to the rings.'

'Go on.'

'I'd say it's more likely it was launched off a trailer, which means we need to ask questions at Swanage, Kimmeridge Bay or Lulworth.' He stood up and glanced towards the west. 'Unless it came out of Chapman's Pool, of course, and then we need to ask how it got there in the first place. There's no public access, so you can't just pull a trailer down and launch a dinghy for the fun of it.' He rubbed his jaw. 'It's curious, isn't it?'

'Couldn't you carry it down and pump it up *in situ*?'

'It depends how strong you are. They weigh a ton these things.' He stretched his arms like a fisherman sizing a fish. 'They come in huge canvas holdalls but, trust me, you need two people to carry them any distance, and it's a good mile from Hill Bottom to the Chapman's Pool slip.'

'What about the boatsheds? The SOCOs took photographs of the whole bay and there are plenty of dinghies parked on the hard standing beside the sheds. Could it be one of those?'

'Only if it was nicked. The fishermen who use the boatsheds wouldn't abandon a perfectly good dinghy. I haven't had any reports of one being stolen but that might be because no one's noticed it's missing. I can run some checks tomorrow.'

'Joyriders?' suggested Galbraith.

'I doubt it.' Ingram touched his foot to the hull. 'Not unless they fancied the hardest paddle of their life to get it out into the open sea. It couldn't have floated out on its own. The entrance channel's too narrow and the thrust of the waves would have forced it back on to the rocks in the bay.' He smiled at Galbraith's lack of comprehension. 'You couldn't take it out without an engine,' he explained, 'and your average joyrider doesn't usually bring his own means of locomotion with him. People don't leave outboards lying around any more than they leave gold ingots. They're expensive items so you keep them under lock and key. That also rules out your pumping up *in situ* theory. I can't see anyone lugging a dinghy *and* an outboard down to Chapman's Pool.'

Galbraith eyed him curiously. 'So?'

'I'm thinking on the hoof here, sir.'

'Never mind. It sounds good. Keep going.'

'If it was stolen out of Chapman's Pool that makes it a premeditated theft. We're talking someone who was prepared to lug a heavy outboard along a mile-long path in order to nick a boat.' He lifted his eyebrows. 'Why would anyone want to do that? And, having done it, why abandon ship? It's a bit bloody odd, don't you think? How did they get back to shore?'

'Swam?'

'Maybe.' Ingram's eyes narrowed to slits against the brilliant orange sun. He didn't speak for several seconds. 'Or maybe they didn't have to,' he said then. 'Maybe they weren't in it.' He lapsed into a thoughtful silence. 'There's nothing wrong with the stern board so the outboard should have pulled it under as soon as the sides started to deflate.'

'What does that mean?'

'The outboard wasn't on it when it capsized.'

Galbraith waited for him to go on and, when he didn't, he made impatient winding motions with his hand. 'Come on, Nick. What are you getting at? I know sweet FA about boats.'

The big man laughed. 'Sorry. I was just wondering what a dinghy like this was doing in the middle of nowhere without an outboard.'

'I thought you said it must have had one.'

'I've changed my mind.'

Galbraith gave a groan. 'Do you want to stop talking in riddles, you bastard? I'm wet, I'm freezing to death here and I could do with a drink.'

Ingram laughed again. 'I was only thinking that the most obvious way to take a stolen rib out of Chapman's Pool would be to tow it out, assuming you'd come in by boat in the first place.'

'In which case, why would you want to steal one?'

Ingram stared down at the collapsed hull. 'Because you'd raped a woman and left her half-dead in it?' he suggested. 'And you wanted to get rid of the evidence? I think you should get your scene-of-crime people out here to find out why it deflated. If there's a blade puncture then I'd guess the intention was to have the boat and its contents founder in the open sea when the tow rope was released.'

'So we're back to Harding?'

The constable shrugged. 'He's your only suspect with a boat in the right place at the right time,' he pointed out.

Tony Bridges listened to Steven Harding's interminable tirade against the police with growing irritation. His friend paced the sitting room in a rage, kicking at anything that got in his way and biting Tony's head off every time he tried to offer advice. Meanwhile, Bibi, a silent and frightened observer to their mounting anger, sat cross-legged on the floor at Tony's feet, hiding her feelings behind a curtain of thick blonde hair and wondering whether it would make the situation better or worse if she announced her intention of going home.

Finally, Tony's patience snapped. 'Get a grip before I bloody *flatten* you,' he roared. 'You're acting like a two-year-old. Okay, so the police arrested you. Big deal! Just be grateful they didn't find anything.'

Steve slammed down into an armchair. 'Who says they haven't? They've refused to release *Crazy Daze* . . . my car's in a pound somewhere . . . What the hell am I supposed to do?'

'Get the solicitor on to it. That's what he's paid to do, for Christ's sake. Just don't keep bellyaching on to us. It's fucking *boring*, apart from anything else. It's not our fault you went to Poole for the sodding weekend. You should have come to Southampton with us.'

Bibi stirred uncomfortably on the floor at his feet. She opened her mouth to say something, then closed it again when caution prevailed. Anger was bubbling in the room like over-heated yeast.

Harding slammed his feet on to the floor in a rage. 'The solicitor's worse than useless, told me the bastards were entitled to hold evidence for as long as is necessary or some legalized crap like that . . .' His voice tailed off on a sob.

There was a long silence.

This time fondness for Tony's friend got the better of

caution and nervously Bibi raised her head. She scraped a gap in her hair to look at him. 'But if you didn't do it,' she said in her soft, rather childish way, 'then I don't see what you're worrying about.'

'Right,' agreed Tony. 'They can't prosecute you without evidence, and if they've released you then there isn't any evidence. QED.'

'I want my phone,' said Harding, surging to his feet again with crackling energy. 'What did you do with it?'

'Left it with Bob,' said Tony. 'Like you told me to do.'

'Has he put it on charge?'

'I wouldn't know. I haven't spoken to him since Monday. He was pretty stoned when I gave it to him, so the chances are he's forgotten all about it.'

'That's all I need.' The angry young man launched a kick at one of the walls.

Bridges took a pull at his lager can, eyeing his friend thoughtfully over the top of it. 'What's so important about the phone?'

'Nothing.'

'Then leave my fucking walls alone!' he bellowed, surging out of his own chair and thrusting his face into Harding's. 'Show some respect, you bastard! This is *my* house, not your crappy little boat.'

'Stop it!' screamed Bibi, cowering back behind the chair. 'What's wrong with you both? One of you's going to get hurt in a minute.'

Harding frowned down at her, then held up his hands. 'All right, all right. I'm expecting a call. That's why I'm twitched.'

'Then use the phone in the hall,' said Bridges curtly, flinging himself into the armchair again.

'No.' He backed towards the wall and leaned against it. 'What did the police ask you?'

'What you'd expect. How well you knew Kate . . . whether I thought the harassment was genuine . . . whether I saw you on Saturday . . . where *I* was . . . what kind of pornography you were into . . .' He shook his head. 'I knew that garbage would come back to haunt you.'

'Leave it out,' said Harding tiredly. 'I told you I'd had enough of your bloody lectures on Monday. What did you tell them?'

Tony frowned warningly at Bibi's bent head, then touched a hand to the back of her neck. 'Do you want to do me a favour, Beebs? Hop down to the off-licence and get an eight-pack. There's some money on the shelf in the hall.'

She rose to her feet with obvious relief. 'Sure. Why not? I'll leave them in the hall then go home. Okay?' She held out a reluctant hand. 'I'm really tired, Tony, and I could do with a decent night's kip. You don't mind, do you?'

'Of course not.' He gripped her fingers for a moment, squeezing them hard. 'Just so long as you love me, Beebs.'

She tore herself free, cradling her hand under her arm, and made for the hall. 'You know I do.'

He didn't speak again until he heard the front door close behind her. 'You want to be careful what you say around her,' he warned Harding. 'She had to give a statement, too, and it's not fair to get her any more involved than she is already.'

'Okay, okay . . . So what did you tell them?'

'Aren't you more interested in what I *didn't* tell them?'

'If you like.'

'Right. Well, I didn't tell them you shagged Kate's brains out.'

Harding breathed deeply through his nose. 'Why not?'

'I thought about it,' Bridges admitted, reaching for a packet of Rizla papers on the floor and setting about rolling himself a joint. 'But I know you too well, mate. You're an arrogant son of a bitch with an over-inflated opinion of yourself' – he squinted up at his friend with a return of good humour in his eyes – 'but I can't see you murdering anyone, particularly not a woman, and never mind she was pissing you off something

150

rotten. So I kept shtoom.' He gave an eloquent shrug. 'But if I live to regret it, I'll have your stinking hide . . . and you'd better believe that.'

'Did they tell you she was raped before she was murdered?'

Bridges gave a low whistle of understanding as if pieces of a jigsaw were finally coming together. 'No wonder they were so interested in your porno shoots. Your average rapist's a sad bastard in a dirty mac who jerks off over that kind of trash.' He pulled a plastic bag out from the recesses of his chair and started to fill the Rizla papers. 'They must have had a field day with those photographs.'

Harding shook his head. 'I got rid of the lot over the side before they came. I didn't want any' – he thought about it – 'confusion.'

'Jesus, you're an arsehole! Why can't you be honest for once? You got shit-scared that if they had evidence of you performing sex acts with an under-age kid, they'd have no trouble pinning a rape on you.'

'It wasn't for real.'

'Chucking the photos away was. You're an idiot, mate.'

'Why?'

'Because you can bet your bottom dollar William will have mentioned photos. *I* sure as hell did. Now the filth will be wondering why they can't find any.'

'So?'

'They'll know you were expecting a visit.'

'So?' said Harding again.

Bridges cast him another thoughtful glance as he licked the edges of the spliff. 'Look at it from their point of view. Why would you be expecting a visit if you didn't know it was Kate's body they'd found?'

Chapter Thirteen

'WE CAN GO to the pub,' said Ingram, locking *Miss Creant* on to her trailer behind his Jeep, 'or I can give you some supper at home.' He glanced at his watch. 'It's 9.30, so the pub'll be pretty raucous by now and it'll be difficult to get anything to eat.' He started to peel off his waterproofs which still streamed water from his immersion in the sea at the bottom of the slip as he had guided *Miss Creant* on to the trailer while Galbraith operated the winch. 'Home, on the other hand,' he said with a grin, 'has drying facilities, a spectacular view and silence.'

'Do I get the impression you'd rather go home?' asked Galbraith with a yawn, levering off his inadequate waders and turning them upside down to empty them in a Niagara Falls over the slip. He was soaked from the waistband down.

'There's beer in the fridge and I can grill you a fresh sea bass if you're interested.'

'How fresh?'

'Still alive Monday night,' said Ingram, taking some spare trousers from the back of the Jeep and tossing them across. 'You can change in the lifeboat station.'

'Cheers,' said Galbraith setting off in stockinged feet towards the grey stone building that guarded the ever-ready Swanage lifeboat, 'and I'm interested,' he called over his shoulder.

Ingram's cottage was a tiny two-up, two-down, backing on to the downs above Seacombe Cliff, although the two downstairs rooms had been knocked into one with an open-plan staircase rising out of the middle and a kitchen extension added to the back. It was clearly a bachelor establishment and Galbraith surveyed it with approval. Too often, these days, he felt he still had to be persuaded of the joys of fatherhood.

'I envy you,' he said, bending down to examine a meticulously detailed replica of the *Cutty Sark* in a bottle on the mantelpiece. 'Did you make this yourself?'

Ingram nodded.

'It wouldn't last half an hour in my house. I reckon anything I ever had of value was smashed within hours of my son getting his first football.' He chuckled. 'He keeps telling me he's going to make a fortune playing for Man United, but I can't see it myself.'

'How old is he?' asked Ingram, leading the way through to the kitchen.

'Seven. His sister's five.'

The tall constable took the sea bass from the fridge, then tossed Galbraith a beer and opened one for himself. 'I'd have liked children,' he said, splitting the fish down its belly, filleting out the backbone and splaying it spatchcock fashion on the grillpan. He was neat and quick in his movements, despite his size. 'Trouble is I never found a woman who was prepared to hang around long enough to give me any.'

Galbraith remembered what Steven Harding had said on Monday night about Ingram fancying the woman with the horse and wondered if it was more a case of the *right* woman not hanging around long enough. 'A guy like you'd do well anywhere,' he said, watching him take some chives and basil from an array of herbs on his window sill and chop them finely before sprinkling them over the sea bass. 'So what's keeping you here?'

'You mean apart from the great view and the clean air?'

'Yes.'

Ingram pushed the fish to one side and started washing the mud off some new potatoes before chucking them into a saucepan. 'That's it,' he said. 'Great view, clean air, a boat, fishing, contentment.'

'What about ambition? Don't you get frustrated? Feel you're standing still?'

'Sometimes. Then I remember how much I hated the rat race when I was in it and the frustrations pass.' He glanced at Galbraith with a self-deprecating smile. 'I did five years with an insurance company before I became a policeman, and I hated every minute of it. I didn't believe in the product, but the only way to get on was to sell more and it was driving me nuts. I had a long think over one weekend about what I wanted out of life, and gave in my notice on the Monday.' He filled the saucepan with water and put it on the gas.

The DI thought sourly of his various life, endowment and pension policies. 'What's wrong with insurance?'

'Nothing.' He tipped his can in the direction of the DI and took a swill. 'As long as you need it . . . as long as you understand the terms of the policy . . . as long as you can afford to keep paying the premiums . . . as long you've read the small print. It's like any other product. Buyer beware.'

'Now you're worrying me.'

Ingram grinned. 'If it's any consolation, I'd have felt exactly the same about selling lottery tickets.'

WPC Griffiths had fallen asleep, fully clothed, in the spare room but woke with a start when Hannah started screaming in the next room. She leapt off the bed, heart thudding, and came face to face with William Sumner as he slunk through the child's doorway. 'What the hell do you think you're doing?' she demanded angrily, her nerves shot to pieces by her sudden awakening. 'You've been told not to go in there.'

'I thought she was asleep. I just wanted to look at her.'

'We agreed you wouldn't.'

'*You* may have done. *I* never did. You've no right to stop me. It's *my* house, and she's *my* daughter.'

'I wouldn't bank on that, if I were you,' she snapped. She was about to add: Your rights take second place to Hannah's at the moment, but he didn't give her the chance.

He clamped fingers like steel bands around her arms and stared at her with dislike, his face working uncontrollably. 'Who have you been talking to?' he muttered.

She didn't say anything, just broke his grip by raising her hands and striking him on both wrists, and with a choking sob he stumbled away down the corridor. But it was a while before she realized what his question had implied.

It would explain a lot, she thought, if Hannah wasn't his child.

Galbraith laid his knife and fork at the side of his plate with a sigh of satisfaction. They were sitting in shirtsleeves on the small patio at the side of the cottage beside a gnarled old plum tree that flavoured the air with the scent of fermentation. A storm lantern hissed quietly on the table between them, throwing a circle of yellow light up the wall of the house and across the lawn. On the horizon, moon-silvered clouds floated across the surface of the sea like windblown veils.

'I'm going to have a problem with this,' he said. 'It's too damn perfect.'

Ingram pushed his own plate aside and propped his elbows on the table. 'You need to like your own company. If you don't, it's the loneliest place on earth.'

'Do you?'

The younger man's face creased into an amiable smile. 'I get by,' he said, 'as long as people like you don't drop in too often. Solitude's a state of mind with me, not an ambition.'

Galbraith nodded. 'That makes sense.' He studied the

other's face for a moment. 'Tell me about Miss Jenner,' he said then. 'Harding gave us the impression he and she had quite a chat before you got back. Could he have said more to her than she's told you?'

'It's possible. She seemed pretty relaxed with him.'

'How well do you know her?'

But Ingram wasn't so easily drawn about his private life. 'As well as I know anyone else round here,' he said casually. 'What did you make of Harding, as a matter of interest?'

'Difficult to say. He gives a convincing performance of wanting nothing to do with Kate Sumner but, as my boss pointed out, dislike is as good a reason for rape and murder as any other. He claims she was harassing him by smearing crap all over his car because he'd rejected her. It might be true, but none of us really believes it.'

'Why not? There was a case down here three years ago when a wife smashed her husband's Jag through the front door of his lover's house. Women can get pretty riled when they're given the elbow.'

'Except he says he never slept with her.'

'Maybe that was her problem.'

'How come you're on his side all of a sudden?'

'I'm not. The rules say keep an open mind, and that's what I'm trying to do.'

Galbraith chuckled. 'He wants us to believe he's a bit of a stud, presumably on the basis that a man who has access to sex on tap doesn't need to rape anyone, but he can't or won't produce the names of women he's slept with. And neither can anyone else.' He shrugged. 'Yet no one questions his reputation for laddish behaviour. They're all quite confident he entertains ladies on his boat even though the SOCOs couldn't come up with any evidence to support it. His bedlinen's stiff with dried semen, but there were only two hairs on it that weren't his, and neither of them was Kate Sumner's. Conclusion, the guy's a compulsive masturbator.' He paused for reflection. 'The problem is his damn boat's positively monastic in every other respect.'

'I don't get you.'

'Not a whisper of anything pornographic,' said Galbraith. 'Compulsive masturbators, particularly the ones who go on to rape, wank their brains out over hard-core porn videos because sensation begins and ends with their dicks, and they need more and more explicit images to help them jerk off. So how does our friend Harding get himself aroused?'

'Memory?' suggested Ingram wryly.

Galbraith chuckled. 'He's done some pornographic photo-shoots himself but claims the only copies he ever kept were the ones he showed William Sumner.' He gave a brief rundown of both Harding's and Sumner's versions of the story. 'He says he threw the magazine in the bin afterwards and, as far as he's concerned, porno shoots become history the minute he's paid.'

'More likely he got rid of everything over the side when it occurred to him I might put his name forward for further questioning.' Ingram thought for a moment. 'Did you ask him about what Danny Spender told me? Why he was rubbing himself with the phone?'

'He said it wasn't true, said the kid made it up.'

'No way. I'll stake my life on Danny getting that right.'

'Why then?'

'Reliving the rape? Getting himself excited because his victim had been found? Miss Jenner?'

'Which?'

'The rape,' said Ingram.

'Pure speculation, based on the word of a ten-year-old and a policeman. No jury will believe you, Nick.'

'Then talk to Miss Jenner tomorrow. Find out if she noticed anything before I got there.' He started to stack the dirty dishes. 'I suggest you use kid gloves, though. She's not too comfortable around policemen.'

'Do you mean policemen in general, or just you?'

'Probably just me,' said Ingram honestly. 'I tipped off her father that the man she'd married had bounced a couple of bad cheques, and when the old boy tackled him about it, the bastard did a runner with the small fortune he'd conned out of Miss Jenner and her mother. When his fingerprints were run through the computer, it turned out half the police forces in England were looking for him, not to mention the various wives he'd acquired along the way. Miss Jenner was number four, although as he never divorced number one, the marriage was a sham anyway.'

'What was his name?'

'Robert Healey. He was arrested a couple of years ago in Manchester. She knew him as Martin Grant but he admitted to twenty-two other aliases in court.'

'And she blames you because she married a creep?' asked Galbraith in disbelief.

'Not for that. Her father had had a bad heart for years and the shock of finding out they were on the verge of bankruptcy killed him. I think she feels that if I'd gone to her instead of him, she could somehow have persuaded Healey to give the money back and the old man would still be alive.'

'Could she?'

'I wouldn't think so.' He placed the dishes in front of him. 'Healey had the whole scam down to a fine art, and being open to persuasion wasn't part of his MO.'

'How did he work it?'

Ingram pulled a wry face. 'Charm. She was besotted with him.'

'So she's stupid?'

'No . . . just overly trusting . . .' Ingram marshalled his thoughts. 'He was a professional. Created a fictitious company with fictitious accounts and persuaded the two women to invest in it, or more accurately persuaded Miss Jenner to persuade her mother. It was a very sophisticated operation. I saw the paper-work afterwards, and I'm not surprised they fell for it. The house was littered with glossy brochures, audited accounts, salary cheques, lists of employees, Inland Revenue statements. You'd have to be very suspicious indeed to assume anyone would go to so much trouble to con you out of a hundred thousand quid. Anyway, on the basis that the company stock was going up by 20 per cent a year, Mrs Jenner cashed in all her bonds and securities and handed her son-in-law a cheque.'

'Which he converted back into cash?'

Ingram nodded. 'It passed through at least three bank accounts on the way, and then vanished. In all, he spent twelve months working the scam – nine months softening up Miss Jenner, and three months married to her – and it wasn't just the Jenners who got taken to the cleaners. He used his connection with them to draw in other people, and a lot of their friends got their fingers burnt as well. It's sad, but they've become virtual recluses as a result.'

'What do they live on?'

'Whatever she can make from the Broxton House livery stables. Which isn't much. The whole place is getting seedier by the day.'

'Why don't they sell it?'

Ingram pushed his chair back, preparatory to standing up. 'Because it doesn't belong to them. Old man Jenner changed his will before he died and left the house to his son, with the proviso that the two women can go on living there as long as Mrs Jenner remains alive.'

Galbraith frowned. 'And then what? The brother throws the sister on the streets?'

'Something like that,' said Ingram dryly. 'He's a lawyer in London, and he certainly doesn't plan to have a sitting tenant on the premises when he sells out to a developer.'

Before he left to interview Maggie Jenner on Thursday morning, Galbraith had a quick word with Carpenter to bring him up to speed on the beached dinghy. 'I've organized a couple of SOCOs to go out to it,' he told him. 'I'll be surprised if they find anything – Ingram and I had a poke around to see what had caused it to deflate and frankly it's all a bit of a mess – but I think it's worth a try. They're going to make an attempt to reflate it and float it off the rocks, but the advice is, don't hold your breath. Even if they get it back, it's doubtful we'll learn much from it.'

Carpenter handed him a sheaf of papers. 'These'll interest you,' he said.

'What are they?'

'Statements from the people Sumner said would support his alibi.'

Galbraith heard a note of excitement in his boss's voice. 'And do they?'

The other shook his head. 'Quite the opposite. There are twenty-four hours unaccounted for, between lunchtime on Saturday and lunchtime on Sunday. We're now blitzing every-one, hotel staff, other conference delegates, but those' – he levelled a finger at the documents in Galbraith's hand – 'are the names Sumner himself gave us.' His eyes gleamed. 'And if they're not prepared to alibi him, I can't see anyone else doing it. It looks as if you could be right, John.'

Galbraith nodded. 'How did he do it, though?'

'He used to sail, must know Chapman's Pool as well as Harding, must know there are dinghies lying around for the taking.'

'How did he get Kate there?'

'Phoned her Friday night, said he was bored out of his mind with the conference and was planning to come home early, suggested they do something exciting for a change, like spend the afternoon on Studland beach, and arranged to meet her and Hannah off the train in Bournemouth or Poole.'

Galbraith tugged at his earlobe. 'It's possible,' he agreed.

A child of three travels free by train, and the record of sales from Lymington station had shown that numerous single adult fares to Bournemouth and Poole had been sold on the Saturday, the trip being a quick and easy one through a change on to regular mainline trains at Brockenhurst. However, if Kate Sumner had purchased one of the tickets she had used cash rather than a cheque or credit card for the transaction. None of the railway staff remembered a small blonde woman with a child but, as they pointed out, the traffic through Lymington station on a Saturday in peak holiday season was so continuous and so heavy because of the ferry link to and from the Isle of Wight that it was unlikely they would.

'The only fly in the ointment is Hannah,' Carpenter went on. 'If he abandoned her in Lilliput before driving back to Liverpool, why did it take so long for anyone to notice her? He must have dumped her by 6 a.m., but Mr and Mrs Green didn't spot her until 10.30.'

Galbraith thought of the traces of benzodiazepine and paracetamol in her system. 'Maybe he fed, watered and cleaned her at six, then left her asleep in a cardboard box in a shop doorway,' he said thoughtfully. 'He's a pharmaceutical chemist, don't forget, so he must have a pretty good idea how to put a three-year-old under for several hours. My guess is he's been doing it for years. By the way the child behaves around him she must have been a blight on his sex life from the day she was born.'

Meanwhile, Nick Ingram was chasing stolen dinghies. The fishermen who parked their boats at Chapman's Pool couldn't help. 'Matter of fact it's the first thing we checked when we heard the woman had drowned,' said one. 'I'd have let you know if there'd been a problem, but nothing's missing.'

It was the same story in Swanage and Kimmeridge Bay.

His last port of call, Lulworth Cove, looked more promising. 'Funny you should ask,' said the voice on the other end of the line, 'because we have had one go missing, black ten-footer.'

'Sounds about right. When did it go?'

'A good three months back.'

'Where from?'

'Would you believe it, off the beach. Some poor sod from Spain anchors his cruiser in the bay, ferries himself and his family in for a pub lunch, leaves the outboard in place with the starter cord dangling, and then tears strips off yours truly because it was hijacked from under his nose. According to him, *no one* in Spain would dream of stealing another chap's boat – never mind he makes it easy enough for the local moron to nick it – and then gives me a load of grief about the aggression of Cornish fishermen and how they were probably at the bottom of it. I pointed out that Cornwall's a good hundred miles away, and that Spanish fishermen are far more aggressive than the Cornish variety and *never* follow European Union rules, but he still said he was going to report me to the European Court of Human Rights for failing to protect Spanish tourists.'

Ingram laughed. 'So what happened?'

'Nothing. I took him and his family out to his sodding great bastard of a fifty-foot cruiser and we never heard another word. He probably put in for twice the dinghy's insurance value and blamed the vile English for its disappearance. We made inquiries, of course, but no one had seen anything. I mean, why would they? We get hundreds of people here during bank holiday week and anyone could have started it up with no trouble. I mean what kind of berk leaves a dinghy with an outboard in place? We reckoned it was taken by joyriders who sank it when they got bored with it.'

'Which bank holiday was it?'

'End of May. School half-term. The place was packed.'

'Did the Spaniard give you a description of the dinghy?'

'A whole bloody manifest more like. All ready for the

insurance. Half of me suspected he wanted it to be nicked just so he could get something a bit more swanky.'

'Can you fax the details through?'

'Sure.'

'I'm particularly interested in the outboard.'

'Why?'

'Because I don't think it was on the dinghy when it went down. With any luck, it's still in the possession of the thief.'

'Is he your murderer?'

'Very likely.'

'Then you're in luck, mate. I've got all sorts of serial numbers here, courtesy of our Spanish friend, and one of them's the outboard.'

Chapter Fourteen

Subject: Steven Harding

Mr and Mrs Harding live at 18 Hall Road, a modest bungalow
to the west of Falmouth. They retired to Cornwall in 1991 after
running a fish and chip shop in Lymington for 20+ years. They
used a considerable proportion of their capital to put their only
child, Steven, through a private drama college following his
failure to gain any A level passes at school, and feel aggrieved
that they now live in somewhat straitened circumstances as a
result. This may in part explain why their attitude towards their
son is critical and unfriendly.

They describe Steven as a 'disappointment' and evince
considerable hostility towards him because of his 'immoral
lifestyle'. They blame his wayward behaviour – 'he is only
interested in sex, drugs and rock and roll' – and lack of
achievement – 'he has never done a day's serious work in his
life' – on laziness and a belief that 'the world owes him a living'.
Mr Harding, who is proud of his working-class roots, says
Steven looks down on his parents which explains why Steven
has been to see them only once in six years. The visit – during
the summer of 1995 – was not a success and Mr Harding's
views on his son's arrogance and lack of gratitude were explo-
sive and earthy. He uses words like 'poser', 'junky', 'parasite',

164

'oversexed', 'liar', 'irresponsible' to describe his son, although it is clear that his hostility has more to do with his inability to accept Steven's rejection of working-class values than any real knowledge of his son's current lifestyle as they have had no contact with him since July 1995.

Mrs Harding cites a schoolfriend of Steven's, Anthony Bridges, as a malign influence on his life. According to her, Anthony introduced Steven to shoplifting, drugs and pornography at the age of twelve and Steven's lack of achievement stems from a couple of police cautions he and Anthony received during their teenage years for drunk and disorderly behaviour, vandalism, and theft of pornographic materials from a newsagent. Steven became rebellious and impossible to control after these episodes. She describes Steven as 'too handsome for his own good', and says that girls were throwing themselves at him from an early age. She says Anthony, by contrast, was always overshadowed by his friend and that she believes this is why it amused Anthony to 'get Steven into trouble'. She feels very bitter that Anthony, despite his previous history, was bright enough to go to university and find himself a job in teaching while Steven had to rely on the funding his parents provided for which they have received no thanks.

When Mr Harding asked Steven how he was able to afford to buy his boat *Crazy Daze*, Steven admitted he had received payment for several hard-core pornography sessions. This caused such distress to his parents that they ordered him from their house in July 1995 and have neither seen nor heard from him since. They know nothing about his recent activities, friends or acquaintances and can shed no light on the events of 9/10 August 1997. However, they insist that, despite all his faults, they do not believe Steven to be a violent or aggressive young man.

Chapter Fifteen

MAGGIE JENNER WAS raking straw in one of the stables when Nick Ingram and John Galbraith drove into Broxton House yard on Thursday morning. Her immediate reaction, as it was with all visitors, was to retreat into the shadows, unwilling to be seen, unwilling to have her privacy invaded, for it required an effort of will to overcome her natural disinclination to participate in anything that involved people. Broxton House, a square Queen Anne building with pitched roof, red-brick walls and shuttered upper windows, was visible through a gap in the trees to the right of the stableyard and she watched the two men admire it as they got out of the car, before turning to walk in her direction.

With a resigned smile, she drew attention to herself by hefting soiled straw through the stable doorway on the end of a pitchfork. The weather hadn't broken for three weeks, and sweat was running freely down her face as she emerged into the fierce sunlight. She was irritated by her own discomfort, and wished she'd put on something else that morning or that PC Ingram had had the courtesy to warn her he was coming. Her checkered cheesecloth shirt gripped her damp torso like a stocking and her jeans chafed against the inside of her thighs. Ingram spotted her almost immediately and was amused to see that, for once, the tables were turned and it was she who was hot and bothered and not he, but his expression as always was unreadable.

She propped the pitchfork against the stable wall and wiped

her palms down her already filthy jeans before smoothing her hair off her sweaty face with the back of one hand. 'Good morning, Nick,' she said. 'What can I do for you?'

'Miss Jenner,' he said, with his usual polite nod. 'This is Detective Inspector Galbraith from Dorset HQ. If it's convenient, he'd like to ask you a few questions about the events of last Sunday.'

She inspected her palms before tucking them into her jeans pockets. 'I won't offer to shake hands, Inspector. You wouldn't like where mine have been.'

Galbraith smiled, recognizing the excuse for what it was, a dislike of physical contact, and cast an interested glance around the cobbled courtyard. There was a row of stables on each of three sides, beautiful old red-brick buildings with solid oak doors, only half a dozen of which appeared to have occupants. The rest stood empty, doors hooked back, brick floors bare of straw, hay baskets unfilled, and it was a long time, he guessed, since the business had been a thriving one. They had passed a faded sign at the entrance gate, boasting: BROXTON HOUSE RIDING & LIVERY STABLES, but, like the sign, evidence of dilapidation was everywhere, in the crumbling brickwork that had been thrashed by the elements for a couple of hundred years, in the cracked and peeling paintwork and the broken windows in the tack room and office which no one had bothered – *or could afford?* – to replace.

Maggie watched his appraisal. 'You're right,' she said, reading his mind. 'It has enormous potential as a row of holiday chalets.'

'A pity when it happens, though.'

'Yes.'

He looked towards a distant paddock where a couple of horses grazed half-heartedly on drought-starved grass. 'Are they yours as well?'

'No. We just rent out the paddock. The owners are supposed to keep an eye on them, but they're irresponsible, frankly, and I usually find myself doing things for their wretched animals that was never part of the contract.' She pulled a rueful smile. 'I can't get it into their owners' heads that water evaporates and that the trough needs filling every day. It makes me mad sometimes.'

'Quite a chore then?'

'Yes.' She gestured towards a door at the end of the row of stables behind her. 'Let's go up to my flat. I can make you both a cup of coffee.'

'Thank you.' She was an attractive woman, he thought, despite the muck and the brusque manner, but he was intrigued by Ingram's stiff formality towards her which wasn't readily explained by the story of the bigamous husband. The formality, he thought, should be on her side. As he followed them up the wooden stairs, he decided the constable must have tried it on at some point and been comprehensively slapped down for playing outside his own league. Miss Jenner was top-drawer material, even if she did live in something resembling a pigsty.

The flat was the antithesis of Nick's tidy establishment. There was disorder everywhere, bean bags piled in front of the television on the floor, newspapers with finished and half-finished crosswords abandoned on chairs and tables, a filthy rug on the sofa which smelt unmistakably of Bertie, and a pile of dirty washing-up in the kitchen sink. 'Sorry about the mess,' she said. 'I've been up since five, and I haven't had time to clean.' To Galbraith's ears, this sounded like a well-worn apology that was trotted out to anyone who might be inclined to criticize her lifestyle. She swivelled the tap to squeeze the kettle between it and the washing-up. 'How do you like your coffee?'

'White, two sugars, please,' said Galbraith.

'I'll have mine black please, Miss Jenner. No sugar,' said Ingram.

'Do you mind Coffeemate?' Maggie asked the Inspector, sniffing at a cardboard carton on the side. 'The milk's off.'

Cursorily she rinsed some dirty mugs under the tap. 'Why don't you grab a seat? If you chuck Bertie's blanket on the floor one of you can have the sofa.'

'I think she means you, sir,' murmured Ingram as they retreated into the sitting room. 'Inspector's perks. It's the best seat in the place.'

'Who's Bertie?' whispered Galbraith.

'The Hound of the Baskervilles. His favourite occupation is to shove his nose up men's crotches and give them a good slobbering. The stains tend to hang around through at least three washes, I find, so it pays to keep your legs crossed when you're sitting down.'

'I hope you're joking!' said Galbraith with a groan. He had already lost one pair of good trousers to the previous night's soaking in the sea. 'Where is he?'

'Out on the razzle, I should think. His second favourite occupation is to service the local bitches.'

The DI lowered himself gingerly into the only armchair. 'Does he have fleas?'

With a grin, Ingram jerked his head towards the kitchen door. 'Do mice leave their droppings in sugar?' he murmured.

'Shit! '

Ingram removed himself to a window sill and perched precariously on the edge of it. 'Just be grateful it wasn't her mother who was out riding on Sunday,' he said in an undertone. 'This kitchen's sterile by comparison with hers.' He had sampled Mrs Jenner's hospitality once four years ago, the day after Healey had fled, and he'd vowed never to repeat the experience. She had given him coffee in a cracked Spode cup that was black with tannin, and he had gagged continuously while drinking it. He had never understood the peculiar mores of the impoverished landed gentry who seemed to believe the value of bone china outweighed the value of hygiene.

They waited in silence while Maggie busied herself in the kitchen. The atmosphere was ripe with the stench of horse manure, wafted in from a pile of soiled straw in the yard outside, and the heat baking the interior of the flat through the uninsulated roof was almost unbearable. In no time at all both men were red in the face and mopping at their brows with handkerchieves, and whatever brief advantage Ingram thought he had gained over Maggie was quickly dispelled. A few minutes later she emerged with a tray of coffee mugs which she handed around before sinking on to Bertie's blanket on the sofa.

'So what can I tell you that I haven't already told Nick?' she asked Galbraith. 'I know it's a murder inquiry because I've been reading the newspapers, but as I didn't see the body I can't imagine how I can help you.'

Galbraith pulled some notes from his jacket pocket. 'In fact it's rather more than a murder inquiry, Miss Jenner. Kate Sumner was raped before she was thrown into the sea, so the man who killed her is extremely dangerous and we need to catch him before he does it again.' He paused to let the information sink in. 'Believe me, any help you can give us will be greatly appreciated.'

'But I don't know anything,' she said.

'You spoke to a man called Steven Harding,' he reminded her.

'Oh, good God,' she said, 'you're not suggesting he did it?' She frowned at Ingram. 'You've really got it in for that man, haven't you, Nick? He was only trying to help in all conscience. You might as well say any of the men who were in Chapman's Pool that day could have killed her.'

Ingram remained blandly indifferent to both her frown and her accusations. 'It's a possibility.'

'So why pick on Steve?'

'We're not, Miss Jenner. We're trying to eliminate him from the inquiry. Neither I nor the Inspector wants to waste time investigating innocent bystanders.'

'You wasted an awful lot of time on Sunday doing it,' she

said acidly, stung by his dreary insistence on treating her with forelock-tugging formality.

He smiled, but didn't say anything.

She turned back to Galbraith. 'I'll do my best,' she said, 'although I doubt I can tell you much. What do you want to know?'

'It would be helpful if you can start by describing your meeting with him. I understand you rode down the track towards the boatsheds and came across him and the boys beside PC Ingram's car. Is that the first time you saw him?'

'Yes, but I wasn't riding Jasper then. I was leading him because he was frightened by the helicopter.'

'Okay. What were Steven Harding and the two boys doing at that point?'

She shrugged. 'They were looking at a girl on a boat through the binoculars, at least Steve and the older brother were. I think the younger one was bored by it all. Then Bertie got overexcited—'

Galbraith interrupted. 'You said *they* were looking through binoculars. How did that work exactly? Were they taking it in turns?'

'No, well, that's wrong. It was Paul who was looking, Steve was just holding them steady for him.' She saw his eyebrows lift in enquiry and anticipated his next question. 'Like this.' She made an embracing gesture with her arms. 'He was standing behind Paul, with his arms round him, and holding the binoculars so Paul could look through the eyepieces. The child thought it was funny and kept giggling. It was rather sweet really. I think he was trying to take his mind off the dead woman.' She paused to collect her thoughts. 'Actually, I thought he was their father, till I realized he was too young.'

'One of the boys said he was playing around with his telephone before you arrived. Did you see him do that?'

She shook her head. 'It was clipped to his waistband.'

'What happened next?'

'Bertie got overexcited, so Steve grabbed him and then suggested we put the boys at ease by encouraging them to pat Bertie and Sir Jasper. He said he was used to animals because he'd grown up on a farm in Cornwall.' She frowned. 'Why is any of this important? He was just being friendly.'

'In what way, Miss Jenner?'

Her frown deepened and she stared at him for a moment, clearly wondering where his questions were leading. 'He wasn't making a nuisance of himself if that's what you're getting at.'

'Why would I think he was making a nuisance of himself?'

She gave an irritated toss of her head. 'Because it would make things easier for you if he was,' she suggested.

'How?'

'You want him to be the rapist, don't you? Nick certainly does.'

Galbraith's grey eyes appraised her coolly. 'There's a little more to rape than making a nuisance of yourself. Kate Sumner had been dosed with a sleeping drug, she had abrasions to her back, strangle marks at her neck, rope burns to her wrists, broken fingers and a ruptured vagina. She was then thrown . . . *alive* . . . into the sea by someone who undoubtedly knew she was a poor swimmer and wouldn't be able to save herself, even assuming she came round from the effects of the drug. She was also pregnant when she died which means her baby was murdered with her.' He smiled slightly. 'I realize that you're a very busy person and that the death of an unknown woman is hardly a priority in your life, but PC Ingram and I take it more seriously, probably because we both saw Kate's body and were distressed by it.'

She looked at her hands. 'I apologize,' she said.

'We don't ask questions for the fun of it,' said Galbraith without hostility. 'Matter of fact, most of us find this sort of case very stressful, although the public rarely recognizes it.'

She raised her head and there was the glimmer of a smile in

her dark eyes. 'Point taken,' she said. 'The problem is, I get the impression you're homing in on Steve Harding just because he was there, and that seems unreasonable.'

Galbraith exchanged a glance with Ingram. 'There are other reasons why we're interested in him,' he said, 'but the only one I'm prepared to tell you at the moment is that he'd known the dead woman for quite some time. For that reason alone we'd be investigating him, whether he was at Chapman's Pool on Sunday or not.'

She was thoroughly startled. 'He didn't say he knew her.'

'Would you have expected him to? He told us he never saw the body.'

She turned to Ingram. 'He can't have done, can he? He said he was walking from St Alban's Head.'

'There's a very good view of Egmont Bight from the coastal path up there,' Ingram reminded her. 'If he had a pair of binoculars, he could have picked her out quite easily.'

'But he didn't,' she protested. 'All he had was a telephone. You made that point yourself.'

Galbraith debated with himself how to put the next question and opted for a straightforward approach. The woman must have a stallion or two in her stables, so she was hardly likely to faint at the mention of a penis. 'Nick says Harding had an erection when he first saw him on Sunday. Would you agree?'

'Either that or he's incredibly well endowed.'

'Were you the cause of it, do you think?'

She didn't answer.

'Well?'

'I've no idea,' she said. 'My feeling at the time was that it was probably the girl on the boat who had got him excited. Walk along Studland beach any sunny day and you'll find a hundred randy eighteen- to twenty-four-year-olds cowering in the water because their dicks react independently of their brains. It's hardly a crime '

Galbraith shook his head. 'You're a good-looking woman, Miss Jenner, and he was standing close to you. Did you encourage him in any way?'

'No.'

'It *is* important.'

'Why? All I know is the poor bloke wasn't in absolute control of himself.' She sighed. 'Look, I'm really sorry about the woman. But if Steve was involved, then he never gave me any indication of it. As far as I was concerned, he was a young man out for a walk who made a phone call on behalf of a couple of children.'

Galbraith laid a forefinger on a page of his notes. 'This is a quote from Danny Spender,' he said. 'Tell me how true it is. "He was chatting up the lady with the horse but I don't think she liked him as much as he liked her." Is that what was happening?'

'No, of course it wasn't,' she said with annoyance, as if the idea of being chatted-up was pure anathema to her, 'though I suppose it might have looked like that to the children. I said he was brave for grabbing Bertie by the collar, so he seemed to think that laughing a lot and slapping Jasper on the rump would impress the boys. In the end I had to move the animals into the shade to get them away from him. Jasper's amenable to most things, but not to having his bottom smacked every two minutes, and I didn't want to be prosecuted if he lashed out suddenly.'

'So was Danny right about you not liking him?'

'I don't see that it matters,' she said uncomfortably. 'It's a subjective thing. I'm not a very sociable person so liking people isn't my strong point.'

'What was wrong with him?' he went on imperturbably.

'Oh, God, this is ridiculous!' she snapped. 'Nothing. He was perfectly pleasant from beginning to end of our conversation.' She cast an angry sideways glance towards Ingram. 'Almost ridiculously polite, in fact.'

'So why didn't you like him?'

She breathed deeply through her nose, clearly at war with herself about whether to answer or not. 'He was a toucher,' she said with a spurt of anger. 'All right? Is that what you wanted? I have a thing against men who can't keep their hands to themselves, Inspector, but it doesn't make them rapists or murderers. It's just the way they are.' She took another deep breath. 'And while we're on the subject – just to show you how little faith you can put in my judgement of men – I wouldn't trust any of you further than I could throw you. If you want to know why, ask Nick.' She gave a hollow laugh as Galbraith lowered his eyes. 'I see he's already told you. Still . . . if you want the juicier details of my relationship with my bigamous husband, apply in writing and I'll see what I can do for you.'

The DI, reminded of Sandy Griffiths's similiar *caveat* regarding her judgement of Sumner, ignored the tantrum. 'Are you saying Harding touched *you*, Miss Jenner?'

She gave him a withering glance. 'Of course not. I never gave him the opportunity.'

'But he touched your animals, and that's what put you against him?'

'No,' she said crossly. 'It was the boys he couldn't keep his hands off. It was all very macho . . . hail-fellow-well-met stuff . . . you know, a lot of punching of shoulders and high fives . . . to be honest it's why I thought he was their father. The little one didn't like it much – he kept pushing him away – but the older one revelled in it.' She smiled rather cynically. 'It's the kind of shallow emotion you only ever see in Hollywood movies so I wasn't in the least bit surprised when he told Nick he was an actor.'

Galbraith exchanged a questioning glance with Ingram.

'I'd say that's an accurate description,' admitted the constable honestly. 'He was very friendly towards Paul.'

'How friendly?'

'*Very,*' said Ingram. 'And Miss Jenner's right. Danny kept pushing him away.'

'*Child seducer?*' wrote Galbraith in his notebook. 'Did you see Steve abandon a rucksack on the hillside before he took the boys down to Nick's car?' he asked Maggie then.

She was looking at him rather oddly. 'The first time I saw him was at the boatsheds,' she said.

'Did you see him retrieve it after Nick drove the boys away?'

'I wasn't watching him.' Her forehead creased into lines of concern. 'Look . . . aren't you jumping to conclusions again? When I said he was touching the boys I didn't mean . . . that is . . . it wasn't inappropriate . . . just, well, *overdone,* if you like.'

'Okay.'

'What I'm trying to say is I don't think he's a paedophile.'

'Have you ever met one, Miss Jenner?'

'No.'

'Well, they don't have two heads, you know. Nevertheless, point taken,' he assured her in a conscious echo of what she'd said herself. Gallantly he lifted his untouched mug from the floor and drank it down before taking a card from his wallet and passing it across. 'That's my number,' he said, getting up. 'If anything occurs to you that you think's important, you can always reach me there. Thank you for your help.'

She nodded, watching as Ingram moved away from the window. 'You haven't drunk *your* coffee,' she said with a malicious gleam in her eyes. 'Perhaps you'd have preferred it with sugar after all. I always find the mouse droppings sink to the bottom.'

He smiled down at her. 'But dog hairs don't, Miss Jenner.' He put on his cap and straightened the peak. 'My regards to your mother.'

Kate Sumner's papers and private possessions had filled several boxes, which the investigators had been working their way through methodically for three days, trying to build a picture of the woman's life. There was nothing to link her with Steven Harding, or with any other man.

Everyone in her address book was contacted without results. They proved, without exception, to be people she had met since moving to the south coast and matched a neat Christmas card list in the bottom drawer of the bureau in the sitting room. An exercise book was found in one of the kitchen cupboards, inscribed: '*Weekly Diary*', but turned out, disappointingly, to be a precise record of what she spent on food and household bills, and tallied, give or take a pound or two, with the allowance William paid her.

Her correspondence was composed almost entirely of business letters, usually referring to work on the house, although there were a few private letters from friends and acquaintances in Lymington, her mother-in-law, and one, with a date in July, from Polly Garrard at Pharmatec UK.

Dear Kate,

It's ages since we had a chat and every time I ring the phone's off the hook or you're not there. Give me a buzz when you can. I'm dying to hear how you and Hannah are getting on in Lymington. It's a waste of time asking William. He just nods and says: 'Fine.'

I'd really love to see the house since you've had all the decorating done. Maybe I could take a day off and visit you when William's at work? That way he can't complain if all we do is sit and gossip. Do you remember Wendy Plater? She got drunk a couple of weeks ago at lunchtime and called Purdy 'a tight-arsed prick' because he was in the hall when she came staggering back late and he told her he was going to dock her wages. God, it was funny! He would have sacked her on the spot if good old Trew hadn't spoken up for her. She had to apologize, but she doesn't regret any of it. She says she's never seen Purdy go purple before!

I thought of you immediately, of course, which is why I've been ringing. It really is ages. Do call. Thinking of you,

Love,

Polly Garrard

Attached to it by paper clip was the draft of an answer from Kate.

Dear Polly,

Hannah and I are doing well, and of course you must come and visit us. I'm a bit busy at the moment, but will ring as soon as I can. The house looks great. You'll love it.

~~You promised on your honour~~ The story about Wendy Plater was really funny!

Hope all's well with you.

Speak soon,

Love,

Kate

The Spender brothers' parents looked worried when Ingram asked if he and DI Galbraith could talk to Paul in private. 'What's he done?' asked the father.

Ingram removed his cap and smoothed his dark hair with the flat of his hand. 'Nothing as far as I know,' he said with a smile. 'It's just a few routine questions, that's all.'

'Then why do you want to talk to him in private?'

Ingram's frank gaze held his. 'Because the dead woman was naked, Mr Spender, and Paul's embarrassed to talk about it in front of you and your wife.'

The man gave a snort of amusement. 'He must think we're the most frightful prudes.'

Ingram's smile broadened. 'Just parents,' he said. He gestured towards the lane in front of their rented cottage. 'He'll probably feel more comfortable if he talks to us outside.'

In the event Paul was surprisingly open about Steven Harding's 'friendliness'. 'I reckon he fancied Maggie and was trying to impress her by how good he was with kids,' he told the policemen. 'My uncle's always doing it. If he comes to our house on his own he doesn't bother to talk to us, but if he brings one of his girlfriends he puts his arms round our shoulders and tells us jokes. It's only to make them think he'd be a good father.'

Galbraith chuckled. 'And that's what Steve was doing?'

'Must have been. He got much more friendly after she turned up.'

'Did you notice him playing with his phone at all?'

'You mean the way Danny says?'

Galbraith nodded.

'I didn't watch him because I didn't want to be rude, but Danny's pretty sure about it, and he should know because he was staring at him all the time.'

'So why was Steve doing that, do you think?'

'Because he forgot we were there,' said the boy.

'In what way exactly?'

Paul showed the first signs of embarrassment. 'Well, you know,' he said earnestly, 'he sort of did it without thinking . . . my dad often does things without thinking, like licking his knife in restaurants. Mum gets really angry about it.'

Galbraith gave a nod of agreement. 'You're a bright lad. I should have thought of that myself.' He stroked the side of his freckled face, considering the problem. 'Still, rubbing yourself with a telephone's a bit different from licking your knife. You don't think it's more likely he was showing off?'

'He looked at a girl through the binoculars,' Paul offered. 'Maybe he was showing off to her?'

'Maybe.' Galbraith pretended to ponder some more. 'You don't think it's more likely he was showing off to you and Danny?'

'Well . . . he talked a lot about ladies he'd seen in the nude, but I sort of got the feeling most of it wasn't true . . . I think he was trying to make us feel better.'

'Does Danny agree with you?'

The boy shook his head. 'No, but that doesn't mean anything. He reckons Steve stole his T-shirt so he doesn't like him.'

'Is it true?'

'I don't think so. It's just an excuse because he's lost it and Mum gave him an earbashing. It's got DERBY FC on the front and it cost a fortune.'

'Did Danny have it with him on Sunday?'

'He says it was in the bundle round the binoculars but I don't remember it.'

'Okay.' Galbraith nodded again. 'So what does Danny think Steve was up to?'

'He reckons he's a paedophile,' said Paul matter-of-factly.

WPC Sandra Griffiths whistled tunelessly to herself as she made a cup of tea in the kitchen at Langton Cottage. Hannah was sitting mesmerized in front of the television in the sitting room, while Sandy was blessing the memory of whatever genius had invented the electronic nanny. She turned towards the fridge in search of milk and found William Sumner standing directly behind her. 'Did I frighten you?' he asked as she gave a little start of surprise.

You know you did, you stupid bastard . . . ! She forced a smile to her face to disguise the fact that he was beginning to give her the creeps. 'Yes,' she admitted. 'I didn't hear you come in.'

'That's what Kate used to say. She'd get quite angry about it sometimes.'

Who can blame her . . . ? She was beginning to think of him as a voyeur, a man who got his rocks off by secretly watching a woman go about her business. She had stopped counting the number of times she'd glimpsed him peering round a door jamb like an unwelcome intruder in his own house. She put distance between herself and him by removing the teapot to the kitchen table and pulling out a chair. There was a lengthy silence during which he sulkily kicked the toe of his shoe against the table leg, shoving the top in little jerks against her belly.

'You're afraid of me, aren't you?' he said suddenly.

'What makes you think that?' she asked as she held the table firm against his kicks.

'You were afraid last night.' He looked pleased, as if the idea excited him, and she wondered how important it was to him to feel superior.

'Don't flatter yourself,' she declared bluntly, lighting a cigarette and blowing the smoke deliberately in his direction. 'Trust me, if I'd been remotely afraid, I'd have taken your fucking balls off. Cripple first and ask questions later, that's my motto.'

'I don't like you smoking or swearing in this house,' he said with another petulant kick at the table leg.

'Then put in a complaint,' she answered. 'It just means I'll be reassigned.' She held his gaze for a moment. 'And that wouldn't suit you one little bit, would it? You're too damn used to having an unpaid skivvy about the place.'

Ready tears sprang to his eyes. 'You don't understand what it's like. Everything worked so well before. And now . . . well, I don't even know what I'm supposed to be doing.'

His performance was amateur at best, diabolical at worst, and it brought out the bully in Griffiths. *Did he think she found male helplessness attractive?* 'Then you should be ashamed of yourself,' she snapped. 'According to the health visitor you didn't even know where the vacuum cleaner was, let alone how to work it. She came here to teach you elementary parenting and housekeeping skills because no one – and I repeat *no one* – is going to allow a three-year-old child to remain in the care of a man who is so patently indifferent to her welfare.'

He moved around the kitchen, opening and shutting cupboard doors as if to demonstrate familiarity with their contents. 'It's not my fault,' he said. 'That's how Kate wanted it. I wasn't allowed to interfere in the running of the house.'

'Are you sure it wasn't the other way round?' She tapped the ash off her cigarette into her saucer. 'I mean you didn't marry a wife, did you? You married a housekeeper who was expected to run this house like clockwork and account for every last penny she spent.'

'It wasn't like that.'

'What was it like then?'

'Living in a cheap boarding house,' he said bitterly. 'I didn't marry a wife *or* a housekeeper, I married a landlady who allowed me to live here as long as I paid my rent on time.'

The French yacht, *Mirage,* motored up the Dart river early on Thursday afternoon and took a berth in the Dart Haven Marina on the Kingswear side of the estuary, opposite the lovely town of Dartmouth and alongside the steam railway line to Paignton. Shortly after they made fast, there was a blast on a whistle and the three o'clock train set off in a rush of steam, raising in the Beneteau's owner a romantic longing for days he himself couldn't remember.

By contrast his daughter sat sunk in gloom, unable to comprehend why they had moored on the side of the river that boasted nothing except the station when everything that was attractive – shops, restaurants, pubs, people, life, *men!* – was on the other side in Dartmouth. Scornfully, she watched her father take out the video camera and search through the case for a new tape in order to film steam engines. He was like a small boy, she thought, in his silly enthusiasms for the treasures of rural England when what really mattered was London. She was the only one of her friends who had never been there, and it mortified her. God, but her parents were *sad*!

Her father turned to her in mild frustration, asking where the unused tapes were, and she had to admit there were none. She'd used them all to film irrelevancies in order to pass the time, and with irritating tolerance (he was one of those understanding fathers who refused to indulge in rows) he played the videos back, squinting into the eyepiece, in order to select the least interesting for reuse.

When he came to a tape of a young man scrambling down the slope above Chapman's Pool towards two boys, followed by shots of him sitting alone on the foreshore beyond the boatsheds, he lowered the camera and looked at his daughter with a worried frown. She was fourteen years old, and he realized he had no idea if she was still innocent or whether she knew exactly what she'd been filming. He described the young man and asked her why she had taken so much footage of him. Her cheeks flushed a rosy red under her tan. No particular reason. He was there and he was – she spoke with defiance – handsome. In any case, she knew him. They'd introduced themselves when they'd chatted together in Lymington. *And* he fancied her. She could tell these things.

Her father was appalled.

His daughter flounced her shoulders. What was the big deal? So he was English? He was just a good-looking guy who liked French girls, she said.

Bibi Gould's face fell as she swung light-heartedly out of the hairdressing salon in Lymington where she worked and saw Tony Bridges standing on the pavement, half-turned away from her, watching a young mother hoist a toddler on to her hip. Her relationship, such as it was, with Tony had become more of a trial than a pleasure and for a brief second she thought about retreating through the door again until she realized he had seen her out of the corner of his eye. She forced a sickly smile to her lips. 'Hi,' she said with unconvincing jauntiness.

He stared at her with his peculiarly brooding expression, taking note of the skimpy shorts and cropped top that barely covered her tanned arms, legs and midriff. A blood vessel started to throb in his head, and he had trouble keeping the temper out of his voice. 'Who are you meeting?'

'No one,' she said.

'Then what's the problem? Why did you look so pissed to see me?'

'I didn't.' She lowered her head to swing her curtain of hair across her eyes in a way he hated. 'I'm just tired, that's all . . . I was going home to watch telly.'

He reached out a hand to grip her wrist. 'Steve's done a vanishing act. Is he the one you're planning to meet?'

'Don't be stupid.'

'Where is he?'

'How would I know?' she said, twisting her arm to try to release herself. 'He's your friend.'

'Has he gone to the caravan? Did you say you'd meet him there?'

Angrily, she succeeded in tugging herself free. 'You've got a real problem with him, you know . . . you should talk to someone about it instead of taking it out on me all the time. And for your information, not everyone runs away to hide in Mummy and Daddy's sodding caravan every time things go wrong. It's a dump, for Christ's sake . . . like your house . . . and who wants to fuck in a dump?' She rubbed her wrist where his fingers had left a Chinese burn on her skin, her immature nineteen-year-old features creasing into a vicious scowl. 'It's not Steve's fault you're so spaced out most nights you can't get it up, so don't keep pretending it is. The trouble with you is you've lost it, but you can't bloody well see it.'

He eyed her with dislike. 'What about Saturday? It wasn't

me who passed out on Saturday. I'm sick to death of being fucked about, Beebs.'

She was on the point of giving a petulant toss of her head and saying sex with him had become so boring that she might as well be comatose as not when caution persuaded her against it. He had a way of getting his own back that she didn't much like. 'Yeah, well, you can't blame me for that,' she muttered lamely. 'You shouldn't buy dodgy E off your dodgy mates, should you? A girl could die that way.'

Chapter Sixteen

FAX:

| From: PC Nicholas Ingram | Date: 14 August – 7.05 p.m. |
| To: DI John Galbraith | Re: **Kate Sumner murder inquiry** |

Sir,

I've had some follow-up thoughts on the above, particularly in relation to the pathologist's report and the stranded dinghy, and as it's my day off tomorrow I'm faxing them through to you. Admittedly they are based entirely on the presumption that the stranded dinghy was involved in Kate's murder, but they suggest a new angle which may be worth considering.

I mentioned this a.m. that: 1) there's a possibility the dinghy was stolen from Lulworth Cove at the end of May, in which case the thief and Kate's murderer could be one and the same person; 2) that if my 'towing' theory was correct, there was a good chance the outboard engine (Make: Fastrigger; Serial No: 240B 5006678) was removed and remains in the thief's possession; 3) you take another look at Steven Harding's log to see if he was in Lulworth Cove on Thursday, 29 May; 4) if he had a second dinghy stowed on board *Crazy Daze* – which only required a foot pump to reflate it – it would solve some of your forensic problems; 5) he probably has a lock-up somewhere which you haven't yet discovered and which may contain the stolen outboard.

***<u>I have since had time to consider the logistics of how the dinghy was actually removed from Lulworth Cove in broad daylight and I've realized that Harding or indeed any boat owner would have had some difficulty.</u>

It's important to recognize that *Crazy Daze* must have anchored in the middle of Lulworth Bay and Harding could only have come ashore in his own dinghy. Joyriders going for a spin would have attracted little attention (the assumption would be that the boat belonged to them) but a man on his own, coping with <u>two</u> dinghies, would have stood out like a sore thumb, particularly as the only way he could have removed them from the Cove (unless he was prepared to waste time deflating them) was to tow them in tandem or parallel behind *Crazy Daze*. It is <u>highly</u> unusual for a yacht to have two dinghies and, once the theft had been reported, that fact is bound to have registered with the coastguards in the lookout point above Lulworth.

I think now that a more likely scenario for the theft was removal by foot. Let's say an opportunist thief spotted that the outboard wasn't padlocked, released its clamps and carried it away quite openly to his car/house/garage/caravan. Let's say he wandered back half an hour later to see if the owners had returned and, finding they hadn't, he simply hoisted the dinghy above his head and carried that away too. I'm not suggesting that Kate Sumner's murder was premeditated at this early stage, but what I am suggesting is that the opportunist theft of the Spanish dinghy in May gave rise to an ideal method in August for the disposal of her body. (NB: thefts <u>of</u> or <u>from</u> boats represent some of the highest crime statistics along the south coast.) I strongly advise, therefore, that you try to find out if anyone connected with Kate was staying in or near Lulworth between 24–31 May. I suspect the sad irony will be that she, her husband and her daughter were – there are several caravan parks and campsites round Lulworth – but I think this will please you. <u>It strengthens the case against the husband.</u>

For reasons that follow, I am no longer confident that you'll find the outboard. Assuming the intention was for the stolen dinghy, plus contents (i.e. Kate) to sink, then the outboard must have been on board.

You may remember my querying the 'hypothermia' issue in the pathologist's report when you showed it to me on Monday. The pathologist's view is that Kate was swimming in the water for some considerable time, prior to drowning, which caused her stress and cold. At the time I wondered why it took her so long to swim a comparatively short distance and I suggested that she was more likely to suffer hypothermia from being exposed to air temperature at night rather than sea temperature – the latter being generally warmer. It would depend of course on how good a swimmer she was, particularly as the pathologist refers to her entering the sea a minimum of half a mile WSW of Egmont Bight, and I assumed she must have swum a great deal further than his estimate. However, you told Miss Jenner this morning that Kate was a poor swimmer, and I have been wondering since how a poor swimmer could have remained afloat long enough in difficult seas to show evidence of hypothermia before death. I have also been wondering why her killer was confident of making it safely back to shore, since there are no lights on that part of the coast and the currents are unpredictable.

One explanation which covers the above is that Kate was raped ashore, her killer presumed her dead after the strangulation attempt and the whole 'drowning' exercise was designed to dispose of her body off an isolated stretch of coast.

Can you buy this reasoning? 1) He bundled her naked and unconscious body into the stolen dinghy, then took her a considerable distance – Lulworth Cove to Chapman's Pool = 8 nautical miles approx. – before he tied her to the outboard and left the dinghy to sink with its contents (wind-chill factor would already have caused hypothermia in a naked woman); 2) once set adrift, Kate came round from the strangulation attempt/ Rohypnol and realized she had to save herself; 3) her broken fingers and nails could have resulted from her struggle to break free of her bonds then release the clamps holding the outboard in place in order to eject its weight, probably capsizing the dinghy in the process; 4) she used the dinghy as a float and only became separated from it when she lapsed into unconsciousness or became too tired to hold on; 5) in all events, I am guessing the dinghy travelled much closer to shore than the pathologist's estimate otherwise the boat would have become swamped and the killer himself would have been in trouble; 6) killer climbed the cliffs and returned to Lulworth/Kimmeridge via the coastal path during the dark hours of the night.

This is as far as my thoughts have taken me, but if the dinghy was involved in the murder then it must have come from the west – Kimmeridge Bay or Lulworth Cove – because the craft was too fragile to negotiate the race around St Alban's Head. I realize none of this explains Hannah, although I can't help feeling that if you can discover where the stolen dinghy was hidden for two months, you may also discover where Kate was raped and where Hannah was left while her mother was being drowned.

(NB: None of the above rules out Harding – the rape may have taken place on his deck with the evidence subsequently washed away, and the dinghy may have been towed behind *Crazy Daze* – but does it make him a less likely suspect?)

Nick Ingram

Chapter Seventeen

THE SUN HAD been up less than an hour on Friday morning when Maggie Jenner set off along the bridleway behind Broxton House, accompanied by Bertie. She was on a skittish bay gelding called Stinger, whose owner came down from London every weekend to her cottage in Langton Matravers to ride hard around the headlands as an antidote to her high-pressured job as a money broker in the City. Maggie loved the horse but loathed the woman whose hands were about as sensitive as steam hammers and who viewed Stinger in the same way as she probably viewed a snort of cocaine – as a quick adrenaline fix. If she hadn't agreed to pay well over the odds for the livery service Maggie provided, Maggie would have refused her business without a second's hesitation but, as with most things in the Jenners' lives, compromise had become the better part of staving off bankruptcy.

She turned right at St Alban's Head Quarry, negotiating her way through the gate and into the deep, wide valley that cleaved a grassy downland passage towards the sea between St Alban's Head to the south and the high ground above Chapman's Pool to the north. She nudged her mount into a canter and sent him springing across the turf in glorious release. It was still cool but there was barely a breath of wind in the air, and as always on mornings like this her spirits soared. However bad existence was, and it could be very bad at times, she ceased to worry about it here. If there was any point to anything, then she came closest to finding it, alone and free, in the renewed optimism that a fresh sun generated with each daybreak.

She reined in after half a mile, and walked the gelding towards the fenced coastal path which hugged the slopes of the valley on either side in a series of steep steps cut into the cliffs. It was a hardy rambler who suffered the agony of the downward trek only to be faced with the worse agony of the upward climb, and Maggie, who had never done either, thought how much more sensible it was to ride the gully in order to enjoy the scenery. Ahead, the sea, a sparkling blue, was flat calm without a sail in sight and she slipped lightly from the saddle while Bertie, panting from the exertion of keeping up, rolled leisurely in the warming grass beside the gelding's hooves. Looping Stinger's reins casually round the top rail of the fence, she climbed the stile and walked the few yards to the cliff edge to stand and glory in the vast expanse of blueness where the line of demarcation between sky and sea was all but invisible. The only sounds were the gentle swish of breakers on the shore, the sigh of the animals' breaths and a lark singing in the sky above . . .

It was difficult to say who was the more startled, therefore, Maggie or Steven Harding, when he rose out of the ground in front of her after hoisting himself over the cliff edge where the downland valley dropped towards the sea. He crouched on all fours for several seconds, his face pale and unshaven, breathing heavily and looking a great deal less pretty than he had five days before. More like a rapist; less like a Hollywood lead. There was a quality of disturbing violence about him, something calculating in the dark eyes that Maggie hadn't noticed before, but it was his abrupt rearing to full height that caused her to shriek. Her alarm transmitted itself immediately to Stinger who pranced backwards, tearing his reins free of the fence, and thence to Bertie who leapt to his feet, hackles up.

'YOU STUPID BASTARD!' Maggie shouted at him, giving vent to her fear in furious remonstration as she heard Stinger's snort of alarm and stamping hooves. She turned away from Harding in a vain attempt to catch the excited gelding's reins before he bolted.

Pray God, he didn't . . . he was worth a fortune to Broxton House Livery Stables . . . she couldn't afford it if he damaged himself . . . pray God, pray God . . .

But Harding, for reasons best known to himself, darted across her path in Stinger's direction and the gelding, eyes rolling, took off like lightning up the hill.

'OH, SHIT!' Maggie stormed, stamping her foot and raging at the young man, her face red and ugly with ungovernable fury. 'How could you be so bloody infantile, you – you CREEP! What the *hell* did you think you were doing! I swear to Christ if Nick Ingram knew you were here he'd *crucify* you! He already thinks you're a fucking PERVERT!'

She was completely unprepared for his backhand slap that caught her a glancing blow across the side of her face and as she hit the ground with a resounding thud, the only thought in her head was: What on earth does this idiot think he's doing . . . ?

Ingram squinted painfully at his alarm clock when his phone rang at 6.30 a.m. He lifted the receiver and listened to a series of high-pitched, unintelligible squeaks at the other end of the line which he recognized as coming from Maggie Jenner.

'You'll have to calm down,' he said when she finally took a breath. 'I can't understand a word you're saying.'

More squeaks.

'Pull yourself together, Maggie,' he said firmly. 'You're not a wimp so don't behave like one.'

'I'm sorry,' she said with a commendable attempt to compose herself. 'Steven Harding hit me so Bertie went for him . . . there's blood everywhere . . . I've rigged up a tourniquet on his arm but it's not working properly . . . I don't know what else to do . . . I think he's going to die if he doesn't get to hospital.'

He sat up and rubbed his face furiously to eradicate sleep. He could hear the white noise of empty space and the sound of birdsong in the background. 'Where are you?'

'At the end of the quarry gully . . . near the steps on the coastal path . . . halfway between Chapman's Pool and St Alban's Head . . . Stinger's bolted and I'm afraid he's going to break a leg if he trips on his reins . . . we'll lose everything . . . I think Steve's dying . . .' Her voice faded as she turned away from the signal. 'Manslaughter . . . Bertie was out of control . . .'

'I'm losing you, Maggie,' he shouted.

'Sorry.' Her voice came back in a rush. 'He's not responding to anything. I'm worried Bertie's severed an artery but I can't get the tourniquet tight enough to stop the bleeding. I'm using Bertie's lead but it's too loose and the sticks here are all so rotten they just keep breaking.'

'Then forget the lead and use something else – something you can get a grip on – a T-shirt maybe. Wind it round his arm as tight as you can above the elbow then keep twisting the ends to exert some pressure. Failing that, try and locate the artery on the underside of his upper arm with your fingers and press hard against the bone to stop the flow. But you've got to keep the pressure on, Maggie, otherwise he'll start bleeding again, and that means your hands are going to hurt.'

'Okay.'

'Good girl. I'll get help to you as fast as I can.' He cut her off and dialled Broxton House. 'Mrs Jenner?' he said, flicking over to the loudspeaker when the receiver was lifted at the other end. 'It's Nick Ingram.' He flung himself out of bed and started to drag on some clothes. 'Maggie needs help and you're the closest. She's trying to stop a man bleeding to death in the quarry gully. They're at the coastal path end. If you take Sir

Jasper and get up there PDQ, then the man stands a chance otherwise—'

'But I'm not dressed,' she interrupted indignantly.

'I couldn't give a shit,' he said bluntly. 'Get your arse up there and give your daughter some support because, by God, it'll be a first if you do.'

'How dare—'

He cut her off, and set in motion the series of calls that would result in the Portland Search and Rescue helicopter being scrambled in the direction of St Alban's Head for the second time in less than a week when the ambulance service expressed doubt about their ability to reach a man in a remote grassy valley before he bled to death.

By the time Nick Ingram reached the scene, having driven his Jeep at breakneck speed along narrow lanes and up the bridle-way, the drama was effectively over. The helicopter was on the ground some fifty yards from the scene of the accident, engine idling, Harding was conscious and sitting up being attended by an SAR paramedic, and another hundred yards to the south of the helicopter and halfway up the hillside, Maggie was busy trying to catch Stinger who rolled his eyes and backed away from her every time she came too close. She was clearly trying to head him off from the cliff edge but he was too frightened of the helicopter to move in its direction, and all she was succeeding in doing was driving him towards the three-foot-high fence and the perilously steep steps that edged the cliff. Celia, clad in a pair of pyjama trousers and a tannin-stained bedjacket, stood arrogantly to one side with one hand grasping Sir Jasper's reins tightly beneath his chin and the other wound into the looped end in case he, too, decided to bolt. She favoured Ingram with a frosty glare, designed to freeze him in his tracks, but he ignored her and turned his attention to Harding.

'Are you all right, sir?'

The young man nodded. He was dressed in Levi's and a pale green sweatshirt, both of which were copiously splattered with blood, and his lower right arm was tightly bandaged.

Ingram turned to the paramedic. 'What's the damage?'

'He'll live,' said the man. 'The two ladies managed to stop the bleeding. He'll need stitching so we'll take him to Poole and get him sorted there.' He drew Nick aside. 'The young lady could do with some attention. She's shaking like a leaf, but she says it's more important to catch the horse. The trouble is he's torn his reins off and she can't get close enough to get a grip on his throat strap.' He jerked his head towards Celia. 'And the older one's not much better. She's got arthritis, and she wrecked her hip riding up here. By rights, we ought to take them with us, but they're adamant they won't leave the animals. There's also a time problem. We need to get moving, but the loose horse is going to bolt in real earnest the minute we take off. It's terrified out of its wits already and damn nearly skidded over the cliff when we landed.'

'Where's the dog?'

'Vanished. I gather the young lady had to thrash him with his lead to get him off the lad, and he's fled with his tail between his legs.'

Nick rumpled his sleep-tousled hair. 'Okay, can you give us another five minutes? If I help Miss Jenner round up the horse, we may be able to persuade her mother to go in for some treatment. How about it?'

The paramedic turned to look at Steven Harding. 'Why not? He says he's strong enough to walk but it'll take me a good five minutes to get him in and settled. I don't fancy your chances much, but good luck.'

With a wry smile, Nick put his fingers to his lips and gave a piercing whistle before scanning both hillsides with narrowed eyes. To his relief, he saw Bertie rise out of the grass on the breast of Emmetts Hill about two hundred and fifty yards away.

He gave another whistle and the dog came like a torpedo towards him. He raised his arm and dropped him to the ground when he was still fifty yards away, then went back to Celia. 'I need a quick decision,' he told her. 'We've got five minutes to catch Stinger before the helicopter leaves, and it strikes me Maggie'll have more chance if she's riding Sir Jasper. You're the expert. Do I take him up to her or do I leave him with you, bearing in mind I know nothing about horses and Jasper's likely to be just as frightened of the noise as Stinger is?'

She was a sensible woman and didn't waste time on recriminations. She handed the loop of the reins into his left hand and guided his right into position under Jasper's chin. 'Keep clicking your tongue,' she said, 'and he'll follow. Don't try and run, and don't let go. We can't afford to lose both of them. Remind Maggie they'll both go mad the minute the helicopter takes off so tell her to ride like the devil for the middle of the headland and give herself some space.'

He set off up the slope, whistling Bertie to follow and gathering him into his left leg so that the dog walked like a shadow beside him.

'I didn't realize it was his dog,' said the paramedic to Celia.

'It's not,' she said thoughtfully, shading her eyes against the sun to watch what happened.

She saw her daughter come stumbling down towards the tall policeman, who had a quick word with her then hefted her lightly into Jasper's saddle before, with a gesture of his arm, he sent Bertie out in a sweeping movement towards the cliff edge to circle round behind the excited gelding. He followed in Bertie's wake, placing himself as an immovable obstacle between the horse and the brink, while directing the dog to hamper Stinger's further retreat up the hillside by dashing to and fro above him. Meanwhile, Maggie had turned Sir Jasper towards the quarry site and had kicked him into a canter. Faced with the unpalatable alternatives of a dog on one side, a helicopter on the other and a man behind, Stinger chose the sensible option of pursuing the other horse towards safety.

'Impressive,' said the paramedic.

'Yes,' said Celia even more thoughtfully. 'It was, wasn't it?'

Polly Garrard was about to leave for work when DI John Galbraith rang her front doorbell and asked if she was willing to answer a few more questions about her relationship with Kate Sumner. 'I can't,' she told him. 'I'll be late. You can come to the office if you like.'

'Fine, if that's the way you want it,' he assured her. 'It might make things difficult for you, though. You probably won't want eavesdroppers to some of the things I'm going to ask you.'

'Oh, shit!' she said immediately. 'I knew this was going to happen.' She opened the door wide. 'You'd better come in,' she said, leading the way into a tiny sitting room, 'but you can't keep me long. Half an hour max, okay? I've already been late twice this month and I'm running out of excuses.'

She dropped on to one end of a sofa, hooking an arm over its back, and inviting him to sit at the other end. She twisted round to face him, one leg curled beneath her so that her skirt rose up to her crotch and her breasts stood out in response to her pulled-back shoulder. The pose was deliberate, thought Galbraith with some amusement, as he lowered himself on to the seat beside her. She was a well-built young woman with a taste for tight T-shirts, heavy make-up and blue nail varnish, and he wondered how Angela Sumner would have coped with Polly as a daughter-in-law in place of Kate. For all her real or imagined sins, Kate seemed to have looked the part of William's wife even if she did lack the necessary social and educational skills that would have satisfied her mother-in-law.

'I want to ask you about a letter you wrote to Kate in July which concerns some of the people you work with,' he told

Polly, taking a photocopy of it out of his breast pocket. He spread it on his knee and handed it to her. 'Do you remember sending that?'

She read it through quickly, then nodded. 'Yup. I'd been phoning on and off for about a week, and I thought, what the hell, she's obviously busy, so I'll drop her a note instead and get her to phone me.' She screwed her face into cartoon pique. 'Not that she ever did. She just sent a scrotty little note, saying she'd call when she was ready.'

'This one?' He handed her a copy of Kate's draft reply.

She glanced at it. 'I guess so. That's what it said, more or less. It was on some fancy headed notepaper, I remember that, but I was pissed that she couldn't be bothered to write a decent letter back. The truth is, I don't think she wanted me to go. I expect she was afraid I'd embarrass her in front of her Lymington friends. Which I probably would have done,' she added in fairness.

Galbraith smiled. 'Did you visit the house when they first moved?'

'Nope. Never got invited. She kept saying I could go as soon as the decorating was finished, but' – she pulled another face – 'it was just an excuse to put me off. I didn't mind. Fact is, I'd probably have done the same in her shoes. She'd moved on – new house, new life, new friends – and you grow out of people when that happens, don't you?'

'She hadn't moved on completely,' he pointed out. 'You still work with William.'

Polly giggled. 'I work in the same building as William,' she corrected him, 'and it gets up his nose something rotten that I tell everyone he married my best friend. I know it's not true – it never was, really – I mean I liked her and all that, but she wasn't the best-friend type, if you know what I mean. Too self-contained by half. No, I just do it to annoy William. He thinks I'm common as muck, and he nearly died when I told him I'd visited Kate in Chichester and met his mother. I'm not surprised. God, she was an old battleaxe! Lecture, lecture, lecture. Do this. Don't do that. Frankly, I'd've wheeled her in front of a bus if she'd been *my* mother-in-law.'

'Was there ever a chance of that?'

'Do me a favour! I'd need to be permanently comatose to marry William Sumner. The guy has about as much sex appeal as a turnip!'

'So what did Kate see in him?'

Polly rubbed her thumb and forefinger together. 'Money.'

'What else?'

'Nothing. A bit of class, maybe, but an unmarried bloke with no children and money was what she was looking for, and an unmarried bloke with no children and money is what she got.' She cocked her head on one side, amused by his expression of disbelief. 'She told me once that William's tackle, even when he had a stiffy, was so limp it was more like an uncooked sausage than a truncheon. So I said, how does he do the business? And she said, with a pint of baby oil and my finger up his fucking arse.' She giggled again at Galbraith's wince of sympathy for another man's problems. 'He loved it, for Christ's sake! Why else would he marry her with his mother spitting poison all over the place? Okay, Kate may have wanted money, but poor old Willy just wanted a tart who'd tell him he was bloody brilliant whether he was or not. It worked like a dream. They both got what they wanted.'

He studied her for a moment, wondering if she was quite as naive as her words made her sound. 'Did they?' he asked her. 'Kate's dead, don't forget.'

She sobered immediately. 'I know. It's a bugger. But there's nothing I can tell you about that. I haven't seen her since she moved.'

'All right. Tell me what you do know. Why did your story about Wendy Plater insulting James Purdy remind you of Kate?' he asked her.

'What makes you think it did?'

He quoted from her letter. '"*She*" – meaning Wendy – "*had to apologize, but she doesn't regret any of it. She says she's never seen Purdy go purple before! I thought of you immediately, of course . . .*"' He laid the page on the bench between them. 'Why that last bit, Polly? Why should Purdy going purple make you think of Kate Sumner?'

She thought for a moment. 'Because she used to work at Pharmatec?' she tried unconvincingly. 'Because she thought Purdy was a prick? It's just a figure of speech.'

He tapped the copy of Kate's draft reply. 'She crossed out, "*You promised on your honour*", in this before going on to write, "*The story about Wendy Plater was really funny!*"' he said. 'What did you promise her, Polly?'

She looked uncomfortable. 'Hundreds of things, I should think.'

'I'm only interested in the one that had something to do with either James Purdy or Wendy Plater.'

She removed her arm from the back of the seat and hunched forward despondently. 'It's got nothing to do with her being killed. It's just something that happened.'

'What?'

She didn't answer.

'If it really does have nothing to do with her murder, then I give you my word it'll go no further than me,' he said reassuringly. 'I'm not interested in exposing her secrets, only in finding her killer.' Even as he spoke, he knew the statement was untrue. All too often, justice for a rape victim meant that she had to endure the humiliation of her secrets being exposed. He looked at Polly with unexpected sympathy. 'But I'm afraid *I'm* the one who has to decide whether it's important.'

She sighed. 'I could lose my job if Purdy ever finds out I told you.'

'There's no reason why he should.'

'You reckon?'

Galbraith didn't say anything, having learnt from experience that silence often exerted more pressure than words.

'Oh, what the hell!' she said then. 'You've probably guessed anyway. Kate had an affair with him. He was crazy about her, wanted to leave his wife and everything, then she blew him away and said she was going to marry William instead. Poor old Purdy couldn't believe it. He's no spring chicken, and he'd been rogering himself stupid to keep her interested. I think he may even have told his wife he wanted a divorce. Anyway, Kate said he went purple and then collapsed on his desk. He was off work for three months afterwards, so I reckoned he must have had a heart attack, but Kate said he couldn't face coming back while she was still there.' She shrugged. 'He started work again the week after she left so maybe she was right.'

'Why did she choose William?' he asked. 'She wasn't any more in love with him than she was with Purdy, was she?'

Polly repeated the gesture of rubbing her thumb and fingers together. 'Dosh,' she said. 'Purdy's got a wife and three grown-up children, all of whom would have demanded their cut before Kate got a look in.' She pulled a wry face. 'Like I said, what she really wanted was an unmarried guy without children. She reckoned if she was going to have to bust a gut to make some plonker happy, she wanted access to everything he owned.'

Galbraith shook his head in perplexity. 'Then why bother with Purdy at all?'

She hooked her arm over the sofa again and thrust her tits into his face. 'She didn't have a father, did she? Any more than I do.'

'So?'

'She had a thing about older men.' She opened her eyes wide in flirtatious invitation. 'Me, too, if you're interested.'

Galbraith chuckled. 'Do you eat them alive?'

She looked pointedly at his fly. 'I swallow them whole,' she said with a laugh.

He shook his head in amusement. 'You were telling me why Kate bothered with Purdy,' he reminded her.

'He was the boss,' she said, 'the guy with the loot. She thought she'd take him for a few bob, get him to pay for improvements on her flat, while she looked around for something better. The trouble was, she didn't reckon on him getting as smitten as he did so the only way to get rid of him was to be cruel. She wanted security, not love, you see, and she didn't think she'd get it from Purdy, not after his wife and children had taken their slice. He was thirty years older than she was, remember. Also, he didn't want any more kids, and that was all she really wanted, kids of her own. She was pretty screwed up in some ways, I guess because she'd had a tough time growing up.'

'Did William know about her affair with Purdy?'

Polly shook her head. 'No one knew except me. That's why she swore me to secrecy. She said William would call the wedding off if he ever found out.'

'Would he have done?'

'Oh, for sure. Look, he was thirty-seven years old, and he wasn't the marrying kind. Wendy Plater nearly got him up to scratch once till Kate put a spanner in the works by telling him she was a lush. He dumped her so quick, you wouldn't believe.' She smiled reminiscently. 'Kate practically had to put a ring through his nose to get him to the registry office. It might have been different if his mother had approved but old Ma Sumner and Will were like Derby and Joan, and Kate had to work her socks off every night to make sex more attractive to the silly sod than having his laundry done on a regular basis.'

'Was it true about Wendy Plater?'

Polly looked uncomfortable again. 'She gets drunk sometimes but not on a regular basis. Still, as Kate said, if Will had wanted to marry her, he wouldn't have believed it, would he? He just seized on the first good excuse to get out.'

Galbraith looked down at Kate Sumner's childish writing in

the draft letter she'd written to Polly and wondered about the nature of ruthlessness. 'Did the affair with Purdy continue after she married William?'

'No,' said Polly with conviction. 'Once Kate made up her mind to something, that was it.'

'Would that stop her having an affair with someone else? Let's say she was bored with William and met someone younger – would she have been unfaithful in those circumstances?'

Polly shrugged. 'I don't know. I sort of thought she might have something going because she hasn't bothered to phone me for ages, but that doesn't mean she did. It wouldn't have been serious, anyway. She was pleased as punch about moving to Lymington and getting a decent house and I can't see her giving all that up very easily.'

Galbraith nodded. 'Have you ever known her use faeces as a means of revenge?'

'What the hell's fee-sees?'

'Crap,' Galbraith explained obligingly, 'turds, dung, number twos.'

'Shit!'

'Exactly. Have you ever known her smear crap over anyone's belongings?'

Polly giggled. 'No. She was much too prissy to do anything like that. A bit of a hygiene freak, actually. When Hannah was a baby she used to swab the kitchen down every day with Dettol in case there were any germs. I told her she was crazy – I mean germs are everywhere, aren't they – but she still went on doing it. I can't see her touching a turd in a million years. She used to hold Hannah's nappies at arm's length after she'd changed her.'

Curiouser and curiouser, thought Galbraith. 'Okay. Give me a rough idea of the timetable. How soon after she told Purdy she was going to marry William did the wedding actually take place?'

'I can't remember. A month maybe.'

He did a quick calculation in his head. 'So if Purdy was off for three months, then it was two months after the wedding that she left work because she was pregnant?'

'Something like that.'

'And how pregnant was she, Polly? Two months? Three months? Four months?'

A resigned expression crossed the young woman's face. 'She said as long as it looked like her it wouldn't matter, because William was so besotted he'd believe anything she told him.' She read Galbraith's expression correctly as one of contempt. 'She didn't do it out of malice. Just desperation. She knew what it was like to grow up in poverty.'

Celia's adamant refusal to go with Harding in the helicopter and her inability to bend at the hip meant that she was either going to have to walk home in extreme pain or travel flat on her back on the floor of Ingram's Jeep which was full of oilskins, waders and fishing tackle. With a wry smile he cleared a space and bent to pick her up. However, she was even more adamant in her refusal to be carried. 'I'm not a child,' she snapped.

'I don't see how else we can do it, Mrs Jenner,' he pointed out, 'not unless you slide in on your front and lie face down where I usually put my fish.'

'I suppose you think that's funny.'

'Merely accurate. I'm afraid it's going to be painful whatever we do.'

She looked at the uncomfortable, ridged floor and gave in with bad grace. 'Just don't make a meal of it,' she said crossly. 'I hate fuss.'

'I know.' He scooped her into his arms and leaned into the Jeep to deposit her carefully on the floor. 'It's going to be a bumpy ride,' he warned, packing the oilskins around her as wadding. 'You'd better shout if it gets too much for you and I'll stop.'

It was already too much but she had no intention of telling him so. 'I'm worried about Maggie,' she said through gritted teeth. 'She ought to be back by now.'

'She'll have led Stinger towards the stables not away from them,' he told her.

'Are you ever wrong about anything?' she asked acidly.

'Not where your daughter's knowledge of horses is concerned,' he answered. 'I have faith in her, and so should you.' He shut the door on her and climbed in behind the wheel. 'I'll apologize in advance,' he called as he started the engine.

'What for?'

'The lousy suspension,' he murmured, letting out the clutch and setting off at a snail's pace across the chewed-up turf of the valley. She didn't make a sound the entire way back and he smiled to himself as he drew into the Broxton House drive. Whatever else she was, Celia Jenner was a gutsy lady, and he admired her for it.

He opened the back door. 'Still alive?' he asked, reaching in for her.

She was grey with pain and fatigue but it took more than a bumpy ride to kill the spark. 'You're a very irritating young man,' she muttered, as she clamped her arm round his neck again and grunted with pain as he shifted her along the floor. 'But you were right about Martin Grant,' she admitted grudgingly, 'and I've always regretted that I didn't listen to you. Does that please you?'

'No.'

'Why not? Maggie would tell you it's the closest I'll ever come to an apology.'

He smiled slightly, hefting her against his chest and stepping away from the Jeep. 'Is being stubborn something to be proud of?'

'I'm not stubborn, I'm principled.'

'Well, if you weren't so' – he grinned at her – 'principled, you'd be in Poole hospital by now getting proper treatment.'

'You should always call a spade a spade,' she said crossly. 'And, frankly, if I was half as stubborn as you seem to think I am, I wouldn't even be in this condition. I object to having my arse mentioned over the telephone.'

'Do you want *another* apology?'

She looked up and caught his eye, then looked away again. 'For goodness sake put me down,' she said. 'This is so undignified in a woman of my age. What would my daughter say if she saw me like this?'

He took no notice of her and strode across the weed-strewn gravel towards her front door, only lowering her to the ground when he heard the sound of running feet. Maggie, flustered and breathless, appeared round the corner of the house, a walking stick in each hand. She handed them to her mother. 'She's not allowed to ride,' she told Nick, bending over to catch her breath. 'Doctor's orders. But thank God she never takes anyone's advice. I couldn't have managed on my own, and I certainly couldn't have got Stinger back without Sir Jasper.'

Nick held supporting hands under Celia's elbows while she balanced herself on the sticks. 'You should have told me to get stuffed,' he said.

She inched forward on her sticks like a large crab. 'Don't be ridiculous,' she muttered irritably. 'That's the mistake I made last time.'

Chapter Eighteen

Statement

Witness: James Purdy, Managing Director, Pharmatec UK
Interviewer: DI Galbraith

Some time during the summer of 1993, I was working late in the office. As far as I was aware, everyone else had left the premises. On my way out at approximately 9.00 p.m., I noticed a light shining in an office at the end of the corridor. The office belonged to Kate Hill, secretary to the Services Manager, Michael Sprate, and, because I was impressed by the fact that she was working late, I went in to commend her on her commitment. She had been drawn to my attention when she first joined the company because of her size. She was slim and small with blonde hair and remarkable blue eyes. I found her very attractive, but that was not my reason for going into her office that night. She had never given any indication that she was interested in me. I was surprised and flattered, therefore, when she got up from her desk and said she had stayed late in the hope that I would come in.

I am not proud of what happened next. I'm fifty-eight years old and I've been married thirty-three years, and no one has ever done to me what Kate did that night. I know it sounds absurd, but it's the sort of thing most men dream of: that they'll walk into a room one day and a beautiful woman, for no reason at all, will offer them sex. I was extremely worried afterwards because I assumed she must have had an ulterior motive for doing it. I spent the next few days in fear. At the very least I expected her to take liberties in her dealings with me; at the worst I expected some sort of blackmail attempt. However, she was extremely discreet, asked nothing in return, and was always polite whenever I saw her. When I realized there was nothing to fear, I became obsessed with her and dreamt about her night after night.

Some two weeks later, she was again in her office when I passed, and the experience was repeated. I asked her why and she said: 'Because I want to.' From that moment on, there was nothing I could do to control myself. In some ways, she is the most beautiful thing that has ever happened in my life, and I do not regret one moment of our affair. In other ways, I look back on it as a nightmare. I did not believe hearts could be broken, but mine was broken several times by Kate, never more so than when I heard she was dead.

Our affair continued for several months until January 1994. For the most part it was conducted in Kate's flat, although once or twice, under the guise of business trips, I took her to hotels in London. I was prepared to divorce my wife in order to marry Kate, even though I have always loved my wife and would never do anything willingly to hurt her. I can only describe Kate as a fever in the blood that temporarily upset my equilibrium because, once exorcized, I was able to return to normal.

On a Friday at the end of January 1994, Kate came into my office at about 3.30 p.m., and told me she was going to marry William Sumner. I was terribly distressed and remember little of what happened next. I know I passed out and when I came round again I was in hospital. I was told I had had a minor heart attack. I have since confessed to my wife everything that happened.

As far as I am aware, William Sumner knows nothing about

my relations with Kate before their marriage. I have certainly not told him, nor have I led him to believe that we were even remotely friendly. It did occur to me that his daughter might be mine, but I have never mentioned it to anyone as I would not lay claim to the child.

I can confirm that I have had no contact with Kate Hill-Sumner since the day in January 1994 when she told me of her decision to marry William Sumner.

James Purdy

Statement

Witness: Vivienne Purdy, The Gables, Drew Street, Fareham
Interviewer: DI Galbraith

....

I first learnt of my husband's affair with Kate Hill some four
weeks after his heart attack in January 1994. I cannot remember
the precise date, but it was either the day she married William
Sumner or the day after. I found James in tears and I was
worried because he had been making such good progress. He
told me he was crying because his heart was breaking, and he
went on to explain why.

I was neither hurt nor surprised by his confession. James
and I have been married a long time, and I knew perfectly well
that he was having a relationship with someone else. He has
never been a good liar. My only emotion was relief that he had
finally decided to clear the air. I felt no animosity towards Kate
Hill-Sumner for the following reasons.

It may sound insensitive but I would not have regarded it
as the worst misfortune that could have happened to me to lose
the man I had lived with for thirty years. Indeed, in some ways
I would have welcomed it as an opportunity to start a new life,
free of duty and responsibility. Prior to the events of 1993/94
James was a conscientious father and husband, but his family
had always taken second place to his personal ambitions and
desires. When I realized that he was having an affair, I made
discreet enquiries about the financial position should divorce
become inevitable, and satisfied myself that a division of our
property would allow me considerable freedom. I renewed my
career as a teacher some ten years ago, and my salary is an
adequate one. I have also made sensible pension provisions for
myself. As a result, I would certainly have agreed to a divorce

had James asked for one. My children are grown up and, while they would be unhappy at the thought of their parents separating, I knew that James would continue to be interested in them.

I explained all this to James in the spring of 1994, and showed him the correspondence I had had with my solicitor and my accountant. I believe it concentrated his mind on the choices open to him and I am confident that he put aside any thought of attempting to rekindle the affair with Kate Hill-Sumner. I hope I don't flatter myself when I say it came as a shock to him to realize that he could no longer take my automatic presence in his life for granted, and that he took this possibility rather more seriously than he took his relationship with Kate Hill-Sumner. I can say honestly that I have no lingering resentment towards James or Kate because it was I who was empowered by the experience. I have a great deal more confidence in myself and my future as a result.

I was aware that William and Kate Hill-Sumner had a child some time in autumn 1994. By simple calculation, I recognized that the child could have been my husband's. However, I did not discuss the issue with him. Nor indeed with anyone else. I could see no point in causing further unhappiness to the parties involved, particularly the child.

I have never met Kate Hill-Sumner nor her husband.

Vivienne Purdy

Chapter Nineteen

INSIDE BROXTON HOUSE, Nick Ingram abandoned both women in the kitchen to put through a call to the incident room at Winfrith. He spoke to Detective Superintendent Carpenter, and gave him details of Harding's activities that morning. 'He's been taken to Poole hospital sir. I shall be questioning him later about the assault but meanwhile you might want to keep an eye on him. He's not likely to go anywhere in the short term because his arm needs stitching, but I'd say he's out of control now or he wouldn't have attacked Miss Jenner.'

'What was he trying to do? Rape her?'

'She doesn't know. She says she shouted at him when her horse bolted so he slapped her and knocked her to the ground.'

'Mmm.' Carpenter thought for a moment. 'I thought you and John Galbraith decided he was interested in little boys.'

'I'm ready to be proved wrong, sir.'

There was a dry chuckle at the other end. 'What's the first rule of policing, son?'

'Always keep an open mind, sir.'

'Legwork first, lad. Conclusions second.' There was another brief silence. 'The DI's gone off in hot pursuit of William Sumner after reading your fax. He won't be at all pleased if Harding's our man after all.'

'Sorry, sir. If you can give me a couple of hours to go back to the headland, I'll see if I can find out what he was up to. It'll be quicker than sending any of your chaps down.'

In the event, he was delayed by the wretched state of the

two Jenner women. Celia was in such pain she was unable to sit down and so she stood in the middle of the kitchen, legs splayed and leaning forward on her two sticks, looking more like an angry praying mantis than a crab. Meanwhile, Maggie's teeth chattered non-stop from delayed shock. 'S-s-sorry,' she kept saying, as she took a filthy, evil-smelling horse blanket from the scullery and draped it round her shoulders, 'I'm j-just s-s-so c-cold.'

Unceremoniously, Ingram shoved her on to a chair beside the Aga and told her to stay put while he dealt with her mother. 'Right,' he said to Celia, 'are you going to be more comfortable lying down in bed or sitting up in a chair?'

'Lying down,' she said.

'Then I'll set up a bed on the ground floor. Which room do you want it in?'

'I don't,' she said mutinously. 'It'll make me look like an invalid.'

He crossed his arms and frowned at her. 'I haven't got time to argue about this, Mrs Jenner. There's no way you can get upstairs, so the bed has to come to you.' She didn't answer. 'All right,' he said, heading for the hall. 'I'll make the decision myself.'

'The drawing room,' she called after him. 'And take the bed out of the room at the end of the corridor.'

Her reluctance, he realized, had more to do with her unwillingness to let him go upstairs than fear of being seen as an invalid. He had had no idea how desperate their plight was until he saw the wasteland of the first floor. The doors stood open to every room, eight in all, and there wasn't a single piece of furniture in any but Celia's. The smell of long-lying dust and damp permeating through an unsound roof stung his nostrils and he wasn't surprised that Celia's health had begun to suffer. He was reminded of Jane Fielding's complaints about selling the family heirlooms to look after her parents-in-law, but their situation was princely compared with this.

The room at the end of the corridor was obviously Celia's own, and her bed probably the only one left in the house. It took him less than ten minutes to dismantle and reassemble it in the drawing room, where he set it up close to the french windows, overlooking the garden. The view was hardly inspiring, just another wasteland, untended and uncared for, but the drawing room at least retained some of its former glory, with all its paintings and most of its furniture still intact. He had time to reflect that few, if any, of Celia's acquaintances could have any idea that the hall and the drawing room represented the extent of her remaining worth. But what sort of madness made people live like this, he wondered? Pride? Fear of their failures being known? Embarrassment?

He returned to the kitchen. 'How are we going to do this?' he asked her. 'The hard way or the easy way?'

Tears of pain squeezed between her lids. 'You really are the most provoking creature,' she said. 'You're determined to take away my dignity, aren't you?'

He grinned as he put one arm under her knees and the other behind her back, and lifted her gently. 'Why not?' he murmured. 'It may be my only chance to get even. '

'I don't want to talk to you,' said William Sumner angrily, barring the front door to DI Galbraith. Hectic spots of colour burned in his cheeks, and he kept tugging at the fingers of his left hand as he spoke, cracking the joints noisily. 'I'm sick of the police treating my house like a damn thoroughfare, and I'm sick of answering questions. Why can't you just leave me alone?'

'Because your wife's been murdered, sir,' said Galbraith evenly, 'and we're trying to find out who killed her. I'm sorry if you're finding that difficult to cope with but I really do have no option.'

'Then talk to me here. What do you want to know?'

The DI glanced towards the road where an interested group

of spectators was gathering. 'We'll have the Press here before you know it, William,' he said dispassionately. 'Do you want to discuss your alleged alibi in front of an audience of journalists?'

Sumner's jittery gaze jumped towards the crowd at his gate. 'This isn't fair. Everything's so bloody public. Why can't you make them go away?'

'They'll go of their own accord if you let me in. They'll stay if you insist on keeping me on the doorstep. That's human nature, I'm afraid.'

With a haunted expression, Sumner seized the policeman's arm and pulled him inside. Pressure was beginning to take its toll, thought Galbraith, and gone was the self-assured, if tired, man of Monday. It meant nothing in itself. Shock took time to absorb, and nerves invariably began to fray when successful closure to a case remained elusive. He followed Sumner into the sitting room and, as before, took a seat on the sofa.

'What do you mean, *alleged* alibi?' the man demanded, preferring to stand. 'I was in Liverpool, for God's sake. How could I be in two places at once?'

The DI opened his briefcase and extracted some papers. 'We've taken statements from your colleagues, hotel employees at the Regal and librarians at the university library. None of them supports your claim that you were in Liverpool on Saturday night.' He held them out. 'I think you should read them.'

Witness statement: Harold Marshall, MD Campbell Ltd, Lee Industrial Estate, Lichfield, Staffordshire

I remember seeing William at lunch on Saturday, 9 August 1997. We discussed a paper in last week's *Lancet* about stomach ulcers. William says he's working on a new drug that will beat the current frontrunner into a cocked hat. I was sceptical, and we had quite a debate. No, I didn't see him at the dinner that evening but then I wouldn't expect to. He and I have been attending these conferences for years, and it'll be a red-letter day when William decides to let his hair down and join the rest of us for some light-hearted entertainment. He was certainly at lunch on Sunday because we had another argument on the ulcer issue.

Witness statement: Paul Dimmock, Research Chemist, Wryton's, Holborne Way, Colchester, Essex

I saw William at about 2.00 p.m. Saturday afternoon. He said he was going to the university library to do some research, which is par for the course for him. He never goes to conference dinners. He's only interested in the intellectual side, hates the social side. My room was two doors down from his. I remember seeing the DO NOT DISTURB notice on the door when I went up to bed about half-past midnight, but I've no idea when he got back. I had a drink with him before lunch on Sunday. No, he didn't seem at all tired. Matter of fact he was in better form than usual. Positively cheerful in fact.

Witness statement: Anne Smith, Research Chemist, Bristol University, Bristol

I didn't see him at all on Saturday but I had a drink with him and Paul Dimmock on Sunday morning. He gave a paper on Friday afternoon and I was interested in some of the things he said. He's researching the drug treatment of stomach ulcers and it sounds like good stuff.

Witness statement: Carrie Wilson, Chambermaid, Regal Hotel, Liverpool

I remember the gentleman in number two-two-three-five. He was very tidy, unpacked his suitcase and put everything away in the drawers. Some of them don't bother. I finished about midday on Saturday, but I made up his room when he went down to breakfast and I didn't see him afterwards. Sunday morning, there was a DO NOT DISTURB notice on his door so I left him to sleep. As I recall he went down at about 11.30 and I made up his room then. Yes, his bed had certainly been slept in. There were science books scattered all over it, and I think he must have been doing some studying. I remember thinking he wasn't so tidy after all.

Witness statement: David Forward, Concierge, Regal Hotel, Liverpool
We have limited parking facilities, and Mr Sumner reserved a parking space at the same time as he reserved his room. He was allocated number thirty-four which is at the back of the hotel. As far as I'm aware the car remained there from Thursday 7 to Monday 11. We ask guests to leave a set of keys with us, and Mr Sumner didn't retrieve his until the Monday. Yes, he could certainly have driven his car out if he had a spare set. There are no barriers across the exit.

Witness statement: Jane Riley, Librarian, University Library, Liverpool
(Shown a photograph of William Sumner)
Quite a few of the conference members came into the library on Saturday, but I don't remember seeing this man. That doesn't mean he wasn't here. As long as they have a conference badge, and know what they're looking for, they have free access.

Witness statement: Les Allen, Librarian, University Library, Liverpool
(Shown a photograph of William Sumner)
He came in on Friday morning. I spent about half an hour with him. He wanted papers on peptic and duodenal ulcers, and I showed him where to find them. He said he'd be back on Saturday, but I didn't notice him. It's a big place. I only ever notice the people who need help.

'You see our problem?' asked Galbraith when Sumner had read them. 'There's a period of twenty-one hours, from two o'clock on Saturday till 11.30 on Sunday, when no one remembers seeing you. Yet the first three statements were made by people whom you told us would give you a cast-iron alibi.'

Sumner looked at him in bewilderment. 'But I was there,'

he insisted. 'One of them must have seen me.' He stabbed a finger at Paul Dimmock's statement. 'I met up with Paul in the foyer. I told him I was going to the library and he walked part of the way with me. That had to be well after two o'clock. Dammit, at two o'clock I was still arguing the toss with that bloody fool Harold Marshall.'

Galbraith shook his head. 'Even if it was four o'clock, it makes no difference. You proved on Monday that you can do the drive to Dorset in five hours.'

'This is absurd!' snapped Sumner nervously. 'You'll just have to talk to more people. Someone must have seen me. There was a man at the same table as me in the library. Ginger-haired fellow with glasses. He can prove I was there.'

'What was his name?'

'I don't know.'

Galbraith took another sheaf of papers out of his briefcase. 'We've questioned thirty people in all, William. These are the rest of the statements. There's no one who's prepared to admit they saw you at any time during the ten hours prior to your wife's murder or the ten hours after. We've also checked your hotel account. You didn't use any hotel service, and that includes your telephone, between lunch on Saturday and pre-lunch drinks on Sunday.' He dropped the papers on to the sofa. 'How do you explain that? For example, where did you eat on Saturday night? You weren't at the conference dinner and you didn't have room service.'

Sumner set to cracking his finger joints again. 'I didn't have anything to eat, not a proper meal anyway. I hate those blasted conference dinners, so I wasn't going to leave my room in case anyone saw me. They all get drunk and behave stupidly. I used the mini-bar,' he said, 'drank the beer and ate peanuts and chocolate. Isn't that on the account?'

Galbraith nodded. 'Except it doesn't specify a time. You could have had them at ten o'clock on Sunday morning. It may explain why you were in such good spirits when you met your friends in the bar. Why didn't you order room service if you didn't want to go down?'

'Because I wasn't that hungry.' Sumner lurched towards the armchair and slumped into it. 'I knew this was going to happen,' he said bitterly. 'I knew you'd go for me if you couldn't find anyone else. I was in the library all afternoon, then I went back to the hotel and read books and journals till I fell asleep.' He lapsed into silence, massaging his temples. 'How could I have drowned her anyway?' he demanded suddenly. 'I don't have a boat.'

'No,' Galbraith agreed. 'Drowning does seem to be the one method that exonerates you.'

A complex mixture of emotions – *relief? triumph? pleasure?* – showed briefly in the man's eyes. 'There you are then,' he said childishly.

'Why do you want to get even with my mother?' asked Maggie when Ingram returned to the kitchen after settling Celia and phoning the local GP. Some colour had returned to her cheeks and she had finally stopped shaking.

'Private joke,' he said, filling the kettle and putting it on the Aga. 'Where does she keep her mugs?'

'Cupboard by the door.'

He took out two and transferred them to the sink, then opened the cupboard underneath and found some washing-up liquid, bleach and pan scourers. 'How long has her hip been bad?' he asked, rolling up his sleeves and setting to with the scourers and the bleach to render the sink hygienic before he even began to deal with the stains in the mugs. From the strong whiffs of dirty dog and damp horse blankets that seemed to haunt the kitchen like old ghosts, he had a strong suspicion that the sink was not entirely dedicated to the purpose of washing crockery.

'Six months. She's on the waiting list for a replacement

operation but I can't see it happening before the end of the year.' She watched him sluice down the draining board and sink. 'You think we're a couple of sluts, don't you?'

''Fraid so,' he agreed bluntly. 'I'd say it's a miracle neither of you has gone down with food poisoning, particularly your mother when her health's not too brilliant in the first place.'

'There are so many other things to do,' she said dispiritedly, 'and Ma's in too much pain most of the time to clean properly . . . or says she is. Sometimes I think she's just making excuses to get out of it because she thinks it's beneath her to get her hands dirty. Other times . . .' She sighed heavily. 'I keep the horses immaculate but cleaning up after myself and Ma is always at the bottom of the list. I hate coming up here anyway. It's so' – she sought a suitable word – 'depressing.'

He wondered she had the nerve to stand in judgement on her mother's lifestyle, but didn't comment on it. Stress, depression and waspishness went together in his experience. Instead, he scrubbed the mugs, then filled them with diluted bleach and left them to stand. 'Is that why you moved down to the stables?' he asked her, turning round.

'Not really. If Ma and I live in each other's pockets we argue. If we live apart we don't. Simple as that. Things are easier this way.'

She looked thin and harassed, and her hair hung in limp strands about her face as if she hadn't been near a shower for weeks. It wasn't surprising in view of what she'd been through that morning, particularly as the beginnings of a bruise were ripening on the side of her face, but Ingram remembered her as she used to be, pre-Robert Healey, a gloriously vibrant woman with a mischievous sense of humour and sparkling eyes. He regretted the passing of that personality – it had been a dazzling one – but she was still the most desirable woman he knew.

He glanced idly around the kitchen. 'If you think this is

depressing, you should try living in a hostel for the homeless for a week.'

'Is that supposed to make me feel better?'

'This one room could house an entire family.'

'You sound like Ava, my bloody sister-in-law,' she said testily. 'According to her, we live in the lap of luxury despite the fact that the damn place is falling down about our ears.'

'Then why don't you stop whingeing about it and do something constructive to change it?' he suggested. 'If you gave this room a lick of paint it would brighten it up and you'd have less to feel depressed about and more to be thankful for.'

'Oh, my God,' she said icily, 'you'll be telling me to take up knitting next. I don't need DIY therapy, Nick.'

'Then explain to me how sitting around moaning about your environment helps you? You're not helpless, are you? Or maybe it's you, and not your mother, who thinks that getting her hands dirty is demeaning?'

'Paint costs money.'

'Your flat over the stables costs a damn sight more,' he pointed out. 'You baulk at forking out for some cheap emulsion, yet you'll pay two sets of gas, electricity and telephone bills just in order to avoid having to get on with your mother. How does that make things easier, Maggie? It's hardly sound economics, is it? And what are you going to do when she falls over and breaks her hip so badly she's confined to a wheelchair? Pop in once in a while to see she hasn't died of hypothermia in the night because she hasn't been able to get into bed on her own? Or will that be so depressing you'll avoid her entirely?'

'I don't need this,' she said tiredly. 'It's none of your business anyway. We manage fine on our own.'

He watched her for a moment, then turned back to the sink, emptying the mugs of bleach and rinsing them under the tap. He jerked his head towards the kettle. 'Your mother would like a cup of tea, and I suggest you put several spoonfuls of sugar in it to bring up her energy levels. I also suggest you make one for yourself. The GP said he'd be here by eleven.' He dried his hands on a tea towel and rolled down his sleeves.

'Where are you going?' she asked him.

'Up to the headland. I want to try and find out why Harding came back. Does your mother have any freezer bags?'

'No. We can't afford a freezer.'

'Cling film?'

'In the drawer by the sink.'

'Can I take it?'

'I suppose so.' She watched him remove the roll and tuck it under his arm. 'What do you want it for?'

'Evidence,' he said unhelpfully, making for the door.

She watched him in a kind of despair. 'What about me and Ma?'

He turned with a frown. 'What about you?'

'God, I don't know,' she said crossly. 'We're both pretty shaken, you know. That bloody man hit me, in case you've forgotten. Aren't the police supposed to stay around when women get attacked? Take statements or something?'

'Probably,' he agreed, 'but this is my day off. I turfed out to help you as a friend, not as a policeman, and I'm only following up on Harding because I'm involved in the Kate Sumner case. Don't worry,' he said with a comforting smile, 'you're in no danger from him, not while he's in Poole, but dial nine-nine-nine if you need someone to hold your hand.'

She glared at him. 'I want him prosecuted which means I want you to take a statement now.'

'Mmm, well, don't forget I'll be taking one from him, too,' Ingram pointed out, 'and you may not be so eager to go for his jugular if he opts to counter prosecute on the grounds that he's the one who suffered the injuries because you didn't have your dog under proper control. It's going to be your word against his,' he said, making for the door, 'which is one of the reasons why I'm going back up there now.'

She sighed. 'I suppose you're hurt because I told you to mind your own business?'

'Not in the least,' he said, disappearing into the scullery. 'Try angry or bored.'

'Do you want me to say sorry?' she called after him. 'Well, okay . . . I'm tired . . . I'm stressed out and I'm not in the best of moods but' – she gritted her teeth – 'I'll say sorry if that's what you want.'

But her words fell on stony ground because all she heard was the sound of the back door closing behind him.

The Detective Inspector had been silent so long that William Sumner grew visibly nervous. 'There you are then,' he said again. 'I couldn't possibly have drowned her, could I?' Anxiety had set his eyelid fluttering and he looked absurdly comical every time his lid winked. 'I don't understand why you keep hounding me. You said you were looking for someone with a boat, but you know I haven't got one. And I don't understand why you released Steven Harding when WPC Griffiths said he was seen talking to Kate outside Tesco's on Saturday morning.'

WPC Griffiths should learn to keep her mouth shut, thought Galbraith in annoyance. Not that he blamed her. Sumner was bright enough to read between the lines of newspaper reports about 'a young Lymington actor being taken in for questioning', and then press for answers. 'Briefly,' he said, 'then they went their separate ways. She talked to a couple of market stallholders afterwards, but Harding wasn't with her.'

'Well, it wasn't me who did it.' He winked. 'So there must be someone else you haven't found yet.'

'That's certainly one way of looking at it.' Galbraith lifted a photograph of Kate off the table beside him. 'The trouble is looks are so often deceptive. I mean, take Kate here. You see this?' He turned the picture towards the husband. 'The first impression she gives is that butter wouldn't melt in her mouth, but the more you learn about her the more you realize that isn't true. Let me tell you what I know of her.' He held up his fingers and ticked the points off as he spoke. 'She wanted money and she didn't really mind how she got it. She manipulated people in order to achieve her ambitions. She could be cruel. She told lies if necessary. Her goal was to climb the social ladder and become accepted within a milieu she admired and, as long as it brought the goalposts closer, she was prepared to play-act whatever role was required of her, sex being the major weapon in her armoury. The one person she couldn't manipulate successfully was your mother, so she dealt with her in the only way possible by moving away from her influence.' He dropped his hand to his lap and looked at the other man with genuine sympathy. 'How long was it before you realized you'd been suckered, William?'

'I suppose you've been talking to that bloody policewoman?'

'Among other people.'

'She made me angry. I said things I didn't mean.'

Galbraith shook his head. 'Your mother's view of your marriage wasn't so different,' he pointed out. 'She may not have used the terms "landlady" or "cheap boarding house", but she certainly gave the impression of an unfulfilled and unfulfilling relationship. Other people have described it as unhappy, based on sex, cool, boring. Are any of those descriptions accurate? Are they all accurate?'

Sumner pressed his finger and thumb to the bridge of his nose. 'You don't kill your wife because you're bored with her,' he muttered.

Galbraith wondered again at the man's naivety. Boredom was precisely why most men killed their wives. They might disguise it by claiming provocation or jealousy but, in the end, a desire for something different was usually the reason – even if the difference was simply escape. 'Except I'm told it wasn't so much a question of boredom, but more a question of you taking her for granted. And that interests me. You see, I wonder what a man like you would do if the woman you'd been taking for granted suddenly decided she wasn't going to play the game any more.'

Sumner stared back at him with disdain. 'I don't know what you're talking about.'

'Or if', Galbraith went on relentlessly, 'you discovered that what you'd been taking for granted wasn't true. Such as being a father, for example.'

Ingram's assumption was that Harding had come back for his rucksack because, despite the man's claim that the rucksack found on board *Crazy Daze* was the one he'd been carrying, Ingram remained convinced that it wasn't. Paul and Danny Spender had been too insistent that it was big for Ingram to accept that a triangular one fitted the description. Also, he remained suspicious about why Harding had left it behind when he took the boys down to the boatsheds. Nevertheless, the logic of why he had descended to the beach that morning, only to climb up again empty-handed, was far from obvious. Had someone else found the rucksack and removed it? Had Harding weighted it with a rock and thrown it into the sea? Had he even left it there in the first place?

In frustration, he slithered down a gully in the shale preci-pice to where the grassy slope at the end of the quarry valley undulated softly towards the sea. It was a western-facing cliff out of sight of the sun, and he shivered as the cold and damp penetrated his flimsy T-shirt and sweater. He turned to look back towards the cleft in the cliff, giving himself a rough idea of where Harding must have emerged in front of Maggie. Shale still pattered down the gully Ingram himself had used, and he noticed what was obviously a recent slide further to the left. He walked over to it, wondering if Harding had dislodged it in his ascent, but the surface was damp with dew and he decided it must have happened a few days previously.

He turned his attention to the shore below, striding down the grass to take a closer look. Pieces of driftwood and old plastic containers had wedged themselves into cracks in the rocks, but there was no sign of a black or green rucksack. He felt exhausted suddenly, and wondered what the hell he was doing there. He'd planned to spend his day in total idleness aboard *Miss Creant*, and he really didn't appreciate giving it up for a wild-goose chase. He raised his eyes to the clouds skudding in on a south-westerly breeze and sighed his frustration to the winds . . .

Maggie put a cup of tea on the table beside her mother's bed. 'I've made it very sweet,' she said. 'Nick said you needed your energy levels raising.' She looked at the dreadful state of the top blanket, worn and covered in stains, then noticed the tannin dribbles on Celia's bedjacket. She wondered what the sheets looked like – it was ages since Broxton House had boasted a washing machine – and wished angrily that she had never introduced the word 'slut' into her conversation with Nick.

'I'd rather have a brandy,' said Celia with a sigh.

'So would I,' said Maggie shortly, 'but we haven't got any.' She stood by the window, looking at the garden, her own cup cradled between her hands. 'Why does he want to get even with you, Ma?'

'Did you ask him?'

'Yes. He said it was a private joke.'

Celia chuckled. 'Where is he?'

'Gone.'

'I hope you thanked him for me.'

'I didn't. He started ordering me about so I sent him away with a flea in his ear.'

Her mother eyed her curiously for a moment. 'How odd of him,' she said, reaching for her tea. 'What sort of orders was he giving you?'

'Snide ones.'

'Oh, I see.'

Maggie shook her head. 'I doubt you do,' she said, addressing the garden. 'He's like Matt and Ava, thinks society would have better value out of this house if we were evicted and it was given to a homeless family.'

Celia took a sip of her tea and leaned back against her pillows. 'Then I understand why you're so angry,' she said evenly. 'It's always irritating when someone's right.'

'He called you a slut and said it was a miracle you hadn't come down with food poisoning.'

Celia pondered for a moment. 'I find that hard to believe if he wasn't prepared to tell you why he wanted to get even with me. Also, he's a polite young man, and doesn't use words like "slut". That's more your style, isn't it, darling?' She watched her daughter's rigid back for a moment but, in the absence of any response, went on: 'If he'd *really* wanted to get even with me, he'd have spiked my guns a long time ago. I was extremely rude to him, and I've regretted it ever since.'

'What did you do?'

'He came to me two months before your wedding with a warning about your fiancé, and I sent him away' – Celia paused to recall the words Maggie had used – 'with a flea in his ear.' Neither she nor Maggie could ever think of the man who had wheedled his way into their lives by his real name, Robert Healey, but only by the name they had come to associate with him, Martin Grant. It was harder for Maggie who had spent three months as Mrs Martin Grant before being faced with the unenviable task of informing banks and corporations that neither the name nor the title belonged to her. 'Admittedly the evidence against Martin was very thin,' Celia went on. 'Nick accused him of trying to con Jane Fielding's parents-in-law out of several thousand pounds by posing as an antiques dealer – with everything resting on old Mrs Fielding's insistence that Martin was the man who came to their door – but if I'd listened to Nick instead of castigating him . . .' She broke off. 'The trouble was he made me angry. He kept asking me what I knew of Martin's background, and when I told him Martin's father was a coffee-grower in Kenya, Nick laughed and said, how convenient.'

'Did you show him the letters they wrote to us?'

'*Supposedly* wrote,' Celia corrected her. 'And, yes, of course I did. It was the only proof we had that Martin came from a respectable background. But, as Nick so rightly pointed out, the address was a PO box number in Nairobi which proved nothing. He said anyone could conduct a fake correspondence through an anonymous box number. What he wanted was Martin's previous address in Britain and all I could give him was the address of the flat Martin was renting in Bournemouth.' She sighed. 'But as Nick said, you don't have to be the son of a coffee-planter to rent a flat, and he told me I'd be wise to make a few enquiries before I allowed my daughter to marry someone I knew nothing about.'

Maggie turned to look at her. 'Then why didn't you?'

'Oh, I don't know.' Her mother sighed. 'Perhaps because Nick was so appallingly pompous . . . Perhaps because on the one occasion that I dared to question Martin's suitability as a husband' – she lifted her eyebrows – 'you called me a meddling bitch and refused to speak to me for several weeks. I think I asked you if you could really marry a man who was afraid of horses, didn't I?'

'Ye-es,' said her daughter slowly, 'and I should have listened to you. I'm sorry now that I didn't.' She crossed her arms. 'What did you say to Nick?'

'More or less what you just said about him,' said Celia. 'I called him a jumped-up little oik with a Hitler complex and tore strips off him for having the brass nerve to slander my future son-in-law. Then I asked him which day Mrs Fielding claimed to have seen Martin and, when he told me, I lied and said she couldn't possibly have done because Martin was out riding with you and me.'

'Oh my God!' said Maggie. 'How could you do that?'

'Because it never occurred to me for one moment that Nick was right,' said Celia with an ironic smile. 'After all, he was just a common or garden policeman and Martin was such a gent. Oxford graduate. Old Etonian. Heir to a coffee plantation. So who wins the prize for stupidity now, darling? You or me?'

Maggie shook her head. 'Couldn't you at least have told me about it? Forewarned might have been forearmed.'

'Oh, I don't think so. You were always so cruel about Nick after Martin pointed out that the poor lad blushed like a beetroot every time he saw you. I remember you laughing and saying that even beetroots have more sex appeal than over-weight Neanderthals in policemen's uniforms.'

Maggie squirmed at the memory. 'You could have told me about it afterwards.'

'Of course I could,' said Celia bluntly, 'but I didn't see why I should give you an excuse to shuffle the guilt off on to me. You were just as much to blame as I was. You were living with the wretched creature in Bournemouth, and if anyone should have seen the flaws in his story it was you. You weren't a child in all conscience, Maggie. If you'd asked to visit his office just once, the whole edifice of his fraud would have collapsed.'

Maggie sighed in exasperation – with herself – with her mother – with Nick Ingram. 'Don't you think I know that? Why do you think I don't trust anyone any more?'

Celia held her gaze for a moment, then looked away. 'I've often wondered,' she murmured. 'Sometimes I think it's bloody-mindedness, other times I think it's immaturity. Usually I put it down to the fact that I spoilt you as a child and made you vain.' Her eyes fastened on Maggie's again. 'You see it's the height of arrogance to question other people's motives when you consistently refuse to question your own. Yes, Martin was a conman but why did he pick on us as his victims? Have you ever wondered about that?'

'We had money.'

'Lots of people have money, darling. Few of them get defrauded in the way that we did. No,' she said with sudden firmness, 'I was conned because I was greedy, and you were conned because you took it for granted that men found you attractive. If you hadn't, you'd have questioned Martin's ridiculous habit of telling everyone he met how much he loved you. It was *so* American and *so* insincere, and I can't understand why any of us believed it.'

Maggie turned back to the window so that her mother wouldn't see her eyes. 'No,' she said unevenly. 'Neither can I – now.'

A gull swooped towards the shore and pecked at something white tumbling at the water's edge. Amused, Ingram watched it for a while, expecting it to take off again with a dead fish in its beak, but when it abandoned the sport and flapped away in disgust, screaming raucously, he walked down the waterline, curious about what the intermittent flash of white was that showed briefly between each wave. *A carrier bag caught in the rocks? A piece of cloth?* It ballooned unpleasantly as each swell invaded it, before rearing abruptly in a welter of spume as a larger wave flooded in.

Chapter Twenty

GALBRAITH LEANED FORWARD, folding his freckled hands under his chin. He looked completely unalarming, almost mild in fact, like a round-faced schoolboy seeking to make friends. He was quite an actor, like most policemen, and could change his mood as occasion demanded. He tempted Sumner to confide in him. 'Do you know Lulworth Cove, William?' he murmured in a conversational tone of voice.

The other man looked startled but whether from guilt or from the DI's abrupt switch of tack it was impossible to say. 'Yes.'

'Have you been there recently?'

'Not that I recall.'

'It's hardly the sort of thing you'd forget, is it?'

Sumner shrugged. 'It depends what you mean by recently. I sailed there several times in my boat, but that was years ago.'

'What about renting a caravan or a cottage? Maybe you've taken the family there on holiday?'

He shook his head. 'Kate and I only ever had one holiday and that was in a hotel in the Lake District. It was a disaster,' he said in weary recollection. 'Hannah wouldn't go to sleep so we had to sit in our room, night after night, watching the television to stop her screaming the place down and upsetting the other guests. We thought we'd wait until she was older before we tried again.'

It sounded convincing, and Galbraith nodded. 'Hannah's a bit of a handful, isn't she?'

'Kate managed all right.'

'Perhaps because she dosed her with sleeping drugs?'

Sumner looked wary. 'I don't know anything about that. You'd have to ask her doctor.'

'We already have. He says he's never prescribed any sedatives or hypnotics for either Kate or Hannah.'

'Well then.'

'You work in the business, William. You can probably get free samples of every drug on the market. And, let's face it, with all these conferences you go to, there can't be much about pharmaceutical drugs you don't know.'

'You're talking rubbish,' said Sumner, winking uncontrollably. 'I need a prescription like anyone else.'

Galbraith nodded again as if to persuade William that he believed him. 'Still . . . a difficult, demanding child wasn't what you signed up for when you got married, was it? At the very least it will have put a blight on your sex life.'

Sumner didn't answer.

'You must have thought you'd got yourself a good bargain at the beginning. A pretty wife who worshipped the ground you trod on. All right, you didn't have much in common with her, and fatherhood left a lot to be desired, but all in all life was rosy. The sex was good, you had a mortgage you could afford, the journey to work was a doddle, your mother was keeping tabs on your wife during the day, your supper was on the table when you came home of an evening, and you were free to go sailing whenever you wanted.' He paused. 'Then you moved to Lymington and things started to turn sour. I'm guessing Kate grew less and less interested in keeping you happy because she didn't need to pretend any more. She'd got what she wanted – no more supervision from her mother-in-law . . . a house of her own . . . respectability – all of which gave her the confidence to make a life for herself and Hannah which didn't include you.' He eyed the other man curiously. 'And suddenly it was your turn to be taken for granted. Is that when you began to suspect Hannah wasn't yours?'

Sumner surprised him by laughing. 'I've known since she was a few weeks old that she couldn't possibly be mine. Kate and I are blood group O, and Hannah's blood group A. That means her father has to be either blood group A or AB. I'm not a fool. I married a pregnant woman and I had no illusions about her, whatever you or my mother may think.'

'Did you challenge Kate with it?'

Sumner pressed a finger to his fluttering lid. 'It was hardly a challenge. I just showed her an Exclusions of Paternity table on the ABO system and explained how two blood group O parents can only produce a group O child. She was shocked to have been found out so easily but, as my only purpose in doing it was to show her I wasn't as gullible as she seemed to think I was, it never became an issue between us. I had no problem acknowledging Hannah as mine which is all Kate wanted.'

'Did she tell you who the father was?'

He shook his head. 'I didn't want to know. I assume it's someone I work with – or have worked with – but as she broke all contact with Pharmatec after she left, except for the odd visit from Polly Garrard, I knew the father didn't figure in her life any more.' He stroked the arm of his chair. 'You probably won't believe me, but I couldn't see the point of getting hot under the collar about someone who had become an irrelevance.'

He was right. Galbraith didn't believe him. 'Presumably the fact that Hannah isn't your child explains your lack of interest in her?'

Once again the man didn't answer and a silence lengthened between them.

'Tell me what went wrong when you moved to Lymington,' Galbraith said then.

'Nothing went wrong.'

'So you're saying that from day *one*' – he emphasized the word – 'marriage was like living with a landlady? That's a pretty unattractive proposition, isn't it?'

'It depends what you want,' said Sumner. 'Anyway, how would *you* describe a woman whose idea of an intellectual challenge was to watch a soap opera, who had no taste in anything, was so houseproud that she believed cleanliness was next to godliness, preferred overcooked sausages and baked beans to rare steak, and accounted voluntarily for every damn penny that either of us ever spent?'

There was a rough edge to his voice which to Galbraith's ears sounded more like guilt at exposing his wife's shortcomings than bitterness that she'd had them, and he had the impression that William couldn't make up his mind if he'd loved his wife or loathed her. But whether that made him guilty of her murder, Galbraith didn't know.

'If you despised her to that extent, why did you marry her?'

Sumner rested his head against the back of his chair and stared at the ceiling. 'Because the *quid pro quo* for helping her out of the hole she'd dug for herself was sex whenever I wanted it.' He turned to look at Galbraith, and his eyes were bright with unshed tears. 'That's all *I* was interested in. That's all any man's interested in. Isn't it? Sex on tap. Kate would have sucked me off twenty times a day if I'd told her to, just so long as I kept acknowledging Hannah as my daughter.'

The memory brought him little pleasure, apparently, because tears streamed in murky rivers down his cheeks while his uncontrollable lid winked . . . and winked . . .

It was an hour and a half before Ingram returned to Broxton House, carrying something wrapped in layers of cling film. Maggie saw him pass the kitchen window and went through the scullery to let him in. He was soaked to the skin and supported himself against the door jamb, head hanging in exhaustion.

'Did you find anything?' she asked him.

He nodded, lifting the bundle. 'I need to make a phone call but I don't want to drip all over your mother's floor. I presume you were carrying your mobile this morning, so can I borrow it?'

'Sorry, I wasn't. So no. I got it free two years ago in return for a year's rental, but it was so bloody expensive I declined to renew my subscription and I haven't used it in twelve months. It's in the flat somewhere.' She held the door wide. 'You'd better come in. There's an extension in the kitchen, and the quarry tiles won't hurt for getting water on them.' Her lips gave a brief twitch. 'They might even benefit. I dread to think when they last saw a mop.'

He padded after her, his shoes squelching as he walked. 'How did you phone me this morning if you didn't have a mobile?'

'I used Steve's,' she said, pointing to a Philips GSM on the kitchen table.

He pushed it to one side with the back of his finger and placed the cling film bundle beside it. 'What's it doing here?'

'I put it in my pocket and forgot about it,' she said. 'I only remembered it when it started ringing. It's rung five times since you left.'

'Have you answered it?'

'No. I thought you could deal with it when you came back.'

He moved across to the wall telephone and lifted it off its bracket. 'You're very trusting,' he murmured, punching in the number of the Kate Sumner incident room. 'Supposing I'd decided to let you and your mother stew in your own juice for a bit?'

'You wouldn't,' she said frankly. 'You're not the type.'

He was still wondering how to take that when he was put

through to Detective Superintendent Carpenter. 'I've fished a boy's T-shirt out of the sea, sir . . . almost certainly belonging to one of the Spender boys. It's got a Derby County FC logo on the front, and Danny claimed Harding stole it from him.' He listened for a moment. 'Yes, Danny could have dropped it by accident . . . I agree, it doesn't make Harding a paedophile.' He held the phone away from his ear as Carpenter's barking beat against his eardrums. 'No, I haven't found the rucksack yet, but as a matter of fact . . . only that I've a pretty good idea where it is.' More barking. 'Yes, I'm betting it's what he came back for . . .' He grimaced into the receiver. 'Oh, yes, sir, I'd say it's definitely in Chapman's Pool.' He glanced at his watch. 'The boatsheds in an hour. I'll meet you there.' He replaced the receiver, saw amusement at his discomfort in Maggie's eyes, and gestured abruptly towards the hall. 'Has the doctor been to see your mother?'

She nodded.

'Well?'

'He told her she was a fool not to take the paramedic's offer to have her admitted as an emergency this morning, then patted her on the head and gave her some painkillers.' Her lips twitched into another small smile. 'He also said she needs a Zimmer frame and wheelchair, and suggested I drive to the nearest Red Cross depot this afternoon and see what they can do for her.'

'Sounds sensible.'

'Of course it does, but since when did sense feature in my mother's life? She says if I introduce any such contraptions into her house, she won't use them and she'll never speak to me again. And she means it, too. She says she'd rather crawl on her hands and knees than give anyone the impression she's passed her sell-by date.' She gave a tired sigh. 'Ideas on a postcard, please, care of Broxton House Lunatic Asylum. What the hell am I supposed to do?'

'Wait,' he suggested.

'What for?'

'A miraculous cure or a request for a Zimmer frame. She's not stupid, Maggie. Logic will prevail once she gets over her irritation with you, me and the doctor. Meanwhile, be kind to her. She crippled herself for you this morning, and a little gratitude and TLC will probably have her on her feet quicker than anything.'

'I've already told her I couldn't have done it without her.'

He looked amused. 'Like mother like daughter, eh?'

'I don't understand.'

'*She* can't say sorry. *You* can't say thank you.'

Sudden light dawned. 'Oh, I see. So that's why you went off in a huff two hours ago. It was gratitude you wanted. How silly of me. I thought you were angry because I told you to mind your own business.' She wrapped her arms about her thin body and gave him a tentative smile. 'Well, thank you, Nick, I'm extremely grateful for your assistance.'

He tugged at his forelock. 'Much obliged I'm sure, Miss Jenner,' he said in a rolling burr. 'But a lady like you don't need to thank a man for doing his job.'

Her puzzled eyes searched his for a moment before it occurred to her he was taking the piss and her overwrought nerves snapped with a vengeance. 'Fuck off!' she said, landing a furious fist on the side of his jaw before marching into the hall and slamming the door behind her.

Two Dartmouth policemen listened with interest to what the Frenchman told them while his daughter stood in embarrassed silence beside him, fidgeting constantly with her hair. The man's English was good, if heavily accented, as he explained carefully and precisely where he and his boat had been the previous Sunday. He had come, he said, because he had read in the English newspapers that the woman who had been lifted off the shore had been murdered. He placed a copy of

Wednesday's *Telegraph* on the counter in case they didn't know which inquiry he was referring to. 'Mrs Kate Sumner,' he said. 'You are acquainted with this matter?' They agreed they were, so he produced a video cassette from a carrier bag and put it beside the newspaper. 'My daughter made a film of a man that day. You understand – I know nothing about this man. He may – how you say – be innocent. But I am anxious.' He pushed the video across the desk. 'It is not good what he is doing, so you play it. Yes? It is important, perhaps.'

Harding's mobile telephone was a sophisticated little item with the capacity to call abroad or be called from abroad. It required an SIM card (Subscriber Identification Module) and a PIN number to use it, but as both had been logged in, presumably by Harding himself, the phone was operational. If it hadn't been, Maggie wouldn't have been able to use it. The card had an extensive memory and, depending on how much the user programmed into it, could store phone numbers and messages, plus the last ten numbers dialled out and the last ten dialled in.

The screen was displaying '5 missed calls' and a 'messages waiting' sign. With a wary look towards the door into the hall, Ingram went into the Menu, located 'Voice mail' followed by 'Mail box', pressed the 'Call' button and held the receiver to his ear. He massaged his cheek tenderly while he listened, wondering if Maggie had any idea how powerful her punch was.

'*You have three new messages,*' said a disembodied female voice at the other end.

'*Steve?*' A lisping, lightweight – *foreign?* – voice, although Ingram couldn't tell if it was male or female. '*Where are you? I'm frightened. Please phone me. I've tried twenty times since Sunday.*'

'*Mr Harding?*' A man's voice, definitely foreign. '*This is the Hotel Angelique, Concarneau. If you wish us to keep your room, you must confirm your reservation by noon today, using a credit card. I regret that without such confirmation the reservation cannot be honoured.'*

'*Hi*,' said an Englishman's voice next. '*Where the fuck are you, you stupid bastard? You're supposed to be kipping here, for Christ's sake. Dammit, this is the address you've been bailed to and I swear to God I'll take you to the cleaners if you get me into any more trouble. Just don't expect me to keep my mouth shut next time. I warned you I'd have your stinking hide if you were playing me for a patsy. Oh, and in case you're interested, there's a sodding journalist nosing round who wants to know if it's true you've been questioned about Kate's murder. He's really bugging me, so get your arse back PDQ before I drop you in it up to your neck.'*

Ingram touched 'End' to disconnect, then went through the whole process again, jotting down bullet points on the back of a piece of paper which he took from a notepad under the wall telephone. Next he pressed the arrow button twice to scroll up the numbers of the last ten people who had dialled in. He discounted 'Voice mail' and made a note of the rest, together with the last ten calls Harding had made, the first of which was Maggie's call to him. For further good measure – *To hell with it! In for a penny in for a pound!* – he scrolled through the entries under 'Names' and took them down together with their numbers.

'Are you doing something illegal?' asked Maggie from the doorway.

He had been so engrossed he hadn't heard the door open, and he looked up with a guilty start. 'Not if DI Galbraith already has this information.' He flattened his palm and made a rocking motion. 'Probable infringement of Harding's rights under the Data Protection Act, if he hasn't. It depends whether the phone was on *Crazy Daze* when they searched it.'

'Won't Steven Harding know you've been playing his messages when you give it back to him? Our answerphone never replays the ones you've already listened to unless you rewind the tape.'

'Voice mail's different. You have to delete the messages if you don't want to keep hearing them.' He grinned. 'But if he's suspicious, let's just hope he thinks you buggered it up when you made your phone call.'

'Why drag me into it?'

'Because he'll know you phoned me. My number's in the memory.'

'Oh God,' she said in resignation. 'Are you expecting me to lie for you?'

'No.' He stood up, lacing his hands above his head and stretching his shoulder muscles under his damp clothes. He was so tall he could almost touch the ceiling and he stood like a Colossus in the middle of the kitchen, easily dominating a room that was big enough to house an entire family.

Watching him, Maggie wondered how she could ever have called him an overweight Neanderthal. It had been Martin's description, she remembered, and it galled her unbearably to think how tamely she had adopted it herself because it had raised a laugh among people she had once regarded as friends but whom she now avoided like the plague. 'Well, I will,' she said with sudden decision.

He shook his head as he lowered his arms. 'It wouldn't do me any good. You couldn't lie to save your life. And that's a compliment, by the way,' he said as she started to scowl, 'so there's no need to hit me again. I don't admire people who lie.'

'I'm sorry,' she said abruptly.

'No need to be. It was my fault. I shouldn't have teased you.' He started to gather the bits and pieces from the table.

'Where are you going now?'

'Back to my house to change, then down to the boatsheds at Chapman's Pool. But I'll look in again this afternoon before

I go to see Harding. As you so rightly pointed out, I need to take a statement from you.' He paused. 'We'll talk about this in detail later, but did you hear anything before he appeared?'

'Like what?'

'Shale falling?'

She shook her head. 'All I remember is how quiet it was. That's why he gave me such a fright. One minute I was on my own, the next he was crouching on the ground in front of me like a rabid dog. It was really peculiar. I don't know what he thought he was doing but there's a lot of scrub vegetation and bushes round there so I think he must have heard me coming and ducked down to hide.'

He nodded. 'What about his clothes? Were they wet?'

'No.'

'Dirty?'

'You mean before he bled all over them?'

'Yes.'

She shook her head again. 'I remember thinking that he hadn't shaved, but I don't remember thinking he was dirty.'

He stacked the cling film bundle, notes and phone into a pile and lifted them off the table. 'Okay. That's great. I'll take a statement this afternoon.' He held her gaze for a moment. 'You'll be all right,' he told her. 'Harding's not going to come back.'

'He wouldn't dare,' she said, clenching her fists.

'Not if he has any sense,' murmured Ingram, moving out of her range.

'Do you have any brandy in your house?'

The switch was so abrupt that he needed time to consider. 'Ye-es,' he murmured cautiously, fearing another assault if he dared to question why she was asking. He suspected four years of angry frustration had gone into her punch, and he wished she'd chosen Harding for target practice instead of himself.

'Can you lend me some?'

'Sure. I'll drop it in on my way back to Chapman's Pool.'

'If you give me a moment to tell Ma where I'm going, I'll come with you. I can walk back.'

'Won't she miss you?'

'Not for an hour or so. The painkillers have made her sleepy.'

Bertie was lying on the doorstep in the sunshine as Ingram drew the Jeep to a halt beside his gate. Maggie had never been inside Nick's little house but she had always resented the neatness of his garden. It was like a reproach to all his less organized neighbours with its beautifully clipped privet hedges and regimented hydrangeas and roses in serried ranks before the yellow-stone walls of the house. She often wondered where he found the time to weed and hoe when he spent most of his free hours on his boat, and in her more critical moments put it down to the fact that he was boring and compartmentalized his life according to some sensible duty roster.

The dog raised his shaggy head and thumped his tail on the mat before rising leisurely to his feet and yawning. 'So this is where he comes,' she said. 'I've often wondered. How long did it take you to train him, as a matter of interest?'

'Not long. He's a bright dog.'

'Why did you bother?'

'Because he's a compulsive digger, and I got fed up with having my garden destroyed,' he said prosaically.

'Oh God,' she said guiltily. 'Sorry. The trouble is he never takes any notice of me.'

'Does he need to?'

'He's *my* dog,' she said.

Ingram opened the Jeep door. 'Have you made that clear to him?'

'Of course I have. He comes home every night, doesn't he?'

He reached into the back for the stack of evidence. 'I wasn't questioning ownership,' he told her. 'I was questioning whether or not Bertie knows he's a dog. As far as he's concerned, he's the boss in your establishment. He gets fed first, sleeps on your sofa, licks out your dishes. I'll bet you even move over in bed in order to make sure he's more comfortable, don't you?'

She coloured slightly. 'What if I do? I'd rather have him in my bed than the weasel that used to be in it. In any case, he's the closest thing I've got to a hot-water bottle.'

Ingram laughed. 'Are you coming in or do you want me to bring the brandy out? I guarantee Bertie won't disgrace you. He has beautiful manners since I took him to task for wiping his bottom on my carpet.'

Maggie sat in indecision. She had never wanted to go inside because it would tell her things about him that she didn't want to know. At the very least it would be insufferably clean, she thought, and her bloody dog would shame her by doing exactly what he was told.

'I'm coming in,' she said defiantly.

Carpenter took a phone call from a Dartmouth police sergeant just as he was about to leave for Chapman's Pool. He listened to a description of what was on the Frenchman's video then asked: 'What does he look like?'

'Five eight, medium build, bit of a paunch, thinning dark hair.'

'I thought you said he was a young chap.'

'No. Mid-forties, at least. His daughter's fourteen.'

Carpenter's frown dug trenches out of his forehead. 'Not the bloody Frenchman,' he shouted, 'the toe-rag on the video!'

'Oh, sorry. Yes, he's young all right. Early twenties, I'd say. Longish dark hair, sleeveless T-shirt and cycling shorts. Muscles. Tanned. A handsome bugger, in fact. The kid who filmed him said she thought he looked like Jean-Claude Van

Damme. Mind you, she's mortified about it now, can't believe she didn't realize what he was up to, considering he's got a rod like a fucking salami. This guy could make a fortune in porno movies.'

'All right, all right,' said Carpenter testily. 'I get the picture. And you say he's wanking into a handkerchief?'

'Looks like it.'

'Could it be a child's T-shirt?'

'Maybe. It's difficult to tell. Matter of fact, I'm amazed the French geezer spotted what the bastard was up to. It's pretty discreet. It's only because his knob's so damn big that you can see anything at all. The first time I watched it I thought he was peeling an orange in his lap.' There was a belly laugh at the other end of the line. 'Still, you know what they say about the French. They're all wankers. So I guess our little geezer's done a spot of it himself and knew what to look for. Am I right or am I right?'

Carpenter, who spent all his holidays in France, cocked a finger and thumb at the telephone and pulled the trigger – bloody racist, he was thinking – but there was no trace of irritation in his voice when he spoke. 'You said the young man had a rucksack. Can you describe it for me?'

'Standard camping type. Green. Doesn't look as if it's got much in it.'

'Big?'

'Oh, yes. It's a full-size job.'

'What did he do with it?'

'Sat on it while he jerked himself off.'

'Where? Which part of Chapman's Pool? Eastern side? Western side? Describe the scenery for me.'

'Eastern side. The Frenchman showed me on the map. Your wanker was down on the beach below Emmetts Hill, facing out towards the Channel. Green slope behind him.'

'What did he do with the rucksack after he sat on it?'

'Can't say. The film ends.'

With a request to send the tape on by courier, together with the Frenchman's name, proposed itinerary for the rest of his holiday and address in France, Carpenter thanked the sergeant and rang off.

'Did you make this yourself?' asked Maggie, peering at the *Cutty Sark* in the bottle on the mantelpiece as Ingram came downstairs in uniform, buttoning the sleeves of his shirt.

'Yes.'

'I thought you must have done. It's like everything else in this house. So' – she waved her glass in the air – '*well behaved.*' She might have said masculine, minimal or monastic, in an echo of Galbraith's description of Harding's boat, but she didn't want to be rude. It was as she had predicted, insufferably clean, and insufferably boring as well. There was nothing to say this house belonged to an interesting personality, just yards of pallid wall, pallid carpet, pallid curtains and pallid upholstery, broken occasionally by an ornament on a shelf. It never occurred to her that he was tied to the house through his job but, even if it had, she would still have expected splashes of towering individualism among the uniformity.

He laughed. 'Do I get the impression you don't like it?'

'No, I do. It's – er—'

'Twee?' he suggested.

'Yes.'

'I made it when I was twelve.' He flexed his huge fingers under her nose. 'I couldn't do it now.' He straightened his tie. 'How's the brandy?'

'Very good.' She dropped into a chair. 'Does exactly what it's supposed to do. Hits the spot.'

He took her empty glass. 'When did you last drink alcohol?'

'Four years ago.'

'Shall I give you a lift home?'

245

'No.' She closed her eyes. 'I'm going to sleep.'

'I'll look in on your mother on my way back from Chapman's Pool,' he promised her, shrugging on his jacket. 'Meanwhile, don't encourage your dog to sit on my sofa. It's bad for both your characters.'

'What will happen if I do?'

'The same thing that happened to Bertie when he wiped his bottom on my carpet.'

Despite another day of brilliant sunshine, Chapman's Pool was empty. The south-westerly breeze had created an unpleasant swell, and nothing was more guaranteed to discourage visitors than the likelihood of being sick over their lunch. Carpenter and two detective constables followed Ingram away from the boatsheds towards an area marked out on the rocky shore with pieces of driftwood.

'We won't know until we see the video, of course,' said Carpenter, taking his bearings from the description the Dartmouth sergeant had given of where Harding had been sitting, 'but it looks about right. He was certainly on this side of the bay.' They were standing on a slab of rock at the shoreline and he touched a small pebble cairn with the toe of his shoe. 'And this is where you found the T-shirt?'

Ingram nodded as he squatted down and put his hand in the water that lapped against the base of the rock. 'But it was well and truly wedged. A gull had a go at getting it out, and failed, and I was saturated doing my retrieval act.'

'Is that important?'

'Harding was dry as a bone when I saw him so it can't have been the T-shirt he came back for. I think that's been here for days.'

'Mmm.' Carpenter pondered for a moment. 'Does fabric easily get wedged between rocks?'

Ingram shrugged. 'Anything can get wedged if a crab takes a fancy to it.'

'Mmm,' said Carpenter again. 'All right. Where's this rucksack?'

'It's only a guess, sir, and a bit of a flaky one at that,' said Ingram standing up.

'I'm listening.'

'Okay, well, I've been puzzling about the ruddy thing for days. He obviously didn't want it anywhere near a policeman or he'd have brought it down to the boatsheds on Sunday. By the same token it wasn't on his boat when you searched it – or not in my opinion anyway – and that suggests to me that it's incriminating in some way and he needed to get rid of it.'

'I think you're right,' said Carpenter. 'Harding wants us to believe he was carrying the black one we found on his boat, but the Dartmouth sergeant described the one on the video as green. So what's he done with it, eh? And what's he trying to hide?'

'It depends on whether the contents were valuable to him. If they *weren't*, then he'll have dropped it in the ocean on his way back to Lymington. If they *were*, he'll have left it some-where accessible but not too obvious.' Ingram shielded his eyes from the sun and pointed towards the slope behind them. 'There's been a mini-avalanche up there,' he said. 'I noticed it because it's just to the left of where Miss Jenner said Harding appeared in front of her. Shale's notoriously unstable – which is why these cliffs are covered in warnings – and it looks to me as though that fall's fairly recent.'

Carpenter followed his gaze. 'You think the rucksack's under it?'

'Put it this way, sir, I can't think of a quicker or more convenient way of burying something than to send an avalanche of shale over the top of it. It wouldn't be hard to do. Kick out a loose rock, and hey presto, you've got a convenient slide of loose cliff pouring over whatever it is you want to hide. No one's going to notice it. Slides like that happen every day. The Spender brothers set one off when they dropped their father's binoculars, and I can't help feeling that might have given Harding the idea.'

'Meaning he did it on Sunday?'

Ingram nodded.

'And came back this morning to make sure it hadn't been disturbed?'

'I suspect it's more likely he intended to retrieve it, sir.'

Carpenter brought his ferocious scowl to bear on the constable. 'Then why wasn't he carrying it when you saw him?'

'Because the shale's dried in the sunshine and become impacted. I think he was about to go looking for a spade when he ran into Miss Jenner by accident.'

'Is that your best suggestion?'

'Yes, sir.'

'You're a bit of a suggestion-junky, aren't you, lad?' said Carpenter, his frown deepening. 'I've got DI Galbraith chasing over half of Hampshire on the back of the suggestions you faxed through last night.'

'It doesn't make them wrong, sir.'

'It doesn't make them right either. We had a team scouring this area on Monday, and they didn't find a damn thing.'

Ingram jerked his head towards the next bay. 'They were searching Egmont Bight, sir, and with respect no one was interested in Steven Harding's movements at that point.'

'Mmm. These search teams cost money, lad, and I like a little more certainty before I commit taxpayers' money to guesses.' Carpenter stared out across the sea. 'I could understand him revisiting the scene of the crime to relive his excitement – it's the sort of thing a man like him might do – but you're saying he wasn't interested in that.'

Ingram had said no such thing, but he wasn't going to argue the point. For all he knew, the Superintendent was right anyway. Maybe that's exactly what Harding had come back for. His own avalanche theory looked horribly insignificant beside the magnitude of a psychopath gloating over the scene of murder.

'Well?' demanded Carpenter.

The constable smiled self-consciously. 'I brought my own spade, sir,' he said. 'It's in the back of my Jeep.'

Chapter Twenty-one

GALBRAITH STOOD UP and walked across to one of the windows which overlooked the road. The crowd of earlier had dispersed, although a couple of elderly women still chatted on the pavement, glancing occasionally towards Langton Cottage. He watched them for several minutes in silence, envying the normality of their lives. How often did they have to listen to the dirty little secrets of murder suspects? Sometimes, when he heard the confessions of men like Sumner, he thought of himself in the role of a priest offering a kind of benediction merely by listening, but he had neither the authority nor the desire to forgive sins and invariably felt diminished by being the recipient of their furtive confidences.

He turned to face the man. 'So a more accurate description of your marriage would be to say it was a form of sexual slavery? Kate was so desperate to make sure her daughter grew up in the sort of security she herself never enjoyed that you were able to blackmail her?'

'I said she *would* have done it, not that she did or that I ever asked her to.' Triumph crept stealthily into Sumner's eyes as if he had won an important point. 'There's no median way with you, is there? Half an hour ago you were treating me like a cretin because you thought Kate had suckered me into marrying her. Now you're accusing me of sexual slavery because I got so tired of her lies about Hannah that I pointed out – very mildly, as a matter of fact – that I knew the truth. Why would I buy her this house if she had no say in the relationship? You said yourself I was better off in Chichester.'

'I don't know. Tell me.'

'Because I loved her.'

Impatiently, Galbraith shook his head. 'You describe your marriage as a war zone, then expect me to swallow garbage like that. What was the real reason?'

'That *was* the real reason. I loved my wife, and I'd have given her whatever she wanted.'

'At the same time as blackmailing her into giving you blow jobs whenever you fancied it?' The atmosphere in the room was stifling, and he felt himself grow cruel in response to the cruelty of Kate and William's marriage. He couldn't rid himself of memories of the tiny, pregnant woman on the pathologist's slab and Dr Warner's casual raising of her hand in order to shake it to and fro in convincing demonstration that the fingers were broken. The noise of grating bone had lodged in Galbraith's head like a maggot, and his dreams were of charnel houses. 'You see, I can't make up my mind whether you loved or hated her. Or maybe it was a bit of both? A love/hate relationship that turned sour?'

Sumner shook his head. He looked defeated suddenly, as if whatever game he was playing was no longer worth the candle. Galbraith wished he understood what William was trying to achieve through his answers, and studied the man in perplexity. William was either extremely frank, or extremely skilful at clouding an issue. On the whole he gave the impression of honesty, and it occurred to Galbraith that, in a ham-fisted way, he was trying to demonstrate that his wife was the sort of woman who could easily have driven a man to rape her. He remembered what James Purdy had said about Kate. '*No one has ever done to me what Kate did that night . . . It's the sort of thing most men dream of . . . I can only describe Kate as a fever in the blood . . .*'

'Did she love you, William?'

'I don't know. I never asked her.'

'Because you were afraid she'd say no?'

'The opposite. I knew she'd say yes.'

'And you didn't want her to lie to you?'

The man nodded.

'I don't like being lied to,' murmured Galbraith, his eyes fixing on Sumner's. 'It means the other person assumes you're so stupid you'll believe anything they say. Did she lie to you about having an affair?'

'She wasn't having an affair.'

'She certainly visited Steven Harding on board his boat,' Galbraith pointed out. 'Her fingerprints are all over it. Did you find out about that? Maybe you suspected that the baby she was carrying wasn't yours? Maybe you were afraid she was going to foist another bastard on to you?'

Sumner stared at his hands.

'Did you rape her?' Galbraith went on remorselessly. 'Was that part of the *quid pro quo* for acknowledging Hannah as your daughter? The right to take Kate whenever you wanted her?'

'Why would I want to rape her when I didn't need to?' he asked.

'I'm only interested in a yes or a no, William.'

His eyes flashed angrily. 'Then no, dammit. I never raped my wife.'

'Maybe you dosed her with Rohypnol to make her more compliant?'

'No.'

'Then tell me why Hannah's so sexually aware?' Galbraith said next. 'Did you and Kate perform in front of her?'

More anger. 'That's revolting.'

'Yes or no, William.'

'No.' The word came out in a strangled sob.

'You're lying, William. Half an hour ago, you described

how you had to sit with her in a hotel bedroom because she wouldn't stop crying. I think that happened at home as well. I think sex with Kate involved Hannah as an audience because you got so fed up with Hannah being given as the excuse for the endless brushes off that you insisted on doing it in front of her. Am I right?'

He buried his face in his hands and rocked himself to and fro. 'You don't know what it's like . . . she wouldn't leave us alone . . . she never sleeps . . . pester, pester all the time . . . Kate used her as a shield . . .'

'Is that a yes?'

The answer was a whisper of sound. 'Yes.'

'WPC Griffiths said you went into Hannah's room last night. Do you want to tell me why?'

Another whisper. 'You won't believe me if I do.'

'I might.'

Sumner raised a tear-stained face. 'I wanted to look at her,' he said in despair. 'She's all I've got left to remind me of Kate.'

Carpenter lit a cigarette as Ingram's careful spadework disclosed the first strap of a rucksack. 'Good work, lad,' he said approvingly. He dispatched one of the DCs to his car to collect some disposable gloves and polythene sheeting, then watched as Ingram continued to remove the shale from around the crumpled canvas.

It took Ingram another ten minutes to release the object completely and transfer it to the polythene sheet. It was a heavy-duty green camper's rucksack, with a waist strap for extra support and loops underneath for taking a tent. It was old and worn, and the integral backframe had been cut out for some reason, leaving frayed canvas edges between the stitched grooves that had contained it. The frays were old ones, however, and whatever had persuaded the owner to remove the frame was clearly ancient history. It sat on the sheeting, collapsed in on itself under the weight of its straps, and whatever it contained took up less than a third of its bulk.

Carpenter instructed one detective constable to seal each item in a forensic bag as he took it out and the other to note what it was, then he squatted beside the rucksack and carefully undid the buckles with gloved fingertips, flipping back the flap. 'Item,' he dictated. 'One pair of 20×60 binoculars, name worn away, possibly Optikon . . . one bottle of mineral water, Volvic . . . three empty crisp packets, Smith's . . . one baseball cap, New York Yankees . . . one blue and white checked shirt – men's – made by River Island . . . one pair of cream cotton trousers – men's – also made by River Island . . . one pair of brown safari-style boots, size seven.'

He felt inside the pockets and took out some rancid orange peel, more empty crisp packets, an opened packet of Camel cigarettes with a lighter tucked in among them, and a small quantity of what appeared to be cannabis, wrapped in cling film. He squinted up at the three policemen.

'Well? What do you make of this little lot? What's so incriminating about it all that Nick mustn't know he had it?'

'The C,' said one. 'He didn't want to be caught in possession.'

'Maybe.'

'God knows,' said the other.

The Superintendent stood up. 'What about you, Nick? What do you think?'

'I'd say the shoes are the most interesting item, sir.'

Carpenter nodded. 'Too small for Harding, who's a good six foot, and too big for Kate Sumner. So what's he doing carrying a pair of size-seven shoes round with him?'

No one volunteered an answer.

*

DI Galbraith was on his way out of Lymington when Carpenter phoned through instructions to locate Tony Bridges and put the 'little bastard' through the wringer. 'He's been holding out on us, John,' he declared, detailing the contents of Harding's rucksack, what was on the Frenchman's video and repeating verbatim the messages that Ingram had taken from the voice mail. 'Bridges *must* know more than he's been telling us so arrest him on conspiracy if necessary. Find out why and when Harding was planning to leave for France, and get a fix on the wanker's sexual orientation if you can. It's all bloody odd, frankly.'

'What happens if I can't find Bridges?'

'He was in his house two or three hours ago because the last message came from his number. He's a teacher, don't forget, so he won't have gone to work, not unless he has a holiday job. Campbell's advice is: check the pubs.'

'Will do.'

'How did you get on with Sumner?'

Galbraith thought about it. 'He's cracking up,' he said. 'I felt sorry for him.'

'Less of a dead cert then?'

'Or more,' said Galbraith dryly. 'It depends on your viewpoint. She was obviously having an affair which he knew about. I think he *wanted* to kill her . . . which is probably why he's cracking up.'

Fortunately for Galbraith, Tony Bridges was not only at home but stoned out of his head into the bargain. So much so that he was completely naked when he came to the front door. Galbraith had momentary qualms about putting anyone in his condition through Carpenter's 'wringer', but they were only momentary. In the end the only thing that matters to a policeman is that witnesses tell the truth.

'I told the stupid sod you'd check up on him,' Bridges said garrulously, leading the way down the corridor into the chaotic sitting room. 'I mean you don't play silly buggers with the filth, not unless you're a complete moron. His problem is he won't take advice – never listens to a word I say. He reckons I sold out and says my opinions don't count for shit any more.'

'Sold out to what?' asked Galbraith, picking his way towards a vacant chair and remembering that Harding was said to favour nudity on board *Crazy Daze*. He wondered gloomily if nakedness had suddenly become an essential part of youth culture, and hoped not. He didn't much fancy the idea of police cells full of smackheads with hairless chests and acne on their bottoms.

'The establishment,' said Bridges, sinking cross-legged on to the floor and retrieving a half-smoked spliff from an ashtray in front of him. 'Regular employment. A salary.' He proffered the joint. 'Want some?'

Galbraith shook his head. 'What sort of employment?' He had read all the reports on Harding and his friends, knew everything there was to know about Bridges, but it didn't suit him at the moment to reveal it.

'Teaching,' the young man declared with a shrug. He was too stoned – or *appeared* to be too stoned, as Galbraith was cynical enough to remind himself – to remember that he had already given the police this information before. 'Okay the pay's not brilliant, but, hell, the holidays are good. And it's got to be better than flaunting your arse in front of some two-bit photographer. The trouble with Steve is he doesn't like kids much. He's had to work with some right little bastards and it's put him off.' He lapsed into contented silence with his joint.

Galbraith assumed a surprised expression. 'You're a teacher?'

'That's right.' Bridges squinted through the smoke. 'And don't go getting hot under the collar. I'm a recreational cannabis user and I've no more desire to share my habit with children than my headmaster has to share his whisky.'

The excuse was so simplistic and so well tutored by the cannabis lobby that it brought a smile to the DI's face. There were better arguments for legalization, he always thought, but your average user was either too thick or too high to produce them. 'Okay, okay,' he said, raising his hands in surrender. 'This isn't my patch so I don't need the lecture.'

'Sure you do. You lot are all the same.'

'I'm more interested in Steve's pornography. I gather you don't approve of it?'

A closed expression tightened the young man's features. 'It's cheap filth. I'm a teacher. I don't like that kind of crap.'

'What kind of crap is it? Describe it to me.'

'What's to describe? He's got a todger the size of the Eiffel Tower and he likes to display it.' He shrugged. 'But that's his problem, not mine.'

'Are you sure about that?'

Bridges squinted painfully through the smoke from his spliff. 'What's that supposed to mean?'

'We've been told you live in his shadow.'

'Who by?'

'Steve's parents.'

'You don't want to believe anything they say,' he said dismissively. 'They stood in judgement on me ten years ago, and have never changed their opinion since. They think I'm a bad influence.'

Galbraith chuckled. 'And are you?'

'Let's put it this way, *my* parents think Steve's a bad influence. We got into a bit of trouble when we were younger, but it's water under the bridge now.'

'So what do you teach?' Galbraith asked, looking around the room and wondering how anyone could live in such squalor. More interestingly, how could anyone so rank boast a girlfriend? Was Bibi as squalid?

257

Campbell's description of the set-up after his interview with Bridges on Monday had been pithy. 'It's a pit,' he said. 'The bloke's spaced out, the house stinks, he's shacked up with a slapper who looks as if she's slept with half the men in Lymington, and he's a teacher for Christ's sake.'

'Chemistry.' He sneered at Galbraith's expression, misinterpreting it. 'And, yes, I do know how to synthesize lysergic acid diethylamide. I also know how to blow up Buckingham Palace. It's a useful subject, chemistry. The trouble is' – he broke off to draw pensively on his spliff – 'the people who teach it are so bloody boring they turn the kids off long before they ever get to the interesting bits.'

'But not you?'

'No. I'm good.'

Galbraith could believe it. Rebels, however flawed, were always charismatic to youth. 'Your friend is in Poole hospital,' he told the young man. 'He was attacked by a dog on the Isle of Purbeck this morning and had to be shipped out by helicopter to have his arm stitched.' He looked at Bridges enquiringly. 'Any idea what he was doing there? In view of the fact he was bailed to this address and presumably you have some knowledge of what he gets up to.'

'Sorry, mate, that's where you're wrong. Steve's a closed book to me.'

'You said you warned him I'd come checking.'

'Not you personally. I don't know you from Adam. I told him the filth would come. That's different.'

'Still, if you had to warn him, Tony, then you must have known he was about to leg it. So where was he planning to go and what did he plan to do?'

'I told you. The guy's a closed book to me.'

'I thought you were at school together.'

'We've grown apart.'

'Doesn't he doss here when he's not on his boat?'

'Not often.'

'What about his relationship with Kate?'

Bridges shook his head. 'Everything I know about her is in my statement,' he said virtuously. 'If I knew anything else I'd tell you.'

Galbraith looked at his watch. 'We've got a bit of a problem here, son,' he said affably. 'I'm on a tight schedule so I can only give you another thirty seconds.'

'To do what, mate?'

'Tell the truth.' He unclipped his handcuffs from his belt.

'Pull the other one,' scoffed Bridges. 'You're not going to arrest me.'

'Too right I am. And I'm a hard bastard, Tony. When I arrest a lying little toe-rag like you, I take him out just as he is, never mind he's got a bum like a pizza and his prick's shrunk in the fucking wash.'

Bridges gave a throaty chuckle. 'The Press would crucify you. You can't drag a naked guy through the streets for illegal possession. It's hardly even a crime any more.'

'Try me.'

'Go on then.'

Galbraith snapped one bracelet on to his own wrist, then leaned forward and snapped the other on to Tony's. 'Anthony Bridges, I am arresting you on suspicion of conspiracy in the rape and murder last Saturday night of Mrs Kate Sumner of Langton Cottage and the grievous bodily assault this morning of Miss Margaret Jenner of Broxton House.' He stood up and started walking towards the door, dragging Bridges behind him. 'You do not have to say anything but it may harm your defence—'

'Shit!' said the young man stumbling to his feet. 'This is a joke, right?'

'No joke.' The DI twitched the spliff out of the young man's fingers and flicked it, still alight, into the corridor. 'The reason Steven Harding was attacked by a dog this morning is because he attempted to assault another woman in the same place that Kate Sumner died. Now you can either tell me what you know, or you can accompany me to Winfrith where you will be formally charged and interviewed on tape.' He looked the man up and down, and laughed. 'Frankly, I couldn't give a toss either way. It'll save me time if you talk to me now, but' – he shook his head regretfully – 'I'd hate your neighbours to miss the fun. It must be hell living next door to you.'

'That spliff's going to set my house on fire!'

Galbraith watched the joint smoulder gently on the wooden floorboards. 'It's too green. You're not curing it properly.'

'You'd know, of course.'

'Trust me.' He yanked Bridges down the corridor. 'Where were we? Oh, yes. It may harm your defence if you do not mention, when questioned, something you later rely on in court.' He pulled open the door and ushered the man outside. 'Anything you do say may be given in evidence.' He prodded Bridges on to the pavement in front of a startled old lady with fluffy white hair and eyes as big as golf balls behind pebble spectacles. 'Morning, ma'am,' he said politely.

Her mouth gaped.

'I've parked behind Tesco's,' he told Bridges, 'so it'll probably be quicker if we go up the High Street.'

'You can't take me up the High Street like this. Tell him, Mrs Crane.'

The elderly woman leaned forward, putting a hand behind her ear. 'Tell him what, dear?'

'Oh, Jesus! Never mind! Forget it!'

'I'm not sure I can,' she murmured in a confidential tone. 'Did you know you were naked?'

'Of course I know!' he shouted into her deaf ear. 'The police are denying me my rights and you're a witness to it.'

'That's nice. I've always wanted to be a witness to something.' Her eyes brimmed with sudden amusement. 'I'll tell my husband about it. He'll be pleased as punch. He's been saying for years that the only thing that happens when you burn the candle at both ends is the wick gets smaller.' She gave a joyful laugh as she moved on. 'And, you know, I always thought it was a joke.'

Galbraith grinned after her. 'What do you want me to do with your front door?' he asked, grabbing the handle. 'Slam it shut?'

'Jesus no!' Bridges lurched backwards to stop the door closing. 'I haven't got a key for Christ's sake.'

'Losing your nerve already?'

'I could sue you for this.'

'No chance. This was your choice, remember. I explained that if I had to arrest you I would take you out as you were and your response was: Go on then.'

Bridges looked wildly up the road as a man rounded the corner, and Galbraith was rewarded with a scrambling stampede for the safety of the corridor. He shut the door and stood with his back to it, halting further flight by a jerk on the handcuffs. 'Right. Shall we start again? Why did Steve go back to Chapman's Pool this morning?'

'I don't know. I didn't even know he was there.' His eyes widened as Galbraith reached for the door handle again. 'Listen, dickhead, that guy coming up the street's a journalist, and he's been pestering me all morning about Steve. If I'd known where the bastard was I'd have sent the bloke after him but I can't even get him to answer his mobile.' He jerked his head towards the sitting room. 'At least let's get out of earshot,' he muttered. 'He's probably listening at the door and you don't want the Press on your back any more than I do.'

Galbraith released the handcuffs on his own wrist and followed Bridges into the sitting room again, treading on the spliff as he went. 'Tell me about the relationship between Steve and Kate,' he said, resuming his seat. 'And make it convincing, Tony,' he added, taking his notebook from his pocket with a sigh, 'because A: I'm knackered; B: you're getting up my nose; and C: it's completely immaterial to me if your name is plastered across the newspapers tomorrow morning as a probable suspect on a rape and murder charge.'

'I never did understand the attraction. I only met her once and, as far as I'm concerned, she's the most boring woman I've ever come across. It was in a pub one Friday lunchtime, and all she could do was sit and look at Steve as if he were Leonardo DiCaprio. Mind you, when she started talking, it was even worse. God, she was stupid! Having a conversation with her was like listening to paint dry. I think she must have lived on a diet of soap operas because whatever I said reminded her of something that had happened in *Neighbours* or *EastEnders*, and it got on my tits after a while. I asked Steve later what the hell he thought he was doing, and he laughed and said he wasn't interested in her for her conversation. He reckoned she had a dream of an arse, and that was all that mattered. To be honest, I don't think he ever intended it to get as serious as it did. She met him in the street one day after the incident with Hannah's buggy, and invited him back to her house. He said it was all pretty mind-blowing. One minute he was struggling to find something to talk about over a coffee in the kitchen, and the next she was climbing all over him. He said the only bad part was that the kid sat in a highchair watching them do it because Kate said Hannah would scream her head off if she tried to take her out.

'As far as Steve was concerned, that was it. That's what he told me anyway. Wham, bam, thank you, ma'am, and bye-bye. So I was a bit surprised when he asked if he could bring her here on a couple of occasions in the autumn term. It was during the day while her husband was at work so I never saw her. Other times, they did it on his boat or in her house, but mostly they did it in his Volvo estate. He'd drive her out into the New Forest and they'd dose the kid with paracetamol so she'd sleep on the front seat while they set to in the back. All in all it went on for about two months until he started to get bored. The trouble was Kate had nothing going for her except her arse. She didn't drink, she didn't smoke, she didn't sail, she had no sense of humour and all she wanted was for Steve to get a part in *EastEnders*. It was pathetic really. I think it was the ultimate dream for her, to get hitched to a soap star and swan around being photographed on his arm.

'In all honesty, I don't think it ever occurred to her that he was only balling her because she was available and didn't cost him a penny. He said she was completely gobsmacked when he told her he'd had enough and didn't want to see her again. That's when she turned nasty. I guess she'd been conning idiots like her husband for so long it really pissed her off to find she'd been taken for a ride by a younger guy. She rubbed crap all over the sheets in his cabin, then she started setting off his car alarm and smearing shit all over his car. Steve got incredibly uptight about it. Everything he touched had crap on it. What really bugged him was his dinghy. He came down one Friday and found the bottom ankle-deep in water and slushy turds. He said she must have been saving them up for weeks. Anyway, that's when he started talking about going to the police.

'I told him it was a crazy idea. If you get the filth involved, I said, you'll never hear the end of it. And it won't be just Kate who's after you, it'll be William, too. You can't go round sleeping with other guys' wives and expect them to turn a blind eye. I told him to cool down and move his car to another parking place. So he said, what about his dinghy? And I said I'd lend him one that she wouldn't recognize. And that was it. Simple. Problem sorted. As far as I know he didn't have any more aggro from her.'

It was a while before Galbraith responded. He had been listening attentively, and making notes, and he finished writing before he said anything. 'Did you lend him a dinghy?' he asked.

'Sure.'

'What did it look like?'

Bridges frowned. 'The same as any dinghy. Why do you want to know that?'

'Just interested. What colour was it?'

'Black.'

'Where did you get it from?'

He started to pluck Rizla papers from their packet and make a patchwork quilt of them on the floor. 'A mail order catalogue, I think. It's the one I had before I bought my new rib.'

'Has Steve still got it?'

He hesitated before shaking his head. 'I wouldn't know, mate. Wasn't it on *Crazy Daze* when you searched it?'

Thoughtfully, the DI tapped his pencil against his teeth. He recalled Carpenter's words of Wednesday: '*I didn't like him. He's a cocky little bastard, and a damn sight too knowledgeable about police interviews.*' 'Okay,' he said next. 'Let's go back to Kate. You say the problem was sorted. What happened then?'

'Nothing. That's it. End of story. Unless you count the fact that she ends up dead on a beach in Dorset the weekend Steve just happens to be there.'

'I do. I also count the fact that her daughter was found wandering along a main road approximately two hundred yards from where Steve's boat was moored.'

'It was a set up,' said Bridges. 'You should be giving William the third degree. He had far more reason to murder Kate than Steve did. She was two-timing him, wasn't she?'

Galbraith shrugged. 'Except that William didn't hate his wife, Tony. He knew what she was like when he married her and it made no difference to him. Steve, on the other hand, had got himself into a mess and didn't know how to get out of it.'

'That doesn't make him a murderer.'

'Perhaps he thought he needed an ultimate solution.'

Bridges shook his head. 'Steve's not like that.'

'And William Sumner is?'

'I wouldn't know. I've never met the bloke.'

'According to your statement you and Steve had a drink with him one evening.'

'Okay. Correction. I don't *know* the bloke. I stayed fifteen minutes tops and exchanged maybe half a dozen words with him.'

Galbraith steepled his fingers in front of his mouth and studied the young man. 'But you seem to know a lot about him,' he said. 'Kate, too, despite only meeting each of them once.'

Bridges returned his attention to his patchwork quilt, sliding the papers into different positions with the balls of his fingers. 'Steve talks a lot.'

Galbraith seemed to accept this explanation because he gave a nod. 'Why was Steve planning to go to France this week?'

'I didn't know he was.'

'He had a reservation at a hotel in Concarneau which was cancelled this morning when he failed to confirm it.'

Bridges' expression became suddenly wary. 'He's never mentioned it.'

'Would you expect him to?'

'Sure.'

'You said you and he had grown apart,' Galbraith reminded him.

'Figure of speech, mate.'

A look of derision darkened the Inspector's eyes. 'Okay, last question. Where's Steve's lock-up, Tony?'

'What lock-up?' asked the other guilelessly.

'All right. Let me put it another way. Where does he store the equipment off his boat when he's not using it? His dinghy and his outboard, for example.'

'All over the place. Here. The flat in London. The back of his car.'

Galbraith shook his head. 'No oil spills,' he said. 'We've

searched them all.' He smiled amiably. 'And don't try and tell me an outboard doesn't leak when it's laid on its side because I won't believe you.'

Bridges scratched the side of his jaw but didn't say anything.

'You're not his keeper, son,' murmured Galbraith kindly, 'and there's no law that says when your friend digs a hole for himself you have to get into it with him.'

The man pulled a wry face. 'I did warn him, you know. I said he'd do better to volunteer information rather than have it dragged out of him piecemeal. He wouldn't listen, though. He has this crazy idea he can control everything when the truth is he's never been able to control a damn thing from the first day I met him. Talk about a loose cannon. Sometimes, I wish I'd never met the stupid bugger because I'm sick to death of telling lies for him.' He shrugged. 'But, hey! He *is* my friend.'

Galbraith's boyish face creased into a smile. The young man's sincerity was about as credible as a Ku Klux Klan assertion that it wasn't an association of racists, and he was reminded of the expression: with friends like this who needs enemies? He glanced idly about the room. There were too many discrepancies, he thought, particularly in relation to fingerprint evidence, and he felt he was being steered in a direction he didn't want to go. He wondered why Bridges thought that was necessary.

Because he knew Harding was guilty? Or because he knew he wasn't?

Chapter Twenty-two

A CALL FROM Dorsetshire Constabulary to the manager of the Hotel Angelique in Concarneau, a pretty seaside town in southern Brittany, revealed that Mr Steven Harding had telephoned on 8 August, requesting a double room for three nights from Saturday, 16 August for himself and Mrs Harding. He had given his mobile telephone as the contact number, saying he would be travelling the coast of France by boat during the week 11–17 August and could not be sure of his exact arrival date. He had agreed to confirm the reservation not less than twenty-four hours prior to his arrival. In the absence of any such confirmation, and with rooms in demand, the manager had left a message with Mr Harding's telephone answering service and had cancelled the reservation when Mr Harding failed to return his call. He was not acquainted with Mr Harding and was unable to say if Mr or Mrs Harding had stayed in the hotel before. Where exactly was his hotel in Concarneau? Two streets back from the waterfront, but within easy walking distance of the shops, the sea, and the lovely beaches.

And the marinas, too, of course.

A complete check of the numbers listed in Harding's mobile telephone, which had been unavailable to the police at the time of his arrest because it had been under a pile of newspapers in Bob Winterslow's house, produced a series of names already known and contacted by the investigators. Only one call remained a mystery, either because the subscriber had deliberately withheld the number or because it had been routed through an exchange – possibly a foreign one – which meant the SIM card had been unable to record it.

'*Steve? Where are you? I'm frightened. Please phone me. I've tried twenty times since Sunday.*'

Before he returned to Winfrith, Detective Superintendent Carpenter took Ingram aside for a briefing. He had spent much of the last hour with his telephone clamped to his ear, while the PC and the two DCs continued to dig into the shale slide and scour the shoreline in a fruitless search for further evidence. He had watched their efforts through thoughtful eyes while jotting the various pieces of information that came through to him into his notebook. He was unsurprised by their failure to find anything else. The sea, as he had learnt from the coastguards' descriptions of how bodies vanished without trace and were never seen again, was a friend to murderers.

'Harding's being discharged from Poole hospital at five,' he told the constable, 'but I'm not ready to talk to him yet. I need to see the Frenchman's video and question Tony Bridges before I go anywhere near him.' He clapped the tall man on the back. 'You were right about the lock-up, by the way. He's been using a garage near the Lymington yacht club. John Galbraith's on his way there now to have a look at it. What I need you to do, lad, is nail our friend Steve for the assault on Miss Jenner and hold him on ice till tomorrow morning. Keep it simple – make sure he thinks he's only being arrested for the assault. Can you do that?'

'Not until I've taken a statement from Miss Jenner, sir.'

Carpenter looked at his watch. 'You've got two and a half hours. Pin her to her story. I don't want her weaselling out because she doesn't want to get involved.'

'I can't force her, sir.'

'No one's asking you to,' said Carpenter irritably.

'And if she isn't as amenable as you hope?'

'Then use some charm,' said the Superintendent, thrusting his frown under Ingram's nose. 'I find it works wonders.'

'The house belongs to my grandfather,' said Bridges, directing Galbraith to pass the yacht club and take the road to the right which was lined with pleasant detached houses set back behind low hedges. It was at the wealthier end of town, not far from where the Sumners lived in Rope Walk, and Galbraith realized that Kate must have passed Tony's grandfather's house whenever she walked into town. He realized, too, that Tony must come from a 'good' family, and he wondered how they viewed their rebellious offspring and if they ever visited his shambolic establishment. 'Grandpa lives on his own,' Tony went on. 'He can't see to drive any more so he lends me the garage to store my rib.' He indicated an entrance a hundred yards farther on. 'In here. Steve's stuff is at the back.' He glanced at the DI as they drew to a halt in the small driveway. 'Steve and I have the only keys.'

'Is that important?'

Bridges nodded. 'Grandpa hasn't a clue what's in there.'

'It won't help him if it's drugs,' said Galbraith unemotionally, opening his door. 'You'll all be for the high jump, never mind how blind, deaf or dumb any of you are.'

'No drugs,' said Bridges firmly. 'We never deal.'

Galbraith shook his head in cynical disbelief. 'You couldn't afford to smoke the amount you do without dealing,' he said in a tone that brooked no disagreement. 'It's a fact of life. A teacher's salary couldn't fund a habit like yours.' The garage was detached from the house and set back twenty yards from it. Galbraith stood looking at it for a moment before glancing up the road towards the turning into Rope Walk. 'Who comes here the most?' he asked idly. 'You or Steve?'

'Me,' said the young man readily enough. 'I take my rib out two or three times a week. Steve just uses it for storage.'

Galbraith gestured towards the garage. 'Lead the way.' As they walked towards it, he caught the twitch of a curtain in one of the downstairs windows, and he wondered if Grandpa Bridges was quite as ignorant about what went into his garage as Tony claimed. The old, he thought, were a great deal more curious than the young. He stood back while the young man unlocked the double doors and pulled them wide. The entire front was taken up with a twelve-foot orange rib on a trailer but, when Tony pulled it out, an array of imported but clearly illicit goods was revealed at the back – neat stacks of cardboard boxes with VIN DE TABLE stencilled prominently on them, trays of Stella Artois lager, wrapped in polythene, and shelves covered in multi-pack cartons of cigarettes. Well, well, thought Galbraith with mild amusement, did Tony really expect him to believe that good old-fashioned smuggling of 'legal' contraband was the worst crime either he or his friend had ever been engaged in? The screed floor interested him more. It was still showing signs of damp where someone had hosed it down, and he wondered what had been washed away in the process.

'What's he trying to do?' he asked. 'Stock an entire off-licence? He's going to have a job persuading Customs and Excise this is for his own use.'

'It's not that bad,' protested Bridges. 'Listen, the guys in Dover bring in more than this every day via the ferries. They're coining it in. It's a stupid law. I mean, if the Government can't get its act together to bring down the duty on liquor and fags to the same level as the rest of Europe, then of course guys like Steve are going to do a bit of smuggling. Stands to reason. Everyone does it. You sail to France and you're tempted, simple as that.'

'And you end up in jail when you get busted. Simple as that,' said the DI sardonically. 'Who's funding him? You?'

Bridges shook his head. 'He's got a contact in London who buys it off him.'

'Is that where he takes it from here?'

'He borrows a mate's van and ships it up about once every two months.'

Galbraith traced a line in the dust on top of an opened box lid, then idly flipped it back. The bottoms of all the boxes in contact with the floor showed a tidemark where water had saturated them. 'How does he get it ashore from his boat?' he asked, lifting out a bottle of red table wine and reading the label. 'Presumably he doesn't bring it in by dinghy or someone would have noticed?'

'As long as it doesn't look like a case of wine there isn't a problem.'

'What *does* it look like?'

The young man shrugged. 'Something ordinary. Rubbish bags, dirty laundry, duvets. If he sticks a dozen bottles into socks to stop them rattling then packs them in his rucksack no one gives him a second glance. They're used to him transporting stuff to and from his boat – he's been working on it long enough. Other times he moors up to a pontoon and uses a marina trolley. People pile all sorts into them at the end of a weekend. I mean if you shove a few trays of Stella Artois down a sleeping bag, who's going to notice? More to the point, who's going to care? Everyone stocks up at the hypermarkets in France before they come home.'

Galbraith made a rough count of the wine boxes. 'There's six-hundred-odd bottles of wine here. It'd take him hours to move these a dozen at a time, not to mention the lager and the fags. Are you seriously saying no one's ever questioned why he's plying to and fro in a dinghy with a rucksack?'

'That's not how he shifts the bulk of it. I was only pointing out that it's not as difficult to bring stuff off boats as you seem to think it is. He moves most of it at night. There are hundreds of places along the coast you can make a drop as long as there's someone to meet you.'

'You, for example?'

'Once in a while,' Bridges admitted.

Galbraith turned to look at the rib on its trailer. 'Do you go out in the rib?'

'Sometimes.'

'So he calls you on his mobile and says I'll be in such-and-such a place at midnight. Bring your rib and the mate's van and help me unload.'

'More or less, except he usually comes in about three o'clock in the morning and two or three of us will be in different places. It makes it easier if he can choose the nearest to where he is.'

'Like where?' asked Galbraith dismissively. 'I don't swallow that garbage about there being hundreds of drop-off points. This whole coast is built over.'

Bridges grinned. 'You'd be amazed. I know of at least ten private landing stages on rivers between Chichester and Christchurch where you can bet on the owners being absent twenty-six weekends out of fifty-two, not to mention slips along Southampton Water. Steve's a good sailor, knows this area like the back of his hand and, providing he comes in on a rising tide in order to avoid being stranded, he can tuck himself pretty close into shore. Okay, we may get a bit wet, wading to and fro, and we may have a trek to the van, but two strong guys can usually clear a load in an hour. It's a doddle.'

Galbraith shook his head, remembering his own soaking off the Isle of Purbeck and the difficulties involved in winching boats up and down slips. 'It sounds like bloody hard work to me. What does he make on a shipment like this?'

'Anything between five hundred and a thousand quid a trip.'

'What do you make out of it?'

'I take payment in kind. Fags, lager, whatever.'

'For a drop?'

Bridges nodded.

'What about rent on this garage?'

'Use of *Crazy Daze* whenever I want it. It's a straight swap.'

Galbraith eyed him thoughtfully. 'Does he let you sail it or just borrow it to shag your girlfriends?'

Bridges grinned. 'He doesn't let *anyone* sail it. It's his pride and joy. He'd kill anyone who left a mark on it.'

'Mmm.' Galbraith lifted a white wine bottle out of another box. 'So when was the last time you used it for a shag?'

'A couple of weeks ago.'

'Who with?'

'Bibi.'

'Just Bibi? Or do you shag other girls behind her back?'

'Jesus, you don't give up, do you? Just Bibi, and if you tell her any different I'll make a formal complaint.'

Galbraith tucked the bottle back into its box with a smile and moved on to another one. 'How does it work? Do you call Steve in London and tell him you want the boat for the weekend? Or does he offer it to you when he doesn't want it?'

'I get to use it during the week. He gets to use it at weekends. It's a good deal, suits everyone.'

'So it's like your house? Anyone and everyone can pile in for a quick shag whenever the mood takes them?' He flicked the young man a look of disgust. 'It sounds pretty sordid to me. Do you all use the same sheets?'

'Sure.' Bridges grinned. 'Different times, different customs, mate. It's all about enjoying life these days, not being tied to conventional views of how to conduct yourself.'

Galbraith seemed suddenly bored with the subject. 'How often does Steve go to France?'

'It probably works out at an average of once every two months. It's no big deal, just booze and fags. If he clears five thousand quid in a year he reckons he's done well. But it's peanuts, for Christ's sake. That's why I told him he should come clean. The worst that can happen is a few months in jail. It would be different if he was doing drugs but' – he shook his head vigorously – 'he wouldn't touch them with a bargepole.'

'We found cannabis in one of his lockers.'

'Oh, come on,' said Bridges with a sigh. 'So he smokes the odd joint. That doesn't make him a Colombian drugs baron. On that basis, anyone who enjoys a drink is smuggling alcohol by the lorry load. Look, trust me, he doesn't bring in anything more dangerous than red wine.'

Galbraith moved a couple of boxes. 'What about dogs?' he asked, lifting a plastic kennel out from behind them and holding it up for Bridges to look at.

The young man shrugged. 'A few times maybe. Where's the harm? He always makes sure they've got their anti-rabies certificates.' He watched a frown gather on Galbraith's forehead. 'It's a stupid law,' he repeated like a mantra. 'Six months of quarantine costs the owner a fortune, the dogs are miserable while it's happening, and not a single one has ever been diagnosed with rabies in all the time this country's been enforcing the rabies regulations.'

'Cut the crap, Tony,' said the DI impatiently. 'Personally, I think it's a crazy law that allows a smackhead like you within a hundred miles of impressionable children, but I'm not going to break your legs to keep you away from them. How much does he charge?'

'Five hundred, and I'm no fucking smackhead,' he said with genuine irritation. 'Smack's for idiots. You should bone up on your drug terminology.'

Galbraith ignored him. 'Five hundred, eh? That's a nice little earner. What does he make per person? Five *thousand*?'

There was a distinct hesitation. 'What are you talking about?'

'Twenty-five different sets of fingerprints inside *Crazy Daze*, not counting Steve's or Kate and Hannah Sumner's. You've just accounted for two – yours and Bibi's – that still leaves twenty-three unaccounted for. That's a lot of fingerprints, Tony.'

Bridges shrugged. 'You said it yourself, he runs a sordid establishment.'

'Mmm,' murmured Galbraith, 'I did say that, didn't I?' His gaze shifted towards the trailer again. 'Nice rib. Is it new?'

Bridges followed his gaze. 'Not particularly, I've had it nine months.'

Galbraith walked over to look at the two Evinrude outboards at the stern. 'It looks new,' he remarked, running a finger along the rubber. 'Immaculate in fact. When did you last clean it?'

'Monday.'

'And you hosed the garage floor for good measure, did you?'

'It got wet in the process.'

Galbraith slapped the inflated sides of the rib. 'When did you last take it out?'

'I don't know. A week ago maybe.'

'So why did it need cleaning on Monday?'

'It didn't,' said Bridges, his expression growing wary again. 'I just like to look after it.'

'Then let's hope Customs and Excise don't rip it apart looking for drugs, my son,' said the policeman with poorly feigned sympathy, 'because they're not going to buy your story about red wine being Steve's most dangerous import any more than I do.' He jerked his head towards the back of the garage. 'That's just a blind in case you're sussed for anything more serious. Like illegal immigration. Those boxes have been in there for months. The dust's so thick I can write my name in it.'

Ingram stopped at Broxton House on his way home to check on Celia Jenner and was greeted enthusiastically by Bertie who bounded out of the front door, tail wagging. 'How's your mother?' he asked Maggie as he met her in the hall.

'Much better. Brandy and painkillers have put her on cloud nine and she's talking about getting up.' She headed for the kitchen. 'We're starving so I'm making some sandwiches. Do you want some?'

He followed with Bertie in tow, wondering how to tell her politely that he'd rather go home and make his own, but kept his counsel when he saw the state of the kitchen. It was hardly up to hospital standards, but the smell of cleaning rising from the floor, worktops, table and units was a huge advance on the ancient, indescribable aroma of dirty dog and damp horse blankets that had shocked his scent and taste buds earlier. 'I wouldn't say no,' he said. 'I haven't had anything to eat since last night.'

'What do you think?' she asked, setting to with a loaf of sliced bread, cheese and tomatoes.

He didn't pretend he didn't know what she was talking about. 'All in all a vast improvement. I prefer the floor this colour.' He touched the toe of one large boot to a quarry tile. 'I hadn't realized it was orange or that my feet weren't supposed to stick to it every time I moved.'

She gave a low laugh. 'It was damned hard work. I don't think it's had a mop on it for four years, not since Ma told Mrs Cottrill she couldn't afford her any more.' She glanced critically around the room. 'But you're right. A coat of paint would make a hell of a difference. I thought I'd buy some this afternoon and slap it on over the weekend. It won't take long.'

He should have brought the brandy up a long time ago, he realized, marvelling at her optimism. He would have done if he'd known she and her mother had been on the wagon for four years. Alcohol, for all its sins, wasn't called a restorative for nothing. He cast an interested eye towards the ceiling which was festooned with cobwebs. 'It'll slap right off again unless you shift that little lot as well. Do you have a stepladder?'

'I don't know.'

'I've got one at home,' he said. 'I'll bring it up this evening when I've finished for the day. In return will you put off your paint-buying trip long enough to give me a statement about Harding's assault on you this morning? I'll be questioning him at five o'clock and I want your version of the story before I do.'

She looked anxiously towards Bertie who, at Ingram's fingered command, had taken up station beside the Aga. 'I don't know. I've been thinking about what you said and now I'm worried he's going to accuse Bertie of being out of control and attacking *him*, in which case I'll be faced with a prosecution under the Dangerous Dogs Act and Bertie will be put down. Don't you think it would be better to let it drop?'

Nick pulled out a chair and sat on it, watching her. 'He'll probably try to bring a counter prosecution, anyway, Maggie. It's his best defence against anything you might say.' He paused. 'But if you let him get in first then you'll be handing him the advantage. Is that what you want?'

'No, of course it isn't, but Bertie *was* out of control. He sank his teeth into the stupid idiot's arm and I couldn't get him off for love or money.' Angrily, she turned a ferocious glare on her dog, then stabbed her knife into a tomato and splattered seeds all over the chopping board. 'I had to thrash him in the end to make him release his hold and I won't be able to deny it if Steve takes me to court.'

'Who attacked first, Bertie or Steve?'

'Me probably. I was screaming abuse at Steve so he lashed out at me, then the next thing I knew Bertie was hanging off his arm like a great hairy leech.' Unexpectedly, she laughed. 'Actually, in retrospect, it's quite funny. I thought they were dancing until red saliva came out of Bertie's mouth. I just couldn't understand what Harding thought he was playing at. First he appears out of nowhere, then he runs at Stinger, then he slaps me and starts dancing with my dog. I felt as if I was in a madhouse.'

'Why do you think he slapped you?'

She smiled uncomfortably. 'Presumably because I made him angry. I called him a pervert.'

'That's no excuse for slapping you. Verbal abuse does not constitute an assault, Maggie.'

'Then maybe it should.'

'The man hit you,' he remarked curiously. 'Why are you making excuses for him?'

'Because, thinking back, I was incredibly rude. I certainly called him a creep and a bastard and I said you'd crucify him if you knew he was there. It's your fault really. I wouldn't have been so frightened if you hadn't come and questioned me about him yesterday. You planted the idea that he was dangerous.'

'*Mea culpa*,' he said mildly.

'You know what I mean.'

He acknowledged the point gravely. 'What else did you say?'

'Nothing. I just screamed at him like a fishwife because he gave me such a shock. The trouble is, he was shocked, too, so we both sort of lashed out without thinking . . . he in his way . . . me in mine.'

'There's no excuse for physical violence.'

'Isn't there?' she asked dryly. 'You excused mine earlier.'

'True,' he admitted, rubbing his cheek reminiscently. 'But if I'd retaliated, Maggie, you'd still be unconscious.'

'Meaning what? That men are expected to show more responsibility than women?' She glanced at him with a half-smile. 'I don't know whether to accuse you of being patronizing or ignorant.'

'Ignorant every time,' he said. 'I know nothing about women except that very few of them could land me a knockout blow.' His eyes smiled at her. 'But I know damn well that I could flatten any of them. Which is why – unlike Steve Harding – I wouldn't dream of raising my hand against one.'

'Yes, but you're so wise and so middle-aged, Nick,' she said crossly, 'and he isn't. In any case, I don't even remember the way it happened. It was all over so quickly. I expect that sounds pathetic, but I've realized I'm not much good as a witness.'

'It just makes you normal,' he said. 'Very few people have accurate recall.'

'Well, the truth is I think he wanted to try and catch Stinger before he bolted and only hit out when I called him a pervert.' Her shoulders sagged despondently as if the brandy-courage in her blood had suddenly evaporated. 'I'm sorry to disappoint you. I used to see everything so straightforwardly before I got taken to the cleaners by Martin, but now I can't make up my mind about anything. I'd have insisted on a prosecution like a shot this morning but now I realize I'd *die* if anything happened to Bertie. I love the stupid animal to distraction, and I absolutely refuse to sacrifice him on a point of principle. He's worth a slap from a toe-rag any day. Goddammit he's *faithful*. All right, he visits you from time to time but he always comes home to love me at night.'

'Okay.'

There was a short silence.

'Is that all you're going to say?'

'Yes.'

She eyed him with suspicion. 'You're a policeman. Why aren't you arguing with me?'

'Because you're intelligent enough to make your own decisions, and nothing I can say will change your mind.'

'That's absolutely right.' She slapped some butter on a piece of sliced bread and waited for him to say something else. When he didn't, she grew nervous. 'Are you still going to question Steve?' she demanded.

'Of course. That's my job. Helicopter rescues don't come cheap, and someone has to account for why this morning's was necessary. Harding was admitted to hospital with dog bites, so I have a responsibility to establish whether the attack on him was provoked or unprovoked. One of you was assaulted this morning and I have to try and find out which. If you're lucky, he'll be feeling as guilty as you are and there'll be a stalemate. If you're unlucky, I'll be back this evening requesting a statement from you in answer to his assertion that you had no control over your dog.'

'That's blackmail.'

He shook his head. 'As far as I'm concerned you and Steven Harding have equal rights under the law. If he says Bertie made an unprovoked attack on him I will investigate the allegation, and if I think he's right I'll submit my findings to the Crown Prosecution Service and suggest they prosecute you. I may not like him, Maggie, but if I think he's telling the truth I will support him. That's what society pays me for, irrespective of personal feeling and irrespective of how it may affect the people involved.'

She turned round, back against the worktop. 'I had no idea you were such a cold fucking bastard.'

He was unrepentant. 'And I had no idea you thought you ranked above anyone else. You'll get no favours from me, not where the law's concerned.'

'Will you favour me if I give you a statement?'

'No, I'll be as fair to you as I am to Harding but my advice is that you'll gain an advantage by getting your statement in first.'

She whipped the knife off the chopping board and waved it under his nose. 'Then you'd bloody well better be right,' she said fiercely, 'or I'll take your testicles off – *personally* – and laugh while I'm doing it. I *love* my dog.'

'So do I,' Ingram assured her, putting a finger on the hilt of the knife and moving it gently to one side. 'The difference is I don't encourage him to slobber all over me in order to prove it.'

*

'I've sealed the garage for the moment,' Galbraith told Carpenter over the phone, 'but you'll have to sort out priorities with Customs and Excise. We need a scene-of-crime team down here pronto, but if you want a hard charge on which to hold Steven Harding, then C and E can probably deliver for you. My guess is he's been ferrying illegal immigrants in wholesale and dropping them off along the south coast . . . Yes, it would certainly explain the fingerprint evidence in the saloon area. No, no sign of the stolen Fastrigger outboard . . .' He felt the young man beside him stir, and he glanced at him with a distracted smile. 'Yes, I'm bringing Tony Bridges in now. He's agreed to make a new statement . . . Yes, very co-operative. William? . . . No, it doesn't eliminate him any more than it eliminates Steve . . . Mmm, back to square one, I'm afraid.' He tucked the telephone into his breast pocket and wondered why he'd never thought of taking up acting himself.

At the other end, Superintendent Carpenter looked at his receiver in surprise for a moment before cutting the line. He hadn't a clue what John Galbraith had been talking about.

Although he hadn't been aware of it, Steven Harding had been under observation by a woman detective constable from the moment he was admitted to the hospital. She sat out of sight in the Sister's office, making sure he stayed put, but in the event he appeared in no hurry to leave. He flirted constantly with the nurses and, much to the WDC's irritation, the nurses reciprocated. She spent the waiting hours pondering the naivety of women, and wondered how many of these selfsame nurses would argue vehemently that they hadn't given him any encouragement if and when he decided to rape them. In other words, what constituted encouragement? Something a woman would describe as innocent flirting? Or something a man would call a definite come-on?

It was with some relief that she handed over responsibility

to PC Ingram in the corridor outside. 'The Sister's discharging him at five but the way things are going, I'm not sure he'll be leaving at all,' she said ruefully. 'He's got every nurse wound round his little finger and he looks set for the duration. Frankly, if they turf him out of this bed, it wouldn't surprise me if he ends up in a nice warm one somewhere else. I can't see the attraction myself but then I've never been too keen on wankers.'

Ingram gave a muted laugh. 'Hang around. Watch the fun. If he doesn't walk out of his own accord on the dot of five, I'll clap the irons on him in there.'

'I'm game,' she agreed cheerfully. 'You never know, you might need a hand.'

The video film was difficult to watch, not because of its content, which was as discreet as the Dartmouth sergeant had promised, but because the picture rose and fell with the movement of the Frenchman's boat. Nevertheless, his daughter had succeeded in capturing considerable footage of Harding in close detail. Carpenter, sitting behind his desk, played it through once, then used the remote to rewind to where Harding had first sat down on his rucksack. He held the image on pause and addressed the team of detectives crammed into his office. 'What do you think he's doing there?'

'Releasing Godzilla?' said one of the men with a snigger.

'Signalling to someone,' said a woman.

Carpenter played back a few frames to follow, in reverse, the panning of the camera lens across the shadowy, out-of-focus glare of the white motor cruiser and the blurry bikini-clad figure lying face down across the bows. 'I agree,' he said. 'The only question is, who?'

'Nick Ingram listed the boats that were there that day,' said another man. 'They shouldn't be too difficult to track down.'

'There was a Fairline Squadron with two teenage girls on

board,' said Carpenter, passing across the report from Bourne-mouth about the abandoned dinghy. '*Gregory's Girl* out of Poole. Start with that one. It's owned by a Poole businessman called Gregory Freemantle.'

Ingram detached himself from the wall and blocked the corri-dor as Steven Harding, arm in sling, came through the door of the ward at 4.45. 'Good afternoon, sir,' he said politely. 'I hope you're feeling better.'

'Why would you care?'

Ingram smiled. 'I'm always interested in anyone I help to rescue.'

'Well, I'm not going to talk to you. You're the bastard who got them interested in my boat.'

Ingram showed his warrant card. 'I questioned you on Sunday. PC Ingram, Dorsetshire Constabulary.'

Harding's eyes narrowed. 'They say they can keep *Crazy Daze* for as long as is necessary but won't explain what gives them the right. I haven't done anything so they can't charge me, but they can sure as hell steal my boat for no reason.' His angry gaze raked Ingram. 'What does "as long as is necessary" mean, anyway?'

'There can be any number of reasons why it's deemed necessary to retain seized articles,' explained the constable helpfully, if somewhat misleadingly. The rules surrounding retention were woolly in the extreme and policemen had few qualms about smothering so-called evidence in mountains of paperwork to avoid having to return it. 'In the case of *Crazy Daze*, it probably means they haven't finished the forensic examination, but once that's done you should be able to effect its release almost immediately.'

'Bollocks to that! They're holding it in case I abscond to France.'

Ingram shook his head. 'You'd have to go a little further

than France, Steve,' he murmured in mild correction. 'Every-one's mighty co-operative in Europe these days.' He stood aside and gestured down the corridor behind him. 'Shall we go?'

Harding backed away from him. 'Dream on. I'm not going anywhere with you.'

'I'm afraid you must,' said Ingram with apparent regret. 'Miss Jenner's accused you of assault which means I have to insist that you answer some questions. I would prefer it if you came voluntarily but I will arrest you if necessary.' He jerked his chin towards the corridor behind Harding. 'That doesn't lead anywhere – I've already checked it out.' He pointed towards a door at the end where a woman was consulting a noticeboard. 'This is the only exit.'

Harding began to ease his arm out of its sling, clearly fancying his chances in a sprint dash against this simple, forelock-tugging, sixteen-stone yokel in a uniform, but something changed his mind. Perhaps it was the fact that Ingram stood four inches taller than he did. Perhaps the woman by the door signalled that she was a detective. Perhaps he saw something in Ingram's lazy smile that persuaded him he might be making a mistake . . .

He gave an indifferent shrug. 'What the hell! I've nothing else to do. But it's your precious Maggie you should be arresting. She stole my phone.'

Chapter Twenty-three

SECURED IN the passenger seat of the police Range Rover where Ingram could keep an eye on him, Harding sat huddled in moody silence for most of the trip back to Swanage. Ingram made no attempt to talk to him. Once in a while their eyes met when the policeman was checking traffic to his left, but he felt none of the empathy for Harding that Galbraith had experienced on *Crazy Daze*. He saw only immaturity in the young man's face and despised him because of it. He was reminded of every juvenile delinquent he'd arrested down the years, not one of whom had had the experience or the wisdom to understand the inevitability of consequence. They saw it in terms of retribution and justice and whether they would do 'time', never in terms of the slow destruction of their lives.

It was as they drove through the little town of Corfe Castle, with its ruined medieval ramparts commanding a gap in the Purbeck chalk ridge, that Harding broke the silence. 'If you hadn't jumped to conclusions on Sunday,' he said in a reasonable tone of voice, 'none of this would have happened.'

'None of what?'

'Everything. My arrest. This.' He touched a hand to his sling. 'I shouldn't be here. I had a part lined up in London. It could have been my breakthrough.'

'The only reason you're here is because you attacked Miss Jenner this morning,' Ingram pointed out. 'What have the events of Sunday got to do with that?'

'She wouldn't know me from Adam but for Kate's murder.'

'That's true.'

'And you won't believe I didn't have anything to do with that – none of you will – but it's not fair,' Harding complained with a sudden surge of bitterness. 'It's just a bloody awful coincidence, like the coincidence of bumping into Maggie this morning. Do you think I'd have shown myself to her if I'd known she was there?'

'Why not?' The car sped up as they exited the thirty-mile speed limit.

He turned a morose stare on Ingram's profile. 'Have you any idea what it's like to have your movements monitored by the police? You've got my car, my boat. I'm supposed to stay at an address you've chosen for me. It's like being in prison without the walls. I'm being treated like a criminal when I haven't done anything, but if I lose my temper because some stupid woman treats me like Jack the Ripper I get accused of assault.'

Ingram kept his eyes on the road ahead. 'You hit her. Don't you think she had a right to treat you like Jack the Ripper?'

'Only because she wouldn't stop screaming.' He gnawed at his fingernails. 'I guess you told her I was a rapist, so of course she believed you. That's what got me riled. She was fine with me on Sunday, then today . . .' He fell silent.

'Did you know she might be there?'

'Of course not. How could I?'

'She rides that gully most mornings. It's one of the few places she can give her horses a good gallop. Anyone who knows her could have told you that. It's also one of the few places with easy access to the beach from the coastal path.'

'I didn't know.'

'Then why are you so surprised she was scared of you? She'd have been scared of any man who appeared out of nowhere on a deserted headland when she wasn't expecting it.'

'She wouldn't have been scared of you.'

'I'm a policeman. She trusts me.'

'She trusted *me*,' said Harding, 'until you told her I was a rapist.'

It was the same point Maggie had made and Ingram conceded it was a fair one – to himself if not to Harding. It was the grossest injustice to destroy an innocent person's reputation, however it was done, and while neither he nor Galbraith had said that the young man was a rapist, the implication had been clear enough. They continued for a while in silence. The road to Swanage led south-east along the spine of Purbeck and the distant sea showed intermittently between folds of pastureland. The sun was warm on Ingram's arm and neck but Harding, sitting in shade on the left-hand side of the car, hunched tighter into himself as if he was cold and stared sightlessly out of the window. He seemed lost in lethargy, and Ingram wondered if he was still trying to concoct some sort of defence or whether the events of the morning had finally taken their toll.

'That dog of hers should be shot,' he said suddenly.

Still concocting a defence then, thought Ingram, while wondering why it had taken him so long to get round to it. 'Miss Jenner claims he was only trying to protect her,' he said mildly.

'It bloody savaged me.'

'You shouldn't have hit her.'

Harding gave a long sigh. 'I didn't mean to,' he admitted as if realizing that continued argument would be a waste of time. 'I probably wouldn't have done it if she hadn't called me a pervert. The last person who did that was my father and I flattened him for it.'

'Why did he call you a pervert?'

'Because he's old-fashioned and I told him I'd done a porno shoot to make money.' The young man balled his hands into fists. 'I wish people would just keep their noses out of my business. It gets on my tits the way everyone keeps lecturing me about the way I live my life.'

Ingram shook his head in irritation. 'There's no such thing as a free lunch, Steve.'

'What's that got to do with anything?'

'Live now, pay later. What goes around, comes around. No one promised you a rose garden.'

Harding turned to stare out of the passenger window, offering a cold shoulder to what he clearly felt was a patronizing police attitude. 'I don't know what the fuck you're talking about.'

Ingram smiled slightly. 'I know you don't.' He glanced sideways. 'What were you doing on Emmetts Hill this morning?'

'Just walking.'

There was a moment's silence before Ingram gave a snort of laughter. 'Is that the best you can do?'

'It's the truth,' he said.

'Like hell it is. You've had all day to work this one out but by God, if that's the only explanation you've been able to come up with, you must have a very low opinion of policemen.'

The young man turned back to him with an engaging smile. 'I do.'

'Then we'll have to see if we can change your mind.' Ingram's smile was almost as engaging. 'Won't we?'

Gregory Freemantle was pouring himself a drink in the front room of his flat in Poole when his girlfriend showed in two detectives. The atmosphere was thick enough to cut with a knife and it was obvious to both policemen that they had walked in on a humdinger of a row. 'DS Campbell and DC Langham,' she said curtly. 'They want to talk to you.'

Freemantle was a Peter Stringfellow lookalike, an ageing playboy with straggling blond hair and the beginnings of desperation in the sagging lines around his eyes and chin. 'Oh God,' he groaned, 'you're not taking her seriously about that bloody oil drum, are you? She doesn't know the first thing about sailing' – he paused to consider – 'or children for that matter, but it doesn't stop her being lippy.' He raised one hand and worked his thumb and forefingers to mimic a mouth working.

He was the kind of man other men take against instinctively, and DS Campbell glanced sympathetically at the girlfriend. 'It wasn't an oil drum, sir, it was an upturned dinghy. And, yes, we took Miss Hale's information very seriously.'

Freemantle raised his glass in the woman's direction. 'Good one, Jenny.' His eyes were already showing alcohol levels well above average, but he still downed two fingers of neat whisky without blinking. 'What do you want?' he asked Campbell. He didn't invite them to sit down, merely turned back to the whisky bottle and poured himself another drink.

'We're trying to eliminate people from the Kate Sumner murder inquiry,' Campbell explained, 'and we're interested in everyone who was in Chapman's Pool on Sunday. We understand you were there on a Fairline Squadron.'

'You know I was. She's already told you.'

'Who was with you?'

'Jenny and my two daughters, Marie and Fliss. And it was a bloody nightmare if you're interested. You buy a boat to keep everyone happy, and all they can do is snipe at each other. I'm going to sell the damn thing.' His drink-sodden eyes filled with self-pity. 'It's no fun going out on your own, and it's even less fun taking a menagerie of cats with you.'

'Was either of your daughters wearing a bikini and lying face-down on the bow between 12.30 and one o'clock on Sunday, sir?'

'I don't know.'

'Does either of them have a boyfriend called Steven Harding?'

He shrugged indifferently.

'I'd be grateful for an answer, Mr Freemantle.'

'Well, you're not going to get one because I don't know and I don't care,' he said aggressively. 'I've had a bucketful of women today, and as far as I'm concerned the sooner they're all genetically engineered to behave like Stepford wives the better.' He raised his glass again. 'My wife serves me with notice that she intends to bankrupt my company in order to take three-quarters of what I'm worth. My fifteen-year-old daughter tells me she's pregnant and wants to run away to France with some long-haired git who fancies himself as an actor, and my girlfriend' – he lurched his glass in Jenny Hale's direction – 'that one over there – tells me it's all my fault because I've waived my responsibilities as a husband and a father. So cheers! To men, eh!'

Campbell turned to the woman. 'Can you help us, Miss Hale?'

She looked questioningly towards Gregory, clearly seeking his support, but when he refused to meet her eyes, she gave a small shrug. 'Ah, well,' she said, 'I wasn't planning on hanging around after this evening anyway. Marie, the fifteen-year-old, was wearing a bikini and was sunbathing on the bow before lunch,' she told the two policemen. 'She lay on her tummy so that her father wouldn't see her bump and she was signalling to her boyfriend who was jerking off on the shore for her benefit. The rest of the time she wore a sarong to disguise the fact that she's pregnant. She has since told us that her boyfriend's name is Steve Harding and that he's an actor in London. I knew she was plotting something because she was hyped up from the moment we left Poole, and I realized it must be to do with the boy on the shore because she became completely poisonous after he left and has been a nightmare ever since.' She sighed. 'That's what the row has been about. When she turned up today in one of her tantrums I told her father he should take some interest in what's really going on because it's been obvious to me for a while that she's not just pregnant but has been taking drugs as well. Now open war has broken out.'

'Is Marie still here?'

Jenny nodded. 'In the spare bedroom.'

'Where does she normally live?'

'In Lymington with her mother and sister.'

'Do you know what she and her boyfriend were planning to do on Sunday?'

She glanced at Gregory. 'They were going to run away together to France, but when that woman's body was found they had to abandon the plan because there were too many people watching. Steve has a boat apparently which he'd left at Salterns Marina, and the idea was for Marie to vanish into thin air out of Chapman's Pool after saying she was going for a walk to Worth Matravers. They thought if she changed into some men's clothes that Steve had brought with him, and slogged it back across land to the ferry, they could be on their way to France by the evening and no one would ever know where she'd gone or who she was with.' She shook her head. 'Now she's threatening to kill herself if her father doesn't let her leave school and go and live with Steve in London.'

While the garage in Lymington, and its contents, were being taken apart systematically by scene-of-crime officers in search of evidence, Tony Bridges was being formally interviewed as a witness and under taped conditions by Detective Superintendent Carpenter and DI Galbraith. He refused to repeat anything he had said to Galbraith about his or Harding's alleged smuggling activities, however, and, as that particular matter was being passed to Customs and Excise, Carpenter was less exercised by the refusal than he might otherwise have been. Instead, he chose to shock Bridges by showing him the videotape of Harding masturbating, then asked him if his friend made a habit of performing indecent acts in public.

Surprisingly, Bridges *was* shocked.

'Jesus!' he exclaimed, wiping his forehead with his sleeve.

'How would I know? We lead separate lives. He's never done anything like that around me.'

'It's not that bad,' murmured Galbraith who was sitting beside Carpenter. 'Just a discreet wank. Why are you sweating over it, Tony?'

The young man eyed him nervously. 'I get the impression it's worse than that. You wouldn't be showing it to me otherwise.'

'You're a bright lad,' said Carpenter, freeze-framing the video at the point where Harding was cleaning himself up. 'That's a T-shirt he's using. You can just make out the Derby FC logo on the front. It belongs to a ten-year-old kid called Danny Spender. He thinks Steve stole it off him around midday on Sunday and half an hour later we see him ejaculating all over it. You know the guy better than anyone. Would you say he has a yen for little boys?'

Bridges looked even more startled. 'No,' he muttered.

'We have a witness who says Steve couldn't keep his hands off the two lads who found Kate Sumner's body. One of the boys describes him using his mobile telephone to bring on an erection in front of them. We have a policeman who says he maintained the erection while the boys were around him.'

'Ah, shit!' Bridges ran his tongue round dry lips. 'Listen, I always thought he hated kids. He can't stand working with them, can't stand it when I talk about teaching.' He looked towards the frozen image on the television screen. 'This has to be wrong. Okay, he's got a thing about sex – talks about it too much – likes blue movies – boasts about three-in-a-bed romps, that kind of thing – but it's always with women. I'd have bet my last cent he was straight.'

Carpenter leaned forward to examine the other man closely, then shifted his gaze to look at the television screen. 'That really offends you, doesn't it? Why is that, Tony? Did you recognize anyone else in the sequence?'

'No. I just think it's obscene, that's all.'

'It can't be worse than the pornography shoots he does.'

'I wouldn't know. I've never seen them.'

'You must have seen some of his photographs. Describe them for us.'

Bridges shook his head.

'Do they include kids? We know he's done some gay poses. Does he pose with children as well?'

'I don't know anything about it. You'll have to talk to his agent.'

Carpenter made a note. 'Paedophile rings pay double what anyone else pays.'

'It's got nothing to do with me.'

'You're a teacher, Tony. You have more responsibility than most people towards children. Does your friend pose with children?'

He shook his head.

'For the purposes of the tape,' said Carpenter into the microphone, 'Anthony Bridges declined to answer.' He consulted a piece of paper in front of him. 'On Tuesday you told us Steve wasn't the kiss-and-tell type, now you're saying he boasts about three-in-a-bed sex. Which is true?'

'The boasting,' he said with more confidence, glancing at Galbraith. 'That's how I know about Kate. He was always telling me what they did together.'

Galbraith wiped a freckled hand around the back of his neck to massage muscles made sore by too much driving that day. 'Except it sounds like all talk and no action, Tony. Your friend goes in for solitary pursuits. On beaches. On his boat. In his flat. Did you ever wonder if he was lying about his relationships with women?'

'No. Why should I? He's a good-looking bloke. Women like him.'

'All right, let me put it another way. How many of these women have you actually met? How often does he bring them to your house?'

'He doesn't need to. He takes them to his boat.'

'Then why is there no evidence of that? There were a couple of articles of women's clothing and a pair of Hannah's shoes on board but nothing to suggest that a woman was ever in the bed with him.'

'You can't know that.'

'Oh, come on,' said Galbraith in exasperation, 'you're a chemist. His sheets have semen stains all over them but nothing that remotely suggests there was anyone else in the bed with him when he ejaculated.'

Bridges looked rather wildly towards the Superintendent. 'All I can tell you is what Steve told me. It's hardly my fault if the stupid sod was lying.'

'True,' agreed Carpenter, 'but you do keep shoving his prowess down our throats.' He produced Bridges' statement from a folder on the table and spread it flat in front of him, holding it down with his palms stretched on either side. 'You seem to have a bit of a thing about him being good-looking. This is what you said at the beginning of the week. "*Steve's a good-looking bloke*",' he read, '"*and has an active sex life. He has at least two girls on the go at the same time . . .*"' He lifted enquiring eyebrows. 'Do you want to comment on that?'

It was clear that Tony had no idea where this line of questioning was leading and needed time to think. A fact which interested both policemen. It was as if he were trying to predict moves in a chess game, and had begun to panic because checkmate looked inevitable. Every so often his eyes flicked towards the television screen, then dropped away rapidly as if the frozen image was more than he could bear. 'I don't know what you want me to say.'

'In simple terms, Tony, we're trying to square your portrayal of Steve with the forensic evidence. You want us to believe your friend had a prolonged affair with an older married woman but we're having difficulty substantiating that any such affair happened. For example, you told my colleague that Steve took Kate to your house on occasion, yet, despite the fact that your house clearly hasn't been cleaned in months, we couldn't find a single fingerprint belonging to Kate Sumner anywhere inside it. There is also nothing to suggest that Kate was ever in Steve's car, although you claim that he drove her to the New Forest on numerous occasions for sex in the back of it.'

'He said they needed out-of-the-way places in case they were spotted together. They were scared of William finding out because, according to Steve, he was so jealous he'd go berserk if he knew he was being two-timed.' He wilted before Carpenter's unconvinced expression. 'It's not my fault if he was lying to me,' he protested.

'He described William to us as middle-aged and straight,' said Carpenter thoughtfully. 'I don't recall him suggesting he was aggressive.'

'That's what he told me.'

Galbraith stirred on his chair. 'So your entire knowledge of Steve's *alleged*' – he put careful stress on the word – 'affair with Kate came from a single meeting with her in a pub and whatever Steve chose to tell you about her?'

Bridges nodded but didn't answer.

'For the purposes of the tape, Anthony Bridges gave a nod of agreement. So was he ashamed of the relationship, Tony? Is that why you only got to meet her once? You said yourself, you couldn't understand what the attraction was.'

'She was married,' he said. 'He was hardly going to parade a married woman around the town, was he?'

'Has he *ever* paraded a woman around town, Tony?'

There was a long silence. 'Most of his girlfriends are married,' he said then.

'Or mythical?' suggested Carpenter. 'Like claiming Bibi as a girlfriend?'

Bridges looked baffled, as if he was struggling with half-heard, dimly understood truths that were suddenly making sense. He didn't answer.

Galbraith levelled a finger at the television screen. 'What we're beginning to suspect is that the talk was a smokescreen for no action. Maybe he was pretending to like women because he didn't want anyone to know that his tastes lay in an entirely different direction? Maybe the poor bastard doesn't want to recognize it himself and lets off steam quietly in order to keep himself under control?' He turned the finger accusingly on Bridges. 'But if that's true, then where does it leave you and Kate Sumner?'

The young man shook his head. 'I don't understand.'

The DI took his notebook from his pocket and flipped it open. 'Let me quote some of the things you said about her: "*I think she must have lived on a diet of soap operas . . .*" "*Kate said Hannah would scream her head off . . .*" "*I guess she'd been conning idiots like her husband for so long . . .*" I could go on. You talked about her for fifteen minutes, fluently and with no prompting from me.' He laid his notebook on the table. 'Do you want to tell us how you know so much about a woman you only met once?'

'Everything I know is what Steve told me.'

Carpenter nodded towards the recording machine. 'This is a formal interview under taped conditions, Tony. Let me rephrase the question for you so there can be no mis-understandings. Bearing in mind that the Sumners are recent newcomers to Lymington, that both Steven Harding and William Sumner have denied there was any relationship between Steven and Kate Sumner, and that you, Anthony Bridges, claim to have met her only once, how do you explain your extensive and accurate knowledge of her?'

Marie Freemantle was a tall, willowy blonde with waist-length wavy hair and huge doe-like eyes which were awash with tears. Once assured that Steve was alive and well and currently answering questions about why he had been at Chapman's Pool on Sunday, she dried her eyes and favoured the policemen with a heavily practised triangular smile. If they were honest, both men were moved by her prettiness when they first saw her, although their sympathies were soon frayed by the self-centred, petulant nature beneath. They realized she wasn't very bright when it became clear that it hadn't occurred to her they were questioning her because Steven Harding was a suspect in Kate Sumner's murder. She chose to talk to them away from her father and his girlfriend, and her spite was colossal, particularly towards the woman whom she described as an interfering bitch. 'I hate her,' she finished. 'Everything was fine till she stuck her nose in.'

'Meaning you've always been allowed to do what you liked?' suggested Campbell.

'I'm old enough.'

'How old were you when you first had sex with Steven Harding?'

'Fifteen.' She wriggled her shoulders. 'But that's nothing these days. Most girls I know had sex at thirteen.'

'How long have you known him?'

'Six months.'

'How often have you had sex with him?'

'Lots of times.'

'Where do you do it?'

'Mostly on his boat.'

Campbell frowned. 'In the cabin?'

'Not often. The cabin stinks,' she said. 'He takes a blanket up on deck and we do it in the sunshine or under the stars. It's great.'

'Moored up to the buoy?' asked Campbell, with a rather shocked expression. Like Galbraith earlier, he was wondering about the generation gap that seemed to have opened, unobserved, between himself and today's youth. 'In full view of the Isle of Wight ferry?'

'Of course not,' she said indignantly, wriggling her

shoulders again. 'He picks me up somewhere and we go for a sail.'

'Where does he pick you up?'

'All sorts of places. Like he says, he'd get strung up if anyone knew he was going with a fifteen-year-old, and he reckons if you don't use the same place too often, no one notices.' She shrugged, recognizing that further explanation was necessary. 'If you use a marina once in two weeks, who's going to remember? Then there's the salt flats. I walk round the path from the Yacht Haven and he just shoots in with his dinghy and lifts me off. Sometimes I go to Poole by train and meet him there. Mum thinks I'm with Dad, Dad thinks I'm with Mum. It's simple. I just phone him on his mobile and he tells me where to go.'

'Did you leave a message on his phone this morning?'

She nodded. 'He can't phone me in case Mum gets suspicious.'

'How did you meet him in the first place?'

'At the Lymington yacht club. There was a dance there on St Valentine's Day and Dad got tickets for it because he's still a member even though he lives in Poole now. Mum said Fliss and me could go if Dad watched out for us, but he got shit-faced as usual and left us to get on with it. That's when he was going out with his bitch of a secretary. I really *hated* her. She was always trying to put him against me.'

Campbell was tempted to say it wouldn't have been difficult. 'Did your father introduce you to Steve? Did he know him?'

'No. One of my teachers did. He and Steve have been friends for years.'

'Which teacher?'

'Tony Bridges.' Her full lips curved into a malicious smile. 'He's fancied me for ages and he was trying to make this pathetic move on me when Steve cut him out. God, he was pissed about it. He's been needling away at me all term, trying to find out what's going on, but Steve told me not to tell him in case he got us into trouble for under-age sex. He reckons Tony's so fucking jealous he'd make life hell for us if he could.'

Campbell thought back to his interview with Bridges on Monday night. 'Perhaps he feels responsible for you.'

'That's not the reason,' she said scornfully. 'He's a sad little bastard – *that's* the reason. None of his girlfriends stay with him because he's stoned most of the time and can't do the business properly. He's been going out with this hairdresser for about four months now, and Steve says he's been feeding her drugs so she won't complain about his lousy performance. If you want my opinion there's something wrong with him – he's always trying to touch up girls in class – but our stupid headmaster's too thick to do anything about it.'

Campbell exchanged a glance with his colleague. 'How does Steve know he's been feeding her drugs?' he asked.

'He's seen him do it. It's like a Mickey Finn. You dissolve a tablet in lager and the girl passes out.'

'Do you know what drug he's using?'

Another shrug. 'Some sort of sleeping pill.'

'I'm not going to explain anything without a solicitor here,' said Bridges adamantly. 'Look, this was one sick woman. You think that kid of hers is weird? Well, trust me, she's as sane as you and me compared with her mother.'

WPC Griffiths heard the sound of smashing glass from the kitchen, and lifted her head in immediate concern. She had left Hannah watching television in the sitting room and, as far as she knew, William was still in his study upstairs where he had retreated, angry and resentful, after his interview with DI Galbraith. With a perplexed frown, she tiptoed along the corridor and pushed open the sitting-room door to find Sumner standing just inside. He turned an ashen face towards her then gestured helplessly towards the little girl who stalked purposefully about the room, picking up pictures of her mother and throwing them with high-pitched guttural cries into the unlit fireplace.

Ingram put a cup of tea in front of Steven Harding and took a chair on the other side of the table. He was puzzled by the man's attitude. He had expected a long interview session, punctuated by denials and counter accusations. Instead Harding had admitted culpability and agreed with everything Maggie had written in her statement. All that awaited him now was to be formally charged and held over till the next morning. His only real concern had been his telephone. When Ingram had handed it to the custody sergeant and formally entered it into the inventory of Harding's possessions, Harding had looked relieved. But whether because it had been returned or because it was switched off, Ingram couldn't tell.

'How about talking to me off the record?' he invited. 'Just to satisfy my own curiosity. There's no tape. No witnesses to the conversation. Just you and me.'

Harding shrugged. 'What do you want to talk about?'

'You. What's going on. Why you were on the coastal path on Sunday. What brought you back to Chapman's Pool this morning.'

'I already told you. I fancied a walk' – he made a good attempt at a cocky grin – 'both times.'

'All right.' He splayed his palms on the edge of the table, preparatory to standing up. 'It's your funeral. Just don't complain afterwards that no one tried to help you. You've always been the obvious suspect. You knew the victim, you own a boat, you were on the spot, you told lies about what you were doing there. Have you any idea how all that is going to look to a jury if the CPS decides to prosecute you for Kate Sumner's rape and murder?'

'They can't. They haven't got any evidence.'

'Oh, for Christ's sake grow up, Steve!' he said in irritation, subsiding on to his chair again. 'Don't you read the news-papers? People have spent years in prison on less evidence than Winfrith have against you. All right, it's only circumstantial but juries don't like coincidence any more than the rest of us and, frankly, your antics of this morning haven't helped any. All they prove is that women make you angry enough to attack them.' He paused, inviting a reply that never came. 'If you're inter-ested, in the report I wrote on Monday, I mentioned that both Miss Jenner and I thought you were having difficulty coping with an erection. Afterwards one of the Spender boys described how you were using your telephone as a masturbation aid before Miss Jenner arrived.' He shrugged. 'It may have had nothing to do with Kate Sumner, but it won't sound good in court.'

A dull flush spread up Harding's throat and into his face. 'That sucks!'

'True nevertheless.'

'I wish to God I'd never helped those kids,' he said with a burst of anger. 'I wouldn't be in this mess but for them. I should have walked away and left them to cope on their own.' He pushed his hair off his face with both hands and rested his forehead in his palms. 'Jesus Christ! Why do you have to put something like that in a report?'

'Because it happened.'

'Not like that it didn't,' he said sullenly, the flush of humiliation lingering in his cheeks.

'Then how?' Ingram watched him for a moment. 'Head-quarters think you came back to gloat over the rape and that's what caused your erection.'

'That's bullshit!' said the young man angrily.

301

'What other explanation is there? If it wasn't the thought of Kate Sumner's body that excited you then it had to be Miss Jenner or the boys.'

Harding raised his head and stared at the policeman, his eyes widening in shocked revulsion. 'The boys?' he echoed.

It crossed Ingram's mind that the facial expression was a little too theatrical, and he reminded himself, as Galbraith had done, that he was dealing with an actor. He wondered what Harding's reaction would be when he was told about the videotape. 'You couldn't keep your hands off them,' he pointed out. 'According to Miss Jenner, you were hugging Paul from behind when she rounded the boatsheds.'

'I don't believe this,' said Harding in desperation. 'I was only showing him how to use the binoculars properly.'

'Prove it.'

'How can I?'

Ingram tilted his chair back and stretched his long legs out in front of him, lacing his hands behind his head. 'Tell me why you were at Chapman's Pool. Let's face it, whatever you were doing can't be any worse than the constructions that are being put on your actions at the moment.'

'I'm not saying another word.'

Ingram stared at a mark on the ceiling. 'Then let me tell you what I think you were doing. You went there to meet someone,' he murmured. 'I think it was a girl and I think she was on one of the boats, but whatever plans you'd made with her were scuppered when the place started jumping with policemen and sightseers.' He shifted his attention back to Harding. 'But why the secrecy, Steve? What on earth were you intending to do with her that meant you'd rather be arrested on suspicion of rape and murder than give an explanation?'

It was two hours before a solicitor arrived, courtesy of Tony's grandfather, and after a brief discussion with his client, and following police assurances that, because of his alibi, Tony was not under suspicion of involvement in Kate Sumner's death, he advised him to answer their questions.

'Okay, yes, I got to know Kate pretty well. She lives – lived – about two hundred yards from my grandfather's garage. She used to come in and talk to me whenever I was in there because she knew I was a friend of Steve's. She was a right little tart, always flirting, always opening those baby blue eyes of hers and telling stories about how this and that man fancied her. I thought it was a come-on, particularly when she said William had a problem getting it up. She told me she went through pints of baby oil to help the poor sod out, and it made her laugh like a drain. Her descriptions were about as graphic as you can get, but she didn't seem to care that Hannah was listening or that I might get to be friendly with William.' He looked troubled, as if the memory haunted him. 'I told you she was sick. Matter of fact, I think she enjoyed being cruel to people. I reckon she made that poor bastard's life hell. It certainly gave her a kick slapping me down when I tried to kiss her. She spat in my face, and said she wasn't that desperate.' He fell silent.

'When was this?'

'End of February.'

'What happened then?'

'Nothing. I told her to fuck off. Then Steve started dropping hints that he was balling her. I think she must have told him I'd made a pass, so he thought he'd swagger a bit just to rub it in. He said everyone had had her except me.'

Carpenter pulled forward a piece of paper and flicked the plunger on his pen. 'Give me a list,' he said. 'Everyone you know who had anything to do with her.'

'Steve Harding.'

'Go on.'

'I don't know of anyone else.'

Carpenter laid his pen on the table again and stared at the

young man. 'That's not good enough, Tony. You describe her as a tart, then offer me one name. That gives me very little confidence in your assessment of Kate's character. Assuming you're telling the truth, we know of only three men who had a relationship with her – her husband, Steven Harding and one other from her past.' His eyes bored into Bridges'. 'By any standards that's a modest number for a thirty-year-old woman. Or would you call any woman who's had three lovers a tart? Your girlfriend, for example? How many partners has Bibi had?'

'Leave Bibi out of this,' said Bridges angrily. 'She's got nothing to do with it.'

Galbraith leaned forward. 'She gave you your alibi for Saturday night,' he reminded him. 'That means she has a great deal to do with it.' He folded his hands in front of his mouth and studied Bridges intently. 'Did she know you fancied Kate Sumner?'

The solicitor laid a hand on the young man's arm. 'You don't need to answer that.'

'Well, I'm going to,' he said, shaking himself free. 'I'm fed up with them trying to drag Bibi into it.' He addressed Galbraith. 'I didn't fucking well fancy Kate. I loathed the stupid bitch. I just thought she was easy, that's all, so I tried it on once. Listen, she was a cock-teaser. It gave her a buzz to get blokes excited.'

'That's not what I asked you, Tony. I asked you if Bibi knew you fancied Kate.'

'No,' he muttered.

Galbraith nodded. 'But she knew about *Steve* and Kate?'

'Yes.'

'Who told her? You or Steve?'

Bridges slumped angrily in his chair. 'Steve mostly. She got really worked up when Kate started smearing Hannah's crap all over his car so he told her what had been going on.'

Galbraith leaned back, letting his hands drop to the table top. 'Women don't give a toss about a car unless the guy who drives it matters to her. Are you sure your girlfriend isn't playing away from home?'

Bridges erupted out of his seat in a fury of movement. 'You are *so* fucking patronizing. You think you know it all, don't you? She got mad because there was shit all over the handle when she tried to open the door. That's what got her worked up. Not because she cares about Steve or the car, but because her hand was covered in crap. Are you so stupid you can't work that out for yourselves?'

'But doesn't that prove my point?' said Galbraith unemotionally. 'If she was driving Steve's car, she must have had more than a nodding acquaintance with him.'

'*I* was driving it,' said Bridges, ignoring the solicitor's restraining hand to lean across the table and thrust his face into the Inspector's. 'I checked the driver's handle and it was clean, so I released the locks. What never occurred to me was that the bloody bitch might have changed tactics. This time the crap was on the passenger's side. Now, get this, dickhead. It was still soft when Bibi touched it so that meant Kate must have put it there minutes before. It also meant that Bibi's hand stank to high bloody heaven. Can you follow all that or do you want me to repeat it?'

'No,' said Galbraith mildly. 'The tape recorder's pretty reliable. I think we got it.' He nodded towards the chair on the other side of the table. 'Sit down, Tony.' He waited while Bridges resumed his seat. 'Did you see Kate walk away?'

'No.'

'You should have done. You said the faeces was still soft.'

Tony pulled both hands across his peroxided hair and bent forward over the table. 'There were plenty of places she could have been hiding. She was probably watching us.'

'Did you ever wonder if you were the target and not Steve? You describe her as sick and say she spat at you.'

'No.'

'She must have known Steve allows you to drive his car.'

'Once in a while. Not often.'

Galbraith flipped another page of his notebook. 'You told me this afternoon that you and Steve had an arrangement regarding your grandfather's garage and *Crazy Daze*. A straight swap, you called it.'

'Yes. '

'You said you took Bibi there two weeks ago.'

'What of it?'

'Bibi doesn't agree with you. I phoned her at her parents' house two hours ago, and she said she's never been on *Crazy Daze*.'

'She's forgotten,' he said dismissively. 'She was drunk as a skunk that night. What does it matter anyway?'

'Let's just say we're interested in discrepancies.'

The young man shrugged. 'I don't see what difference it makes. It's got nothing to do with anything.'

'We like to be accurate.' Galbraith consulted his notebook. 'According to her, the reason she's never been on *Crazy Daze* is because Steve banned you from using it the week before you met her. "*Tony trashed the boat when he was drunk,*"' he read, '"*and Steve blew his stack. He said Tony could go on using the car but* Crazy Daze *was off limits.*"' He looked up. 'Why did you lie about taking Bibi on board?'

'To wipe the stupid smirk off your face, I expect. It pisses me off the way you bastards behave. You're all fascists.' He hunched forward, eyes burning angrily. 'I haven't forgotten you were planning to drag me through the streets in the buff even if you have.'

'What's that got to do with Bibi?'

'You wanted an answer so I gave you one.'

'How about this for an answer instead? You knew Bibi had been on board with Steve, so you decided to offer an explanation for why her fingerprints were there. You knew we'd find yours because you went out to *Crazy Daze* on Monday, and you thought you'd be safe pretending you and Bibi had been there together. But the only place we lifted your prints in the cabin, Tony, was on the foreward hatch, while Bibi's were all over the headboard behind the bed. She likes being on top, presumably?'

He dropped his head in misery. 'Fuck off.'

'It must drive you up the wall the way Steve keeps stealing your girlfriends.'

Chapter Twenty-four

MAGGIE LOWERED HER aching arms and tapped pointedly on her watch when Nick shouldered his way through the scullery door, carrying an aluminium stepladder. She was perched precariously on a garden chair on top of the kitchen table, her hair sticky with cobwebs, her rolled-up sleeves saturated with water. 'What sort of time do you call this?' she demanded. 'It's a quarter to ten and I have to be up at five o'clock tomorrow morning to see to the horses.'

'Good God, woman!' he declared plaintively. 'A night without sleep won't kill you. Live dangerously and see how you enjoy it.'

'I expected you hours ago.'

'Then don't marry a policeman,' he said, setting up his ladder under the uncleaned part of the ceiling.

'Chance'd be a fine thing.'

He grinned up at her. 'You mean you'd contemplate it?'

'Absolutely not,' she said, as if offering him a challenge to even try and chat her up. 'All I meant was that no policeman has ever asked me.'

'He wouldn't dare.' He opened the cupboard under the sink and hunkered down to inspect it for cleaning implements and buckets. She was above him – like the rare occasions when she met him on horseback – and she felt an awful temptation to take advantage of the fact by dripping water on to the back of his neck. 'Don't even think about it,' he said, without looking up, 'or I'll leave you to do the whole bloody lot on your own.'

308

She chose to ignore him, preferring dignity to humiliation. 'How did you get on?' she asked, stepping down from the chair to dunk her sponge in the bucket on the table.

'Rather well.'

'I thought you must have done. Your tail's wagging.' She climbed back on to the chair. 'What did Steve say?'

'You mean apart from agreeing with everything in your statement?'

'Yes.'

'He told me what he was doing at Chapman's Pool on Sunday.' He looked up at her. 'He's a complete idiot, but I don't think he's a rapist or a murderer.'

'So you were wrong about him?'

'Probably.'

'Good. It's bad for your character to have everything your own way. What about paedophile?'

'It depends on your definition of paedophilia.' He swung forward a chair and straddled it, resting his elbows along the back, content to watch her work. 'He's besotted with a fifteen-year-old girl who's so unhappy at home she keeps threatening to kill herself. She's an absolute stunner apparently, nearly six feet tall, looks twenty-five, ought to be a supermodel and turns heads wherever she goes. Her parents are separated and fight like cat and dog – her mother's jealous of her – her father has a string of bimbos – she's four months pregnant by Steve – refuses to have an abortion – weeps all over his manly bosom every time she sees him' – he lifted a sardonic eyebrow – 'which is probably why he finds her attractive – and is so desperate to have the baby and so desperate to be loved that she's twice tried to slit her wrists. Steve's solution to all this was to whisk her off to France in *Crazy Daze* where they could live' – another sardonic lift of an eyebrow – 'love's young dream without her parents having any idea where she'd gone or who she'd gone with.'

Maggie chuckled. 'I told you he was a good Samaritan.'

'Bluebeard, more like. She's fifteen.'

'And looks twenty-five.'

'If you believe Steve.'

'Don't you?'

'Put it this way,' he said dispassionately, 'I wouldn't let him within half a mile of a daughter of mine. He's oversexed, deeply enamoured with himself and has the morals of an alleycat.'

'A bit like the weasel I married in other words?' she asked dryly.

'No question about it.' He grinned up at her. 'But then I'm prejudiced of course.'

There was a glint of amusement in her eyes. 'So what happened? He got sidetracked by Paul and Danny and the whole thing went pear-shaped?'

He nodded. 'He realized, when he had to identify himself, that there was no point going on with it and signalled to his girlfriend to abandon it. Since when, he's had one tearful conversation with her over his mobile on his way back to Lymington on Sunday night, and hasn't been able to talk to her since because he's either been under arrest or separated from his phone. The rule is, she always calls him, and as he hasn't heard from her he's terrified she's killed herself.'

'Is it true?'

'No. One of the messages on his mobile was from her.'

'Still . . . poor boy. You've locked him up again, haven't you? He must be worried sick. Couldn't you have let him talk to her?'

He wondered at the vagaries of human nature. He would have bet on her sympathies being with the girl. 'Not allowed.'

'Oh, come on,' she said crossly. 'That's just cruel.'

'No. Common sense. Personally, I wouldn't trust him further than I could throw him. He's committed several crimes, don't forget. Assault on you, sex with an under-age girl, conspiracy to abduct, not to mention gross indecency and committing lewd acts in public . . .'

'Oh my God! You haven't charged him with having an erection, have you?'

'Not yet.'

'You *are* cruel,' she said in disgust. 'It was obviously his girlfriend he was looking at through the binoculars. On that basis you should have arrested Martin every time he put his hand on my arse.'

'I couldn't,' he said seriously. 'You never objected, so it didn't constitute an assault.'

There was a twinkle in her eye. 'What happened to indecency?'

'I never caught him with his trousers down,' he said with regret. 'I did try, but he was too bloody quick every time.'

'Are you winding me up?'

'No,' he said. 'I'm courting you.'

Half-asleep, Sandy Griffiths squinted at the luminous hands on her clock through gritty eyes, saw that it was three o'clock, and tried to remember if William had gone out earlier. Yet again, something had disturbed her intermittent dozing. She thought it was the front door closing, although she couldn't be sure if the sound had been real or if she'd dreamt it. She listened for footfalls on the stairs but, hearing only silence, stumbled out of bed and dragged on her dressing gown. Babies she thought she could probably cope with – a husband, *NEVER* . . .

She switched on the landing lamp and pushed open Hannah's bedroom door. A wedge of light cut across the cot, and her alarm subsided immediately. The child sat in the concentrated immobility that seemed to be her nature, thumb in mouth, staring wide-eyed with her curiously intense gaze. If she recognized Griffiths, she didn't show it. Instead she looked through her as if her mind saw images behind and beyond the woman that had no basis in reality, and Griffiths realized she was fast asleep. It explained the cot and the locks on all the doors. They were there to protect a sleepwalker, she understood belatedly, not to deprive a conscious child of adventure.

From outside, muffled by closed doors, she heard the sound of a car starting, followed by gears engaging and the scrunch of tyres on the drive. What the hell did the bloody man think he was doing now, she wondered? Did he seriously believe that abandoning his daughter in the early hours of the morning would endear him to social services? *Or was that the whole point?* Had he decided to ditch the responsibility once and for all?

Wearily she leaned against the door jamb and studied Kate's blank-eyed, blonde-haired replica with compassion and thought about what the doctor had said when he saw the smashed photographs in the fireplace. *'She's angry with her mother for deserting her . . . it's a perfectly normal expression of grief . . . get her father to cuddle her . . . that's the best way to fill the gap . . .'*

William Sumner's disappearance raised a few eyebrows in the incident room at Winfrith when Griffiths notified them of it, but little real interest. As so often in his life, he had ceased to matter. Instead, the spotlight turned on Beatrice 'Bibi' Gould who, when police knocked on her parents' door at 7.00 a.m. on Saturday morning, inviting her back to Winfrith for further questioning, burst into tears and locked herself in the bathroom, refusing to come out. When threatened with immediate arrest for obstruction, and on the promise that her parents could accompany her, she finally agreed to come out. Her fear seemed out of proportion to the police request and when asked to explain it she said, 'Everyone is going to be angry with me'.

Following a brief appearance before magistrates on his assault charge, Steven Harding, too, was invited for further questioning. He was chauffeured by a yawning Nick Ingram who took the opportunity to impart a few facts of life to the immature young man at his side. 'Just for the record, Steve, I'd break your legs if it was my fifteen-year-old daughter you'd got pregnant. As a matter of fact, I'd break your legs if you even laid a finger on her.'

Harding was unrepentant. 'Life's not like that any more. You can't order girls to behave the way you want them to behave. They decide for themselves.'

'Watch my lips, Steve. I said it's *your* legs I'd be breaking, not my daughter's. Trust me, the day I find a twenty-four-year-old man besmirching a beautiful child of mine is the day that bastard will wish he'd kept his zip done up.' Out of the corner of his eye he watched words begin to form on Harding's lips. 'And don't tell me she wanted it just as much as you did,' he snarled, 'or I'd be tempted to break your arms as well. Any little jerk can persuade a vulnerable adolescent into bed with him as long as he promises to love her. It takes a man to give her time to learn if the promise is worth anything.'

Bibi Gould refused to have her father in the interview room with her, but begged for her mother to sit with her and hold her hand. On the other side of the table, Detective Superintendent Carpenter and DI Galbraith took her through her previous statement. She quailed visibly in front of Carpenter's frown, and he only had to say: 'We believe you've been lying to us, young lady,' for the floodgates of truth to open.

'Dad doesn't like me spending weekends at Tony's . . . says I'm making myself cheap . . . He'd have gone spare if he'd known I'd passed out. Tony said it was alcohol poisoning because I was vomiting blood, but I think it was the bad E that his friend sold him . . . I was sick for hours after I came round . . . Dad would have killed me if he'd known . . . He hates Tony . . . He thinks he's a bad influence.' She laid her head on her mother's shoulder and sobbed heartily.

'When was this?' asked Carpenter.

'Last weekend. We were going to this rave in Southampton

so Tony got some E from this bloke he knows . . .' She faltered to a stop.

'Go on.'

'Everyone's going to be angry,' she wailed. 'Tony said why should we get his friend into trouble just because Steve's boat was in the wrong place.'

With considerable effort Carpenter managed to smooth his frown into something approaching fatherly kindness. 'We're not interested in Tony's friend, Bibi, we're only interested in getting an accurate picture of where everyone was last weekend. You've told us you're fond of Steven Harding,' he said disingenuously, 'and it will help Steve considerably if we can clear up some of the discrepancies around his story. You and Tony claimed you didn't see him on Saturday because you went to a rave in Southampton. Is that true?'

'It's true we didn't see him.' She sniffed. 'At least I didn't . . . I suppose Tony might have done . . . but it's not true about the rave. It didn't start till ten, so Tony said we might as well get in the mood earlier. The trouble is I can't remember much about it . . . We'd been drinking since five and then I took the E . . .' She wept into her mother's shoulder again.

'For the record, Bibi, you're telling us you took an Ecstasy tablet supplied to you by your boyfriend, Tony Bridges?'

She was alarmed by his tone. 'Yes,' she whispered.

'Have you ever passed out before in Tony's company?'

'Sometimes . . . if I drink too much.'

Pensively, Carpenter stroked his jaw. 'Do you know what time you took the tablet on Saturday?'

'Seven, maybe. I can't really remember.' She blew her nose into a Kleenex. 'Tony said he hadn't realized how much I'd been drinking, and that if he had he wouldn't have given it to me. It was awful . . . I'm never going to drink or take Ecstasy ever again . . . I've been feeling ill all week.' She raised a wan smile. 'I reckon it's true what they say about it. Tony thinks I was lucky not to die.'

Galbraith was less inclined to be fatherly. His private opinion of her was that she was a blousy slag with too much puppy fat and too little self-control, and he seriously pondered the mysteries of nature and chemistry that meant a girl like this could cause a previously sane man to behave with insanity. 'You were drunk again on Monday,' he reminded her, 'when DS Campbell visited Tony's house in the evening.'

She flicked him a sly up-from-under look that curdled any remnants of sympathy he might have had. 'I only had two lagers,' she said. 'I thought they'd make me feel better – but they didn't.'

Carpenter tapped his pen on the table to bring her attention back to him. 'What time did you come round on Sunday morning, Bibi?'

She shrugged self-pityingly. 'I don't know. Tony said I was sick for about ten hours, and I didn't stop till seven o'clock on Sunday evening. That's why I was late back to my parents'.'

'So about nine o'clock on Sunday morning then?'

She nodded. 'About that.' She turned her wet face to her mother. 'I'm ever so sorry, Mum. I'm never going to do it again.'

Mrs Gould squeezed the girl's shoulder and looked pleadingly at the two policemen. 'Does this mean she'll be prosecuted?'

'What for, Mrs Gould?'

'Taking Ecstasy?'

The Superintendent shook his head. 'I doubt it. As things stand, there isn't any evidence that she took any.' *Rohypnol, maybe* . . . 'But you're a very stupid young woman, Bibi, and I trust you won't come whining to the police with your troubles the next time you accept unknown and unidentified tablets from a man. Like it or not, you bear responsibility for your own behaviour, and the best advice I can offer you is to listen to your father once in a while.'

Good one, guv, thought Galbraith.

Carpenter tented his fingers over Bibi's previous statement. 'I don't like liars, young woman. None of us does. I think you told another lie last night to my colleague DI Galbraith, didn't you?'

Her eyes stretched in a kind of panic but she didn't answer.

'You said you've never been on *Crazy Daze* when we think you have.'

'I haven't.'

'You volunteered a set of your fingerprints at the beginning of the week. They match several sets found in the cabin of Steve's boat. Would you care to explain their presence in light of your denial that you've never been there?' He scowled at her.

'It's . . . Tony doesn't know, you see . . . oh God!' She shook with nerves. 'It was just . . . Steve and I got drunk one night when Tony was away. He'd be so *hurt* if he found out . . . he's got this thing about Steve being good-looking, and it'd *kill* him if he found out that we . . . well, you know . . .'

'That you had intercourse with Steven Harding on board *Crazy Daze?*'

'We were drunk. I don't even remember much about it. It didn't *mean* anything,' she said desperately, as if disloyalty could be excused when alcohol loosened inhibitions. But perhaps the concept of *in vino veritas* was too obscure for an immature nineteen-year-old to understand.

'Why are you so frightened of Tony finding out?' asked Carpenter curiously.

'I'm not.' Her eyes stretched wider in a visible demonstration that she was lying.

'What does he do to you, Bibi?'

'Nothing. It's just . . . he gets really jealous sometimes.'

'Of Steve?'

She nodded.

'How does he show it?'

316

She licked her lips. 'He's only done it once. He jammed my fingers in the car door after he found me in the pub with Steve. He said it was an accident, but . . . well . . . I don't think it was.'

'Was that before or after you slept with Steve?'

'After.'

'So he knew what you and Steve had done?'

She pressed her hands to her face. 'I don't see how he could have done . . . he wasn't around for the whole week but he's been – well, *odd* – ever since . . .'

'When did this happen?'

'Last half-term.'

Carpenter consulted his diary. 'Between 24 and 31 May?'

'It was a bank holiday, I know that.'

'Fine.' He smiled encouragingly. 'Only one or two more questions, Bibi, and then we're done. Do you remember an occasion when Tony was driving you somewhere in Steve's car and Kate Sumner had smeared the passenger door handle with her daughter's faeces?'

She pulled an expression of disgust. 'It was horrible. I got it all over my hand.'

'Can you remember when that was?'

She thought about it. 'I think it was the beginning of June. Tony said he'd take me to the flicks in Southampton but I had to wash my hands so much to get all the filth off that in the end we never went.'

'After you'd slept with Steve then?'

'Yes.'

'Thank you. Last question. Where did Tony stay while he was away?'

'*Miles* away,' she said with emphasis. 'His parents have a caravan at Lulworth Cove and Tony always goes there on his own when he needs to recharge his batteries. I keep telling him he should give up teaching because he really *hates* children. He says if he has a nervous breakdown it'll be *their* fault, even though everyone else will say it was because he smoked too much cannabis.'

Steven Harding's interview was tougher. He was informed that Marie Freemantle had given the police a statement about her relationship with him and that, because of her age, he could well face charges. Nevertheless, he declined the services of a solicitor, saying he had nothing to hide. He seemed to assume that Marie had been questioned as a result of his off-the-record conversation with Nick Ingram the previous evening, and neither Carpenter nor Galbraith disabused him of the fact.

'You are currently in a relationship with a fifteen-year-old by the name of Marie Freemantle?' said Carpenter.

'Yes.'

'Whom you knew to be under-age when you first had sexual intercourse with her?'

'Yes.'

'Where does Marie live?'

'Fifty-four Dancer Road, Lymington.'

'Why did your agent tell us you have a girlfriend called Marie living in London?'

'Because that's where he thinks she lives. He got her some work and, as she didn't want her parents to know about it, we gave the address of a shop in London that acts as a postal drop.'

'What sort of work?'

'Nude work.'

'Pornography?'

Harding looked uncomfortable. 'Only soft porn.'

'Video or stills?'

'Stills.'

'Were you in the shots with her?'

'Some,' he admitted.

'Where are those photographs now?'

'I dropped them over the side of my boat.'

'Because they showed you performing indecent acts with an under-age girl?'

'She doesn't look under-age.'

'Answer the question, Steve. Did you put them over the side because they showed you performing indecent acts with an under-age girl?'

Harding nodded.

'For the purposes of the tape, Steven Harding nodded agreement. Did Tony Bridges know you were sleeping with Marie Freemantle?'

'What's Tony got to do with it?'

'Answer the question, Steve.'

'I don't think so. I never told him.'

'Did he see the photographs of her?'

'Yes. He came out to my boat on Monday and they were on the table.'

'Did he see them before Monday?'

'I don't know. He trashed my boat four months ago.' He ran his tongue round his dry mouth. 'He might have found them then.'

Carpenter leaned back, his fingers toying with his pen. 'Which would have made him angry,' he said, more as a statement than a question. 'She's a pupil of his and he had a fondness for her himself, albeit a hands-off one because of his position, which you knew about.'

'I – er – guess so.'

'We understand you met Marie Freemantle on 14 February. Was that while you were having a relationship with Kate Sumner?'

'I didn't have a relationship with Kate.' He blinked nervously, trying like Tony the night before to pre-guess the direction the questions were going. 'I went back to her house one time and she kind of . . . well . . . threw herself at me. It was okay, but I've never been that keen on older women.

I made it clear I wasn't interested in anything long term and I thought she understood. It was just a quick shag in her kitchen – nothing to get excited about.'

'So when Tony tells us the relationship went on for three or four months, he's lying?'

'Oh, Jesus!' Harding's nervousness increased. 'Listen, I may have given him that impression. I mean I knew Kate . . . you know, as an acquaintance . . . for quite a while before we actually got it together, and I may have . . . well, given Tony the idea there was a bit more to it than there actually was. It was a joke, really. He's a bit of a prude.'

Carpenter watched him for a moment, before lowering his eyes to a piece of paper on the table in front of him. 'Three months after meeting Marie, some time during the week 24–31 May, you had a one-night stand with Bibi Gould, Tony Bridges' girlfriend. Is that right?'

Harding gave a small groan. 'Oh, come on! That really *was* nothing. We got drunk in the pub and I took her back to *Crazy Daze* to sleep it off because Tony was away and his house was locked up. She came on to me a bit strong and . . . well, to be honest, I don't remember much about it. I was rat-arsed and couldn't swear that anything happened worth recording.'

'Does Tony know?'

He didn't answer immediately. 'I don't – look, why do you keep going on about Tony?'

'Answer the question, please. Does Tony know that you slept with his girlfriend?'

'I don't know. He's been a bit off recently, so I've been wondering if he saw me ferrying her back to the slip the next morning.' With a worried gesture, he pulled at the hair that flopped across his forehead. 'He was supposed to be staying the whole week in his folks' caravan, but Bob Winterslow said he saw him that day at his grandad's place, getting ready to tow his rib out.'

'Can you remember which day it was?'

'Bank holiday Monday. Bibi's hairdressing salon doesn't open on bank holidays which is why she was able to stay over on Sunday night.' He waited for Carpenter to speak, and when he didn't, he gave a small shrug. 'Listen, it was no big deal. I planned to square it with Tony if he ever said anything' – another shrug – 'but he never did.'

'Does he normally say something when you sleep with his girlfriends?'

'I don't make a habit of it, for Christ's sake. The trouble is . . . well, Bibi was like Kate. You try and be nice to a woman, and the next minute they're climbing all over you.'

Carpenter frowned. 'Are you saying they forced you to have intercourse with them?'

'No, but—'

'Then spare me the excuses.' He consulted his notes again. 'How did your agent get the idea Bibi was your girlfriend?'

Harding tugged at his hair again and had the grace to look embarrassed. 'Because I told him she was a bit of a goer.'

'Meaning she'd be amenable to pornographic stills?'

'Yes.'

'Would your agent have mentioned that to Tony?'

Harding shook his head. 'If he had, Tony would have taken me apart.'

'Except he didn't take you apart over Kate Sumner, did he?'

The young man was clearly baffled by the question. 'Tony didn't know Kate.'

'How well did *you* know her, Steve?'

'That's the crazy thing,' he said. 'Hardly at all . . . okay, we did it once but . . . well, it doesn't mean you get to know someone, does it? I avoided her afterwards because it was embarrassing. Then she started treating me as if I'd wronged her in some way.'

Carpenter pulled out Harding's statement. 'You claimed she was obsessed with you, Steve. "*I knew she had a serious crush on me . . .*"' he read. '"*She used to hang around by the yacht club waiting for me to come ashore . . . Most of the time she just stood and watched me, but sometimes she'd deliberately bump into me and rub her breasts against my arm . . ."*' 'Is any of that true?'

'I may have exaggerated a bit. She did hang around for about a week till she realized I wasn't interested. Then she sort of . . . well, abandoned the idea, I suppose. I didn't see her again till she did the thing with the nappy.'

Carpenter sorted Tony Bridges' statement from the pile. 'This is what Tony said: "*He told me on more than one occasion this year that he was having problems with a woman called Kate Sumner who was stalking him . . .*" Did you decide to exaggerate a bit when you told Tony?'

'Yes.'

'Did you refer to Kate as a "tart"?'

He hunched his shoulders. 'It was just an expression.'

'Did you tell Tony Kate was easy?'

'Listen, it was a joke. He used to have a real hang-up about sex. Everyone used to tease him, not just me . . . then Bibi came along and he . . . well, lightened up.'

Carpenter studied him closely for a moment. 'So did you sleep with Bibi for a joke?'

Harding stared at his hands. 'I didn't do it for any particular reason. It just happened. I mean she really *was* easy. The only reason she hangs around with Tony is because she's got a thing about me. Look' – he hunched further into his seat – 'you don't want to get the wrong idea about all of this.'

'What wrong idea's that, Steve?'

'I don't know, but you seem to have it in for Tony.'

'With reason,' said Carpenter, easing another piece of paper from the pile in front of him and hiding the contents with cupped fingers. 'We've been told you watched him feed Bibi a drug called' – he lowered his eyes to the paper, as if the word were written there – '*Rohypnol* so she wouldn't complain about his performance. Is that true?'

322

'Oh, shit!' He rested his head in his hands. 'I suppose Marie's been spouting her mouth off?' His fingers caressed his temples in soft, circular movements, and Galbraith was fascinated by the gracefulness of his actions. He was an extraordinarily beautiful young man and it didn't surprise him that Kate had found him more attractive than William.

'Is it true, Steve?'

'Sort of. He told me he slipped it to her once when she was giving him a load of grief but I didn't see him do it, and for all I know he was lying through his teeth.'

'How did he know about Rohypnol?'

'Everyone knows.'

'Did you tell him?'

Harding lifted his head to look at the paper in front of the Superintendent, clearly wondering how much information was written there. 'His grandad hasn't been sleeping too well since his wife died so the GP prescribed him Rohypnol. Tony was telling me about it, so I laughed and said it could sort all his problems if he could get hold of some of it. It's not my fault if the stupid fucker used it.'

'Have you used it, Steve?'

'Do me a favour! Why would I need to?'

A faint smile crossed Carpenter's face as he changed tack. 'How soon after the incident with the nappy did Kate start smearing Hannah's faeces on your car and setting the alarm off?'

'I don't know. A few days, maybe.'

'How did you know it was her?'

'Because she'd left Hannah's crap on the sheets in my boat.'

'Which was some time towards the end of April?' Harding nodded. 'But she didn't start this' – Carpenter sought a suitable phrase – ' "dirty campaign" until after she realized you weren't interested in pursuing a relationship with her?'

'It's not my *fault*,' he said despairingly. 'She was . . . *so* . . . *fucking . . . boring.*'

'The question I asked you, Steve,' repeated Carpenter patiently, 'was did she start her "dirty" campaign after she realized you weren't interested in her?'

'Yes.' He jabbed the heels of his palms against his eyelids in an effort to recall detail. 'She just made my life hell until I couldn't stand it any longer. That's when I thought of persuading William to tell her I was an arse-bandit.'

The Superintendent ran a finger down Harding's statement. 'Which was in June?'

'Yes.'

'Any particular reason why you waited a month and a half to put a stop it?'

'Because it was getting worse not better,' the young man said with a sudden rush of anger as if the memory still rankled deeply. 'I thought she'd run out of steam if I was patient, but when she started targeting my dinghy, I decided enough was enough. I reckoned she'd start on *Crazy Daze* next, and there was no way I was going to let her do that.'

Carpenter nodded as if he thought the explanation a reasonable one. He pulled out Harding's statement again and ran his finger down it. 'So you sought out William and showed him photographs of yourself in a gay magazine because you wanted him to tell his wife you were gay?'

'Yes.'

'Mmm.' Carpenter reached for Tony Bridges' statement. 'Tony, on the other hand, says that when you told him you were going to report Kate to the police for harassing you, he advised you to move your car instead. According to him *that's* what sorted the problem. In fact, he thought it was pretty funny when we told him last night that your solution to Kate's harassment was to show William gay pictures of yourself. He said: "*Steve always was as thick as two short planks.*"'

Harding shrugged. 'So? It worked. That's all I was interested in.'

Slowly, Carpenter squared the papers on the table in front

of him. 'Why do you think that was?' he asked. 'I mean, you're not seriously suggesting that a woman who was so angry at being rejected that she was prepared to harass and intimidate you for weeks would meekly give up when she found out you were gay? Or are you? Admittedly I'm no expert in mental disorders but I'd guess the intimidation would become mark-edly worse. No one likes to be made a fool of, Steve.'

Harding stared at him in perplexity. 'Except she *did* stop.'

The Superintendent shook his head. 'You can't stop some-thing you never started, son. Oh, she certainly wiped Hannah's nappy on your sheets in a moment of irritation, which probably gave Tony the idea, but it wasn't Kate who was getting her own back on you, it was your friend. It was a peculiarly apt revenge after all. You've been crapping on his doorstep for years. It must have given him a hell of a buzz to pay you back in your own coin. The only reason he stopped was because you were threatening to go to the police.'

A sickly smile washed across Harding's face like wet water colour. He looked ill, thought Carpenter with satisfaction.

William Sumner's mother had long since given up trying to induce her son to talk. Her initial surprise at his unheralded appearance in her flat had given way to fear and, like a hostage, she sought to appease and not to confront. Whatever had brought him back to Chichester was not something he wanted to share with her. He seemed to alternate between anger and anguish, rocking himself to and fro in bouts of frenetic move-ment only to collapse in tear-sodden lethargy when the fit passed. She was unable to help him. He guarded the telephone with the singlemindedness of a madman and, handicapped by immobility and dread, she withdrew into silent observation.

He had become a stranger to her in the last twelve months and a kind of subdued dislike drove her towards cruelty. She found herself despising him. He had always been spineless, she thought, which was why Kate had gained such an easy ascendancy over him. Her mouth pinched into lines of contempt as she listened to the dry sobs that racked his thin frame and, when he finally broke his silence, she realized with a sense of inevitability that she could have predicted what he was going to say. '. . . I didn't know what to do . . ."

She guessed he had killed his wife. She feared now he had also killed his child.

Tony Bridges rose to his feet as the cell door opened and viewed Galbraith with an uneasy smile. He was diminished by incarceration, a small insignificant man who had discovered what it meant to have his life controlled by others. Gone was the cocksure attitude of yesterday, in its place a nervous recognition that his ability to persuade had been blunted by the stone wall of police distrust. 'How long are you going to keep me here?'

'As long as it takes, Tony.'

'I don't know what you want from me.'

'The truth.'

'All I did was steal a boat.'

Galbraith shook his head. He fancied he saw a momentary regret in the frightened gaze that briefly met his before he stood back to let the young man pass. It was remorse of a kind, he supposed.

'. . . I didn't mean to do it. I didn't do it – not really. Kate would still be alive if she hadn't tried to push me over the side. It's her fault she's dead. We were getting on fine until she made a lunge at me, then the next thing I knew she was in the water. You can't blame me for that. Don't you think I'd have drowned Hannah too if I'd intended to kill her mother . . . ?'

Chapter Twenty-five

BROXTON HOUSE SLUMBERED peacefully in the afternoon sunshine as Nick Ingram pulled up in front of the porticoed entrance. As always he paused to admire its clean, square lines and, as always, regretted its slow deterioration. To him, perhaps more than to the Jenners, it represented something valuable, a living reminder that beauty existed in everything; but then he, despite his job, was enduringly sentimental, and they were not. The double doors stood wide open, an invitation to any passing thief, and he picked up Celia's handbag from the hall table as he passed on his way to the drawing room. Silence lay across the house like a blanket of dust, and he worried suddenly that he had come too late. Even his own footfalls on the marble floor were just a whisper in the great emptiness that surrounded him.

He eased open the drawing-room door and stepped inside. Celia was propped up in bed, bifocals slipping off the end of her nose, mouth open, snoring quietly, with Bertie's head on the pillow beside her. They looked like a tableau out of *The Godfather*, and Nick was hard-pushed not to laugh out loud. The sentimentalist in him viewed them fondly. Maybe Maggie was right, he thought. Maybe happiness was more to do with bodily contact than with hygiene. Who cared about tannin in teacups when you had a hairy hot-water bottle who was prepared to lie with you and love you when no one else would? He tapped lightly on one of the door panels and watched with amusement as Bertie opened a cautious eye then closed it again in obvious relief when he realized Nick wasn't going to make any demands on his loyalty.

'I'm not asleep, you know,' said Celia, raising a hand to adjust her spectacles. 'I heard you come in.'

'Am I disturbing you?'

'No.' She hoisted herself into a more upright position, tugging her bedjacket across her chest in a belated attempt to safeguard her dignity.

'You shouldn't leave your bag on the hall table,' he told her, walking across to put it on the bed. 'Anyone could steal it.'

'They're welcome to it, my dear. There's nothing in it worth taking.' She examined him closely. 'I prefer you in uniform. Dressed like that, you look like a gardener.'

'I said I'd help Maggie with the painting and I can't paint in my uniform.' He pulled forward a chair. 'Where is she?'

'Where you told her to be. In the kichen.' She sighed. 'I worry about her, Nick. I didn't bring her up to be a manual labourer. She'll have navvy's hands before she's finished.'

'She already has. You can't muck out stables and scrub horse buckets day after day and keep your hands pretty. The two are mutually exclusive.'

She tut-tutted disapprovingly. 'A gentleman doesn't notice that kind of thing.'

He'd always been fond of her. He didn't know why except that her forthright approach appealed to him. Perhaps she reminded him of his own mother, a down-to-earth Cockney who had been dead for ten years. Certainly he found people who spoke their minds easier to get on with than those who cloaked their feelings in hypocritical smiles. 'He probably does, you know. He just doesn't mention it.'

'But that's the whole point, you silly fellow,' she said crossly. 'A gentleman is known by his manners.'

He grinned. 'So you prefer a man who lies to a man who is

honest? That's not the impression you gave me four years ago when Robert Healey did his bunk.'

'Robert Healey was a criminal.'

'But an attractive one.'

She frowned at him. 'Have you come here to annoy me?'

'No, I came to see if you were all right.'

She waved a hand in dismissal. 'Well, I am. Go and find Maggie. I'm sure she'll be pleased to see you.'

He made no move to go. 'Were either of you ever called as a witness in Healey's trial?' he asked her.

'You know we weren't. He was only tried for his last fraud. All the rest of us had to take a back seat in case we confused the issue, and that made me more angry than anything. I wanted my day in court so that I could tell the little beast what I thought of him. I was never going to get my money back, but at least I could have taken my pound of flesh.' She folded her arms across her chest like armour plating. 'However, it's not a subject I wish to dwell on. It's unhealthy to rake over the past.'

'Did you read the reports of the trial?' he went on, ignoring her.

'One or two,' she said curtly, 'until I gave up in fury.'

'What made you furious?'

A small tic started above her lip. 'They described his victims as lonely women, desperate for love and attention. I've never been so incensed about anything. It made us look such fools.'

'But your case wasn't tried,' he pointed out, 'and that description applied to his last victims – two elderly unmarried sisters who lived alone in an isolated farmhouse in Cheshire. A perfect target for Healey, in other words. It was only because he tried to speed up the fraud by forging their names on cheques that he was discovered. The sisters' bank manager was worried enough to go to the police.'

The tic fluttered on. 'Except I sometimes think it was true,' she said with difficulty. 'I never thought of us as lonely, but we did rather blossom when he came into our lives and I'm humiliated every time I remember it.'

Ingram reached into the back pocket of his jeans and pulled out a newspaper clipping. 'I brought something I want to read to you. It's what the judge told Healey before he passed sentence.' He smoothed the paper on his lap. '"*You're an educated man with a high IQ and an engaging manner*",' he read, '"*and these qualities make you extremely dangerous. You display a ruthless disregard for your victims' feelings while at the same time exercising considerable charm and intelligence to convince them of your sincerity. Too many women have been taken in by you for anyone to believe that THEIR*"' – he stressed the word – '"*gullibility was the only reason for your success, and I am persuaded that you represent a real menace to society.*"' He laid the clipping on the bed. 'What the judge recognized is that Healey *was* a charming and intelligent man.'

'It was pretence,' she said, reaching for the comfort of Bertie's ears and tugging at them. 'He was an actor.'

Ingram thought of Steven Harding's very moderate acting skills, and shook his head. 'I don't think so,' he said gently. 'No one could keep up a pretence like that for a year. The charm was genuine which is what you and Maggie were attracted by, and it seems to me that the problem you both have is coming to terms with that. It makes his betrayal so much worse if you liked him.'

'No.' She pulled a tissue from under her pillow and blew her nose. 'What upsets me more is that I thought he liked *us*. We're not so difficult to love, are we?'

'Not at all. I'm sure he adored you both. Everyone else does.'

'Oh, don't be absurd!' Celia snapped. 'He wouldn't have stolen from us if he had.'

'Of course he would.' Ingram propped his chin in his hands and stared at her. 'The trouble with you, Mrs J, is that you're a conformist. You assume everyone does and should behave the same way. But Healey was a professional conman. Theft was his business. He'd made a ten-year career out of it, don't forget. That doesn't mean he wasn't fond of you, any more than it would mean I wasn't fond of you if I had to arrest you.' His mouth twitched into a crooked smile. 'We do what we're good at in this life if we don't want to starve, and we cry all the way to the bank if it upsets us.'

'That's nonsense.'

'Is it? Do you think I take pleasure arresting a ten-year-old kid for vandalism when I know he comes from a lousy home, truants because he can't read, and is likely to get a belting from his drunken mother because she's too stupid to deal with him in any other way? I caution the boy because that's what I'm paid to do, but I'm always a damn sight fonder of him than I am of his mother. Criminals are human like everyone else, and there's no law that says they aren't likable.'

She peered at him over her bifocals. 'Yes, but *you* didn't like Martin, Nick, so don't pretend you did.'

'No, I didn't,' he admitted, 'but it was a personal thing. I thought the guy was a grade A prat. If I'm honest, though, I never believed for one moment that Mrs Fielding was telling the truth when she accused him of trying to steal her antiques. As far as I was concerned he was whiter than white . . . bloody perfect, in fact . . . every young woman's dream.' The smile became even more crooked. 'I assumed – and still do because it didn't fit Healey's MO – that it was Mrs Fielding's senility talking, and the only reason I came to you about it was because I couldn't resist the opportunity to take him down a peg or two.' He raised his eyes to hers. 'It certainly didn't give me any insights into what he was really up to. Even when Simon Farley told me he'd passed a couple of dud cheques in the pub and asked me to get it sorted quietly because he didn't want any fuss, it never occurred to me that Martin was a professional. If it had, I'd have approached it differently, and maybe you wouldn't have lost your money and maybe your husband would still be alive.'

'Oh, for God's sake!' she said gruffly, pulling so hard on Bertie's ears that the poor animal furrowed his brow in pain. 'Don't you start feeling guilty, too.'

'Why not? If I'd been older and wiser I might have done my job better.'

With an uncharacteristic display of tenderness, she laid a hand on his shoulder. 'I have enough trouble coping with my own guilt without carrying yours and Maggie's as well. According to Maggie, her father dropped dead because she was shouting at him. *My* recollection is that he threw a two-week tantrum then dropped dead after a drinking bout in his study. If my son is to be believed, he died of a broken heart because Maggie and I treated him like a cipher in his own house.' She sighed. 'The truth is Keith was a chronic alcoholic with a history of heart disease who could have died at any moment, although clearly Martin's shenanigans didn't help. And it wasn't as though it was Keith's money that was stolen. It was mine. My father left me ten thousand in his will twenty years ago, and I managed to work it up to over a hundred thousand by playing the stock market.' She frowned in irritation at the memory, before giving Ingram's shoulder a sudden sharp rap. 'This is ridiculous. When all's said and done, the only person to blame is Robert Healey and I refuse to let anyone else take responsibility.'

'Does that include you and Maggie or are you going to go on wearing sackcloth and ashes so that the rest of us feel guilty by association?'

She regarded him thoughtfully for a moment. 'I was right about you yesterday,' she said. 'You are a *very* provoking young man.' She flapped a hand towards the hall. 'Go away and make yourself useful. Help my daughter.'

'She's doing a fine job on her own. I'll probably just stand back and watch.'

'I wasn't talking about painting the kitchen,' Celia retorted.

'Neither was I, but the answer's still the same.'

She peered at him blankly for a moment, then gave a throaty chuckle. 'On the principle that everything comes to him who waits?'

'It's worked up till now,' he said, reaching for one of her hands and holding it lightly. 'You're a gutsy lady, Mrs J. I always wanted to know you better.'

'Oh, for goodness sake, get on with you!' she said, smacking him away. 'I'm beginning to think Robert Healey was a novice compared with you.' She wagged a finger at him. 'And don't call me Mrs J. It's appallingly *infra dig* and makes me sound like a cleaner.' She closed her eyes and took a deep breath as if she were about to bestow the crown jewels on him. 'You may call me Celia.'

'... I couldn't think properly, that was the trouble ... if she'd just listened to me instead of shouting all the time ... I suppose what surprised me was how strong she was ... I wouldn't have broken her fingers otherwise ... it was easy ... they were tiny, like little wishbones, but it's not the kind of thing a man wants to do ... put it this way, I'm not proud of it ...'

Nick found Maggie in the kitchen, arms crossed, staring out of the window at the horses in the drought-starved paddock. The ceiling had received a coat of brilliant white emulsion but none of the walls had yet been touched, and the paint-roller had been abandoned to harden in the tray. 'Look at those poor brutes,' she said. 'I think I'm going to phone the RSPCA and have their beastly owners prosecuted.'

He knew her too well. 'What's really bugging you?'

She swung round defiantly. 'I heard it all,' she said. 'I was listening outside the door. I suppose you thought you were being clever?'

'In what way?'

'Martin took the trouble to seduce Mother before he seduced me,' she said. 'At the time I was impressed by his tactics. Afterwards, I decided it was the one thing that should have warned me he was a cheat and a liar.'

'Perhaps he found her easier to get on with,' Nick suggested mildly. 'She's good news, your ma. And, for the record, I have no intention of seducing you. It'd be like fighting my way through half a mile of razor wire – painful, unrewarding, and bloody hard work.'

She favoured him with a twisted smile. 'Well, don't expect *me* to seduce *you*,' she said tartly, 'because you'll be waiting for ever if you do.'

He prized the paint-roller out of the tray and held it under a running tap in the sink. 'Trust me. Nothing is further from my mind. I'm far too frightened of having my jaw broken.'

'Martin didn't have a problem.'

'No,' he said dryly. 'But then Martin wouldn't have had a problem with the Elephant Man as long as there was money in it. Does your mother have a scrubbing brush? We need to remove the hardened paint from this tray.'

'You'll have to look in the scullery.' She watched in an infuriated silence while he scrabbled around among four years' detritus in search of cleaning implements. 'You're such a hypocrite,' she said then. 'You've just spent half an hour boosting Ma's self-esteem by telling her how lovable she is, but I get compared with the Elephant Man.'

There was a muffled laugh. 'Martin didn't sleep with your mother.'

'What difference does that make?'

He emerged with a bucket full of impacted rags. 'I'm having trouble with the fact that you sleep with a dog,' he said severely. 'I'm buggered if I'll turn a blind eye to a weasel as well.'

There was a brief silence before Maggie gave a splutter of laughter. 'Bertie's in bed with Ma at the moment.'

'I know. He's about the worst guard dog I've ever encountered.' He took the bundle of cloth out of the bucket and held it up for inspection. 'What the hell is this?'

More laughter. 'They're my father's Y-fronts, you idiot. Ma uses them instead of J-cloths because they don't cost anything.'

'Oh, right.' He put the bucket in the sink to fill it with water. 'I can see the logic. He was a big fellow, your dad. There's enough material here to cover a three-piece suite.' He separated out a pair of striped boxer shorts. 'Or a deckchair,' he finished thoughtfully.

Her eyes narrowed suspiciously. 'Don't even think about using my father's underpants to seduce me, you bastard, or I'll empty that entire bucket over your head.'

He grinned at her. 'This isn't seduction, Maggie, this is courtship. If I wanted to seduce you I'd have brought several bottles of brandy with me.' He wrung out the boxer shorts and held them up for inspection. 'However . . . if you think these would be effective . . . ?'

'. . . most of the time it's just me, the boat and the sea . . . I like that . . . I feel comfortable with space around me . . . people can get on your nerves after a while . . . they always want something from you . . . usually love . . . but it's all pretty shallow . . . Marie? She's okay . . . nothing great . . . sure I feel responsible for her, but not for ever . . . nothing's for ever . . . except the sea . . . and death . . .'

Chapter Twenty-six

JOHN GALBRAITH PAUSED beside William Sumner's car in the Chichester street and stooped to look in through the window. The weather was still set fair and the heat from the sun-baked roof warmed his face. He walked up the path towards Angela Sumner's flat and rang the doorbell. He waited for the chain to rattle into place. 'Good afternoon, Mrs Sumner,' he said when her bright eyes peered anxiously through the gap. 'I think you must have William in there.' He gestured towards the parked car. 'May I talk to him?'

With a sigh, she released the chain and pulled the door wide. 'I wanted to phone you but he pulled the wire out of the wall when I suggested it.'

Galbraith nodded. 'We've tried your number several times but there was never any answer. If the phone wasn't plugged in, that explains it. I thought I'd come anyway.'

She turned her chair to lead him down the corridor. 'He keeps saying he didn't know what to do. Does that mean he killed her?'

Galbraith laid a comforting hand on her shoulder. 'No,' he said. 'Your son isn't a murderer, Mrs Sumner. He loved Kate. I think he'd have given her the earth if she'd asked him for it.'

They paused in the sitting-room doorway. William sat huddled in an armchair, arms wrapped protectively about himself and the telephone in his lap, his jaw dark with stubble and his eyes red-rimmed and puffy from too much weeping and too little sleep. Galbraith studied him with concern, recognizing that he bore some of the responsibility for pushing him towards the brink. He could excuse his prying into William's and Kate's secrets on the grounds of justice, but it was a cold logic. He could have been kinder, he thought – one could always be kinder – but, sadly, kindness rarely elicited truth.

He squeezed Angela Sumner's shoulder. 'Perhaps you could make us a cup of tea,' he suggested, moving aside for her wheelchair to reverse. 'I'd like to have a few words with William alone, if that's possible.'

She nodded gratefully. 'I'll wait till you call me.'

He closed the door behind her and listened to the whine of the battery fading into the kitchen. 'We've caught Kate's killer, William,' he said, taking the seat opposite the man. 'Steven Harding has been formally charged with her abduction, rape and murder and will be remanded to prison shortly to await trial. I want to stress that Kate was not a party to what happened to her, but on the contrary fought hard to save herself and Hannah.' He paused briefly to search William's face, but went on when there was no reaction. 'I'm not going to pretend she didn't have sex with Steven Harding prior to the events of last week because she did. However, it was a brief affair some months ago, and followed a prolonged campaign by Harding to break her down. Nevertheless – and this is important' – he glossed the truth deliberately in Kate's favour – 'it's clear she made up her mind very quickly to put an end to the relationship when she recognized that her marriage was more important to her than a mild infatuation with a younger man. Her misfortune was her failure to recognize that Steven Harding is self-fixated and dangerously immature and that she needed to be afraid of him.' Another pause. 'She was lonely, William.'

A strangled sob issued from the other man's mouth. 'I've been hating her so much . . . I knew he was more than a casual acquaintance when she said she didn't want him in the house any more. She used to flirt with him at the beginning, then she turned vicious and started calling him names . . . I guessed he'd got bored with her . . .'

'Is that when he showed you the photographs?'

'Yes.'

'Why did he do that, William?'

'He said he wanted me to show them to Kate but . . .' He lifted a trembling hand to his mouth.

Galbraith recalled something Tony had said the previous evening. '*The only reason Steve does pornography is because he knows it's inadequate guys who're going to look at it. He doesn't have any hang-ups about sex so it gives him a buzz to think of them squirming over pictures of him . . .*'

'But he really wanted to show them to you?'

Sumner nodded. 'He wanted to prove that Kate would sleep with anyone – even a man who preferred other men – rather than sleep with me.' Tears streamed down his face. 'I think she must have told him I wasn't very good. I said I didn't want to see the pictures, so he put the magazine on the table in front of me and told me to' – he struggled with the words, closing his eyes in pain, as if to blot out the memory – ' "suck on it".'

'Did he say he'd slept with Kate?'

'He didn't need to. I knew when Hannah let him pick her up in the street that something was going on . . . she's never let me do that.' More tears squeezed from his tired eyes.

'What *did* he say, William?'

He plucked at his mouth. 'That Kate was making his life hell by smearing Hannah's nappies on his possessions, and that if I didn't make her stop he'd go to the police.'

'And you believed him?'

'Kate was – like that,' he said with a break in his voice. 'She could be spiteful when she didn't get her own way.'

'Did you show her the magazine?'

'No.'

'What did you do with it?'

'Kept it in my car.'

'Why?'

'To look at . . . remember . . .' He rested his head against the back of the chair and stared at the ceiling. 'Have something to hate, I suppose.'

'Did you tackle Kate about it?'

'There was no point. She'd have lied.'

'So what did you do?'

'Nothing,' he said simply. 'Went on as if nothing had happened. Stayed late at work . . . sat in my study . . . avoided her . . . I couldn't *think*, you see. I kept wondering if the baby was mine.' He turned to look at the policeman. 'Was it?'

Galbraith leaned forward and clamped his hands between his knees. 'The pathologist estimated the foetus at fourteen weeks, making conception early May, but Kate's affair with Harding finished at the end of March. I can ask the pathologist to run a DNA test if you want absolute proof, but I don't think there's any doubt Kate was carrying your son. She didn't sleep around, William.' He paused to let the information sink in. 'But there's no doubt Steven Harding accused her wrongly of harassment. Yes, she lashed out once in a moment of pique, but probably only because she was annoyed with herself for having given in to him. The real culprit was a friend of Harding's. Kate rejected him, so he used her as a shield for his own revenge without ever considering the sort of danger he might be putting her into.'

'*I never thought he'd do anything to her . . . Jesus! Do you think I wanted her killed? She was a sad person . . . lonely . . . boring . . . God, if she had anything going for her she kept it well hidden . . . Look, I know this sounds bad – I'm not proud of it now – but I found it funny the way Steve reacted. He was shit-scared of her. That stuff about dodging round corners was all true. He thought she was going to attack him in the middle of the street if she managed to catch him unawares. He kept talking about the movie* Fatal Attraction, *and saying Michael Douglas's mistake was not to let the Glenn Close character die when she tried to kill herself.'*

'Why didn't you tell us this before?' Carpenter had asked.

'Because you have to believe someone's guilty before you get yourself into trouble. In a million years I wouldn't have thought Steve had anything to do with it. He doesn't go in for violence.'

'Try violation instead,' Carpenter had said. 'Off-hand, can you think of anything or anyone your friend has not violated? Hospitality ... friendship ... marriage ... women ... young girls ... every bloody law you can think of ... Did it never occur to you, Tony, that someone so intensely sociopathic as Steven Harding, so careless of other people's sensibilities, might represent a danger to a woman he thought had been terrorizing him?'

Sumner continued to stare at the ceiling, as if answers lay somewhere within its white surface. 'How did he get her on to his boat if she wasn't interested any more?' he asked flatly. 'You said no one had seen her with him after he spoke to her outside Tesco's.'

'She smiled at me as if nothing had happened,' Harding had told them, 'asked me how I was and how the acting was going. I said she had a bloody nerve even talking to me after what she'd done, and she just laughed and told me to grow up. "You did me a favour," she said. "You taught me to appreciate William, and if I don't hold any grudges why should you?" I told her she knew fucking well why I held a grudge, so she started to look cross. "It was payment in kind," she said. "You were crap." Then she walked away. I think that's what made me angry – I hate it when people walk away from me – but I knew the woman in Tesco's was watching so I crossed the High Street and went down behind the market stalls on the other side of the road, watching her. All I planned to do was have it out with her, tell her she was lucky I hadn't gone to the police ...'

'Saturday's market day in Lymington High Street,' said Galbraith, 'so the place was packed with visitors from outside.

People don't notice things in a crowd. He followed her at a distance, waiting for her to turn towards home again.'

'*She looked pretty angry so I think I must have upset her. She turned down Captain's Row, so I knew she was probably going home. I gave her a chance, you know. I thought if she took the top road I'd let her go, but if she took the bottom road past the yacht club and Tony's garage I'd teach her a lesson . . .*'

'He has the use of a garage about two hundred yards from your house,' Galbraith went on. 'He caught up with her as she was passing it and persuaded her and Hannah to go inside. She'd been in several times before with Harding's friend, Tony Bridges, so it obviously didn't occur to her there was anything to worry about.'

'*Women are such stupid bitches. They'll fall for anything as long as a bloke sounds sincere. All I had to do was tell her I was sorry, and squeeze a couple of tears out – I'm an actor so I'm good at that – and she was all smiles again and said, no, she was sorry, she hadn't meant to be cruel and couldn't we let bygones be bygones and stay friends? So I said, sure, and why didn't I give her some champagne out of Tony's garage to show there were no hard feelings? You can drink it with William, I said, as long as you don't tell him it came from me. If there'd been anyone in the street or if old Mr Bridges had been at his curtains, I wouldn't have done it. But it was so bloody easy. Once I'd closed the garage doors, I knew I could do anything I wanted . . .*'

'You need to remember how little she knew about him, William. According to Harding himself, her entire knowledge of him came from two months of constant flattery and attention while he wanted to get her into bed, a brief period of unsatisfactory love-making on both sides which resulted in *him* giving her the cold shoulder and *her* taking petty revenge with Hannah's nappy on his cabin sheets, then four months of mutual avoidance. As far as she was concerned, it was old history. She didn't know his car was being daubed with faeces, didn't know he'd approached you and told you to warn her off, so when she accepted a glass of champagne in the garage, she genuinely thought it was the peace-offering he said it was.'

'*If she hadn't told me William was away for the weekend I wouldn't have gone through with it, but you kind of get the feeling that some things are meant to happen. It was her fault really. She kept on about how she had nothing to go home for, so I offered her a drink. If I'm honest, I'd say she was up for it. You could tell she was pleased as bloody punch to find herself alone with me. Hannah wasn't a problem. She's always liked me. I'm about the only person, other than her mother, who could pick her up without her screaming . . .*'

'He put her to sleep, using a benzodiazepine hypnotic drug called Rohypnol which he dissolved in the champagne. It's been called the date-rape drug because it's easy to give to a woman without her knowing. It's powerful enough to keep her out for six to ten hours, and in the cases reported so far, women claim intermittent periods of consciousness when they know what's happening to them but an inability to do anything about it. We understand there are moves to change it to a schedule 3 controlled drug in 1998, add a blue dye to it and make it harder to dissolve, but at the moment it's open to abuse.'

'*Tony keeps his drug supplies in the garage, or did until he heard you'd arrested me, then he went in and cleared the whole lot out. He'd taken the Rohypnol off his grandad when the poor old bugger kept falling asleep during the daytime. He found him in the kitchen once with the gas going full blast because he'd nodded off before he had time to put a match to it. Tony was going to chuck the Rohypnol out but I told him it could do him some good with Bibi so he kept it. It worked like a treat on Kate. She went out like a light. The only problem was, she let Hannah drink some of the champagne as well, and when Hannah went out she fell over backwards with her eyes wide open. I thought she was dead . . .*'

'He's very unclear what he was intending to do to Kate. He

talks about teaching her a lesson but whether the intention was always to rape her then kill her, he can't or won't say.'

'*I wasn't going to hurt Kate, just give her something to think about. She'd been pissing me off with the crap thing, and it had been really bugging me. Still, I had to have a rethink when Hannah keeled over. That was pretty frightening, you know. I mean, killing a kid, even if it was an accident, is heavy stuff. I thought about leaving them both there while I scarpered to France with Marie but I was afraid Tony might find them before I met up with her, and I'd already told him I was going to Poole for the weekend. I guess it was the fact that Kate was so small that made me think about taking them both with me . . .*'

'He took them on board under everyone's noses,' said Galbraith. 'Just motored *Crazy Daze* into one of the visitors' pontoons near the yacht club and carried Kate on in the canvas holdall that takes his dinghy when it's not in use. They're substantial items, apparently, big enough to take eight feet of collapsed rubber, plus the seat and the floor boarding, and he says he had no trouble folding Kate into it. He took Hannah on board in his rucksack and carried the buggy quite openly under his arm.'

'*People never question anything if you're up front about what you're doing. I guess it has something to do with the British psyche, and the fact we never interfere unless we absolutely have to. But you kind of want them to sometimes. It's almost as if you're being forced to do things you don't really want to do. I kept saying to myself, ask me what's in the bag, you bastards, ask me why I'm carrying a baby's buggy under my arm. But no one did, of course . . .*'

'Then he left for Poole,' said Galbraith. 'The time was getting on for midday by then and he says he hadn't thought what he was going to do beyond smuggling Kate and Hannah aboard. He talks about being stressed out, and being unable to think properly' – he raised his eyes to Sumner – 'rather like your description of yourself earlier, and it does seem as if he opted to do nothing, left them imprisoned and unconscious inside the bags on the principle of out of sight out of mind.'

'*I guess I'd realized all along I was going to have to dump them over the side but I kept putting it off. I'd sailed out into the Channel to get some space around me, and it was around seven o'clock when I hauled them up on deck to get it over with. I couldn't do it, though. I could hear whimpering coming out of the rucksack so I knew Hannah was still alive. I felt good about that. I never wanted to kill either of them . . .*'

'He claims Kate started to come round at about 7.30 which is when he released her, and let her sit beside him in the cockpit. He also claims it was her idea to take her clothes off. However, in view of the fact that her wedding ring is also missing, we think the truth is he decided to strip her body of anything that could identify her before he threw her overboard.'

'*I know she was frightened, and I know she probably did it to try to get into my good books, but I never asked her to strip and I never forced her to have sex with me. I'd already made up my mind to take them back. I wouldn't have altered course otherwise, and she'd never have ended up in Egmont Bight. I gave her something to eat because she said she was hungry. Why would I do that if I was going to kill her . . .?*'

'I know this is distressing for you, William, but we believe he spent hours fantasizing about what he was going to do with her before he killed her, and when he'd stripped her he went ahead and played out those fantasies. However, we don't know how conscious Kate was or how much she knew about what was going on. One of the difficulties we have is that *Crazy Daze* shows no recent signs of Kate and Hannah being on board. What we think happened is that he kept Kate naked on the deck for about five hours between 7.30 and half-past midnight which would explain the evidence of hypothermia and the lack of forensic evidence connecting her with the interior. We're still looking for evidence on the topsides but

I'm afraid he had hours during the trip back to Lymington on Sunday to scrub the deck clean with buckets of salt water.'

'*Okay, I was way out of line at the beginning, I'll admit that. Things got out of control for a while – I mean I panicked like hell when I thought Hannah was dead – but by the time it was dark I'd got it all worked out. I told Kate that if she promised to keep her mouth shut I'd take her to Poole and let her and Hannah off there. Otherwise, I'd say she came on board willingly, and as Tony Bridges knew she had the hots for me, no one would believe her word against mine, particularly not William . . .*'

'He says he promised to take Kate to Poole, and she may have believed him, but we don't think he had any intention of doing it. He's a good sailor, yet he steered a course that brought him back to land to the west of St Alban's Head when he should have been well to the east. He's arguing that he lost track of his position because Kate kept distracting him, but it's too much of a coincidence that he put her into the sea where he did, bearing in mind he was planning to walk there the next morning.'

'*She should have trusted me. I told her I wasn't going to hurt her. I didn't hurt Hannah, did I . . . ?*'

'He says she lunged at him and tried to push him overboard, and in the process went over herself.'

'*I could hear her shouting and thrashing about in the water, so I brought the helm round to try and locate her. But it was so dark I couldn't see a damn thing. I kept calling to her but it all went silent very quickly and in the end I had to give up. I don't think she could swim very well . . .*'

'He's claiming he made every attempt to find her but thinks she must have drowned within a few minutes. He refers to it as a terrible accident.'

'*Of course it was a coincidence we were off Chapman's Pool. It was pitch black, for Christ's sake, and there's no lighthouse at St Alban's Head. Have you any idea what it's like sailing at night when there's nothing to tell you where you are? I hadn't been concentrating, hadn't taken the tidal drift and wind changes into account. I was pretty sure I'd sailed too far west which is why I altered course to sail due east, but it wasn't until I came within sight of the Anvil Point lighthouse that I had any idea I was within striking distance of Poole. Look, don't you think I'd have killed Hannah as well if I'd meant to kill Kate . . .?*

When Galbraith fell silent, Sumner finally dragged his gaze away from the ceiling. 'Is that what he'll say in court? That she died by accident?'

'Probably.'

'Will he win?'

'Not if you stand up for her.'

'Maybe he's telling the truth,' said the other man listlessly.

Galbraith smiled slightly. Kindness *was* a mug's game. 'Don't ever say that in my presence again, William,' he said with a rasp in his throat. 'Because, so help me God, I'll beat the fucking daylights out of you if you do. I saw your wife, remember. I wept for her before you even knew she was dead.'

Sumner blinked in alarm.

Galbraith straightened. 'The bastard drugged her, raped her – several times we think – broke her fingers because she attempted to release her daughter from the rucksack, then put his hands round her neck and throttled her. But she wouldn't die. So he tied her to a spare outboard his friend had given him and set her adrift in a partially inflated dinghy.' He thumped his fist into his palm. 'Not to give her a chance of life, William, but to make sure she died slowly and in fear, tormenting herself about what he was going to do to Hannah and regretting that she'd ever dared to take revenge on him.'

'The kid never cried once after I took her out of the rucksack. She wasn't frightened of me. As a matter of fact I think she felt sorry for me because she could see I was upset. I wrapped her in a blanket and laid her on the floor in the cabin and she went to sleep. I might have panicked if she'd started crying in the marina,

but she didn't. She's a funny kid. I mean she's obviously not very bright, but you get the feeling she knows things . . .'

'I don't know why he didn't kill Hannah, except that he seems to be afraid of her. He says now that the fact she's alive is proof he didn't want Kate to die either, and he may have decided that as she was never going to be a threat to him he could afford to let her live. He says he changed her, fed her and gave her something to drink from the bag that was on the back of the buggy, then took her off the boat in his rucksack. He left her asleep in the front garden of a block of flats on the Bournemouth to Poole road, a good mile from Lilliput, and seems to be more shocked than anyone that she was allowed to walk all the way back to the marina before anyone questioned why she was on her own.'

'There was some paracetamol in the buggy bag so I dosed her up with it to make sure she was asleep when I took her off the boat. Not that I really needed to. I reckon the Rohypnol was still working because I sat and watched her in the cabin for hours and she only woke up once. There's no way she could have known where Salterns Marina was, so how the hell did she find her way back to it? I kept telling you she was weird. But you wouldn't believe me . . .'

'On the trip back to Lymington he put everything overboard that could connect him in any way at all with Kate and Hannah – the dinghy holdall, Kate's clothes, her ring, the buggy, Hannah's dirty nappy, the rug he wrapped her in – but he forgot the sandals that Kate left behind in April.' Galbraith smiled slightly. 'Although the odd thing is he says he did remember them. He took them out of a locker after he left Hannah asleep on the cabin floor and put them in the buggy bag, and he says now that the only person who could have hidden them under the pile of clothes was Hannah.'

'I got sidetracked worrying about fingerprints. I couldn't make up my mind whether to clean the inside of Crazy Daze or not. You see I knew you'd find Kate and Hannah's fingerprints

from when they were on board in April and I wondered if it would be better to pretend that visit had never happened. In the end I decided to leave it exactly the way it's been for the last three months because I didn't want you lot imagining I'd done something worse than I had. And I was right, wasn't I? You wouldn't have released me on Wednesday if you'd found any evidence that I set out to hurt Kate the way you're saying I did . . .'

Sumner's eyes welled again but he didn't say anything.

'Why didn't you tell me Kate and Harding had had an affair?' Galbraith asked him.

It was a moment before William answered and, when he did, he lifted a trembling hand in supplication, like a beggar after charity. 'I was ashamed.'

'For Kate?'

'No,' he whispered, 'for myself. I didn't want anyone to know.'

To know what? Galbraith wondered. That he couldn't keep his wife interested? That he'd made a mistake marrying her? He reached over and took the telephone from Sumner's lap. 'If you're interested, Sandy Griffiths says Hannah's been walking round the house all day, looking for you. I asked Sandy to tell her I'd be bringing you home, and Hannah clapped her hands. Don't make a liar out of me, my friend.'

He shook with grief. 'I thought she'd be better off without me.'

'No chance.' He raised the man to his feet with a hand under his arm. 'You're her father. How could she possibly be better off without you?'

Chapter Twenty-seven

MAGGIE LAY ON the floor stretching her aching back while Nick meticulously poked a loaded paint brush into all the nooks and crannies that she'd missed. 'Do you think Steve would have done it if Tony Bridges hadn't wound him up by smearing crap all over the place?'

'I don't know,' said Nick. 'The Superintendent's convinced he's an out-and-out psychopath, says it was only a matter of time before his obsession with sex spilled over into rape, so maybe he'd have done it anyway, with or without Tony Bridges. I suppose the truth is Kate was in the wrong place at the wrong time.' He paused, remembering the tiny hand waving in the spume. 'Poor woman.'

'Still . . . does Tony walk away scot-free? That's hardly fair, is it? I mean he must have known Steve was guilty.'

Nick shrugged. 'Claims he didn't, claims he thought it was the husband.' He dabbed gently at a spider and watched it scurry away into the shadows. 'Galbraith told me he and Carpenter hung Tony up to dry last night for keeping quiet the first time they interviewed him, and Tony's excuse was that Kate was such a bitch he didn't see why he should help the police screw her husband. He reckoned Kate got what she deserved for spouting off about the poor bastard's performance. He has trouble on that front himself, apparently, so his sympathies were with William.'

'And this man's a *teacher*?' she said in disgust.

'Not for much longer,' Nick reassured her, 'unless his fellow inmates have a yen for chemisty. Carpenter's thrown the book at him – perverting the course of justice, supplying drugs, false imprisonment of his girlfriend, rape of said girlfriend under the influence of Rohypnol, incitement to murder . . . even' – he chuckled – 'criminal damage to Harding's car . . . and that's not to mention whatever Customs and Excise choose to throw at him.'

'Serves him right,' said Maggie unsympathetically.

'Mmm.'

'You don't sound convinced.'

'Only because I can't see what prison will do for someone like Tony. He's not a bad guy, just a misguided one. Six months' community service in a home for the disabled would do him more good.' He watched the spider sink into a pool of wet emulsion. 'On a scale of one to ten, spasmodic impotence doesn't even register compared with severe physical or mental handicap.'

Maggie sat up and clasped her arms about her knees. 'I thought policemen were supposed to be hard bastards. Are you going soft on me, Ingram?'

He looked down at her with a gleam of amusement in his dark eyes. 'Courtship's like that, I'm afraid. The hardness comes and goes whether you like it or not. It's nature.'

She lowered her face to her knees, refusing to be diverted. 'I don't understand why Steve drowned Kate off Chapman's Pool,' she said next. 'He knew he was going there the next morning and he must have realized there was a chance she'd wash up on the beach. Why would he want to put his meeting with Marie in jeopardy?'

'I'm not sure you can apply logic to the actions of someone like Harding,' he said. 'Carpenter's view is that, once he had Kate on board, there would only ever be one place he'd kill her. He says you can tell from the Frenchman's video how hyped-up he was by all the excitement.' He watched the spider lift his legs from the wet paint and wave them in useless protest.

'But I don't think Steve expected her body to be there. He'd broken her fingers and tied her to an outboard so it must have been a hell of a shock to find she'd managed to free herself. Presumably the intention was to gloat over her grave before absconding with Marie. Carpenter thinks Harding's an embryo serial killer so in his view Marie's lucky to be alive.'

'Do you agree with him?'

'God knows.' He mourned the spider's inevitable death as the exhausted creature dipped its abdomen into the paint. 'Steve says it was a terrible accident, but I've no idea if he's telling the truth. Carpenter doesn't believe him and neither does DI Galbraith, but I have a real problem accepting that anyone so young can be so evil. Let's just say I'm glad you had Bertie with you yesterday.'

'Does Carpenter think he wanted to kill me, too?'

Nick shook his head. 'I don't know. He asked Steve what was so important about the rucksack that he'd risked going back for it, and do you know what Steve said? "My binoculars." So then Carpenter asked him why he'd left it there at all, and he said: "Because I'd forgotten the binoculars were in it." '

'What does that mean?'

Nick gave a low laugh. 'That there was nothing in it he wanted, so he decided to dump it. He hadn't had any sleep, he was knackered and Marie's desert boots kept banging against his back and giving him blisters. All he wanted to do was get rid of it as fast as possible.'

'Why is that funny?'

'It's the exact opposite of why I thought he'd left it there.'

'No, it's not,' she contradicted him. 'You told me it would incriminate him because he used it to carry Hannah off his boat.'

'But he didn't kill Hannah, Maggie, he killed Kate.'

'So?'

'All I did by finding it was help the defence. Harding will argue it proves he never intended to murder anyone.'

He sounded depressed, she thought. 'Still,' she said brightly, I suppose they'll be offering you a job at headquarters. They must be awfully impressed with you. You homed in on Steve as soon as you saw him.'

'And homed straight out again the minute he spun me a plausible yarn.' Another low laugh, this time self-deprecating. 'The only reason I took against him was because he got up my nose, and the Superintendent knows that. I think Carpenter thinks I'm a bit of a joke. He called me a suggestion-junky.' He sighed. 'I'm not sure I'm cut out for CID work. You can't take a wild guess then invent arguments to support the theory. That's how miscarriages of justice happen.'

She cast him a speculative glance. 'Is that something else Carpenter said?'

'More or less. He said the days are long past when policemen could play hunches. It's all about putting data into computers now.'

She felt angry on his behalf. 'Then I'll phone the bastard and give him a piece of my mind,' she said indignantly. 'If it hadn't been for you, it would have taken them months to make the connection between Kate and Harding – if ever, frankly – and they'd never have found that stranded dinghy or worked out where it was stolen from. He ought to be congratulating you, not finding fault. *I'm* the one who got it all wrong. There's obviously a flaw in my genes that makes me gravitate towards scumbags. Even Ma thought Harding was the most frightful creep. She said: "Fancy making such a performance over a dog bite. I've had far worse, and all anyone offered me was TCP."'

'She'll have my guts for garters when she finds out I made her wreck her hip for a murderer.'

'No, she won't. She says you remind her of James Stewart in *Destry Rides Again*.'

'Is that good?'

'Oh, yes,' said Maggie with a sardonic edge to her voice.

'She goes weak at the knees every time she sees it. James Stewart plays a peace-loving sheriff who brings law and order to a violent city by never raising his voice or drawing his gun. It's fantastically sentimental. He falls in love with Marlene Dietrich who throws herself in front of a bullet to protect him.'

'Mmm. Personally, I've always fancied myself as Bruce Willis in *Die Hard*. The heroic, bloodstained cop with his trusty arsenal who saves the world and the woman he loves by blasting hell out of Alan Rickman and his gang of psychopaths.'

She giggled. 'Is this another attempt at seduction?'

'No. I'm still courting you.'

'I was afraid you might be.' She shook her head. 'You're too nice, that's your trouble. You're certainly too nice to blast hell out of anyone.'

'I know,' he said despondently. 'I don't have the stomach for it.' He climbed down the stepladder and squatted on the floor in front of her, rubbing his tired eyes with the back of his hand. 'I was beginning to like Harding. I still do in a funny kind of way. I keep thinking what a waste it all is and what a difference it would have made if someone, somewhere, had warned him that everything has a price.' He reached up to put the paint brush in the tray on the table. 'To be fair to Carpenter, he *did* congratulate me. He even said he'd support me if I decided to apply for the CID. According to him, I have potential' – he mimicked the Superintendent's growl – 'and he should know because he hasn't been a Super for five years for nothing.' He smiled his crooked smile. 'But I'm not convinced that's where my talents lie.'

'Oh, for God's sake!' she declared, revealing more of her genes than she knew. 'You'd make a brilliant detective. I can't think what you're worried about. Don't be so bloody cautious, Nick. You should seize your chances.'

'I do . . . when they make sense to me.'

'And this one doesn't?'

He smiled and stood up, removing the tray to the sink and

running water into it. 'I'm not sure I want to move away.' He glanced about the transformed room. 'I rather like living in a backwater where the odd suggestion makes a difference.'

Her eyes fell. 'Oh, I see.'

He rinsed the emulsion out of the brush in silence, wondering if she did, and if 'I see' was going to be her only response. He propped the brush to dry on the draining board, and seriously considered whether fighting his way through half a mile of razor wire wouldn't be the more sensible option after all. 'Shall I come back tomorrow? It's Sunday. We could make a start on the hall.'

'I'll be here,' she said.

'Okay.' He walked across to the scullery door.

'Nick?'

'Yes?' He turned.

'How long do these courtships of yours usually take?'

An amiable smile creased his eyes. 'Before what?'

'Before . . .' She looked suddenly uncomfortable. 'Never mind. It was a silly question. I'll see you tomorrow.'

'I'll try not to be late.'

'It doesn't matter if you are,' she said through gritted teeth. 'You're doing this out of kindness, not because you have to. I haven't asked you to paint the whole house, you know.'

'True,' he agreed, 'but it's a courtship thing. I thought I'd explained all that.'

She clambered to her feet with flashing eyes. 'Go *away*,' she said, pushing him through the door and bolting it behind him. 'And for God's sake bring some brandy with you tomorrow,' she yelled. 'Courtship stinks. I've decided I'd rather be seduced.'

The television was on and Celia, remote control in hand, was chuckling to herself when Maggie tiptoed into the drawing room to see if she was all right. Bertie had abandoned the stifling heat of the bed and was stretched out on his back on the sofa, legs akimbo. 'It's late, Ma. You ought to be asleep.'

'I know, but this is so funny, darling.'

'You said it was wall-to-wall horror movies.'

'It is. That's why I'm laughing.'

Maggie fixed her mother with a perplexed frown, then seized the remote control and killed the picture. 'You were listening,' she accused her.

'Well . . .'

'How *could* you?'

'I needed a pee,' said Celia apologetically, 'and you weren't exactly whispering.'

'The doctor said you weren't to walk around on your own.'

'I had no option. I called out a couple of times but you didn't hear me. In any case' – her eyes brimmed with humour – 'you were getting on so well that I decided it would be tactless to interrupt you.' She appraised her daughter in silence for a moment, then abruptly patted the bed. 'Are you too old to take some advice?'

'It depends what it is,' said Maggie, sitting down.

'Any man who invites the woman to make the running is worth having.'

'Is that what my father did?'

'No. He swept me off my feet, rushed me to the altar, and then gave me thirty-five years to repent at leisure.' Celia smiled ruefully. 'Which is why the advice is good. I fell for your father's over-inflated opinion of himself, mistook obstinacy for masterfulness, alcoholism for wit, and laziness for charisma . . .' She broke off apologetically, realizing that it was her daughter's father she was criticizing. 'It wasn't all bad,' she said robustly. 'Everyone was more stoical in those days – we were taught to put up with things – and look what I got out of it. You . . . Matt . . . the house . . .'

Maggie leaned forward to kiss her mother's cheek. 'Ava . . . Martin . . . theft . . . debts . . . heartache . . . a wonky hip . . .'

'Life,' countered Celia. 'A still-viable livery stable . . . Bertie . . . a new kitchen . . . a future . . .'

'Nick Ingram?'

'Well, why not?' said Celia with renewed chuckles. 'If I was forty years younger and he showed the remotest interest in me, I certainly wouldn't need a bottle of brandy to get things moving.'